THE GRECIAN GODDESS
THE COMPLETE SERIES

TESSA COLE
CLARA WILS

Gryphon's Gate Publishing

The Grecian Goddess

Copyright © 2023 Tessa Cole and Clara Wils

Gryphon's Gate Publishing

550 King St. N.

PO Box 42088 Conestoga

Waterloo, ON

N2L 6K5

Print ISBN: 978-1-990587-37-5

KISS OF THE GODDESS

GRECIAN GODDESS: BOOK 1

KISS OF THE GODDESS

GRECIAN GODDESS: BOOK 1

CHAPTER 1

ANNIE

MY PHONE RANG. WITH HANDS NUMB FROM THE COLD, I PULLED IT from my purse, fumbled, and dropped it onto the icy sidewalk.

"Fuck!"

Several of those around me on the early morning crowded Chicago street turned my way with expressions varying from shock to annoyance at my outburst, and I flashed them my winningest grin, which I hoped said "sorry, go about your business" before turning my attention back to my phone.

Except before I could kneel to get it, another pedestrian unknowingly kicked it across the sidewalk.

"Fuck!" I snapped again and this time didn't care who heard it or what they thought.

My life was on that phone.

More importantly, my *job* was on that phone.

The start-up I worked for didn't have work phones, so everything went on our personal ones. And I had a lot on there.

As the Operations Coordinator for Siren's Call Software, I was the "everything else" person at the company. With only seven of us in the office and five of those being developers, that left myself and my cohort Diane, to take care of the rest of the business. We were HR, office managers, finance, shipping-receiving, and most importantly internal sales. We reached out to all the police in the area to set up demos of the software, so they'd hopefully buy it.

And that meant I had the contact information for every police service in all of the Chicago area on my phone.

Something I couldn't afford to lose.

Siren's Call wasn't that big yet, but we were growing and I needed that information — not to mention I was sure some of my police contacts wouldn't have wanted their phone numbers available to just anyone.

I huffed out a breath, misting a cloud of cold air around my head, and scrambled after it.

But moving through the thick crowd of people who were all hurrying to their jobs to start their day wasn't easy. I may have been tall for a woman, but I wasn't particularly forceful. So, by the time I reached where my phone had been, it had been kicked again, skittering away... into a dark alley.

Wonderful.

This was the icing on top of a very foul cake, which had been the last month for me.

To start, I'd only just managed to save my job after messing up the paychecks at the beginning of the month. I'd been working overtime during the holidays at the end of December, and it had been on my list of things to do, but that list had been far too long for one person. The rest of the company was off. The checks were usually Diane's thing, but she'd been in Mexico, and with everything else and my family commitments, I'd been so frazzled that I'd simply forgotten.

My boss, *the* boss, had been furious, but I'd managed to resolve that quick enough to avoid getting fired. Except the late check meant I hadn't had enough in my account and my rent check had bounced. Then my landlord was furious. I had only just gotten that sorted out when my heater had died and the sadistic landlord — perhaps as payback for the late payment — had taken a week to fix it. Which meant my place had been freezing, so I'd stayed at my brother's place.

Except he was getting ready for his wedding, and that meant my ex — one of his friends and a groomsman — had been there a lot, so of course I was interrogated and harassed about my pipe dream of living and working quietly in the tropics, which reminded me why we'd broken up in the first place. Not to mention that the aforementioned wedding was in two days, and I still didn't have anything to wear.

And now, to top it all off, my phone was in some creepy alley-way, probably already broken and beyond repair.

Fuck, fuck, fuck, fuck!

I finally reached the mouth of the alley and stood there for a long moment. I wasn't in the worst part of town, but I also wasn't in the best. And smart girls didn't walk into dark alleys — even a pre-dawn dark alley — alone.

Behind me, the barely risen sun sent long shadows stretching through the Chicago streets.

Okay, so it wasn't exactly pre-dawn, and my phone was only about a dozen feet in, but still. Dark alley. At least my phone looked to be undamaged. Though perhaps some snow had gotten into it. God, I hoped not.

I pulled my thick coat tighter around me and slipped beyond the bustling sidewalk just one step into the alley. No mugging so far.

A warm wind blew out from the depths of the narrow lane... smelling of garbage. The warmth was welcome, as much as the smell was off-putting. I didn't know why it was warm either. Perhaps there was a sewer grate back there somewhere?

"You can do this," I muttered to myself. But I wasn't about to do it unprepared. My father would say, 'this is how good women get taken by predators.' And he might be right. Admittedly he was talking about dark alleys at one in the morning, but I'd rather be over prepared than under.

I slipped my hand into my purse and felt around for a moment, before I recalled that I'd left my taser at home.

"Well, double fuck." If anyone had been seriously listening to me for the last minute, they'd probably be wondering about my limited vocabulary.

Finding my small umbrella, I latched onto that and pulled it out. I kept the umbrella in my purse because you never knew what a Chicago winter would bring. It wasn't much of a weapon, but it was something, and I felt a little better about holding it as I shuffled a couple feet into the alley.

I inched forward, searching for danger, my nerves on high alert even though this situation didn't demand *high alert*.

Had that garbage bag shifted? Was there movement in the shadows farther in?

This was ridiculous. I had no idea why I was suddenly panicking. My heart raced, my fear a lot stronger than it should have been, and I was sweating through my many layers of wool. I was going to be a right royal mess by the time I got to work.

I reached my phone, glanced down quickly, making sure I knew where it was, then snapped my gaze back up. No one was going to get the drop on me today.

Kneeling slowly, I patted the ground, hoping to feel the phone. Nothing yet, and I wasn't going to risk looking down again and be caught unawares.

I shifted to the side, causing my coat and heavy skirt to bunch uncomfortably around my left leg, forcing me to adjust slightly. But my foot hit a patch of ice and slipped out from under me, throwing me head first toward a brick wall.

With a yelp, I lurched forward, sending my wool hat sliding down over my eyes. I flailed my arms out, trying to catch myself before I smashed my skull, and instead thumped face first onto soft ground, my breath knocked out of me—

Wait a minute.

Soft?

Where was that wall?

Sure, I was thrilled I hadn't crashed into a solid wall, and yet what the hell had happened?

I sat up, reaching to adjust the hat, and got a face full of sand.

Sand?

Now I was blind for a different reason. Also, some had gotten into my mouth.

"Gah."

I tried to spit it out and blink my eyes clear — I wasn't going to use my hands again, since that was what I'd done the first time. Yet as my stinging, watery vision slowly cleared, I felt around me and grew even more confused.

The sand was hot.

Had I fallen through an unseen door into someone's secret Zen garden?

It was the only thing that made sense, and yet it didn't make any kind of sense at all, and not knowing what was going on was the last straw in a long line of frustrating, exhausting, stressful straws.

I'd almost lost my job. I'd almost lost my apartment. I'd had to spend time with my ex and my family who didn't really understand me. And if I had now lost my phone, there was still a chance I'd lose my job.

Tears, not just from the sand, welled in my eyes. I sat enveloped in heat, getting far too warm in all my winter clothes and having — I'm ashamed to say — a mini pity party. This was the topper, the perfect end to a month from hell. I could only hope February would be better.

After a moment, I sucked in a breath and carefully wiped the grit and tears from my eyes.

There wasn't anything I could do about what had already happened. The only thing I could do was keep moving forward. And to do that, I had to take stock and find my phone.

Except when I looked around everything had changed.

The alley was gone. The darkness was gone. Hell, all of Chicago was gone!

Sand stretched ahead of me as far as I could see, green-brown hills sat to my left and...was that the wash of waves I heard?

I looked to my right and indeed, a vast span of water with distant islands stretched away beyond the light-brown sandy beach.

Beach?

I was on a beach?

What... the... fuuuuck?

This had to be a dream. There was nowhere else on this world I'd rather be than on a sunny beach. It was my deepest desire, my *pipe dream,* and had been as long as I'd been an adult.

I hated winter, hated the cold. I had family in Chicago, a home, a life, but it wasn't where I wanted to live.

And that was a major source of division between me and my family. I loved them and they me, but they didn't understand. My skin burned at the drop of a hat. My ex had taken me to Barbados on vacation. I'd loved every minute of it, up until I'd gotten a sunburn so bad, I'd had to go to the hospital. He'd thought that had taught me a lesson, and changed my mind. It hadn't. I didn't know how I'd make it work, but there was nothing I wanted more than to be a virtual assistant on some beach somewhere.

And here I was.

But... how?

A dream, yes, it had to be a dream.

"Pardon, stranger, are you in need of aid?"

I yelped and spun at the sound of the voice behind me. It took a long moment for my brain to actually hear what had been said. The voice hadn't sounded threatening, but it had been a burly baritone, and I didn't want any man from some dark alley — or some mystery beach — too close to me right now, since I had no idea what the hell was going on.

But when I did see the guy who'd spoken — or so I assumed since he was the only one around — I blurted, "Holy-what-the-fuck?"

The man was stunning.

He lay on a long flat slab of black rock at the water's edge that was part of a collection of jagged rocks, jutting up from the sand, some over a dozen feet tall. With his torso levered up on his arms so he could look at me, it was clear he wasn't wearing anything above the waist, and I could see his broad chest and heavily muscled shoulders and arms. His face was clean-shaven, with a curious smile below startling blue-green eyes and framed by thick, blue-black hair that fell in waves past his shoulders.

In short, he was one of the most gorgeous men I'd ever seen.

But my exclamation had been more from seeing his legs, or more precisely his lack of legs. Where his legs should have been was a massive fish tail.

"I... ah..." I flashed him my hopefully-winning smile again, flustered.

He'd said something a second ago and I couldn't recall it, and everything was just a little... too much for me right now. The sun, the sand, the handsome fish-man. I should be in a dark alley, in Chicago, in winter... not here, wherever here was.

"Do you need help?" the man asked.

"Yes?" I said, just a little too defensively. Instantly the image of me in his arms, lost in bliss, screaming that same word, came to mind and the heat of a flush rose to my face, making me far too warm in this sunny paradise with all my winter clothes on.

The man levered himself up farther and swung his not-legs over the side of the rock. Yep, that was a long fish's tail... I wasn't delusional.

Or at least I wasn't delusional in my delusion?

"A mermaid?" I asked, the question slipping out.

No that wasn't the right word.

"Mer... man?"

"We prefer merfolk, or *tritons*," he said with a grin. "And from your voice, I think you're a woman of some sort? It's hard to tell with all those strange clothes. You must be quite hot."

He thought I was sexy? No, he meant...

Hot. Yes. Burning up.

I'd hit my head.

I'd fallen into that wall after all, and hit my head and now I was lying unconscious — probably bleeding out and feverish — in that alley, fantasizing about... merfolk.

Would anyone find me? Would I wake up? At the very least, I was going to be *very* late for work.

"It's a dream," I said softly. But hearing the words out loud didn't seem to change anything. "It's all just a dream." Repeating it didn't help.

And if it *was* a dream, why was I still in my winter woolies? Why — if I'd chosen to dream of sexy fish-guy here — wasn't I in his arms? Hell, he didn't even have a cock! Some dream-man he was.

Perhaps that was some comment on my psyche. I couldn't even get laid in my dreams.

"How do... merfolk have sex?" I blurted out, and my cheeks

burned, even though this *was* a dream and I had no reason to be embarrassed by my own subconscious.

But that was the frustrating illogic of dreams.

He chuckled and flashed me a mischievous grin. "That's a little forward, don't you think? But I'd be happy to show you if you wanted to shed some of those heavy things you're wearing."

My blush turned searing at his proposition... or had that been in response to *my* proposition?

And ah, hell, it was a dream after all.

If I was unconscious and freezing to death in an alley some-where, I'd be an idiot to deny my dream.

I began stripping off my things, but I was wearing a lot — and not a lot in the dream sense where the dream just kept adding clothes and I never got past the undressing stage. Winter in the Windy City wasn't great for sexy clothes. Not that I cared much for such things anyway. I just wanted to be warm. So, there were a lot of layers: heavy down coat, boots, wool socks, long woolen skirt, thick knitted sweater. Now I was just down to a long-sleeved shirt, woolen leggings and my underthings.

Distracted by shedding my clothes, I paused at this point to look back at the man. And there it was. The thick shaft of an oh-my-God sized dick had appeared from somewhere amidst those scales.

"Holy shit! Where did that come from?" Why did such embar-rassing words keep slipping out of my mouth? Because I was dreaming. And it seemed I was still awkward as hell in my dreams.

But... wow... this dream had just taken a turn for the... erotic.

Again, without much thought, I said, "That thing can't be real."

It reminded me of a dildo I had at home. My friend Lacey had given it to me as a joke. Not something I'd use... usually, so it stood proudly on a shelf, and that's where I must have gotten this image from.

"It is," he said with a cocky grin. Then he leaned forward a little, those sea-green eyes burrowing into me. "And you are an extra-ordinary woman. Your skin is such an odd shade. I'm not sure I've seen that coloring before. Are you some rock nymph?" He drew in a sudden shock of breath, eyes going wide. "Or perhaps a goddess come to have your way with me in a fit of lust?" His grin grew wider, edged with a hint of awe. "I'd heard of such things, but never thought it would happen to me."

Nymph? Goddess? Me?

That was positive proof this was a dream. No man had ever used those words to describe me before. Certainly, no hunky half-fish-man with a massive cock.

And I was *not* going to complain.

"Yep, that's me. Goddess Extraordinaire, Annie Chambers. Come and ravish me, you... whatever you are."

"A goddess? Truly? Amazing!" He looked down his body and my gaze followed, stalling on his massive cock. "But I can't come to you as I am. You would have to come to me." Right... fish couldn't walk.

Of course.

I peeled off my shirt and began the short trek across the blazing hot sands to hunky-fish-guy.

"Although, perhaps..." His grin darkened and turned flirty and he pushed himself off from the rock on which he sat.

In my head I saw an awkward landing... but that didn't happen. His fish tale vanished and legs appeared in a haze which lasted only an instant before he landed.

I stopped, blinking.

Suddenly this dream didn't feel right.

Why it had felt *right* a moment before when he'd been half-fish, I wasn't quite sure. It was dream logic, or something like that. But now he was just a man. A man with a cock that belonged in porn videos, who was looking at me just a little too expectantly. Yeah, sure, it was still a dream, but somehow him being just a man

— with an erection I couldn't quite take my eyes off— changed things.

Then there was this strange niggling feeling.

In some dreams things felt real, but they didn't often hurt, like the sand burning the bottoms of my feet, or the intense sun on my skin.

I was a strawberry blonde with fair skin — except for the freckles from nose to navel — so I burned far too easily.

A breeze swept off the waters, cooling, refreshing, ruffling my hair. The way the wind raised goose bumps on my bare arms, or how my hair tickled my face as it blew about... something about all of this felt just a little too not-dreamlike.

It was amazing, so much better than winter in Chicago, but still...

"What's your name?" I don't know why I asked. Guys in dreams had names didn't they? Him having a name wouldn't disprove that this was a dream.

"Delphon of Galniosia," he said with a bit of a formal bow. The gesture was slightly less gracious with his cock out.

But that name... I didn't think I'd come up with a name like that for my dream guy. I'd always liked the name Kevin. Sexy men had names like Kevin: Kevin Bacon and oh... Kevin Sorbo. My younger self had even had a crush on Kevin Costner, specifically his sensitive, yet determined character from Field of Dreams. Or there was Charles. A very regal name. I didn't think I'd ever met a man named Delphon before. It sounded Greek. Maybe he was Greek. And what was the other part of his name... Gal-something? If I dreamed it, I should remember it, right?

I was starting to get just a little self-conscious standing there in my bra and leggings, and him standing there, so very... upright and—

I pressed my legs together at the thought of *that* inside me. I'd never been with a man so well-endowed before. Okay, so there'd been once when I'd taken that dildo off my shelf, lubed it up, and—

I was getting *way* off track.

But what was on track?

Was this a dream or... the other option was just a little too unreal... literally.

I'd been in Chicago, in winter, just moments ago, and now I was quickly getting a burn!

Was I unconscious in that alley?

Or...

"Is this real?" Again, I wasn't quite sure why I asked that. It wasn't as if a dream was going to tell me it was a dream.

Delphon's brow furrowed as he looked at me with a bit of confusion. "I'm not sure what you mean, Goddess Extraordinaire, Annie Chambers." He tilted his head to one side, blue-black locks tumbling with it, sea-green eyes curious. "I assure you I'm very real. Are you not attracted to me, my goddess?"

That would be a resounding *hell yes!* I was attracted to him. But none of this felt right.

I knelt and scooped up some sand into my hand. It burned as it slid through my fingers.

Still...

What could I do to prove this was a dream? Dreams were sketchy things. You could convince yourself it was reality, if only for a short time. Yet I seemed to be aware of this being a dream. And sometimes those were the best dreams! Sometimes I could even make myself fly!

Yes! That would be a great way to determine if this was a dream: I would fly.

I got up and headed to the large rocks — just to the right of Mr. Happy-fish-pants, scrambled, hopped, and climbed from one to another to get atop the largest. From there I'd jump off and fly.

That idea suddenly seemed just a little iffy though, because if this wasn't a dream — as crazy as that might be — I'd be throwing myself down a dozen or so feet onto sand. At least it was sand and not rock.

Delphon, erection now mostly gone, had walked closer, standing below me. "Goddess? What do you intend?"

"Oh, screw it!" I whispered. This had to be a dream.

I spread my arms out to either side and stepped off.

CHAPTER 2

ANNIE

AIR RUSHED PAST MY FACE AND EARS, AND I FELT A PURE, JOYOUS JOLT of adrenaline for a split second before I started to plummet to the ground.

Oh shit oh shit oh shit.

Maybe this wasn't a dream.

"What are you doing, woman?" came a startled voice from behind me, and, with a heavy whoosh of air and flap of wings, strong hands caught me under each arm and swept me up higher.

Startled, I looked up and saw a man, no— an angel.

Holy crap, an angel!

He held me firmly as he flew out over the beach before gently bringing us down fifty feet from where I'd stepped off the rock.

And now I was certain this was a dream, because only someone as stunning and perfect as him could be a dream.

His blond hair, tussled and yet still perfect, framed a long angular face with pale blue eyes like a summer's sky, a straight nose, and a square jaw. Then there was everything below his neck. Unlike Delphon, he wore clothes... sort of. A strange wrap skirt covered him from waist to knees, leaving his chest and arms bare for my eyes to devour. And from what I could see, he was all hard, gorgeous planes of rigid muscle on a tall, lean frame that was as tall as fish-guy but not quite as broad.

I threw myself at him, the rush of having flown — or rather, having been flown — filling me and wrapped my arms around him.

Yep, definitely a dream. He smelled like fresh morning air with a hint of sweat, and with our bodies pressed tight, I could feel an oh-so-tantalizing long something hardening under that skirt of his.

"Pardon," he said, grabbing my shoulders to hold me in place and easing away from my embrace.

I let my hands slide over his skin as he stepped back, my pulse pounding. I was already hot, but I was getting all manner of wet just looking at this guy. A dream man, an angel.

"What was that for? Saving your life?" he asked, his voice a silky, smooth tenor.

"Hey, hands off, Rion. I saw the goddess first!" fish-guy snapped.

I turned to see him stalking toward us, still naked.

Two glorious men fighting over me, one of them an angel. Yep, definitely a dream and I was going to enjoy it. Mostly because I was fairly certain now that when I woke up, I was going to have one hell of a headache, or a concussion, or something, and probably frostbite.

"It's okay, guys. No need to fight. You can both have me. I've never had a threesome before, but I'd be willing to give it a go. Hell, the guys I've been with have barely known how to do twosomes." I looked around to find a place to fully enjoy my dream before I woke up. Dream or not, I'd never found the idea of sex on a beach that appealing with all that gritty sand getting in very sensitive places. "Let's get off the beach though."

"Who is this strange woman? A goddess you say?" the angel

asked, his smooth sensual tenor sending a shiver of desire rushing down my spine and making me think, just for a second, that it might be worth getting grit in the wrong places.

"This is Goddess Extraordinaire Annie Chambers," Delphon said behind me. "A very odd one indeed. I saw her emerge from the rocks back there, as if she were a stone titan, yet she doesn't have the coloring to be one. And I've never seen a stone titan looking quite... like that."

"Agreed. She is rather odd, isn't she?"

"Hey!" I might be odd, but this was my dream. Weren't my dream men supposed to find me alluring, beautiful, and stunning?

Of course, I *knew* I wasn't really any of those things. I was just plain old Annie with strange career goals that no one understood. Apparently even my dream men knew it.

"I'd have used the word exquisite," Delphon said.

Well, okay! I'd take exquisite. Things that were exquisite were special and unique and sought after by many.

I studied the grassy hill to my left. It was a little farther than I wanted to go just to have sex, but I bet there was less grit.

The angel — what had Delphon called him? Rion? — snorted. "Every woman is exquisite to you."

"Well yes, but—"

Swell. So much for being unique. But still, even if one of my dream men was a womanizer that just meant he was experienced. I wasn't sure how *that* would translate in my dream but there was only one way to find out.

Please let this be one of the good kind of dreams.

I swung back to them. "I've found a spot. We'll still want a blanket though. Do either of you have one?" I asked. It wasn't likely given that Delphon was naked and Rion only had a skirt, but hey, it was worth asking. And really, this was a dream. I shouldn't have bothered asking. A blanket would appear once needed. I could probably will one into existence right now if I really concentrated.

I blinked and realized the angel was wearing more than just his skirt. He had a strange harness around his torso and, half-turned as he was toward Delphon, I could see an odd long pack on his back between his wings. That and Delphon now had a satchel with him, and I didn't know if he'd grabbed it when Angel-dude was rescuing me or if it had just magically appeared.

I frowned, the dream suddenly not feeling right again. And I had no idea why. Nothing had really changed and yet...

"Goddess?" the angel said softly, also noticing that somehow the dream had changed. "I'm Hyperion of the Phyllidian Forest, son of Eonas, the Sky General." He bowed slightly.

It was a very long name for some dream-angel. Where the hell was my subconscious getting these names from? Some book I read on Greece as a child, perhaps? Unless this wasn't a dream... which was impossible because this strange place and these strange men... were well... impossible. So it *had* to be a dream.

"Most who know me well, call me Rion."

"Rion." I repeated the name. "And Delphon." I glanced at the once-merfolk, now just naked-guy. "Sure. Who am I to question a dream?"

"Dream?" Rion asked, glancing at Delphon.

Delphon shrugged. "She's mentioned this being a dream, several times."

Rion turned back to me. "Are you a goddess of dreams, then?" He looked around. "This feels real enough. I don't recall falling asleep."

"Not your dream, *my* dream." How had we come to this conversation? Weren't we supposed to be heading to the hills to have sexy times before I woke up?

To that point. Why weren't they all over me, doing everything in their power to please me? Wasn't that the only reason to dream of men like these? It certainly wasn't to have a conversation about whether or not this was a dream.

I had to get this dream back on track.

"You should ravish me before I wake up. But, over there, and on a blanket." I pointed to the spot I'd picked out on the hills beyond the beach.

"Ravish you?" Rion raised a brow.

"She's mentioned *that* a few times as well. Before you came along, she seemed quite intent on mounting me." Delphon's erection stirred to life a little and he smiled at me, then winked.

"Exactly," I said. "But I'm perfectly fine if you want to share. Or take turns. Whatever."

"We'll be late for our meeting," Rion said to Delphon.

"Meeting?" I blurted out.

Oh, come on!

This had to be my subconscious trying to remind me I was lying in an alley and was going to be late for work. I hated it when reality intruded on perfectly good dreams.

"I'd be willing to be a little late," Delphon said with a shrug.

"Of course you would." Rion rolled his eyes at Delphon and swept a hand through his golden locks, brushing them back from his forehead. He looked at me, far too serious. "I do apologize for my friend, Goddess..." He frowned.

"Annie," Delphon said.

"Goddess Annie. He's always been a bit too eager with women." He gave Delphon a scathing look.

No.

No no no no. This was *not* going to be one of *those* dreams where I woke hot and bothered and completely unsatisfied.

I opened my mouth to argue with him, but he cut me off.

"We have a meeting with two others in the town of Masia," he said. "Just beyond those dunes." He pointed down the beach.

I looked. The beach seemed to curve around, and I thought I

could see structures in the distance as well as a few boats out on the waters near that area.

"I think they'd understand if we were delayed by a goddess," Delphon said and stepped in. "Relax for once, Rion. Don't be a cold wind about this." Delphon's erection swayed in front of me, so close I could touch it.

And damn it. I needed to keep this dream on track and not let it turn into something else.

With a boldness I'd never had in real life, I reached out and wrapped my hand around Delphon's thick shaft, just below the tip, drawing a low, masculine groan.

"The goddess has a firm grip," he purred.

Rion's brows shot up and the bulge under his wrap grew larger.

Desire tightened in my core at the thought of having both of them. This was going to be one hell of a dream... if I could keep the damn thing on track.

Except they'd said they were meeting two others. Maybe my subconscious hadn't been trying to sidetrack my desire. Maybe it had been adding to the fantasy.

If two men were good, wouldn't more be better? "You said you were meeting others? Would they want to help with ravishing me?"

I'd thought a threesome risqué. What would a five-some be like? If they were all as gorgeous as these two were, I didn't think I'd mind it at all. My mind slipped into a fantasy of four men — in this case two looked like Rion and two like Delphon, all over me, caressing, fondling, large cocks out and rigid and ready. I drew in a shuddering breath as my body tingled from those imagined hands and bodies. Suddenly, my remaining bra, undies, and leggings were too much. I wanted to be naked and free and thrown into continuous fits of bliss by a harem of large, hot men.

"Goddess!" Delphon's voice was strained, and broke me from my daydream. I was squeezing his cock.

"Oh," I released it and he gasped with relief, but quickly recovered. "I'm certain our friends would love to join in the ravishing," he said. "Aethan certainly. And I'm sure we could convince Keph to join in." Turning to me, he added, "You'd like Keph, he's... big."

That shocked me a little. "Bigger than you?" I couldn't help but look at his erection again and shiver with anticipation. I tried picturing a larger cock and had to press my legs together at the thought. "Oh my."

"Indeed."

I was on fire, within and without, especially with the sun raging down on my fair skin. I was sweating through my wool leggings. Hooking my thumbs into the waistband I slipped them down and kicked them off. The sun be damned! This was a dream. I wasn't going to get a burn in my dream. Perhaps I'd actually tan for once! And I was going to get this four-man action going as soon as possible.

I began marching down the beach to the town. "Yep, let's go. I would like all of you to ravish me! Also, it would be nice to have a bed for all this glorious sex. I'm assuming we'll find one in that town you mentioned. And a drink. I could use a drink. I'm parched."

Behind me I heard Delphon chuckle. "A drink it is! Then the ravishing."

"Del— I—" Rion said, then sighed. "As the goddess wishes."

It sounded like angel-boy was in. Good. It was time to get this dream going.

CHAPTER 3

ANNIE

UNFORTUNATELY WE DIDN'T JUST INSTANTLY ARRIVE AT THE TOWN and once again I feared the dream was turning into one of *those* dreams. The kind where I searched for something — usually it was a bathroom, but in this case it was two more lovers and a bed — and never actually found it.

We walked for what felt like a good thirty minutes with the heat beating down on me, and I was covered in sweat and my calves ached with the exertion of walking through the sand before I'd even reached the dunes Rion had mentioned... which was something I didn't want to think about.

People didn't sweat in dreams and even if they did, my sore legs felt all too real.

We reached the apex of the sandy hills and beyond I could see the town in more detail now that it was much closer.

It didn't look like much. 'Town' seemed a bit liberal a word for it. It was more of a village. A really small village. There were a few larger buildings near the shoreline and at the center of town, but the rest of the buildings were huts. Actual honest to goodness huts. And there couldn't have been more than a couple hundred people there. I was sure, though, that — as in most dreams — it would change by the time I reached it and it would end up being something else entirely. Something with a comfy bed big enough to fit me and all soon-to-be four men.

Except the village didn't change.

It stayed the same small, too-rugged-to-be-quaint village, and by the time we walked up from the beach onto a packed sandy-earth road between some huts toward the center of town, I was getting woozy. Something, along with everything else — the heat, my sweating, and my sore calves — that also felt a little too real.

I swayed, bumping into the reed-woven wall of the hut next to me, and bounced off to march forward once again.

"Are you well, goddess?" Rion asked from behind me. "You don't seem to be accustomed to the heat."

"The gods live on a high mountain, don't they?" Delphon said. "It's probably much cooler up there."

"Exactly," I replied. Though I wasn't sure what I was agreeing to. My thoughts were hazy and muddled. This was usually how I felt when I'd been out in the sun too long. Just like that time in Barbados.

My gaze slowly dropped to my arm, and I couldn't tell if it was because I'd thought to look to see how bad of a burn I'd gotten or if it had just fallen of its own volition.

I frowned.

I wasn't lobster red yet. Odd. In fact, I seemed to be only just a tad darker... I was actually tanning! How odd. But then dreams were strange things.

Rion drew close and placed a strong, steadying hand against the small of my back, guiding me as we moved deeper into the town. I snaked my arm behind his waist, letting it slip down over his wrap to clutch at one iron-hard butt-cheek.

He made a bit of a humming noise at that, but didn't dissuade me, and we stepped out onto what I guessed was a main street.

"Wha...?"

The street was filled with all manner of strange and wonderful beings.

My subconscious was going crazy and I had no idea what any of it meant... other than I was horny.

A group of three half-men-half-horses walked by. What were they called again?

Jeez. With the heavy haze muddling my thoughts everything was so hard to remember.

Centaurs.

That was it. They were centaurs.

Going in the opposite direction were a gaggle of slight, slender girls, their skin and hair curious shades of blue and green. They passed by a woman with wings for arms and the legs of a bird haggling with a merchant selling fruit at the side of the road. The merchant himself was a giant of a man with only one eye above his nose, who was crouching down to be a bit less intrusive.

Then there was a large fellow with the head of a bull—

There was a name for them... mini-towers!

I giggled.

It wasn't the right word, but the man certainly towered over almost everyone else here. Maybe the mythology professors, or whoever it was who decided those things, should rename them.

Everyone seemed to be some odd creature from mythology or fairy tales, and the really startling thing was that — like my two companions — everyone was either naked or barely clothed, and nobody seemed to care.

I giggled again, my head swimming. There was something I was supposed to remember...

"I think we need to get you some water," Rion said.

He scooped me up — what a gentleman... angel... gentle-angel? — and carried me across the square to one of the larger buildings. It looked like some kind of pub with a large awning shading the front door and the rough-hewn tables and benches placed underneath. And with the raucous sound of many voices coming from within, it sounded like a pub, too.

And sure enough, the sign nailed over the door said "cantina."

Which only reaffirmed my belief that this was a dream.

Wouldn't the place have a proper name?

Funny how I could come up with all manner of strange people and a weird name like— whatever the hell Rion's full name was, but my subconscious couldn't come up with a name for the cantina.

Delphon opened the door for Rion and we entered the darkened interior.

The sights, now harder to see in the dim light, and sounds all began to blend together for me and my mind was on the verge of turning into mush. Which was very un-dreamlike... or maybe it was very dreamlike. I couldn't figure out which.

Rion laid me on a long bench and two other men appeared. It was hard to make out much, but one seemed shorter, scruffy, with horse's legs? He was introduced as Aethan. The other was the big one Delphon had mentioned. A brick wall of a man with shiny black skin, huge in every way and had to duck to keep from hitting his head on the ceiling. He gave a small smile as he was introduced, Kephas, or Keph.

Is this the one who's bigger than Delphon?

I looked between his legs, there was a shadow there, hard to see the dark skin in the darkened interior. But the swaying shadows certainly suggested he was... aptly proportioned for his massive size.

"I'm Goddess Extraordinaire Annie Chambers," I said, or tried to. The words were a bit slurred and sloppy. "Ravish me!"

Then I blacked out and was floating in a dark place weightless, bodyless, with nothing and no one around me.

This was more like the dreams I was used to.

The other dream had been so very... odd. Yet a part of me wanted to go back to it. It seemed a much more preferable option to waking up cold and bleeding in that alley.

A hint of light and sound and a cool, refreshing liquid whispered across my senses, and I was suddenly aware that I was drinking.

A rough wooden cup was softly pressed to my lips, gently tilted forward, and a trickle of water dribbled its way into my mouth... most of the time. Otherwise I could feel the wetness where it had gone down my chin.

Even before I opened my eyes, my other senses seemed to be on high alert. The cool and refreshing water was the best thing I'd ever tasted, a cacophony of noise surrounded me, hurting my ears and making my head throb, and I sat, reclined back, my torso and head resting on something hard, while the reek of old beer, wine, roasting meat, and sweat assaulted my sense of smell.

I crinkled my nose as my eyes fluttered open, and I fell into a stunning, dark silver-rimmed gaze.

It belonged to an enormous man, his flesh as near to midnight black as I'd ever seen. His face was kind, with rounded cheeks, and even though he was bald, I got the sense that he was around my age. He cradled me, holding me gently against his large body as if I was a doll, and while I felt delicate and fragile, I also felt completely safe.

"Feeling better?" he asked, his voice soft and incredibly deep, as he took the cup from my lips. A cup which seemed quite tiny compared to his massive, thick-fingered hand.

My thoughts instantly leaped in a highly inappropriate direction given that I'd just passed out — probably from heat stroke. But his large fingers made me think of other large things, which had me thinking of that large... *member* filling me and—

"I, ah..."

My thoughts leaped again and I remembered this was a dream.

There wasn't anything inappropriate about my thoughts toward this man at all. He was a figment— a very *large* figment of my imagination.

I tried to adjust a little to see how impressive he actually was, but wasn't at a good angle and moving made my head swim and my thoughts swirl back toward the dark nothing part of the dream.

"Did you want up?" he asked.

I wanted *him* up.

But it was probably better if I made sure I didn't pass out again first.

I pressed my forehead against his bare chest, closed my eyes, and sucked in a long, slow breath, trying to steady myself.

"Just breathe, little goddess," the man said, his deep voice rumbling through me as his hand, so large it seemed to span my entire back, swept slow, gentle circles on my back.

I sucked in another breath

"That's it."

"Thank you—" I searched my memory for his name. I'd heard it before I'd passed out. And besides, this was my dream. I'd named him.

It floated around in my mind for a second, just out of reach before I captured it.

Keph.

His name was Keph... and I had no idea why my subconscious had decided that was a good name for him.

I raised my head to look him in his stunning eyes again. "Thank you, Ke—"

Something oddly shaped about the length of my forearm flew by my head, hit the wall beside Keph's shoulder with a heavy *thunk*, and dropped to the floor.

Keph's gaze jerked up, while mine followed whatever it was that had hit the wall.

It looked like a piece of wood.

No, it looked like a piece of table leg.

My senses lurched and the magical little bubble I'd fallen into when I'd looked into Keph's eyes popped. Noise roared around me. Noise I *knew* I'd been hearing, but hadn't been paying attention to before.

I turned in Keph's embrace and became suddenly aware of two things.

The first was that the room was in chaos. Everyone except me and Keph were in the middle of a massive brawl. Chairs and tables were smashed and people wrestled and punched and went flying in all directions.

Food and beverages were tossed about with abandon, sometimes as a result of being knocked off a table, other times on purpose, thrown into someone's face.

The other thing I became aware of was Keph's aforementioned member that I'd been curious about.

Moving had shifted me to the side and I had a perfect view of it because the man was completely naked!

Delphon had been right. Keph was huge, and it was just lying there. It wasn't even erect.

Man. My subconscious was really trying to tell me something if even in the middle of a bar brawl I was getting hot and bothered thinking about a guy's monster cock and what it would look like when it was standing proud.

I wrenched my attention up and tried to pretend that I hadn't just gotten an eyeful, though I was fairly certain I was in the throes of a full-body blush and was very hot and very bothered.

Why did no one wear any clothes in this God-damned-uber-sexy dream?

Though, I wasn't wearing much myself.

I'd been too warm. Perhaps that was it. Everyone was too hot for clothes.

I giggled a bit at that unable to help myself then heaved my attention back to the fight.

"So ah... what's happening?" I asked Keph who didn't seem at all ruffled by the fight even after he'd nearly been hit by a table leg.

"The others got tired of waiting, so they started a brawl. It's common when we meet like this." The words rumbled out from him, deep and soft, and made a shiver of desire rush over me.

I couldn't quite imagine what part of me wanted my dream men to be brutish and go start fights, but apparently that's where this dream had gone. Though... Keph was quiet and calm and didn't look one bit worried.

A few feet away, a man — also naked — swung a chair at another guy, who ducked, and the chair swept toward me and the quiet giant holding me.

Keph caught the chair one handed and shoved, sending the man stumbling back a good five feet, then wrapped that large arm protectively back around me.

In the dim light it was hard to tell, but his skin looked shiny, more like black stone than skin, and when I ran my hand over his muscular forearm, it felt like stone, too.

He was literally rock hard, bringing a whole new meaning to the idea of *chiseled* muscles, and from that one-handed shove, he was strong, too. He could win this brawl in the blink of an eye.

"Why don't you fight?" I asked.

He gave a single low chuckle. "I'd break people."

Hunh. Yeah. I bet he would.

Large, strong, and gentle. I couldn't think of a more perfect combination. And I was sure he could be just a little bit rough when he needed to, because, hey, this was my dream.

I leaned back into him. He seemed content to let the fight run its course, and I knew without a doubt he'd protect me. Until the others were done messing around, it was just him and me, and I was okay with that.

I slid my hand up his arm and onto his chiseled chest. God, but my hand seemed so tiny compared to everything of his, and I wasn't a small woman. Sure, he was less defined than Rion, more rounded, with impossibly massive, rolling shoulders, but that didn't make him any less attractive.

A green-skinned woman threw a mug that somehow still had liquid in it at another woman with horse legs, making her sputter with rage and reminding me that no one was actually human in this dream.

"So what are you?" I asked.

"Stone titan," he rumbled.

"Yes, you are." I couldn't help myself as my gaze dipped to his lap again. "You're so very... hard."

He smiled and his massive hand shifted along the outside of my thigh, his palm alone was as wide across as my leg, and my thighs weren't small. "And you are very soft."

And now all I could think about was having that hand slide to the inside of my thigh, and his thick fingers driving me crazy.

I was more than ready. And this *was* a dream after all.

The bar fight— hell, the rest of this dream world didn't matter. I wanted this man. I needed to know what sex with him would be like. I reached down and ran a single finger along the length of his cock. It twitched and rose and swelled and... holy fuck!

I was trembling with anticipation and a hint of fear. Would that massive thing even fit inside me? Even as wet as I was now, I was uncertain. I was about to climb into his lap when a large form smashed into the wall on the other side of me. He'd hit with his back and landed in a sitting position, his legs outstretched as if he'd just sat and hadn't been thrown there.

It was my merman, Delphon.

"Oh, hey, you're awake!" he said. He wore a wild grin, despite blood oozing from his nose and from a cut in his forehead. "And I see you've gotten to know Keph. Didn't I tell you he was big?"

God yes, but... my desire and passion abated as reality — whatever strange dream 'reality' this was — returned to me.

I was in a room full of people, and I'd been about to mount Keph.

That, and Delphon was bleeding.

"You're hurt." I reached to check the wound — not that I'd know what to do with it. I'd tried to be a nurse, trouble was, I was pretty squeamish around blood. Except this was a dream and I couldn't seem to stop myself.

The instant my fingers touched his forehead a strange rush of something swept over me, and his eyes widened. It felt as if energy passed from me to him and right before my eyes the cut on his forehead closed.

He blinked and reached up to touch the wound, probing tentatively then more seriously. "You healed me?"

"I did?" But the results were clear. "I did."

I looked at my hand and the blood on my fingertips. I'd healed him. This wasn't something I'd dreamed of before. Generally, if I had powers at all in my dreams, it was flight or invisibility, not... healing?

And yet, long ago I'd wanted to be a nurse or a doctor. My mother had been a nurse, and my father was a doctor. For the longest time, as a child, that's what I'd wanted to be as well. Then I'd started taking biology courses and dissecting things. Taking care of people was one thing, but dealing with blood and vomit and all the other nasty things that came out of people... that wasn't for me. And as much as I had an analytical mind, being good at math and puzzles and organizing things, I never got the grades in chemistry or biology to take that route, even if I'd changed my mind.

At the time, I'd figured it was for the best and taken business courses in college.

Except now I could heal.

Which had to be some deeply repressed desire from my psyche. It was only then that I realized that despite my long trek across the beach — wearing next to nothing — I hadn't gotten a burn. Perhaps I could heal myself too? Nice!

Yep. I was some healing-powered-goddess in this dream. I could get behind that.

Delphon wiped the blood from his face and looked at me with so much more than the excitement and interest he'd shown on the beach. There was true wonder and admiration in his eyes.

"A goddess, indeed," he whispered.

I gave him a knowing smile and winked.

"Amazing," Keph added.

I turned back to him, unable to stop my gaze from dipping to his lap again, and my breath caught at seeing his half-aroused cock. All the heat and passion from a moment before returned to me.

"I am, and I think I deserve a reward, don't you, gentlemen?" I started to rise. I felt strong enough, and the room didn't spin. That was a good sign. "Why don't we find a room and—"

The other two men joined us at that moment, the fight seemingly winding down.

Rion was everything I remembered. He hadn't changed in the way that people in dreams sometimes did. He was still tall and lean and chiseled and now had a sheen of sweat on him, not to mention a couple of bruises, one on his cheek, the other on his side, that were starting to bloom a bright red.

I could soothe those. And the thought of running my hands over his hard muscles to do so only added to my heat and urgency.

I turned my attention to the other man, who, like Delphon and

Keph was also naked. I'd been delirious when I was introduced to him — what was his name? Aethan, yes — and hadn't gotten a good look at him. Now I let my gaze slide appreciatively down his body.

He was the shortest of the four, stocky and broad-chested, with ruddy red-brown skin, and his hair was a wild, spiky dark-red mane like a mohawk that ran from his forehead, down the back of his neck to his shoulder blades. His soft brown eyes seemed to devour me as we both looked each other over, hungrily. He was crouching, which was easy, given his backward horse-like legs. And yep, he had hooves.

"Hello again," he said, those brown eyes sparkling with mischief. "You're a sex goddess, I hear? I'm ready when you are." And he most certainly was. The expression 'hung like a horse' came to mind, but even so, he had nothing on Keph.

"Shut up, Aethan," Rion said. His angel wings were gone, which was kind of disappointing, and he looked me over critically and not sexually like I would have wanted. "Are you feeling better? I think the heat got to you on the walk here."

It certainly had. And with these four hunky guys surrounding me now, it was getting to me once again.

"She healed Del," Keph said in that slow, deep rumbling way, which made my skin tingle.

"She did," Del confirmed. "Definitely a goddess." His gaze at me was a little wild and still full of awe.

Aethan's grin grew. "A true goddess? A healing sex goddess?" His eyes went wide. There was something in that look, more than sexual desire — though judging by his erection he was more than ready — but there was also a yearning, a soul-deep need in his gaze that surprised me.

I smiled at him, and gave a wink.

Suddenly I had Marvin Gaye's 'sexual healing' running through my head.

"Well let's find our goddess a soft place to... rest, shall we?"

Aethan said as he turned toward the door. "The Sailor's Rest should have a room available."

Del rose, though his gaze, still full of awe and now a burning desire, never left me. The look in those intense blue-green eyes sent a thrill down my spine and made my legs weak. No one had ever looked at me like that before.

"Goddess," he said, holding out a hand, which I took.

"Before that," Keph said, sending another thrill trembling through me. God, I loved his voice. "As much as we may want to please the goddess and receive her healing gift. There may be others who need it more."

Others? How many more were going to join in pleasuring me?

"Remember that camp we saw coming into town?" Keph said to Aethan as he carefully stood... or rather, sort of stood, since he was too tall for the low ceiling.

"Camp?" Del asked.

"Yeah," Aethan said, his expression turning grim. Whatever he'd seen, it hadn't been good. "You're right. They need her more than we do."

Who were they?

"They?" Rion asked.

Keph gave a shrug of his massive boulder-shoulders. "Don't really know. They're sick or something. We asked one of the locals and he said recently people have been falling ill. And when they do, they go there. They probably have a wise woman to help them, but I'm guessing they don't have a goddess."

Oh, well yes, I could see how that might have elicited some pity from Aethan. Poor souls. Good thing I was a superhero-healing goddess. "Great, I'll go heal these folks, then you four can give me my... reward." I made sure to make eye contact with each of them.

Del's gaze was eager and full of fire. Aethan nodded, his pity fading back to heated desire as his gaze swept over me again, and man, I liked the way his eyes seemed to devour me. Rion's expression was stalwart and his smile seemed to say 'you have a good heart.' Then he winked, a signal that he'd be more than happy to oblige helping in my 'reward,' while, Keph's gaze was filled with a heated curiosity.

"And a reward you shall have." His soft, silver-lined eyes shimmered, and he trailed a finger down my arm, sending anticipation shivering through me.

"Let's get this healing done!" I said.

CHAPTER 4

ANNIE

THE CAMP WAS SMALL, NO MORE THAN A DOZEN TENTS, AND ONLY A few people wandered around, some dressed all in white.

I marched off the dirt road, heading for it, only to realize a moment later, I was alone. Turning back, I saw the four men standing at the edge of the road.

"Come on," I called out to them, not sure why they'd stopped.

None of them moved. They were scared. It was clear on their expressions.

I sighed. My shoulders fell, head tilting. "Really, guys?" So much for brave and stalwart souls.

I marched back.

"Listen up, you sexy hunks of man-meat," I said, shocking myself at that choice of words. I'd never have said that to a man's face in real life. Though, to be fair, I hadn't met many men who'd warranted it, either. But then, this was a dream, and I was feeling emboldened. I was a sexy-healing-superhero after all. "If you want any of this," I motioned to myself, waving a hand down my form. "Then you'd better come with me."

I smiled at my inadvertent pun. Here was hoping that once this healing gig was over they would *come with me* — after I'd had a few other orgasms of course. This was a fantasy after all, might as well make it a good one.

"But they're sick. What if we catch it?" Aethan said. He actually seemed worried. Odd for my dream men to be so preoccupied with dream-sickness.

"I'm a healer, remember. I'll heal you." It was obvious.

That changed their expressions, well most of them. Del, Rion, and Keph all nodded and seemed to relax. Aethan wasn't so easily swayed.

"I didn't really see you heal Del the first time. Perhaps—"

Keph snapped his fist out and tapped Aethan in the face with a resounding crack, making the small man stumble and fall onto his butt.

I wasn't sure who was more shocked. Aethan that Keph had hit him without warning, or me because it hadn't looked like Keph had hit him that hard.

"Ow, Zeus's balls!" Aethan exclaimed, blood running from his now-broken nose. "Why'd you do that?"

"Heal him," Keph said to me. "Then he'll believe."

I suppressed a laugh. It had happened so fast. For all his bulk, Keph was quick. And certainly, Aethan had deserved it for doubting my awesomeness.

I sauntered — just a little slowly, letting him suffer for a moment — back to the men and laid a gentle hand on Aethan's cheek, trying not to look at the blood gushing from his nose.

As much as I like this super-healing goddess thing. I wish it involved less blood.

Again, I felt the energy flow from me to him, and again, with startling speed, the man's nose reformed, straightened, and the bleeding stopped.

Aethan blinked, reached up to his reformed nose, and spat out a mouthful of blood, his eyes wide with awe.

He stood and bowed deeply. "I'll never doubt you again, Goddess Annie."

"You'd better not." Again, emboldened and feeling distant from my real-life self, I slapped him on his hairy ass, noticing only then he had a horse-like tail.

Hunh. Unable to help myself, I gave it a quick tug, half expecting it to come off. I didn't know why I expected it might come off — this was a dream after all — but it didn't.

"Come on, boys, let's heal some folks!" I said, turning as Aethan's eyes grew wider and his cock a little stiffer.

Then I marched back toward the camp with my men following.

A woman, looking similar to Aethan — except with hairy goat-like legs, cloven hooves, and tight-spiraling horns atop her head — came rushing out toward us.

Unlike most of the people I'd seen so far, this woman wore clothes, a white dress which came to her 'knees' backward as they were. The dress covered just her front with a loop that hooked behind her neck to keep her loose covering in place. She had thick brown hair, falling in waves past her shoulders, and wide square-ish eyes, which made her look a bit startled.

"You shouldn't come closer," she warned. "Those here are very sick, quite contagious. Do not enter unless you're already like them and seek aid."

Nope. "I'm here to heal everyone," I called out, perhaps a little too loudly. A few others from the small tent-village looked my way as well.

"She's a true healer indeed," Del said before the woman or anyone else could question us. "A goddess come to us from the heavens."

I flashed a brilliant smile. It felt good to have a herald. I hadn't realized I'd always wanted one, until I had one.

I strode forward, past the shocked goat-woman and pushed

into the nearest tent, flagrantly throwing the flap to one side—and froze.

Before me were two woman, one much older than the other, perhaps a mother and daughter. They looked human — no fish tails or goat's legs — but with colorful skin. The older woman had rose colored hair and skin beautifully patterned and mottled in bright reds, oranges, and yellows. The younger woman had bright pink hair, her skin darker, maroons, deep purple, and violet.

Except that was only part of what had stopped me. The other part was much less beautiful. Dark spots covered their skin, the younger one seemingly much further along than the elder, her patches were larger and at the center of a few of them the skin had burst, the wounds weeping blood.

The elder woman turned to me with shock — and possibly hope — in her eyes. She was kneeling at the top of a woven straw mat, the only thing between her and the hard ground, cradling the younger woman's torso on her lap. The young one was less responsive, head lolling to one side, eyes searching, but not seeing me.

"Oh God," I whispered.

This was horrible. In the matter of seconds my dream had gone from fun, sexy, and empowering, to dour, sad, and gruesome. It hadn't fully turned into a dark and scary nightmare, but the scene before me was certainly far from pleasant and could easily go that way.

"Can you help us?" the woman asked.

The goat-woman-nurse rushed over and pushed me aside at that moment. "I don't know what or who you are." Her gaze was intense. "But don't give these people false hope. Can you truly heal as you say?"

I hoped so.

Although now that I was there, I didn't particularly want to get any closer to the women in the tent.

But I'd committed myself, and I *had* healed Aethan's broken nose. Surely I could heal whatever this was.

I went to the mother first.

The men and the nurse crowded into the entranceway of the small tent, watching me but not coming any closer. I would have made some comment about them looking away for modesty's sake — since the women in the tent were naked — but then half the people I'd seen so far, man or woman, had been naked, so modesty wasn't much of a thing in this particular dream.

I stood beside the mother and laid a hand atop her head. Even there, I could feel the heat radiating from her, most likely from a fever.

"I really hope this works," I whispered, only just barely breathing the words, and pushed energy into the woman. I felt it take, latching onto something inside her and forcing it out of her.

The woman gasped, her eyes going wide like my guys when they'd experienced my magic, and the spots vanished from her vibrant skin.

I stepped back, a bit lightheaded for a moment.

"Is that water?" Rion ask, drawing my attention to him as he pointed to a clay jug on the ground a few feet from the entranceway.

The nurse nodded and he grabbed it and rushed to my side, wrapping a strong arm around me, which felt ever-so-good, even if I was mostly certain I didn't need it.

He lifted the jug to my lips and I took a long swig of the cool, refreshing water before pushing it away and turning my attention to the young woman.

Rion stepped back, but stayed close, and I knelt next to the girl.

The mother reached out a tentative hand to brush my shoulder. "You are indeed a goddess," she said softly. "If unlike any I've ever seen before."

Yep, frumpy and freckled. I'm sure most goddesses were much more beautiful than I was. Luckily this was a dream, so everyone here thought I was beautiful.

Laying hands upon one of the few unblemished spots on the young woman, I took a deep breath and focused on healing her. This took a lot longer. The young woman's illness was much further along, and her body thirstily drank the healing energy from me.

This time I was the one who gasped when it was done, my head spinning, my vision blurring.

I sat back heavily on my butt, and Rion rushed back to me, kneeling beside me and offering me more water. But the young woman's eyes fluttered open, and I couldn't help but stare, the water forgotten for a second.

Her eyes were a deep, stunning scarlet, and while I'd have thought red eyes would have been scary — the embodiment of evil in horror and fantasy movies — there was nothing terrifying about them. They were gorgeous.

"How...?" she asked her mother, her voice weak.

"You were saved by the grace of a kind goddess," her mother replied, then turned to me. "What is your name so we might worship you in thanks for this service?"

"Annie Chambers. Goddess Extraordinaire." Then, light-headed as I was, I giggled.

Worship?

Me?

Rion helped me drink from the jug again and that helped to strengthen me a little, though even after I'd had my fill, the room was still spinning ever so slightly.

"Help me up," I said to Rion, and he did. Standing, the world whirled a little faster and I had to keep leaning to the right to try to correct it, while Rion held me close. I probably would have fallen if he hadn't.

"You're tired," he said softly. "Perhaps you should rest before you tend to the others."

I smiled, a bit of a sloppy grin. It occurred to me that the sensations I was feeling were very similar to being drunk.

"I'm fine," I said with a weak wave of my hand. "Take me to the others so I can heal them all, then we can get on with the pleasuring of me."

"As you wish," he said, though he looked more concerned than happy at that prospect.

Except as I staggered out of the tent steadied by Rion's strong arms and headed to the next tent, doubt began to creep into my mind. This dream was getting stranger and stranger and some distant part of my consciousness whispered, *perhaps it's not a dream after all.*

But that... was still just a little too farfetched to believe.

CHAPTER 5

HYPERION

TRULY THIS WOMAN WAS A GODDESS UNLIKE ANY I'D EVER SEEN OR known. The gods and goddesses of legend were powerful, yes, but often selfish and self-serving. I didn't know why Aethan still insisted on cursing upon Zeus. Those gods hadn't done anything for any of our peoples in hundreds of years. The few — alleged — gods or goddesses I'd seen in my lifetime, had probably all been fakes and frauds. They hadn't done anything like what Annie was doing. As much as her name was odd, her deeds were pure and her power very clear.

Yet, she was growing weak.

She'd healed nearly two dozen poor souls in the camp and insisted she be taken to the next, but now I was fully carrying her while the others waited at the edge of the camp for us. She seemed to slip in and out of consciousness. And still, she wouldn't give up, wouldn't rest.

I set her down in the last tent where three people huddled together. Luckily none of them seemed as far gone as that young *anthousae* woman Annie had first healed. A few others along the way had been as bad or worse, but luckily not many.

Whatever the origins of this nasty disease, it was particularly horrible to see. I'd never seen anything like this in Nikandra, nor any of the Okanid islands around it. And I thanked all the gods for that.

The gods...

I stepped back as Annie began to work, barely able to sit upright. Certainly no god had done so much good for any of the people here in recent memory. All the glorious tales of the gods were hundreds if not thousands of years old. And most of the *glory* was for the gods themselves, spiteful and petty as they were. They'd done some good for men and women, but they'd been more of an annoyance than a boon.

Annie finished with the last of the three *epimelidai* in the tent then slumped to her side. When I knelt next to her, her life-beat was still strong within her, at neck and wrist, but she'd passed out, probably exhausted. I slipped my arms under her shoulders and legs to lift her, but before I did, one of the *epimelidai* spoke up.

"Please, good *erinai*. Could you convey a message to the goddess? I'm gifted with the sight," the young man said, keeping his voice low, and I could understand why. Such people — *prophissi* as they were known — were generally shunned. As much as seeing the future might have been a gift, it was often more of a curse, as what was seen was rarely good. "When she healed me, I had a vision."

Bloody crows!

I clenched my jaw tight. As much as I wanted to leave this man, I knew what he had to say could be very important, so I nodded for him to go on.

"There is a darkness, an oozing filth. It's behind what infected us. It's aware of this healing goddess now and is furious with her for halting its work here. It will come for her and bring this terrible death to all around her when it does."

Well that was just great.

"Is that all?" I asked

The young man nodded, and I picked Annie up and left.

Del, Aethan, and Keph waited in the shade of a nearby tree. The sun sat low on the horizon, turning the few wisps of clouds in an otherwise clear sky, a soft pink. Goddess Annie had spent almost all day healing everyone.

"She's exhausted," I told them.

Del and Keph nodded, while Aethan looked a little put out. Of the four of us, the *satyr* was the worst around women. He had the unfortunate combination of being easily aroused and awkward with the opposite sex. That meant that, as much as he wanted to be with every woman he saw, he was often disappointed.

"Let's get a room and rest, then we can talk," Keph said in that usual slow and steady manner of his, his deep voice always calming.

"Agreed," I said and we began to make our way back to Masia. "And you should all know. There is more going on here."

"Oh?" Del asked.

"One of the last to be healed was a seer and had a prophetic vision when the goddess healed him. Something about there being a darkness behind this disease. It knows of her now and will come for her... And it's not going to be nice when it does."

They stared at me as if they didn't know what to say about that, and I understood their predicament. I didn't know what to say about Goddess Annie or the prophesy, either.

The quiet solemnity with which we walked back to town was indeed odd for us. We were sent to Masia to meet with our three counterparts, partly because we enjoyed a rousing conversation or argument. This silence spoke to our immediate and intense reverence for this strange woman among us and our fear of the darkness now hunting her.

I looked down at the form in my arms and shook my head. The Goddess Annie Chambers was an enigma. First, she was taller by a head than most of the women in these parts, almost as tall as Aethan. Second, her form was that of a woman caught between maiden and matron. She had the narrow waist of a maiden, combined with the full hips, thighs, and bust of a matron. It was an alluring combination, perhaps hinting at the goddess's sexual prowess and youthful energy.

At the thought, I felt the stirrings of arousal just as I had when I'd first met her on the beach and when she'd embraced me, pressing her divine body against mine.

My heart quickened. I was not usually one who caroused and sought women to pleasure. That was more Del and Aethan's thing. There had to be something special about a woman for me to join with them, and so very much about Annie was special.

There was her pale red hair, a color I'd not seen before. Certainly, many of the *nymphai* peoples had brightly colored hair, but not anything like Annie's. My own people had a fairly uniform blond or pale brown. *Tritons*, like Del, tended to darker shades, blacks, or deep blue or greens, or shades of coral, while Aethan's people, the *satyrs* of the Theophylian Plains had varied coloring, from white to black, as well as light brown to Aethan's dark red.

Odder still was the fine speckling over Annie's cheeks, shoulders, arms, back, chest and stomach. This dappled skin was similar to some of Aethan's kind, when in horse form. A dappled hide wasn't uncommon, but it generally didn't transfer to the *satyr* form. These spots seemed to accentuate her beauty, the perfect accent on the pale skin beneath.

She was like the legends of amazon women of old: tall and strong, beautiful in their surety and confidence, ferocious in battle. I had yet to see Annie Chambers in battle, but given how she'd thrown herself into the healing of those sick people, I had no doubt of her fierceness.

Then there were her strange garments: lacey webbing over her breast and loins that was so very seductive. There was little reason for people to cover themselves in this warm climate. Generally, there were only two reasons a woman might do so, and both applied to Annie. Some healers wore coverings, like that *panai* woman back at the sick camp, and Annie was a healing goddess... though the nurse's coverings were usually white and Annie's were pink.

The second reason a woman might cover herself was to make herself more alluring to men. It made her mysterious and seductive — causing a man's mind to imagine her features, think about her, instead of passing over her like all the other women.

And I was certainly thinking about the goddess in my arms. These strange coverings at her breasts and loins hid just enough to make my blood boil, while also showing enough to make imagining the rest very easy. A thoroughly captivating combination.

Yet another in her long list of mysteries, was her obsession with dreams. Though I wondered if perhaps this was how the gods came to us. In their dreams?

That made a certain sense to me. The gods had not been here in many generations. Perhaps they had not slept or dreamed in that time.

Or perhaps it was just Annie Chambers who slipped into the mortal realm in her dreams.

I didn't know, and I knew trying to understand the ways of the gods in general was a good way to make my head spin.

We reached the Sailor's Rest Public House, and Del — always the most generous with his ample wealth — paid for a room for the night.

We took Annie up to our assigned room on the second floor. It was small, barely wide enough to hold two beds and a small table between them, but it was also probably the largest room in the inn.

I gently laid her on one of the beds, and, feeling protective and wishing to stay close and guard her, I sat at the foot of the bed.

Keph sat on the floor, as usual, his back to the closed door, while Del and Aethan each sat on opposite ends of the other bed.

"I call to order the sixteenth session of the meeting of emissaries," Del said formally. "Well, my good men, other than the excitement of today, what have you been up to?"

"Pardon," I interrupted. "Shouldn't we speak of *this* excitement? I'm concerned about the goddess and this coming darkness. We were the ones who told her about the camp. It's our fault she's drawn the attention of this foul entity, whatever it is."

"Agreed," Aethan said. "She's certainly the most exciting thing that's happened to me in the last six months." His *excitement* was plain to see. Of course I knew several *satyrs* and they always seemed half aroused. Even the women among them seemed in a near perpetual state of stimulation, so Aethan's current condition wasn't unexpected.

I'd been interested in a *satyr* woman once, long ago when'd I'd been young. She'd been a beautiful roan with the most exquisite blue-gray skin and blue-black hair. And very lusty. I'd nearly always come away exhausted from our encounters.

I dragged my mind back to the topic at hand. "Aethan, please. She's been targeted by this sickness-bringing entity because of us. We told her to go to that camp and now she's in danger." I couldn't stop a little passion slipping into my voice despite wanting to appear calm and serious.

"Agreed," Keph said in that leisurely, rumbling bass of his. "Do you or Del know where she came from?"

"I do," Del said. "Sort of. There I was, enjoying some sun on a hot rock, fresh from my trip up from Galniosia when I heard something and turned. Truth be told, I didn't see it happen in the moment, but she was stumbling away from what had been a tall standing stone next to me. She couldn't have come from anywhere other than the heavens or out of that rock. I'd made sure I was alone before I began my sunning. I like the silence of listening to the waves. Then there she was, out of nowhere."

"My folk can move through stone," Keph said with an intrigued look.

"But she looks nothing like your people," Del said quickly. "Her skin is soft and pale and she's nowhere near as big as any of your titan women."

"Small," Keph agreed. Though he then gave a half-smile. "But... not too small."

I caught the heat in those silver-lined black eyes of his. For a moment I was just a bit jealous. One session with Keph would ruin the goddess for the rest of us. None of us could compete with his... size. Yet, I could understand his attraction. I felt it too. Which was odd. Both Keph and I were the least likely to seek out a woman for casual sex, yet both of us were caught up with Annie's energy.

"So, she's a goddess of healing and sex and dreams and stone?" Aethan mused, his gaze sliding up to the ceiling in thought. "I've never heard of anything like that before."

"And her name," Del said with a shake of his head. "It's unlike any goddess I've ever heard of. Ani. Anichambers. I supposed that's sort of like Aphrodite."

"Odd name aside, you can't deny what she did today," I said, the events still fresh in my mind. "She cured those people of that devastating illness."

"But do the gods often get so... tired?" Aethan asked.

That seemed odd to me as well. She'd fought through her exhaustion with great conviction, but in all the tales I knew of gods, the gods didn't tire.

But then perhaps that's just how those old tales came across after hundreds of years of telling.

"Can we really know the gods? I've certainly never met one. Perhaps they are more like us than we know," I said.

The others, having never met any other gods either, all nodded or shrugged, generally accepting this.

"So, what do we do with her?" Del asked.

"She demanded our pleasure," Aethan said, quick to remind everyone. "We must oblige her. I'll go first." He rose and took a step to cross the room.

I rose to meet him before he could wake her.

"Let her sleep." I would have asked if he'd want some overly excitable woman to interrupt his sleep, but I feared his answer to that question would not be the same as mine.

He huffed, but backed off. "I'll be first when she wakes then."

"We'll let her choose which of us will begin," Keph said, ending the debate in a single sentence because no one argued with Keph. The large man's love-tap to Aethan's face earlier that day had been extremely restrained and had still had the man reeling and broken his nose. The titan could punch through solid stone and not even bruise his rock-like knuckles.

I sat back at Annie Chamber's feet, my gaze drawn to her once again. Indeed, all our gazes were upon her.

So mysterious and magical, strange and wonderful.

"We need to protect her," I said, knowing it in my heart.

"Agreed," Del said. "You're right. It's our fault she's in danger. We need to keep her close and keep this darkness, whatever it is, away from her."

"Agreed," Keph rumbled.

"I'm in," Aethan said eagerly. His choice of words didn't escape me. I was certain he very much wanted to be *in*.

I rolled my eyes at him. "Then it's set. We'll keep her from the darkness."

The others nodded, sealing the pact.

"So," Del said, lounging back against the wall behind him. "Seeing as our goddess isn't going anywhere for a while, I figure we have some time to go over any news from the realms of

Nikandra. I'll go first. Things are going swimmingly in Galniosia." Del snorted at his own joke while Aethan groaned and I rolled my eyes. "We've heard back from the court of the Atargatine merfolk and secured a political alliance. Our dashing prince narrowly escaped a political marriage. That honor will fall to his younger brother, now fated to marry some distant princess." He shuddered and I couldn't help shuddering with him.

I understood the necessity of a political marriage. Peace between various factions among our peoples rested on family bonds, but I hated the idea of spending the rest of my life with someone I didn't know and from his shudder, Del did as well.

"For his sake," Del said, "I hope she's kind and gentle. He's not an overly forward man, the young prince. It's sad really. But he's accepted his fate, actually seems to be looking forward to it. He's sent the princess one of his works of art as a betrothal present."

"At least he's trying to make the situation more comfortable," Keph said.

"Yeah, for what it's worth," Del replied, his tone clear that he thought a piece of art wasn't going to make the situation less awkward. He shrugged and continued with his report. "The Whale-folk of the deep Poseidic Ocean are worried about the many storms this year out on the open waters. They fear it portends dark times ahead. I think they're a superstitious lot and these are just storms." He pursed his lips and frowned. "Anything else?" he asked himself, lost in thought for a moment then shrugged. "Closer to home, all is quiet in the Okanid archipelago. The waters are clear and calm and the other islands are still no fun at all. Mostly backward folk, still caught up in rites to the gods and such."

I could attest to this last bit. The other smaller islands of the Okanid Island Chain were not as progressive in their beliefs and thinking. The folk still strongly believed in the old gods and followed their rituals — gruesome as some of them might be — to the letter.

I sighed. Yet there were some here on Nikandra who sought to return to those old ways. Mostly elders, and mostly men. I didn't understand it, personally.

I listened as the others went through their reports. Aethan spoke of a disease beginning to affect the people on the plains, and I couldn't help wondering if this was the same illness that Goddess Annie had just healed. This wasn't a good omen at all. Yet that seemed the most pressing of his concerns. The rest of his time he spoke of women he'd been with. I highly suspected — knowing him as I did — that most of what he said were just tales and fantasies.

Keph's report was slow and stoic, like the large man himself. It seemed not much was affecting the stone titans who lived under the Ophion Mountains.

Then it came to me, and with a sigh, I leaned forward to rest my elbows on my knees and set my chin atop my clasped hands. I sat there for a long moment before I spoke, not looking forward to what I had to announce.

"The council of elders has chosen who will replace my father as sky general when he retires."

"You sound upset," Aethan said cautiously. "Did they not choose you?"

"I'm upset because they *did* choose me." And that meant everything was going to change. I'd tried to forget about it, pretend I was still just a captain, commanding a flight of one hundred *erinai*, and the excitement with Annie Chambers earlier that day had done well to distract me. But now it all came back. "This will probably be my last meeting with you all." And that's what I hated the most about this promotion.

"Oh?" Del asked with a furrow brow. "But...?" He left the question hanging.

"Who will replace me? I don't know yet. Given the *erinai* nature, I'm sure he'll be no fun at all. And don't get your hopes up that it might be a woman. Again, given some of our backward ways, that's unlikely. Even if it were a woman, I highly doubt she'd be interested in entertaining any of you."

There were nods from the others. From my own reports as well as general awareness, they knew what my people were like. Of all those on Nikandra, the *erinai* were the most outdated in their thinking. They were insular and cold to most other races, and thought themselves superior because of their ability to fly. Something about being lords of the skies made them think they were lords of all peoples.

I wasn't particularly fond or proud of my family and heritage. It hadn't even been that long ago that we'd warred with the plains-folk — Aethan's people. These meetings of the four largest nations of Nikandra were a direct result of those wars and a hope on all parts to keep such things from happening again.

With me leaving this position as emissary, I was afraid such talks would cease to be.

The four of us had all been told by our elders that we needed to be strong in these talks, negotiate trade deals and political alliances — to the advantage of our home nations. And the four of us generally ignored such negotiations and spent our time together drinking, talking, and carousing. It was how we'd become such fast friends.

There was the occasional talk of trade and politics, but it generally went smoothly because of our tightknit group. Mostly we went back to our respective peoples and told them that no negotiations were possible, perhaps next season. And they accepted that, thinking the other nations were all too staunch in their ways.

I had no clue what would happen if any one of us was replaced. It could be catastrophic to keeping the balance — albeit not moving forward balance, but balance nonetheless — between our nations.

A heavy silence filled the room for a long moment, then Keph, in his way, simply said, "We'll miss you."

That comment, and the earnestness that I knew was behind it, nearly brought me to tears. "I'll miss you all as well."

We didn't speak any more of it after that.

Since we all wished to watch over Goddess Annie Chambers, and since we all desperately needed a drink, we ordered wine and ale and had it sent up to the room.

It was late — perhaps even early the next morning — when we all fell into a hazy drunken sleep. I half-thought-half-dreamed of Goddess Annie healing those people, a soft sheen of sweat making her pale skin glisten as her body slowly sagged with exhaustion.

She'd given too much, healing too many people too quickly and—

Someone yelped and I jerked upright, my pulse suddenly racing, my senses yanking me awake, and my eyes flying open.

Far-too-bright sunlight streamed through the single window of the room — which we'd forgotten to shutter — making me hiss and squint, my gaze instantly jumping to the goddess.

She sat in the bed, backed up against the wall as far away from me as she could get, her knees pulled up, her arms around them hugging them tight against her chest. She looked terrified, her large golden-brown eyes wild.

"This isn't a dream is it?" she said, voice trembling.

CHAPTER 6

ANNIE

I WAS SURE OF IT NOW. THIS WASN'T A DREAM. AND IF IT WASN'T A dream, then where in hell was I and who were these naked men in my room?

I had just been dreaming, living in a world of strange and wonderful and scary things, and now I was awake.

I *knew* I was awake.

Except I was still in the world of strange, wonderful, and scary things.

And while I'd had that experience before of waking in a dream and still being in the dream, this time felt different.

Because it had remained consistent. That was it. My dreams were never this linear, the characters and places and times shifted and jumped around — as they'd been doing just a moment before, while I'd slept.

And now I was back, *awake*, finding that things hadn't really changed — other than my location — and was suddenly sure this wasn't a dream any more.

"Who are you?" I asked, squishing myself into the corner, trying to make myself smaller, which was kind of stupid. If I needed to run, I shouldn't be hugging myself in a ball. But then there was no way I could escape with the four men in the small room and Keph leaning against the door.

They were the same men — or sort-of-men — I'd been with before. I knew their names, but suddenly that wasn't enough. The fact that they were all naked — or close to it — in this way-too-small room, making them all too close to me and still essentially strangers, was just too much in this moment.

"Goddess?" Rion asked slowly.

He looked rough, his eyes squinting in the sunlight. In fact, as they slowly woke, they all looked rough.

It was then I noticed the jugs and pitchers and cups strewn all over the floor. A lot of jugs and cups. These guys had gone on one hell of a bender.

And for some reason that was what solidified my certainty that this wasn't a dream.

Dream men didn't get hangovers, and they didn't cram themselves into a small room while you slept and have a drinking party.

"It's us," Rion said. "Did the healing yesterday affect your memory?"

"No, I remember you all, but why are you real?" I realized as soon as I said it that it was a silly question. Except I desperately needed to know the answer.

How could men with wings or fish tails or the legs of horses be real?

Perhaps if I reworded it a little. "How are *you* real?"

Rion frowned at me.

Nope that still sounded insane.

"What are you?" Now I was just digging myself a hole. I stopped while I was still — hopefully — ahead.

"Real?" Keph asked, in that slow bass rumble. Even in my shock and despite my fear it still sent a thrill through me — somehow both soothing and arousing at the same time.

"Goddess, you seem confused and afraid. Fear not. We won't harm you. We've stayed here to protect you," Rion said. All of that sounded very nice and gentlemanly and logical, but it didn't explain why he'd had wings for a while yesterday...

Had wings.

My thoughts lurched. "Where are your wings?"

Rion's eyes widened just a little. "I've shed them."

"Shed? Like a cat sheds fur?"

"What's a cat?" Aethan asked. "Is that a being of the heavens?"

Most cats would probably think so, yes. But the more important thing was, how could they not know what a cat was?

I turned to Del. "Where's your fish tail?" Then to Aethan. "Can you change your legs to people legs?" Then to Keph. "And... you seem normal, if huge, so I guess... why are you huge?"

"Goddess," Del began slowly. "Are you not aware of the types of peoples of the Okanid Islands?"

"Let's assume for the moment that I'm not," I said, my gaze still darting from man to man, my mind whirling.

"Oh." Rion blinked. Then he sat up a little straighter. There was an odd look in his eyes as he gazed at me. It was an assessment, that much I knew. Men had a certain look when they were *assessing* a woman. Except this wasn't the usual kind of assessment. There wasn't lust or desire behind it. No, it was as if he were somehow comparing me to some image in his mind, and after a moment he nodded.

"I'm an *erinai*," he said.

Eh-rin-eye? I sounded it out in my head.

"The *erinai* are peoples of the air and kin to the great hawks and eagles. We can take the form of men, as you see me now, or possess wings, for our natural domain is the air above. We can also take the shape of birds of prey, hawks and eagles mostly."

Ah, okay. Bird-men.

Yep, that made no sense at all.

"Next." I turned to Del.

"I'm a *triton*," he said. He'd said that before. That was a word I recognized — vaguely. Greek, perhaps? "I can be a man, or a merfolk, as you originally saw me, or a large fish. Some of my people have an alternate merfolk shape in which they possess the head of a fish with the remainder of the body as a man."

Fish-face? I couldn't imagine that, at least not on Del — gorgeous as he was. Still, he *was* half-fish, and that *was* impossible.

Swell. I had two impossibilities so far, so, I turned my attention to Aethan. Might as well just get all the impossibilities out of the way, then try some rational thought with Keph.

"I'm a *satyr*."

Say-ter? "You mean satire?"

"No, that's a type of play. My people are *satyrs*."

I nodded, not really understanding.

Rising, Aethan's legs shimmered and became those of a man.

I blinked. His legs had shimmered. It had really happened.

Logic said this had to be a dream, but it wasn't, and I was growing more and more certain of that despite all the impossibilities around me.

As much as it was strange, it was still far too real and *normal* where it really counted. Even this conversation didn't fit the idea that this was a dream. People didn't explain what they were in dreams, they just were.

"I can take the form of a man, but usually don't." His legs shimmered again and returned to being the horse-like legs... with a tail. A tail! "I like my legs. Human feet are too small and the knees are too low, it always confuses me. I can also take the shape of a horse."

"Like a centaur?"

Aethan's eyebrows shot up. "A centaur? No! Zeus's balls! They can't change their shape. They're stuck as they are, half horse, half man. I can't imagine what that would be like."

Said the half-horse half-man.

Blinking, I turned to Keph. He was still huge and striking with great lumps of muscle for shoulders and heaving slabs for a chest. His arms were thicker than my not-skinny thighs and then there was that... impossibility... between his legs. I got wet — and a little sore — just looking at it.

"I'm a stone titan," he rumbled.

Sure. "And what do you turn into?"

"Stone."

"Not an animal?"

He shook his head.

"So, a stone man?"

"Like a statue," Rion said. "When he's fully stone, he can't move."

I nodded, my head bobbing up and down, and I couldn't seem to stop it. I had hoped that some explanations would clear things up. I'd been so terribly wrong.

"I, ah... I need to go," I said, starting to inch off the bed. But I stopped when I'd gotten as far as throwing my legs over the side. "That is... if any of you know how I got here?"

CHAPTER 7

ANNIE

I DIDN'T THINK I WAS SHOWING IT, BUT I WAS IN FULL PANIC MODE. These guys seemed nice, strange as they were, and had the bodies of Greek gods, but still—

I didn't belong here. Wherever here was.

I needed to get back to a place where my life made sense. It may not have been perfect, but it at least made sense.

Also... I was mostly naked.

"Where are...?" My clothes were scattered all over a beach somewhere. Oddly, I wasn't uncomfortable in what I was wearing. I certainly wasn't too hot, and my underwear covered me as well as any bikini would. "Screw it. Sorry guys. I gotta go. I, ah..." Oh wait! Crap! "How long was I asleep?" Had I missed my brother's wedding? I felt pretty sure I'd missed a day of work— Except I had no idea how time worked wherever I was. Fuck!

"It's been a day," Del said.

"My day or your day?" I asked, making them frown.

God. I just had to hope their day was like my day and I hadn't been gone too long.

"I really have to go." If time worked the same wherever I was, then my brother's wedding was tomorrow.

"Goddess, please. Stay with us," Aethan said. "We need to protect you from the darkness."

But it wasn't dark out, so that had to be some kind of ploy to keep me there.

And everything within me was screaming with panic, begging me to get out of there — now now now — get home.

I jumped from the bed and rushed across the small room to the door.

Keph hurried to stand, but in his rush, misjudged how low the ceiling was and put his head through it. Someone yelled at him from the room above us, making him jerked back and crash through the door behind him and out into the hall.

And now I had an opening.

I rushed out into the hall, jerked right — even though I had no idea if that would get me out of there or not — found a set of stairs and rushed down them.

At the bottom was a large room filled with tables and chairs and a bunch of *people* who stopped eating and talking to stare at me. They were all strange and naked and—

And I wasn't going to think about it.

I dashed out the door into brilliant midday sun, picked a direction at random, and started running, ignoring the sting of the hard, stony ground on my bare feet.

I had to get out of there, had to get home, had to—

I raced across the high dunes and down onto the beach. Far off in the distance, I could see the odd tall rock formation where everything had started and where my clothes would be — hopefully.

I wasn't much of a runner. I mostly walked on the treadmill at the gym, maybe an awkward jog now and then, but I put on the jets now. Oddly I wasn't even that winded when I got to the pile of stones and — luckily — all my discarded clothes.

This is where I'd arrived, this had to be the way back.

Except there wasn't a doorway or big sign or anything indicating how I'd arrived in this strange place.

I gathered up my things and put them in a pile. It was far too hot to put any of them back on again. It was then that I realized I was missing my leggings. I'd taken them off farther down the beach.

I turned back to get them even though they weren't really important, getting home was, but the guys were running over the sand toward me — well three of them. Rion, who was way ahead of the others was flying because, of course! He had wings!

He reached me as I found my leggings and landed lightly in the sand beside me.

"Goddess—"

"Can't talk, gotta go." *Got to get the hell out of here before I lose my mind.* And I sure as hell couldn't look at the gorgeous man with his chiseled muscles, because I couldn't get distracted and he might convince me to stay.

Except a part of me kept asking why not? Why couldn't I stay?

Sure, my life made sense... because it was normal. But I wasn't anyone special there. Here, these men thought I was a goddess and that was more alluring than anything I'd felt in a long, long time.

Goddess. Every time one of these hot guys said that word in reference to me my heart skipped a beat. Hunks didn't say that to girls like me.

I was so wound up and confused that I began to put on my leggings, despite the heat. I got them half way on, then realized what I was doing and decided, *fuck it*, and kept going. Hopefully I'd be back in a Chicago winter soon enough, where I'd need them.

Except there was sand in the leggings and with their tight fit, they chaffed almost instantly. Just great.

"Goddess, please!" Rion said as I forced myself away from him and marched back to the rocks and the rest of my clothes. "You can't leave. We need to protect you."

"From the darkness, yeah. I don't think that will be a problem for a while. It's quite bright at the moment. If you want to help, find me a way home," I said my voice still sharp with a panic I didn't want to completely acknowledge, because if I did I was sure I was going to have a mental breakdown. "I'm sure the darkness won't find me at home."

"In the heavens?"

"In Chicago."

Rion frowned. "She-ka-go?"

"Yes."

"Do you not know how you came here?" Rion asked.

"No."

"Oh." His frown deepened. "Very intriguing."

"Very intriguing?" I spun on him, my panic turning into sharp frustration. "Very intriguing? I'm not intriguing. I'm just Annie Chambers from Chicago. I'm not a goddess, I'm a normal person. Only here, wherever here is, you don't seem to have normal people. You have fish-people and horse-people and bright, multi-colored people. Haven't you noticed that I'm different?"

His lips quirked with a hint of a smile. "I have, yes."

Aethan and Del had almost caught up to us, while Keph, who was a little slower, was still fast-trudging across the beach.

"Don't leave us, goddess," Aethan called out. "We haven't plea-sured you yet." He reached me, huffing just a little. "I was really looking forward to satisfying a goddess." After a scathing look from Rion he added, "Oh, yeah, and we need to protect you from the darkness, but don't you worry about that. We'll keep you nice and close, and there's nowhere closer than on my—" Rion punched his shoulder making him yelp in pain and shutting him up.

And yet I was still stuck on, *I was really looking forward to satisfying a goddess.*

And I was really looking forward to being satisfied by you, is something I didn't say.

I don't know why I was so attracted to a man with horse-legs. Perhaps it was the other horse parts down there and wondering just how satisfied I'd be with it inside me.

Was it getting hot out here? Like hotter than hot?

I really needed to shake off those sorts of thoughts and concentrate on getting home. "I've gotta go. Gotta get home." The words helped focus me.

"Home?" Aethan asked.

"She-ka-go," Rion said.

"Yep, there." I moved over to the rocks. Hadn't Del said something about me coming from the rocks? That didn't seem likely, but then nothing here did.

I put my hands on the large flat surface of the tallest rock. It was the one I'd tried to jump off. Something about it, the way the side was so... flat and smooth... made me wonder.

One of my hands landed solidly on its surface. The other passed right into it.

"Holy-what-the-fuck?" I pulled my hand out. It had felt cold in the rock... on the other side? "No fucking way," I breathed.

"What is it, Annie Chambers?" Rion asked, drawing closer.

"Put your hand there." I grabbed his wrist and guided his hand to the rock that wasn't a rock, making him lean into me.

He did, except I think he expected the rock to be solid, because he lost his balance when his hand didn't hit the rock's surface and with a yelp, he stumbled forward and kept going, vanishing through the rock.

My heart pounded.

This was it.

This was my way home.

And I'd just dumped a nearly-naked angel into some dark alley in Chicago.

CHAPTER 8

DELPHON

I WATCHED RION VANISH THROUGH THE FACE OF THE STONE AND stopped dead, gaping. As much as I knew — somewhere in my mind — that this had to be some sort of portal, I couldn't make sense of it. Added to this was the runaway goddess now gathering up her many clothes so she could leave through that same portal.

"Annie Chambers," I called out. I needed to stop her. From her reaction to everything since she'd awoken, it was clear something wasn't right. Yesterday, she'd been fearless and adventurous. Today she seemed terrified. I didn't know what had changed, but I wanted to help. Somewhere, deep down, I felt like this was my fault.

Had I somehow messed up this chance meeting? I felt responsible for the divine woman. I'd been the one to whom she'd come to initially, whether on purpose or not. And through my interactions with her, she'd ended up in that sick camp, and now had some *darkness* out to get her.

"You can't leave," I gasped, nearly out of breath from sprinting across the beach. I probably could have crossed the distance in the nearby water in half the time, but hadn't thought to change back to my *triton* form. "Please."

I grabbed one of her arms, stopped her, but she flinched, trying to jerk away.

Gods, she seemed so afraid of us.

I released her, but I moved to stand between her and the portal. "Tell us what's wrong. We only want to help you. We need to protect you." *And you are the most fascinating and wonderous woman — goddess, whatever — I've ever met.*

She stared at me, barely able to see over the pile of heavy clothes in her arms.

"I..." Confusion filled her eyes. "I don't know what's happening. I... I thought this was a dream, but now I know it's not and that's just... I have to go home."

"Then we'll go with you." I didn't know where she was going, but I was willing to go anywhere with this woman. Rion had already gone through.

Annie Chambers nearly choked then had a coughing fit. "No... you can't," she managed to sputter out between gasps. "Look at you! All of you!"

I glanced at myself then Aethan who stood beside me. I couldn't see anything wrong with any of us.

She shoved past me, heading toward the invisible portal where Rion had disappeared. "You're naked."

Naked? What was wrong with that? Though I did recall something about the gods being on a high mountain. And mountains were cold.

I nodded, understanding. That would explain why Annie Chambers had been so overdressed when she'd arrived.

"And it's cold where you are from?"

Annie hefted her pile of clothes and gave me a dry look. "Clearly."

Well, that wouldn't be too much of a problem for me. As a

triton, I was resistant to the effects of temperature. The depths were cold, but that didn't affect me too much. I was fairly certain Keph would be fine. Stone titans did not mind such things. *Erinai* were also somewhat protected against the elements, as the high skies could be cold. It was Aethan who'd be most affected.

"We'll be well, goddess. Few of us are affected by such things."

"No," she said firmly as she turned to me, awkwardly, given the bundle she carried. "You can't come with me."

"Rion has already crossed over," Aethan said, inspecting the rock wall, hands roving the flat surface. He hadn't slipped through like Rion had, not yet anyway.

"I'll make sure he comes back." Annie Chambers stopped before the rock face and began to don her many layers once again. It looked like she would be quite hot, while she was here at least. Also, sand had gotten into much of what she wore. That couldn't be comfortable. Indeed, she was grimacing as she dressed. Yet she kept going.

Keph finally caught up to us.

"Where's Rion?" he asked.

"In the heavens," Aethan said, still fixated on that stone.

Annie Chambers, now fully bulked up in her many clothes turned to me. "Look, you can't come because... where I come from, it isn't normal to walk around naked."

Oh. "Would it offend the gods?" I asked. I didn't see how the natural form of any creature could be so upsetting. Also, most of the depictions of the gods had them being naked or close to it. But perhaps their ways had changed in the many hundred years since they'd been active among us.

"Yes!"

"Then we need to find some coverings," Keph said. Then to Annie, "You have many, might we borrow some?"

"No! My clothes won't—" She cut herself off. "You can't come with me!"

I was about to ask why not, when she anticipated such a question.

"That's my world, not yours. This is your world, not mine. Neither of us belongs in the other's world. I'm sorry I came here and got you all... worked up."

Which was one way of putting it. The run here had tempered any arousal I'd felt, but looking at the goddess now, even with all her clothes on, she still captivated me. Those golden eyes and speckled cheeks. Her commanding surety and something more that I couldn't explain. Something deeper which called to an equally deep place in me.

"We're not sorry you came," Keph said slowly. "Those sick people needed your help. You must have been sent to help them. And now we need to protect you from the coming darkness."

"Darkness? What darkness? You keep mentioning it."

"After you healed the last of the sick yesterday, one of them, a seer, said he'd had a vision as you'd healed him. He said there was a darkness that would come for you. It didn't much like what you did healing all those people."

"Well fuck." She spat out the word. I wasn't familiar with the saying. "No good deed goes unpunished." I hadn't heard that before, either. It sounded rather appropriate, if a little morose.

"So, you see..." I tried to capture her eyes to let her see my sincerity, but it was hard to get a good look at her face with the thick scarf covering her mouth and jaw and a heavy hat pulled down to her eyebrows. I moderated my tone, trying to sound reasonable. "We need to go with you to protect you. It's our fault you went to those people. Now we need to make sure you're safe."

Keph nodded. "I'd thought she'd be safe in the heavens, but if this darkness is some other god, then we should go with her."

"I..." She looked up at the sky. "God!" It was odd to hear the word as a singular. Was that how the gods cursed? To perhaps only themselves? It was an odd thought. "You can't..." But her words had less conviction that before. "I'll..." She sighed heavily. "Fuck me, I'm not going to dissuade you, am I?"

"No." My voice was soft but firm.

"I'm going to regret this," she said, deflated. "Fine. You can come, but you're going to need to cover yourselves, at least a little." I think I was the only one close enough to hear her next whispered words. "I hope no one I know sees me on the way home."

We took a few moments then to figure out the best way for us to cover ourselves. Annie Chambers demanded that Aethan switch to his non-horse legs, and using her skirt, which was unfortunately torn up, as well as her scarf, we all managed to cover our loins — if only just.

"Let's go," she said shaking her head, clearly doing this against her better judgement.

But I knew this was the right course. There wouldn't be any place she'd be safe. From the old legends, even the mountain of the gods wasn't immune to dark forces.

Aethan tried to move through the stone, but couldn't. It was a solid wall.

Annie approached, touching the stone where she had before, and Aethan tried again and nearly fell through.

"It's your touch," I murmured to her.

She grimaced at me. "Swell. Now go."

I stepped through... and stopped dead.

A massive, high, dark wall loomed before me, and despite my resistance to the weather, a sharp chill bit my exposed skin. Loud noises assailed me from my right and I looked to see many people passing by the mouth of the tunnel I was in. Beyond them flashed fast moving... somethings, roaring by with the odd honking sounds, like those of a dying whale.

Aethan was as stunned as I, and Rion huddled next to a large bin of some sort, which smelled foul.

"What is this place?" I asked him.

"She-ka-go," he said, teeth chattering.

Then I was bumped from behind as Keph came through and finally Annie Chambers.

"Oh, thank God that worked," she said with relief, but then she huffed an exasperated sigh. "What the hell am I going to do with you lot?"

I was beginning to sense that this wasn't the mountain of the gods, but something far stranger, and suddenly I wasn't so sure we should have come.

But it was too late now and I needed to get out of the cold as soon as possible.

"Lead the way to your estate, goddess," I said. Perhaps her servants would be able to clothe me and my friends.

"Just... put away your wings and everything odd," she said with a shake of her head. "And act normal."

But I was pretty sure *my* normal and *her* normal were two very different things.

CHAPTER 9

ANNIE

I SHUT AND LOCKED THE DOOR TO MY APARTMENT BEHIND ME, breathing hard, my heart pounding, and expecting a knock at any moment from a neighbor or friend who'd seen me with these four men. Men who looked like they'd walked off the set of some barbarian or caveman movie. Looking at the four of them milling around my small apartment, I instantly regretted letting them come with me. It had been a bad idea at the time, but they'd been so damned persistent and considerate and sexy.

Okay, so some small part of me had been having this fantasy since I'd been old enough to buy my first vibrator. And if I was honest, not all of my racing heart was due to the fear of having been spotted with them. A part of me loved the idea of these guys wanting to be near me, protect me, and pleasuring me until I was a quivering mess.

As much as I had no clue how these guys were real, or how that other world was real, they were. It was hard to accept, alternate worlds and all that, and it was just too much to contemplate right now. I felt like my mind would explode if I did. It would be easier to accept that I was hallucinating, yet the longer these four stayed with me, the less I considered that an option.

Perhaps harder to accept was that they wanted to help me, be with me, and even considered me a sex goddess.

Standing there, still waiting for something terrible to happen, I watched as Aethan stripped off the bit of my torn skirt he'd worn as a loin cloth. Almost instantly his legs were back in horse-form.

"Much better," he said and I couldn't entirely disagree. In here, safe, locked in my apartment, I didn't necessarily mind having four sexy guys who wanted to get naked and have sex — assuming that was still on the table. And by the way Aethan was looking at me — and the fullness of his erection — it was.

"God, this is a glorious mess," I breathed. I couldn't quite figure out if it was more glorious or more a mess.

For a long moment, I couldn't move from the door, couldn't get my mind to work. I just didn't know what I was going to do with these men — other than what a certain burning desire deep in my body wanted me to do. My life had been a bit of a mess before all of this and...

"Fuck!" My phone was still back in that alley. I'd completely forgotten about it when we'd come back from wherever we'd been.

I was torn between wanting to run back out to get it, which meant leaving the guys in my apartment alone — or heaven forbid they'd want to come with me, which they probably would — and staying here, ripping off my clothes, and getting lost in this fantasy just a little longer before returning to real life.

As with so many other times in my life, practicality won.

"Hey, guys, I've... ah... got to run out and do some... stuff—" Get my phone, pick up clothes for them, call people who'd probably been trying to get ahold of me, get a dress for my brother's wedding — which was tomorrow! The only positive in all of this was that I'd caught a date on a newspaper at a newsstand and now knew that time seemed to work the same in my world as theirs. I'd only lost a day and a half — the whole day being a Friday, which wasn't great as far as keeping my job was concerned — but better than having lost weeks or even months. "If I leave you here, are you going to behave?"

"We will come with you and—"

"Nope," I said before they could argue with me. "You're not coming, not this time. I'm putting my foot down. As you saw, there are a lot of people in my world, and you all stand out like—" *Sex gods.* "A sore thumb. I won't be too long," I said before they could argue with me. "There's food in the fridge. Help yourself. Feel free to have a shower and freshen up." I waved toward the bathroom. "Just don't leave."

"Goddess, we—"

I unlocked my door and left before they could argue with me, hurrying down the hall and out of sight before they could follow me.

God, I hoped they stayed put.

Running back to the alley — thank God it wasn't far from my home — I did a quick search for my phone. I wasn't even concerned about people jumping out of the darkness at me this time. I had too many other things to worry about and too many things that I didn't even want to think about.

Thinking was bad. There was just too much to think about and none of it made sense.

I found the phone, crushed with a large Keph-sized foot print over it, and could only pray the SIM card and the memory card inside were still good.

I quickly ran to a consignment store for several bags full of old clothes that would hopefully fit the guys then to a corner store for a new phone. I'd hoped to take a bus downtown to get a dress for my brother's wedding but didn't think they guys would wait that long for me. So instead, I stopped in at the tiny boutique store around the corner from my building and paid way too much for a gorgeous red dress — which I'd been eyeing for weeks, and already tried on a half-dozen times. Then I rushed back to my apartment.

As I did, I swapped the SIM card from my old phone to the new and made a few quick calls. First to Diane at work. Luckily, I hadn't been fired for missing the one day of work — and thank goodness it had only been one day. She'd covered for me, telling everyone I'd called her to say I was sick. I told her that was exactly it, and I'd been so ill I hadn't even been able to get to my phone.

Second to my brother to confirm that everything was on schedule for the wedding. I'd missed the rehearsal, but I used the same excuse: sick as a dog and not able to even get to my phone, but I was feeling much better now. Luckily, I wasn't in the wedding party, so my absence wasn't a big deal. I didn't know my brother's fiancé well and her maids of honor were all close friends of hers.

Then I made a couple more calls to friends, in case they'd been worried even though a day out of touch wasn't uncommon for me, and the world was set right once again... or as right as things could get with four hot, strange men waiting for me in my apartment.

I didn't quite know what I expected to find when I returned, but Del, Keph, and Rion, their hair in various stages of drying most likely from having a shower, sitting around my tiny kitchenette table, quietly picking away at some leftover Chinese food wasn't quite it... though it wasn't a perfect scene.

The chair Keph had tried to sit on had broken beneath him and he sat — as it seemed he often did — on the floor. Still, he was tall enough to rest his elbows on the table which looked like it might break under his weight at any moment.

They all looked up at me when I rushed back in, their expressions filled with relief.

"Thank God," I said, relieved myself, that they hadn't done anything stupid. I could handle having one less chair. At least they were all still there. "Good."

"Your world is a strange and wonderful place," Del said standing, revealing that he was, of course, naked. "The bathing room is pristine and the automatic water is incredible."

It sure was. I was glad they liked it.

I dumped the bags of clothes on the floor by my feet. "I hope you'll all find stuff that fits in here so the next time we go out you won't be so—" Hot, sexy, attention-drawing. "Cold."

I was still in my coat and boots and hat, and I hadn't started to take any of it off because I was just a little worried that once I started taking things off, I wouldn't stop until I was as naked as they were — and that included Rion who'd lost his wrap sometime after he'd arrived at my apartment.

The trouble was, I'd taken care of all the pressing matters and was utterly exhausted and really just wanted these four to cuddle and pamper me all night.

And the more my mind played that scenario out, the more my body wanted it.

"Ah, screw it. After the day I've had, I deserve this." And by *day* I meant everything since I'd fallen into their world.

I started taking my things off, and as I'd feared... anticipated? ... I didn't stop, and by the time I was naked, I wanted more than just cuddling.

"Okay guys," I said, my voice breathy and hopefully sexy. "You want me, you got me."

That had Keph and Rion standing as well and shooting questioning glances between them.

Then Rion cleared his throat. "Which of us would you like to pleasure you first, goddess?"

Wow. Those were words I never thought I'd ever hear, and they made me feel both desirable and powerful, melting what little crumbling resistance I had left to this idea. Rion himself had always been stalwart and kind, carrying me from healing to healing in the sick-camp.

"You," I said, my heart thundering with fear and anticipation.

"As you wish, goddess," he replied, his skin flushing and his cock rising. His hardening erection was a thing of wonder. Taller than Del, but not as broad, seemed to describe Rion *and* his cock — and a quick glance at Del confirmed that suspicion.

Rion came to me, and with each step, my heart felt like some wild beast trying to break out of my ribcage. I was so very hot, probably flushed and completely red.

He bent and swiftly scooped me up into his strong arms just like he had the day before. Wordlessly, he carried me to my bedroom — the group must have scouted out my place when I was gone, since he knew the way — and sat me on the edge of the bed.

His sky-blue gaze, filled with a sizzling heat, slowly trailed down my naked body, making my breath hitch.

I couldn't believe I had a gorgeous man in my bedroom and looking at me like I was beautiful, *desirable* — and with a hard-on that proved his look wasn't just an act.

"How would you like to be pleasured, my goddess?" he asked, his silken tenor sending a shiver of anticipation rushing through me.

"I ah..." I didn't know what to say. If I'd still thought I was in a dream, I might have been brave and proclaimed exactly what I wanted... if I'd actually known what I wanted. But knowing this wasn't a dream anymore stole my courage. That, and all I could think about was feeling good. *That* was what I wanted and I didn't care how that happened. "I ah... however you'd normally please a goddess?"

"As you wish," he breathed, sending a stronger shiver of antici-pation rushing through me to pool hot and needy between my thighs.

CHAPTER 10

ANNIE

RION'S PUPILS DILATED WITH HIS DESIRE, TURNING HIS PALE EYES into deep, bottomless blue pools, and he trailed his fingers along my jaw and the side of my neck.

It was a whisper of a touch, tender, reverent. It made my pulse stutter in desire and, if I was being honest with myself, a little bit of unease. He thought he was making love to a goddess and I wasn't one. But as much as I knew I had to tell him, the words stalled on my lips. I'd never had a man look at me like I was special and beautiful, and I wasn't ready for the fantasy to end.

When this was over — whatever this was — I was going to stay in my world and he was going to go back to his. I knew he had no expectations for a relationship so he never had to know the truth. And really, in his world, with my superpower, I could be a goddess.

I shoved my worry aside and focused on him. His fingers teased across my collarbone as he sank to his knees, now no longer towering over me, but looking up at me. I opened my legs so he could draw closer, and he took the invitation, sliding his other hand up the inside of my thigh as he leaned in, drawing close.

"I've never met anyone like you," he murmured.

My gaze dipped to his lips, and I couldn't help wondering what he'd taste like, how his lips would feel against mine.

I slid my fingers into his blond hair and urged him close, but instead of raising his lips to meet mine, he dipped down and brushed the tip of his tongue over my nipple.

My breath stalled. I wasn't sure why. I'd had guys lick and suck my nipples before, but there was something about his touch, how his hand on my collarbone slid down to my other breast and his other hand on my thigh inched higher, his fingers now only an inch away from my wet and aching core. Maybe it was how he still gazed up at me, his eyes filled with worship, never leaving mine.

Then he sucked on my nipple and my thoughts scattered. It didn't matter how he looked at me or anything else. There was just overwhelming, sizzling, sensation. His mouth teased my nipple into a tight bud with a firm insistent pressure, his hand kneaded the other breast, and his fingers on my thigh teased closer and closer to where I desperately wanted him.

My breath picked up and so did his, and a faraway part of me knew that meant he was enjoying himself too.

He teased a finger through my folds and slid the slickened tip over my clit with another whisper of a touch that made my whole body hitch, not just my breath.

A low sensual moan fell from my lips, drawing a hum of pure masculine pleasure from him that twisted my desire even tighter.

With the hand on my breast, he gently pressed, urging me to lie back, and then slowly swept his lips down my stomach, sinking lower and lower, until his breath teased my curls and my pulse pounded in anticipation.

Oh, God! Was he really?

He looked up, his eyes catching mine, as if to ask permission.

Yes he was!

"Please," I breathed.

His expression heated, and he dipped lower.

A few of the previous men I'd been with had done some perfunctory fingering, but never oral, and I'd always wanted to know what it would be like to have a man — especially one who knew what he was doing — kiss me down there.

And Rion knew exactly what he was doing.

His warm breath caressed my sensitive flesh, making me squirm, before he started tormenting me in the most amazing way with this tongue, teasing it through my folds, flicking over my clit, and then — oh, God yes — sliding it into me.

A low moan escaped with one of my shaky breaths. I tangled my fingers in his hair, holding on for dear life, savoring the sensation and not wanting it to end. I wanted him to make me come with just his mouth alone. And I was already so very close. Just a little more. Just a little harder and faster.

But he didn't pick up the pace, just kept tormenting me, building my need into a simmering ball that grew bigger and tighter.

I squirmed, my fingers digging into his scalp, until the ball burst in a glorious release more powerful than anything I'd experienced before.

My head tipped back as my muscles contracted tight and I half-cried half-moaned my satisfaction.

"That was—" I breathed, my thoughts spinning, my breath ragged, and a voice inside me growing louder and louder begging for more. More more more.

Rion lifted his lips away and looked up at me through the veil of his blond hair falling across his eyes, his gaze, full of desire, sliding over my body, making every inch of me burn.

His blue eyes captured mine and held me there for a long moment, stealing all breath and thought. Then he slowly stood, his long thick erection rising above the edge of the bed, making my pulse pound and my mouth dry with anticipation.

My heart thundered in my chest, my blood rushing in my ears, and I raised my gaze back to his.

Breathtaking, heated need filled his eyes, sending a shiver of another climax racing through me. I shifted back on the bed, making room for him, and opened my legs in invitation again.

He didn't hesitate, claiming the space and running his hands up the insides of my thighs, urging me to open wider.

His thumb brushed my clit again, nearly sending me over the edge, and tiny tremors raced through me, promising me another incredible climax.

The desire in his eyes turned into a vortex, pulling me in, worshiping me, making me feel like I was the only woman in the world for him, and with a rush of wind, his wings swept out behind him.

My thoughts stuttered, filled with awe and longing.

Right. Wow. I'm about to be fucked by an angel.

He leaned down, his wings flapping slightly so he didn't need his arm to support him, and his face hovered over mine, that curtain of hair creating a private space, where only we existed.

"For my goddess," he whispered, as he pressed the tip of his cock against my entrance.

I squirmed, trying to inch closer to him, urging him to enter me. But he captured my hips in his large hands, his thumb still tormenting my clit, and held me in place as he slowly, oh so agonizingly, incredibly, slowly, pushed into me.

Every sensitive nerve in my channel, already awakened from my first orgasm, thrummed with sensation. I'd never felt like this before, like I'd burst into flames if he didn't start moving, but I also knew he was taking his time to let my body adjust to him, as well as to torturously draw out this incredible moment.

I was panting with need, my body twitching on the verge of

release again by the time he'd fully sheathed himself inside me. Then, held aloft by his wings, he began to rock his hips with long slow thrusts. Out and in. Out and back in.

His thumb swirled circles on my clit in time with his thrusts, while his other hand swept over my stomach and back to my breast, teasing my nipple again.

It was sensation overload with the friction of him moving inside me, the insistent pressure against my clit, and the rough kneading on my breast. It stole my breath and twisted me tighter than I'd ever been before with the promise of an even more powerful climax.

His pace picked up, the pressure from his hands growing as his own desire started to overtake him. His breath came fast, his masculine groans fueling my own, until my eyes rolled back and another orgasm rolled over me in a stunning, breathtaking wave.

A whimper of bliss mixed with heartache escaped my lips and a tear seeped from beneath my lashes.

I'd been sleeping with all the wrong guys. No one had ever made me feel so satisfied and so beautiful before. A part of me whispered that was because he thought I was a goddess, but I shoved that fear deep down. Right now, in this moment, to this incredible, sexy man, I was special and adored. I mattered.

"Goddess?" he whispered.

"More," I managed to gasp out. More more more. I never wanted this feeling to end.

"As you wish," he said, his hot breath caressing my lips.

He drew himself out so very slowly and I felt at the same time empty, and in great anticipation of his next passage into me. This continued, the slow filling then withdrawing of that amazing length of his as he gradually picked up pace. His face moved from over mine to kiss my neck and shoulders, breasts and nipples.

I lost track of time, of meaning, of everything except the purity of pleasure he brought me. I cracked my eyes open and watched in awe as Rion moved above me, his wings sweeping forward and back, brushing air over my hypersensitive skin. A white light radiated from his body, making him look even more like an angel. The glow grew brighter and brighter, until my eyes watered and I had to shut them.

But shutting my eyes only made my senses lock into the sensation of him moving inside me and how he'd already brought me back to the highest point of need again. So quickly, so amazing.

Every muscle in my body thrummed, my desire twisted tight, and another powerful orgasm crashed over me, burning away all breath and thought with raw, glorious, satisfaction.

With a few more powerful strokes, he groaned and tensed inside me, our bodies locked together, sending another rippling orgasm rushing through me. I cried out, gripped in the final waves of release and the world behind my closed lids spun around and around and around, filled with bright, flashing stars.

My back arched off the bed—

No all of me arch from the bed. I felt nothing below me, only Rion's strong arms around me, holding me close, my breasts pressed to his hard chest.

With a sigh, I opened my eyes and fell into intense, bright blue eyes, filled with adoration and desire, then glanced to the side and realized we were flying, hovering over my bed as he finished in concert with my final ecstatic climax.

We stayed aloft for some time, as he shuddered and moan, my core clenching tight around him, his heartbeat pounding in his cock against my sensitive channel.

After a long heavy glorious moment, we sank back to the bed, our chests pressing against each other with heavy breaths, tiny tremors still rushing through my muscles.

"Does my goddess require more?" he asked, his voice dark with masculine satisfaction.

Hell, yes! But I wasn't sure if I could take much more in that moment. I was wrung out, weak as a kitten, and still spinning on elation and flashing starts and satisfaction.

"No, Rion," I gasped. "Thank you. Oh God, thank you so much." I reached around his neck and pulled him closer. It occurred to me only then, that in all that, he hadn't kissed me on the lips even once.

I raised my head and pressed my lips against his. He gasped and I slid my tongue into his mouth, teasing it against his, and showing him with my lips how much I'd enjoyed what we'd done, how much it meant to me to feel so thoroughly satisfied.

He jerked back, his eyes filled with confusion and surprise. "Goddess?"

"Yes?"

"You kissed me."

"Yes."

"Do you mean it?"

That was a silly question.

"Of course I did," I giggled, my mind and body still whirling with my incredible releases.

He nodded slowly. "I accept."

I had no idea what he was accepting, but I went with it, too far gone into warm, exhausted joy. "Good, 'cause here's another."

I pulled his face down to mine again and this time, when his lips touched mine, I felt a spark, like a static shock. For a moment it was painful, burning my lips, then as our mouths crushed together it soothed and from my lips a warm tingling sensation spread out, filling my body and seeping into my soul. I was the most accepted and fulfilled I'd ever felt. Tears of joy left my eyes as peace swept over me. For the first time in a very long time, I felt completely relaxed, serene, and loved.

I didn't want this moment to end, so I didn't release him for a while. By the time I did, he was glowing again, only faintly this time.

"My angel," I said as my arms fell away from him and a deliciously delighted dreaminess came over me. My eyes fluttered shut as he lifted away from me.

I felt blankets put over me, and I wafted away into soft, sensual dreams.

CHAPTER 11

AETHAN

RION STRODE FROM THE GODDESS'S BEDROOM, AND I COULD SWEAR he was glowing. The lean man was never smug, but he stood tall and proud with a slightly awed and bewildered look on his face.

Zeus's balls, how I envied him.

It hadn't been right that I'd been in the bathing room, cleaning up when the goddess had made her choice. I knew, if I'd been there, she'd have chosen me, but the fates had decided that wasn't to be.

"The goddess is resting," Rion said softly. Of course she was. He'd tired her out and now the rest of us would have to wait. Crow-eaten bastard!

We were gathered around the kitchen table and Rion came to stand before us. I could smell the tang of sex and sweat on him, making me even more jealous.

A slow, silly grin spread on his face, something I'd never seen on him before. "And, she has chosen me as her bonded mate."

"What?" I blurted. This couldn't be true. How could she have picked her mate before having tried the rest of us?

Del made a similar surprised exclamation. Keph, of course,

since the large man had never been one for extreme emotions, only gave a soft huff.

"She kissed me." Rion's fingers drifted up to his lips as if he still couldn't believe what had happened. "It was unlike anything I've ever felt before. The bonding rang through me, like I was a bell. I can still feel it." He drew in a long breath and as he exhaled, his shoulders rolled back. I think this was the first time I'd ever seen him fully relaxed, and now I was sure he was glowing.

With the sinking sun of the late afternoon wrapping Goddess Annie's residence in dusky twilight, it was becoming clear that Rion really was the sole source of light in the room.

"A bonding kiss?" Del said, surprised, jerking me away from Rion's glow and back to the point. "A true kiss?"

Rion nodded. "Indeed. I wasn't sure if she'd just been caught up in passion. When I asked her if she meant it, she said yes and kissed me again. It was upon the second kiss that I felt the bonding claim me. I'm hers now and she's mine. Irrevocably."

I bit back a groan of frustration. That was it. The rest of us were just dead weight now. She'd made her choice and a bonding kiss was sacred. It was a formal pact between man and woman, a vow for all eternity of love and fidelity.

Some said there was actually ancient magic in a true kiss, but I didn't much believe in magic.

Although from the way Rion was talking about his experience, perhaps when a bonding kiss came from a goddess there was a higher power involved in sealing the vow.

Agitated, I rose from where I'd been squatting — since the chairs in her apartment were meant for legs of a different shape than mine. I could have shifted into my man form, but I hadn't liked it when I'd been forced to trudge through the cold as one, and had reverted back to a *satyr* as quick as I could. It just felt so much more natural, more balanced and agile. Though, oddly, I hadn't felt quite as awkward with my man-legs for that short period between stepping out of the alley and arriving at Goddess Annie's residence, which was a first for me.

Needing to get away from the not-even-smug bastard Rion, I strode across the room. Except it wasn't far, not nearly far enough to ease the frustration churning inside me, and certainly not as far as I would have expected for a goddess's residence.

Man! I couldn't believe this. I'd been waiting for a chance to pleasure the goddess since yesterday. My cock ached in anticipation, like it had been aching since I'd first laid eyes on her, and now, if I was going to get any relief, I had to do it myself.

Far too often I'd had to take control of my own release. Some might say that was because I got aroused far too easily, which... may be true. But it wasn't my fault there were far too many attractive women in the world. And far too few who wished to be with me.

I clenched my jaw and bit back another groan.

The trouble was, I couldn't really be angry at Rion. I knew why he'd been chosen first. Some small part of me knew that even if I hadn't been in the shower, she'd have chosen him. He was the noblest of us all, the most forthright and pure.

Most of the time, when the four of us got together, we went carousing: drinking and wenching. Rion drunk his fair share, but he and Keph were always more sedate with the women, rarely being with one and taking their pleasure.

And when Rion did take a woman, he actually took them to a room instead of coupling with them in the cantina, like nearly everyone else. Even Keph, the few times he'd found a woman who was willing to try his massive cock, coupled casually. The women would sit astride him as he sat upon the floor because it was only sex after all. It didn't mean anything. It wasn't like they were kissing these women on the lips. No such grand gestures were made, no promises, and the women were well aware of it.

Most were eager to be with someone like Del or Keph — since

those two were both extraordinarily well hung. But it wasn't like I was lacking in that area. Sure, I was the smallest of the group in every way, but I could still please a woman.

Yet there was something about Rion beyond his cock that seemed to draw women.

Perhaps it was that slight standoffishness, the difficulty in landing him.

Although I suspected it was more than that. Something to do with that noble nature of his.

It wasn't like I treated women poorly. I just... lost control of myself sometimes, led around by my cock instead of my head or heart. *Lusty* was how I put it. Yet I also knew that even among other *satyrs* — who were a sensual people — I was a bit more taken with passions than usual.

I told myself it was because I was still young and full of life. Yet I could also see how my overly lusty nature scared some women. I just... didn't know how to control it.

And I'd hoped...

My shoulders fell. I'd hoped that Goddess Annie would help to heal me. Perhaps sex with her would help to heal whatever it was that was wrong with me, help me gain some measure of control.

But now that was impossible. She'd chosen Rion.

I desperately wished to return to my world and forget all about the amazing goddess that I'd thought would change my life.

My stomach churned with disappointment and frustration and my gaze leaped to Rion. As much as he was a dear friend, I felt betrayed. And Gods! I couldn't look at him, couldn't stand to be in the same room.

I jerked away and marched back to the bathing room. After bringing myself to a release, I had another shower, this one cold and uncomfortable, but that at least helped to tame my raging desires.

I was in a more level mind, if still a foul mood, when I stepped out of the bathroom to rejoin the others.

Except the second I stepped into the common room, the world around me stuttered to a halt. The strange sounds of the street outside became drawn out, the three other guys, who'd been turning to look at me, froze suddenly trapped in time.

Was this the darkness that was after Goddess Annie? Was she in trouble?

I rushed over to Del and waved a hand in front of his face, except he was still looking at the bathroom door.

"Del?"

What was happening?

"Guys?" I started to turn to Rion when Del's gaze slowly, agonizingly slowly, started to shift from the bathroom door.

Oh thank the Gods, he wasn't frozen. But he was moving extremely slowly and that was still a serious problem. If the darkness was this powerful, I, alone, wasn't going to be strong enough to protect our— *Rion's* goddess.

The world snapped, the force like a punch in the gut, stealing my breath. Del's gaze jerked to me, suddenly back to normal speed, and I staggered to the side, catching myself on the long bar between the cooking area and the eating area.

"The darkness," I gasped.

Del jerked to his feet and grabbed my arm to help steady me. "What just happened?"

"You moved so fast I could hardly see you," Rion said, grabbing my other arm. "You were only a blur."

Only a blur?

Keph remained sitting. He wasn't much good to anyone in confined spaces, always in danger of breaking something — which, in this case he already had.

My blood rushed through me and I felt more alive and energized than I had in a long time, but oddly not aroused which was when I usually felt alive and energized.

But that, of course, was because the darkness had attacked.

Except—

"Moving fast?" I searched the barely-lit living quarters for whatever it was that was coming after Goddess Annie.

But everything was normal, or as normal as this strange place had been before the attack, making me question if it had actually *been* an attack. Wouldn't the darkness have kept going, pressed its advantage? We'd been helpless. So, did that mean something else had happened?

"You were all moving slowly. It was like time stopped or was drawn out or something."

"For you maybe," Rion said, "But for us, you zipped around the room, almost too fast to see. Definitely too fast to keep up with."

I was fast?

Could what have happened actually have been me and not some darkness? It would explain why the attack had stopped when I'd stopped.

Okay, so if it was me—

I drew in a quick breath and tried running to the far side of the room and back as fast as I could.

Again, everyone froze, their gazes on the spot where I'd been and not following me across the small room.

I touched the far wall, then ran back to where I'd been as their attention, comically, jumped to the middle of the room for a second, confused, before jerking back to me at my starting point.

"What in the Heavens—" Del gasped, taking a large step away from me. Rion took a step back as well, both of their expressions shocked.

"That was incredible," Keph said from where he sat. "I could barely see you."

I grinned, unable to help myself, as the same rush of energy from before flooded me. I felt great, like I could do anything, and surely an attack from the darkness wouldn't leave me feeling energized and powerful.

"When did you get so fast?" Rion asked.

I had no clue, but then—

Rion had been glowing earlier. He didn't seem to be anymore and the room was growing quite dark as evening set in, but I was sure he'd been glowing.

"When did you start glowing?" I asked him.

He frowned. "Glowing?"

"You noticed it, too?" Del said. "I thought it was a trick of the light."

Rion took another step away from me as if I was crazy and it was contagious. "Notice what?"

"When you came from the goddess—" And with just mentioning her, the rush of power flooding me vanished and I was brought back to my sad reality. "You were glowing."

"I was?" Rion's frown deepened, then realization flashed over his face and I knew, with his quick mind, that he'd figured something out. "I thought I'd noticed something when I was with the goddess. It was like something sparked within me even before the bonding, and I was glowing brightly when I was with her, but I thought it was an effect of coupling with a goddess."

"Perhaps I should mention," Del said hesitantly, "that when I was in the shower, something happened. The water... I could feel it."

I rolled my eyes at him. "We could all *feel* it. It rains down upon you. Hard to miss."

"No, I mean, I could *feel* where it came from, hidden in the walls and in the bowl of the self-washing toilet. Then... I made it stop and flow in different directions around me. I controlled it."

"Why didn't you say anything?" Rion asked.

"Well, why didn't you say anything about glowing?" Del countered.

The muscles in Rion's jaw flexed, but he didn't argue back.

"We've come to the realm of the gods," I said. "We must have all been granted powers, boons, whatever you wish to call them." I didn't quite believe it, but since it clearly wasn't the darkness attacking, being granted magic was the next most obvious explanation. I turned to Keph. "What can you do?"

The large man shrugged, his massive shoulders rolling with the gesture. "Don't know. Though... I have felt... lighter since I've come here."

Lighter? Given how easily that chair had crumbled beneath him when he'd first sat in it, he couldn't be *that* much lighter. But still—

"This is indeed a strange and curious place," I said softly.

Too bad I wasn't meant to stay. The goddess would send me back. She had Rion now.

And that brought to mind something else. Before a moment ago, I hadn't much believed in magic, or powers. Now I'd been proven wrong, and I had clear evidence of strange forces at work. And if that was the case, if this world had granted us abilities, then perhaps there was magic in Rion's bonding with the goddess. A true bonding. A mystical vow made with their lips.

I bit back a huff of frustration. How could he? How could she? She'd promised—

Well, no. She'd promised nothing.

She'd asked for us to pleasure her and it seemed she'd only needed one of us. She'd chosen her bonded mate.

Zeus's balls.

I didn't want to be furious with Rion, a brother, a friend, but in this moment, I couldn't help it. Powers or no, I couldn't stop thinking about how he'd taken a precious opportunity from all of us... from me.

The door to the goddess's sleeping chambers opened and she stepped out wrapped in a strange pink fuzzy robe. She looked half asleep, and her lush lips spread into a silly grin as she looked over at us. With a giggle, she made her way to the next door over, the bathing room, then went in and closed the door.

We'd all been silent, following her with our gazes until she vanished once again.

From her actions, if I hadn't known better, I'd have assumed she was drunk. Perhaps it was some effect of sex with Rion, or the bonding itself.

Perhaps the power of the true kiss had left her giddy. Certainly Rion seemed far giddier than he had before.

"You're a lucky man," Del whispered to Rion, and I could hear the disappointment in his voice. At least I wasn't the only one.

That silence hung over us all until the goddess emerged from the bathing room.

She frowned. "Why is it so dark in here?"

"Goddess?" Rion asked as she turned to an odd piece of decoration on the wall next to her, a small knob protruding from the wall in the center of a rectangular plate no bigger than my palm. There'd been another one just inside the door of the bathing room, but I had no idea what they represented.

With a quick flick, she pushed the knob into an upright position and light blossomed from several sources around us. Except they weren't torches or lanterns. They seemed like small balls of light, though it was hard to tell since I couldn't look at any one for too long.

"Hounds of Hades," Rion breathed.

"What an astounding magic," Del added.

"It's not magic, it's—" Her frown deepened, her gaze ever-so-slightly out of focus. "You don't have lights? No, I guess I didn't see any in your world. But then how do you light your houses at night?"

"Torches or lanterns," Keph said. "Though my people rarely require such things." It was true. Stone titans had exceptional vision in the dark, which probably came from living deep in the mountains their entire lives.

"But no electricity?" Goddess Annie said, using a word I didn't recognize, her voice slightly slurred. "Hunh."

"This illumination, is it sorcery?" Keph asked, awe softening his deep rumbling voice.

"No, though it might take me a while to fully explain it, and even then—" She sighed and offered a soft dopey smile. "How about we just say it is and move on."

Keph grunted at that, nodding and accepting that, even though she'd just said it wasn't magic.

Which, I supposed was for the best. Some of the wonders of this place had been easy to figure out like the flowing waters in the... what had she called it? Right. Shower. Or the cold box with food, even though it didn't have any ice and wasn't buried in the ground like it should have been, or the self-cleaning toilet. I suspected there were far more wonderous and amazing things in this world than any of us from Nikandra would understand.

And I wanted to learn all about them and the amazing world.

Except if I couldn't have the goddess, then there really wasn't a place for me here.

Goddess Annie drew herself up and that silly grin that made me frustratingly hard, lit up her face.

"So," she purred. "Who's next to pleasure the goddess?"

I stared at her.

Everyone did.

"But, goddess, we bonded," Rion said, aghast.

"Yep, we certainly did," she said, and her grin got larger. Gods, she was so beautiful. "And that was—" She released a low sexy sigh.

The sound went straight to my cock, and I had to drop my

hands and shift to the side to hide my hard-on. Not because I was embarrassed, but because she and Rion had bonded.

"That was amazing. Thank you," she said, her voice breathy with desire, and she slid a steamy, still slightly out-of-focused gaze over us, stopping at Del. "I think I'd like to try a *triton* next. Ohhhh, in the shower! That could be interesting."

I could practically hear Rion's heart crumbling. Poor *erinai*. The goddess had just casually dismissed him and requested another. For some reason the magic of the bond — if there indeed was any magic or bond for that matter — had no effect on her.

Perhaps gods and goddesses were immune to such things? They could claim a mortal's soul, as she had done with Rion, and then go on to claim another?

Which would be cruel indeed. Torture for the mortal involved and yet I couldn't help but smile.

The ways of the gods were strange to be sure, but that meant, there was still hope for me!

CHAPTER 12

ANNIE

HAZY, FOGGY DARKNESS MUDDLED MY THOUGHTS AND I COULDN'T get them to focus no matter how hard I tried. Apparently Rion had actually fucked my brains out. Blown my mind!

I giggled at that thought.

Yes, he had!

I felt like I'd had too much to drink. I was literally weak in the knees, using the wall to help support me, my vision was blurry, showing me double of everything, and I didn't really know what I was saying. Words came out, and, as if from some echo, I heard them a moment later and only then known what I'd said.

Triton in the shower...

A shiver of desire rushed through me at the thought and Del certainly seemed up for it given his instant arousal at my words.

Yeah. Del in the shower was a great idea.

Still leaning on the wall to keep my balance, I carefully turned back toward the bathroom.

My thoughts tripped over that. Given shower sex involved standing up and keeping my balance, mixing it with how tired and dopey I was, it was probably a bad idea. Once the warm water hit me, I'd probably dissolve into a satisfied puddle of goo. Also, if all the guys had had showers, there might not be much warm water left and a cold shower certainly wouldn't be pleasant.

"Actually, ah... maybe tomorrow?" I said, hoping that wouldn't hurt his man-ego too much while attempting to reinforce my desire to have sex with him with a smile and a wink.

I did the slow turn back to my bedroom when another thought hit me.

I had my brother's wedding tomorrow. And the thought of weak-knee-making sex before the wedding seemed like a bad idea, too. I didn't want to feel sex-drunk and giddy for my brother's special day.

But the image of me and Del in the shower was stuck in my head now and come hell or high water, it was going to happen... I just wasn't sure when.

"After the wedding," I said more to myself than him. "I've got to get ready in the morning. But we're definitely having some sexy times in the shower tomorrow, I promise."

All the guys kept staring at me as if I had two heads or something. Had I said something wrong? I didn't think so. I—

My stomach gave a very loud and long rumble.

Oh... I tried to remember the last time I'd eaten. My thoughts stalled as I dragged them back in time. Not when we arrived at my apartment... not when I'd woken that morning in their world... not when I'd finished healing those people... not—

Holy fuck. I hadn't eaten anything since yesterday morning! No wonder I was tired and loopy and hungry. "Also, I'm famished. Who wants something to eat?"

Except I knew I didn't have much in my fridge, especially if the guys had eaten the last of that Chinese food. There were some other leftovers, but they were stale as hell by now and I just hadn't gotten around to tossing them out.

I'd just order something.

What did I want? Pizza? Chinese?

For some reason sausage kept leaping to mind.

Way to be subtle, psyche.

Still, the thought made me giggle as I gazed at the sausage fest in my dining room.

Given my current state, it shouldn't have surprised me that I then imagined each of the guys as a type of sausage. Aethan was a jumbo, Rion a foot-long, Del a thick kielbasa, and Keph a whole salami.

Oh, God. I was getting wet just thinking about their *sausages.*

I leaned back against the wall and the image of one of the guys — it didn't matter which —pressing me against the wall, pulling up my housecoat, and fitting their *sausage* between my ample buns flashed through me.

I waited for a moment to see if the vision would come true, but alas, it didn't. Still the thought of it made my knees so weak, I slid down the wall to sit on the floor.

My stomach rumbled again, but I was in no condition to even reach my phone. I'd have to crawl.

"Then again, maybe I'll just go back to bed," I said, my voice slurred and sloppy, like the rest of me. "I might need some help."

But the guys were still staring at me like I had a third eye, which was far different from how they'd looked at me before... like a goddess.

And I still didn't know what was wrong.

Del acted first, moving toward me, his expression filled with hesitation and worry. "Goddess, are you unwell?"

"Del," Rion hissed, shooting him a look full of daggers and making him stop halfway between the kitchen table and me.

"I'm only trying to help her," Del said. "You heard her. She's not interested in me right now. You can help her, if that's what you'd like."

Except Rion didn't move. He looked at me, his gaze sliding from my eyes to down my body and stalling on...

I dragged my gaze down to see what had captured his attention and realized I was sitting with my knees up and slightly separated, showing him and the others everything down there.

Swell—

Oh, well. They were all going to see it eventually.

I dragged my gaze back up as Rion jerked his attention away and Del huffed and finished hurrying to my side.

"What happened, goddess?" he asked, his voice low, although I was pretty sure the others could still hear him. My apartment wasn't that big.

I snorted at him as he helped me stand, and turned me in the direction of my bedroom. If he wasn't aware of what Rion and I had done, I was kind of concerned for my time with him. "We had *sex*, fish-man," I said, my slurring drawing out the word sex, as I shuffled forward.

"I mean, what's wrong? You seem unwell."

"Nope, I'm very good. Super good. Uber good. Awesome." I smiled up at him then lowered my voice, trying to whisper as well. "Is Rion upset? Did I... was I—"

Oh, God! Was I a horrible lay?

Rion had certainly seemed satisfied when he'd left me. I was certainly satisfied with his performance, but—

"Goddess, you chose him and then—"

"Yes, I did!" I proclaimed, forgetting to whisper. "And I'm choosing you next, but not until tomorrow, after the wedding."

"But, goddess—" Del started.

"You all wanted to be with me," I interrupted. I couldn't figure out why he was acting so weird. "You asked me to choose. Did I choose the wrong guy first?"

"That's not what I meant. You kissed Rion, on the lips, a true kiss, claiming him, didn't you?"

"Oh, yes I did." I'd definitely claimed him, and he'd claimed me. And what a glorious kiss it had been. Though I had just been given more orgasms at once then I think I'd had in my entire life so that might have colored my memory of it.

A shiver of remembered bliss swept through me, reigniting my desire despite my exhaustion, and a soft moan escaped my lips. "He kissed me in all manner of places before that." The memory of Rion's blond head bobbing between my thighs made my breath hitch and another soft moan escaped. "He's quite good with his mouth."

"So, you did bond with him," Del pressed, "lip to lip, a sacred vow?"

A sacred what now?

Another flash of memory of Rion's intense look at me just before he went down on me, stole the rest of my thoughts, and I stumbled.

Del steadied me before I fell and the feel of his strong hands on my hips made me think of Rion's strong hands on me and how I'd felt and—

The memory of my last orgasm whispered through me, stealing my breath and making my world spin... again.

"But then you said you wished to be with me, in the shower," Del said, his voice softer than before, as if he were far away and not right beside me.

"Tomorrow after the wedding," I replied. Though I was seriously reconsidering waiting. Perhaps it didn't have to be in the shower. Perhaps I could just lay exhausted on my bed and he could... "You're strongly making me reconsider though."

"What?"

I turned to face him, pressed my palms against his chiseled chest, and leaned in. He smelled of water and my lilac-scented bath-soap. It wasn't a particularly masculine scent, but it was clean and fresh and delicious and—

"Okay, you've convinced me," I said, my voice husky. He was so close and strong and gorgeous. Yep, I didn't want to wait for the shower. I wanted him right now.

"My bedroom," I breathed.

"Goddess—" He glanced back at the others. I didn't bother looking with him, no one else mattered in this moment.

Except he wasn't doing anything and I was sure I gave him more than enough time for the guys to give him that macho manly hey-you're-going-to-get-laid look.

"Take me to bed," I insisted, sliding my hands down his chest toward his—

He scooped me into his arms before I could grab his fully erect cock.

"She's unwell," he announced and carried me into the bedroom, not bothering to nudge the door shut with his heel like Rion had.

Did he want the others to watch? An exhibitionist, was he?

Kinky.

He set me on the bed and I threw open my housecoat, spreading my legs for him. "I may not move too much, but I'm all yours."

Del's cock twitched and he groaned as his gaze roamed my naked body.

"Delphon, please," Rion said, his voice gruff and distant, in the other room. "Don't."

"Ignore him, he's had his turn," I said, giving him my best alluring gaze, letting out all the pent-up desire thrumming through me in that one look.

"I ah... I can't," Del said. "You and Rion—"

I dropped my gaze to his cock, giving it a pointed look, before raising my eyes back to his. "It certainly looks like you can."

Except what had he said about Rion?

I was sure there was something. Something I'd forgotten. But at the moment there was nothing in the room, nothing in the world for me, except this stunningly hot naked man before me. I had to have him inside me even if my body could barely move.

"Please," I begged.

But he just stood there, his expression pained, his gaze shifting from me to the others then back to me.

"I'm sorry, Goddess Annie. I can't," he said and he turned away and left.

What?

The door closed behind him.

What the fuck had just happened?

I ached with a need that I *had* to have fulfilled, but the man who'd been promising to pleasure me since the moment we'd met had just walked out.

It felt like the air had been sucked out of the room. I couldn't breathe and could barely think. All I really knew was that I needed a release and wouldn't get it, which left me throbbing and alone and confused and frustrated as hell.

Was this some cruel joke?

Get me all worked up and leave me hanging?

Well, fine.

I wouldn't let him win... at whatever stupid game he was playing. Before Rion, I hadn't had a man in three years and I didn't need one now.

I reached over to the drawer in my bedstand and fumbled inside for my lucky vibrator, Richard. But the sludge in my head made the room spin and my arm was stupidly weak.

And when I finally — *finally!* — got ahold of the thing and flicked the on switch, nothing happened.

The batteries were dead.

"Fuck! Me!"

I threw the vibrator across the room. It hit the wall with a heavy thud and I curled up in a ball, feeling cold and alone and frustrated.

Which, if I was thinking straight should have shocked me, since I barely knew these guys and had just had the most amazing sex with Rion. But I wasn't thinking straight, and I couldn't move past my throbbing desire and the sense that Del had betrayed me.

CHAPTER 13

KEPHAS

AFTER SPENDING THE NIGHT UNCERTAIN WHAT TO DO ABOUT Goddess Annie, Aethan decided to make her breakfast. He found some eggs in the tall cold box and a frying pan, and had fussed with one of the large devices in the kitchen, but had been unable to get it to work as he wanted. So, he'd taken the bits of the wooden chair I'd crushed and searched for a reasonable place to put a small fire. Del had pointed out that the built-in basin in the cooking area had easily available water hidden in the wall, just like there'd been in the shower, so Aethan had started it there.

I marveled at the quick minds of my friends. On my own, I wouldn't have known what to do with that shower. Del had shown me how to use it, turning the knobs to bring forth hot and cold water. And while I was among the smartest of the stone titans — one of the reasons I'd been chosen as emissary — that, unfortunately, wasn't saying much. My kind were slow and ponderous — in mind and body — like the rocks from which we'd supposedly been spawned.

Except a few seconds after lighting the fire, a high-pitched, ear-piercing, constant beeping screamed through the common area.

"We're under attack," Aethan yelped, and the guys turned, back to back, creating a triangle, their fists up and their gazes sweeping over the room, searching for whoever or whatever was screaming its battle cry.

"Where is it coming from?" Del asked.

"I can't see anyone," Aethan replied.

Rion's gaze jerked to the ceiling. "Above us?"

Then the door to Goddess Annie's bedroom crashed open, and she stormed into the common area, that strange pink fuzzy robe tied tight about her small frame like armor.

She looked ferocious and beautiful, with her hands clenched into fists, her pale red hair hanging loose and wild around her small face, and the speckles on her cheeks dark against her fair skin like war paint.

There was fire in her eyes, but it wasn't the good kind. It wasn't the passionate kind that she'd had when we'd first met her. No, this was an angry fire. And that fire was directed entirely at us and not searching for any danger.

"What the hell is going on?" she yelled over the screeching.

Her body trembled with fury, but there was more emotion within her than just rage. I didn't think she'd slept well. She seemed tired and there was... a resentment or frustration behind her anger. I might not have been as quick of mind as my friends, but I'd always been good at sensing how others were feeling.

Annie stalked over to the cooking area, turned on the water and put out the fire. "There's a perfectly good stove, right there!" She pointed at the device Aethan had been trying to work earlier.

"Goddess," Aethan said, "I'd suspected as much, but—"

She glared at him. "You couldn't have just waited for me to get up and asked?"

"We thought you might be tired and wished to have a meal ready for you when you woke," Aethan replied.

"Well, you've fucked it up now." Annie left him there and moved to the two large windows in her common area and pushed open the strange see-through shutters, letting in cold gusts of air, causing Annie to repeat that word *fuck* over and over again.

After a few moments, the screeching stopped and she turned to face us, her expression hard, but I could still sense her frustration.

A tirade was coming, and while I was brave and could face her anger, it stung knowing I'd disappointed her.

"And now I'm freezing," she ground out as she moved back to the windows and reclosed the see-through shutters. "I don't know what I was thinking letting you all come here. It was a mistake. I'd send you all back now, but I have a wedding to get ready for. So, here's the deal. You all just stay here, and don't do anything, don't touch anything, don't fuck up my life more than you already have. Then when I get back from the wedding, I'm sending you all back."

"Goddess—" Del tried, but even I knew that was a mistake.

She spun on him, the look in her eyes even harder than before. "What? What is it you cold-hearted bastard? Do you want to get me all worked up again then leave me sad and alone? I'm not falling for that twice. I can't recall all of what happened last night, but I remember that much."

Rion spoke, hope in his voice. "Does that mean—?" Sadly, another mistake. The goddess had not been kind to him, and that deserved an explanation, but not while she was so upset.

"Shut up. All of you." She turned to Rion, and an odd mix of emotions played over her features mixing with her fury: lust, joy, sadness, grief. "I don't want to be seduced again. I don't care how sexy you all are. Once was enough." I could sense a duality in this, a confusion.

But then, we were all confused. The bonding kiss was a sacred thing and yet she'd discarded it so easily.

She hadn't seemed like herself when she had, but still, that had really hurt Rion. Trying to give herself to Del had been a slap in the *erinai*'s face, a sword to his soul. I didn't know much about how the bonding kiss might work in her world, but it seemed it was not treated with the respect and honor as it was in our world.

Annie put a hand to her head, running it through her tangled hair. "I don't know what you guys did to me last night, but it was cruel." Some of her anger fled from her and she just seemed tired and hurt now. I didn't fully understand this. She claimed we'd been cruel, when she'd been the one to crush Rion's heart. There must be some vast misunderstanding here.

I didn't know if now was the best time to speak, but I had to try. "Goddess—"

"Don't call me that."

"Annie," I tried again, and she didn't immediately stop me. That was a good sign. "I think there is a misunderstanding here."

"I'll say," she huffed.

But before I could go on, Del interrupted me. It seemed he'd grown angry as well. "Misunderstanding? Is that what you call luring me into your bed after you've bonded with one of my closest friends?"

Annie gaped, her eyes wide. "I lured you? No, you were the one... weren't you?" She looked away, confusion flashing across her expression.

Ah, so there was definitely confusion and misunderstanding there. They'd both thought the other to be attempting seduction. I didn't see how Annie could think that's what Del had been doing, but she had seemed quite disoriented at the time.

"It doesn't matter," Annie snapped, and with that, I felt a solid door slam shut on this argument. She wasn't going to hear any more. "What matters is I have a wedding to get ready for. And after that, you're all leaving. I can't take any more of whatever this is." She turned and marched into the bathing room, slamming the door behind her.

I sighed, that was that.

Del turned and leaned heavily on the counter between the dining and cooking areas. "I don't understand any of this."

I wanted to help. I knew there was more, a mystery of emotions to solve, but I'd needed more information to get to the heart of it. Now it seemed I wouldn't have a chance.

Rion went to him. The bond between those two friends had strengthened last night when Del had denied the goddess. Even I knew that must have been hard for the *triton*. We were all taken with Goddess Annie, more than a little captivated by her and her strange ways. Del had been one of the first to see her and had remained desirous of her. She had offered herself to him and he'd refused. Rion had greatly appreciated that. Though I was also fairly certain the goddess hadn't been in her right mind last night. Coupling with her would have been wrong, even if she'd been asking for it.

"I don't know what to make of any of this," Rion said. "She seems so erratic and has been ever since we arrived in her world. Perhaps it was a mistake to come here."

"No, we need to protect her," Aethan said, firm.

I hadn't heard what the seer had said about Annie and the darkness, but Rion had been greatly concerned for her after he'd heard the proclamation. Perhaps the seer was wrong and there was no danger to her, but I didn't think any of us wanted to take that chance.

Even with what had happened last night to Rion and how upset she was at us at the moment, we still wished to protect her. But I got the feeling she'd insist this time and send us back.

"We can at least protect her until she sends us back," Aethan said, as if reading my mind.

"I don't think she wants us at this wedding, though," I said, and from the corner of my eye, I caught the door to the bathing room jerk open.

"That's right. I don't," Annie said from the doorway. She must have overheard us, not that we'd been trying to be quiet.

Del didn't turn, didn't look at her, but his voice was firm when he said, "We need to protect you, wherever you go, even if you don't wish that of us. Even if we are... frustrated with you, and you with us. It doesn't matter. We've made a pact."

"Fuck your pact. You're not going to the wedding. I couldn't bring all of you if I wanted. I'm only allowed a plus *one*. And frankly I don't want to bring any of you."

Aethan piped up. "But you *can* bring *one* of us?"

"I can, but—"

"Then we shall select one of us to escort you," Del said, still not looking at her. "Or *you* can select one of us if you wish."

"No."

Del spun then. He wasn't angry — although even with my usually good sense for emotions I couldn't tell exactly what he was feeling — but his voice was raised. "I'm sorry, goddess. You can banish us back to our realm if you wish, but even while you're angry at us, we'll still protect you for as long as we can."

She glared back at him. "No."

"It *will* happen. We'll find a way. So, either you allow us or we'll do something on our own, and as you've already seen, that doesn't seem to go well in your world."

Annie's eyes narrowed and Del held her glare as if daring her to say no again so we could follow her on our own.

Which was something that even *I* knew was a terrible idea. Her world was strange and terrifying and everything we did seemed to cause problems or upset her.

Annie jerked her gaze to the ceiling. "Fuck me," she hissed. "You're— You have to be—" She let out a long growl then slammed her fist against the door beside her. "Fuck, fuck, fuck, fuck, fuck!"

She hit the door again. Then her look turned sour, her frustration deepening with the realization that she was trapped and had to let us go with her. "Fine! *One* of you can come. But God help me, this is a mistake!" She turned, slamming the bathing room door shut behind her again.

We all stared at where she'd been, no one saying anything for a long moment.

"Well—" Del said, but Annie burst from the bathing room again and stalked over to her bag, muttering something about how this was going to end badly.

She pulled out a small device and looked at us. "Rion can come. I have a friend with a husband who's about his size. Hopefully she can lend me a suit for him to borrow." She jabbed her finger repeatedly against the device before putting it to her ear and heading back to the bathing room, slamming the door for a third time.

There came a loud, drawn out cry of, "Fuck!" from the bathing room, then a softer, "Oh, no Margie, sorry, that wasn't for you." After that I couldn't hear anything else.

This was it. Rion would go to the wedding and after that the goddess would return us to our world.

None of this sat right with me. I knew there was more going on in the underlying emotions, some confusion causing this mayhem. But I didn't think I was going to get the chance to set it right.

CHAPTER 14

KEPHAS

GODDESS ANNIE LEFT WITH RION. THE THREE OF US REMAINING IN her home had watched through the windows as they'd walked down the street before finally turning a corner and stepping out of sight.

I still felt unsettled, but knew there wasn't anything I could do about it for now. I only hoped that when Annie returned, she might be in a better mood and willing to listen and talk.

That's what was needed. A conversation not confused by heated emotions. Yet I feared that wouldn't happen.

The other two paced the small area, while I remained seated. I'd already broken one chair. I didn't want to move around too much for fear of breaking something else. The table or counters, even the walls, who knew what else might crumble under my great weight. Luckily the ceiling was high enough that I wasn't at risk of accidentally poking my head through it if I stood, though it was close.

Aethan's pacing was hard to watch, his every movement was frenetic and twitchy. Every now and then he'd seem to skip from one spot to another, a blur in between. He seemed to be having some inner conversation with himself, arms moving as if making a point to someone, but he didn't say anything out loud.

Del's pacing was more sedate. He was sad, distressed, head shaking from time to time. He knew we'd messed up our time with the goddess, but like me, he didn't really know why or how.

After the argument that morning, Annie hadn't given us much more to go on. She'd showered, then ordered some food for us all, something called 'breakfast burritos.' They'd been quite good, though not enough had been ordered for my appetite and I was left hungry.

Annie had wolfed down two of them with a drink she'd called *kah-fee*, and Aethan had had some of that dark liquid as well, loving it, while the rest of us had opted for water from the tap.

It still amazed me that water could come when called, simply by turning a knob. But there were many wonders in this strange world. The walk to Goddess Annie's place had been a feast of marvels, so many people, buildings reaching high into the sky, and those fast-moving beasts upon the roads. Cars Annie had called them. It didn't seem right to me that something so large and dangerous should move so fast. I was large and potentially danger-ous, but I remained slow. It seemed a balance which these strange metal devices ignored.

After the morning meal, Annie had disappeared to get ready, first doing her hair and applying something to her face, covering the beautiful speckles on her cheeks, making her look even more pale. Then she'd put on an alluring red dress.

People wore little clothing in Nikandra, it wasn't necessary for most, and women only covered themselves if they were nurses, or to be alluring and mysterious. And the goddess had been all of that. Poor Aethan had been instantly aroused when she'd come from her room in that stunning covering, and I felt bad for the *satyr*. He seemed to have such little control over his emotions and his body.

Annie's friend had arrived — not allowed to come in — and dropped off clothes for Rion. He'd looked very mysterious and uncomfortable once they'd been put on: dark pants, white shirt with buttons on the front, and a dark jacket. All of it just a little too tight on him, obviously made for a man of similar height, but with a lesser build.

Annie hadn't said more than a dozen words to any of us, and I'd been able to sense her frustration and anger, her confusion and the desire she was trying desperately to hide, but this didn't tell me more than what I already knew.

And I needed more if I was going to find out the true reason for the tension among us.

She and Rion had left and the rest of us had settled in.

I sighed, replaying the emotions I'd sense from her over and over again in my mind, hoping that I'd be able to see something I'd missed that would let me know what was really going on, when a tight, burning spark ignited in my chest.

It was small, but powerful and growing, something that had only happened a handful of times in my entire life and something I hadn't felt in years.

I was about to have a vision.

I knew it was futile to resist or try to stop it, and in this moment I actually — for once — accepted it. Perhaps it would tell me more of what I'd need to know about Annie and what had happened between us.

The spike of pain in my chest grew, and lines of fire traced from my heart to my head. This was the process. It was always the same. Next it would explode behind my eyes and I'd be taken away, captured by the vision.

I sent a quick prayer to Hephaestus. I wasn't one who believed much in the gods, but Hephaestus was the one who was supposed to have created the stone titans long ago, and when I was in dire need, I would sometimes whisper prayers to him.

"Help me see true," I breathed.

Then the pain exploded in my head and the room before me vanished.

I floated in darkness, free and weightless — a very uncomfortable feeling for a stone titan.

Then light blossomed with another spike of pain. It was a diffuse illumination and nothing was clear. I hoped it would come into better focus, but the vague shapes, moving around and mingling, and the rumble of many voices talking, didn't become clearer.

Then sharp cracks, like thunder, rang out for an instant and a single person snapped into focus. Annie. She was being carried by someone and vomiting, but the vision didn't clarify who was carrying her, and everyone and everything else remained out of focus.

Then more sharp cracks of violent thunder and a great crash as a darkness burst onto the scene. People screamed, running from it as it broke through what seemed like a wall, charging into the midst of the people.

My heart skipped a beat. The darkness. It had found Annie.

The light around me flared, blinding me.

My vision cleared and I was back in my body in Annie's residence, the pain in my head fading. Yet even as it faded, a secondary pain of *knowing* burst through me and I was given instant insight into where Annie and Rion were. It wasn't far, perhaps a walk of a dozen minutes from here, a place called Silver Birch Hall.

"Hades," I hissed and the other two stopped their pacing and stared at me.

"We need to go," I said, carefully rising as quickly as I could without bumping and breaking anything. "Annie and Rion are in danger. The darkness has found her."

Aethan nodded turning for the door and reaching for the latch.

Del frowned. "How do you know this?"

My visions were rare. I'd had perhaps five in my entire life and it wasn't something I'd spoken to anyone about, only my parents. Now I had to tell my friends, and I wasn't sure how they'd take knowing that I could see the future.

"I have visions. Not often. Sometimes I see things that haven't happened yet." I dropped my gaze to my large hands, afraid of their reaction. I was a stone titan, and my kind didn't have mystic abilities. I was... unnatural. "I hope this doesn't change your view of me."

"Why would you say that?" Aethan asked. "It's not like you've grown a second head or something."

"Yeah," Del agreed. "If anything, I'm sorry for you. Visions can't be easy to live with."

"They aren't. But as I said, they're rare." I'd managed to fully stand now without breaking anything, but knew I needed to stay mindful of my surroundings.

"Which makes me grateful that you've had one and hopefully given us time to save Goddess Annie and Rion," Aethan said opening the door.

"We should probably dress first," Del said, as I made my way across the room to them.

Aethan glanced down his naked body then out the partially open door as if he was struggling with the idea of spending the few seconds it took to put clothes on.

"It's cold out and everyone I saw outside wore clothes," Del added.

"Right." Aethan shut the door and zipped to the clothes the goddess had left for us piled on the seat of a large, cushioned couch.

Del and I joined him and we rooted through it.

The others found clothes quick enough, but there wasn't much that fit me and in the end, I put on a pair of strange, gray pants made from a fabric that incredibly stretched to fit my large frame and a similarly stretchy pull-over shirt with a blue and red crest on the chest. Both items were skin-tight on me, near to bursting, but they held. The pants only covered me to mid-calf, but I wasn't too worried about the cold. The deep caves where I lived were far underground and very chilly all year round and stone titans were used to the cold.

"Do we know where we're going?" Del asked as he pulled on a pair of loose black pants.

"I do," I said. "That was part of my vision."

"Then it must be fated," Aethan said. He looked like an *anthousae*, in vibrant green pants, a yellow shirt with a hood attached, and a bright blue and purple coat that was too small to properly close. He was a rainbow of color if you included his ruddy-red skin. "Let's go."

We rushed out into the street, and I could only hope that we wouldn't be too late.

CHAPTER 15

ANNIE

RION WAS RIGID AND COLD SITTING NEXT TO ME IN THE WEDDING hall, and I tried to concentrate on the ceremony to distract me from the mess that had suddenly become my life.

By bringing Rion — who looked stunning in a suit, of course — everyone now thought I had a new boyfriend. A hot boyfriend. And I'd already fended off so many questions about him — mostly from other women while his back was turned — that I was even more frustrated and angry.

"Where'd he come from?"

"His name is what? Ryan?"

"Does he have a brother?"

"What's he like in bed?"

And my personal favorite — for its ever-so-condescending tone, "How'd you managed to land him?"

Then there was the obvious, "What does Carter think of him?"

Carter was my ex, and the son of a friend of my father's, our family's lawyer. Carter and I had known each other since we were kids and everyone had thought I was so lucky to 'land him' once we were adults. He was a lawyer in his father's firm, and doing well for himself.

I, of course, was the black sheep of my family, barely scraping by. My father was a doctor, my mother had been a nurse. My brother, Daniel — the one getting married — was an accountant, and my sister, Sheri, was a successful business owner, running her own flower shop. She'd supplied all the flowers for the wedding, of course.

Then there was me, an administrative assistant — even though my job was so much more than that. My family and friends didn't understand. I didn't want what they wanted. I hated living in the city. My dream was to be a virtual assistant, living somewhere warm and working on the beach. A simple life. Yet my family thought that was a silly dream. They kept bringing up the same questions and concerns.

"How can you support yourself?"

"The tropics? Won't you burn?"

"You'll be all alone down there, why would you want to leave Chicago?"

"How will you get your clients? You won't be able to meet in person. That's very important." *As if they'd never heard of the internet.*

"It will never work. You'll be back living at dad's place soon enough."

Carter and I had broken up over the exact same thing. He wanted me to be a house wife, staying home and taking care of our future kids, as his job could easily support a wealthy lifestyle.

He'd taken me to Barbados, so I could 'see what it was like.' And I swear he'd let me get burned that day just to prove I wasn't meant for a warm climate.

We'd come back and he'd thought he'd made his point. But I'd loved the sun and sand. Even after a burn so bad I'd been hospitalized, I wanted it more than ever.

So what if I had to reek of sunscreen? I'd slather on some one-hundred-and-ten SPF and be ready to go. But he'd never understood and I'd not been able to take his patronizing anymore. I'd known then that he didn't understand me and didn't want to try.

And when Carter had met Rion just before the wedding had started, he'd made a face and said, "I didn't think Chicago had a rent-a-date service."

That had boiled my blood, but I hadn't known what to say. The woman on his arm was gorgeous of course, but I had more class than to suggest *she* was a working girl. So, I'd gritted my teeth, trying very hard not to make a scene and ruin my brother's special day. I'd turned to walk away from him, but his voice had followed me. "Still want to be an admin assistant in the tropics? I hope this guy likes spending lots of time in the hospital!" And he'd laughed.

"He's an ass," Rion had said. Some of the few words he'd spoken to me since last night, and ones I actually agreed with.

Let everyone wonder about Rion. He wasn't saying anything, which helped the mysterious air about him and peaked everyone else's speculation.

And besides. I could have a man like him if I wanted.

At least that's what I told myself.

I'd done my best to be a picture of perfection today. My dress was gorgeous, hugging my curves and cinched tight at the waist. I didn't always love my hips, but give me a good form fitting dress, and I'd happily show off my hourglass figure. The neck was low cut, showing an abundance of cleavage, and I'd spent nearly an hour styling my hair in the one sexy up-do I knew how to do to accentuate my long neck. Most of my hair was pinned up, held aloft by dozens of pins, but I'd kept a few locks loose and curled them so they'd frame my face.

My freckles were covered up with foundation — well most of them — I'd made sure the freckles on my face, chest, and shoulders were covered up, but I didn't wanted make-up all down my arms, so those ones were still showing, and anyone who knew me, knew I was just hiding the rest.

Actually, now that I thought about it. I hadn't thought to cover the back of my neck and with my hair up... and this dress was mostly backless... everyone behind me could see all the freckles I'd missed back there. Well, fuck.

Still, I knew I was as hot as I could be and that made a small part of me feel sexy, even if the rest of me was feeling awkward.

I loved Rion and hated him.

Both emotions that shocked and infuriated me. I didn't know what had happened between the guys last night and this morning, but suddenly everything was like pulling teeth with them, difficult and weird and frustrating.

Next to me, Rion was stiff and I didn't know what I'd done to upset him, and the more I tried to think about it, the more confused and upset I got. I didn't really know, nor did I want to know, what had happened. We'd had mind-blowing sex and then...

Then I'd been loopy as hell for some reason and didn't remember much except talking to Del and feeling horny all over again and nothing coming of it.

Now Rion seemed to have the possessiveness of a guy who didn't want his girl around other men, but he was still giving me the cold shoulder. Which didn't make sense because all of the guys had seemed perfectly willing to share me when we'd been in their world. Yet now he was acting like that wasn't an option. Apparently, he'd done a hard one-eighty in how he saw things sometime between having sex with me and now.

A part of me wondered if sex with me had somehow changed his mind and made him want me even more, to the point of possessiveness. But the rest of me thought that was crazy.

No man had ever fallen that hard for me, and he certainly

didn't seem to want me now. As possessive as he was, he was also pushing me away, as if I'd done something wrong, but I had no clue what that was.

So there I was, mocked by friends and family for my dreams, with a gorgeous man who hadn't said more than a few words to me because I'd somehow blown it with him.

I couldn't quite fathom how the man who'd been so tender and passionate in bed with me had turned into this cold, unfeeling statue. It brought back all the anger I'd felt that morning with the abrupt wakeup call from the fire alarm and reminded me that I was sending the guys back as soon as the wedding was done.

Except I was conflicted.

They'd caused trouble for me, but they'd also been trying to help. Apparently, I needed protecting from something, and up until that morning, they'd all been desperate to pleasure me.

Except that seemed to have gone away now too.

I bit back a sigh.

I just didn't know anymore.

All I knew was that I was done with this fantasy. It wasn't even much of a fantasy anymore, and I should have known things wouldn't have worked out for me. My life would be simpler and back to normal with them gone.

And right now, that was what I wanted... really.

"Do you, Lisa, take Daniel to be your lawfully wedded husband..." I pulled my attention back to the wedding. This was the important part, and I let myself be swept away by the fairytale wedding.

Lisa was gorgeous in a white, very modern, form-fitting dress, that was simple and elegant, while my brother was dashing — as dashing as an accountant could get — in his tux, hair coifed to within an inch of its life. And the way they looked at each other...

I sighed.

That sort of caring and love...

I'd seen a hint of it in Rion's eyes last night, but nothing like what these two had. Theirs seemed enduring and solid, and I could only wish for such a love.

Which brought me right back to Rion.

Who I didn't want to think about, damn it.

So, I concentrated on this magical moment in front of me and tried to live vicariously through my soon to be sister-in-law.

"You may now kiss the bride," the officiant announced and the two leaned in for a chaste kiss.

"Gods!" Rion breathed next to me, his eyes wide with shock. "I—"

He jerked up to his feet and swiftly walked out of the row of chairs.

Luckily that coincided with everyone else standing and cheering for the couple at the front, but it was that very same cheering that made it harder for me to follow along behind Rion and ask him what was so offensive about the ceremony.

I got to the end of our row in time to see him reach a door at the side of the hall, and I hurried after him as fast as I could in my best red stilettos, before he stepped out of sight. I'd miss the receiving line, but that wasn't too big a deal. Making sure Rion didn't do anything stupid was more important.

He marched out the door, and I caught it just before it clicked closed and rushed after him to find him just on the other side, leaning head-first against the wall, half-heartedly punching the wall, again and again. We were in a narrow hall, thankfully void of people, with chairs stacked against the wall.

"Rion, what is it?" I asked. "What's wrong with you?"

He spun on me, his long-blond hair flying out at the sudden movement about him. His sky-blue eyes were rimmed in red — had he been crying? — were somehow cold and burning hot at the same time.

"What's wrong with me?" he demanded, his anger shocking me and making me take a hesitant step away from him. "What's wrong with you? You kiss me and I accept your bond only to have you throw it away and ask Del to join you? Was I nothing to you? We were bonded, united, hearts locked, and you threw it away as if it were nothing!"

"What?" I stumbled back another step.

What was he talking about? What was this about bonds and locked hearts? It didn't make sense.

"Then you bring me here." Rion jerked his hand toward the door behind me. "To witness the bonding of your brother and his beloved. To witness their *bonding kiss* when you so flagrantly denied ours."

"Ours?" My eyes went wide. These guys were from some primitive culture. Did they think I'd married Rion because we'd had sex?

"Wait, do you think we're... *bonded* because we had sex?"

He blinked and frowned in confusion. "What? No. Sex is nothing. A pleasure, fun. No, we were bonded by our kiss."

"Kiss? Which one?" There'd been a lot of... *lip work* last night.

"Your kiss on my lips." His confusion deepened, overwhelming more of his rage. Now he seemed as confused as I was. "You pressed your lips to mine. Lips are sacred. The lips speak of promises and a kiss upon the lips is a true kiss, a bonding kiss. It signifies—"

"Oh, fuck," I groaned as realization hit me.

Somehow all the other kisses hadn't meant anything, but my kissing him on the lips — which *I'd* instigated — *had* meant something to him. And just now my brother's marriage had been sealed with a kiss.

Hunh. Was that something that transcended our worlds? Had the kiss-on-the-lips in our world just come to mean something less?

"Rion, I didn't know."

"How could you not know?" he demanded. "It's part of your bonding ceremony. We just saw it."

And now I had no idea what to say to him, because, fuck, he thought he was my *husband*.

CHAPTER 16

AETHAN

I HATED MY MAN-LEGS.

Del had insisted I change to them when we went out, even though they'd be covered by pants. I suppose I could understand. Everyone here seemed to have man-legs and I'd have stood out with my equine legs, even with pants on.

Still, I was as awkward as a newborn foal.

Add to that my inability to fully control my new speed, and I was a literal walking mess.

Thankfully, most people on the street were ignoring me and looking at Keph.

And Gods, was he a sight! Those gray stretchy pants and the white shirt with the blue and red crest barely fit him. They were pulled tight over his massive frame, and the large man was hesitant and apprehensive of everything around him despite the urgency of his vision.

He'd always been careful around others, afraid of hurting people, and there were so many more people here than back in our world. He wasn't so much walking down the street as carefully shuffling along when we should have been running.

Which only made me more agitated. I couldn't walk right, and the fear that we'd be too late to save Goddess Annie from the darkness made my chest tight. Not to mention everything around me was fascinating, drawing my attention from trying to control my body to stare at the wonders around me.

To top it off, I didn't know what to make of everything that had happened. A part of me could understand why the goddess had seemed so out of place in our world after seeing hers. This was a truly fantastical place. It was a confusion of oddities and I was the quickest among our group to take to new things. I couldn't imagine what it must be like for the rest of them. Keph had seemed overwhelmed the moment we'd stepped into her world and still did.

Except that didn't excuse the goddess's behavior toward Rion. Much as I hoped it meant she might be open for other options, I also didn't want to hurt my friend. These three men had been good to me. They hadn't shunned me for my quick wit, as most of my clan did, and they didn't care about my sexual awkwardness when we were carousing.

They were more like brothers than friends, a distant family I saw far too infrequently. And I didn't want a brother to suffer.

And as much as I hoped I could be healed by the goddess, her behavior had been odd since we'd returned.

"Do you think something is wrong with the goddess?" I asked as the three of us stopped behind a group of other people waiting at a large intersection that, like many intersections, had a strange set of lights.

I'd observed the correct interactions at such a crossing during our trip to the goddess's home. Symbols lit up with a walking figure or a hand, indicating when a person could cross the stream of self-propelled carts, something which I found absolutely fascinating — the goddess had called them... cars?

Del glanced at me then turned his attention back to sweeping the area around us as if he was searching for trouble. "I'm afraid we might be seeing her true colors."

The light changed and the group ahead of us crossed the intersection and the cars rushed past in the other direction, but Keph didn't move.

"Come on," I said, but Keph tensed and the walking figure was replaced by the flashing red hand, indicating that we were running out of time.

And we weren't just running out of time with the light. Even if Keph's vision hadn't specifically told him when the darkness would attack, at his current pace there was no way we'd make it in time to protect the goddess.

I grabbed the big guy's sleeve to get him to move but the red hand stopped flashing and the direction of the cars changed.

"I've read—" Del said as two men reached the intersection and waited behind us for the light to change again. He glanced back at them then shifted closer to me and dropped his voice. "I've read many tales of the ancients."

"Like Zeus and Heracles?" I asked, my voice just as soft. I knew some of the folklore on the gods, those tales passed on through stories by minstrels and storytellers, but I hadn't actually read any of them.

Del nodded. "Those same, yes. But the stories I read were not glorious tales, not for the most part. They portrayed the gods like men, petty, selfish, and often cruel. They were rarely benevolent. So, when I met Goddess Annie and she'd been so kind and giving of herself to help the sick—" Del ran a hand through his long blue-black hair, pushing it out of his eyes and sighed. "I'd thought she was different. Now I'm not so sure. And if she is as petty and cruel as those gods of old, I don't know if I want to anger her further."

Del was right, she'd been kind and giving in our world, and

now she was erratic, one minute a seductress, the next furious. So, what did that mean?

I could foresee two outcomes to our current course of action. Either we'd rescue the goddess and she'd be grateful, perhaps taking us back — though we'd need to figure out how she felt about Rion. Or, she'd be furious we'd disobeyed her command to stay at her home and we'd have sealed our fates, banished from this world. Both seemed just as likely in my mind.

The walking figure appeared and I started across the intersection, but Keph still didn't move.

"Keph," I hissed, standing a quarter of the way across. We didn't have time for this!

The men behind him hesitated, waiting for him to go, while a woman and her child, both bundled up against the chill, walked past me in the opposite direction toward the big guy. Except they hesitated as they drew close to him, their eyes wide as if they were afraid of him, then scurried past.

"Come on," I insisted as the light changed to the flashing hand. People were staring and we needed to get moving.

One of the men said something under his breath and both of them shot Keph a dark look before hurrying around him and crossing, and I returned to the big man's side to wait for the light to change. Again.

At this rate we were never going to get there, and we were running out of time.

I bit back a yell of frustration and yanked my gaze to the massive buildings towering around me. I was certain now that not all of these people were gods. Most of them must be the servants to the gods, like the men who'd waited with us to cross the intersection. It made sense that Gods would have many servants. I just hadn't realized how many.

The light changed again and finally — finally! — Keph decided it was safe and we continued down the street before stopping at the next intersection with its red hand telling us to wait our turn.

"You're crossing when the walking figure appears," I ordered. "If the darkness has found Rion and the goddess then we don't have time for you to hesitate at every intersection."

"Unless his power of foresight knows just how slow he's going to move through this strange land and has given us enough forewarning," Del said.

I glared at him. "You're not helping."

The light changed and much to my surprise, Keph started shuffling across the intersection without any more hesitation, as if having spent all that time at the previous intersection to figure out the lights had been enough to quell his concerns.

But then one of the cars that was turning toward us gave a blaring horn sound.

Keph jumped, clearing a good dozen feet, and making Del's mouth drop open in surprise — and I had no doubt my mouth was hanging open as well. Stone titans weren't known for their leaping ability, they certainly couldn't jump that high, and Keph had done it as if were nothing.

He landed and stumbled into the car that had made the shocking noise waiting for us to cross. The self-propelled cart made the blaring sound again and the big titan, clearly reacting on instinct, put a hand on either side of the car. I hadn't thought Keph's arm span was that wide, but he easily boxed in its front then lifted it clear off the ground.

Off. The. Ground!

By Zeus and all the gods!

I knew Keph was strong, but those cars looked heavy and he'd lifted it like it was nothing.

"Keph!" Del shouted — and a good thing too, because I was too stunned to react. "Put that down."

Del's voice snapped Keph out of his shock and he set the

contraption back on the ground. The three of us hurried across the intersection and back onto the designated walking area, but now *everyone* was looking at us. Not the least of which were the people in the car Keph had picked up, who'd forgotten to go when the light had changed.

"Ah... sorry," I called to them, but I couldn't take my eyes off the massive hand prints crunched into the metal on either side of the thing.

So much for avoiding too much notice. I should have known Keph would be a liability, but it was too late now, so we rushed onward to our destination.

CHAPTER 17

DELPHON

WE FOUND THE HALL AND RUSHED IN. KEPH, AS MUCH AS HE'D BEEN slow and hesitant at the beginning of our journey was now in such a hurry that he forgot to duck and banged his head on the doorframe. Luckily, he had a hard head. Legend was that stone titans were partially made of stone. I didn't know if that was true, but I'd never seen the man bleed. Though, to be fair, he was a softhearted fellow in general and rarely joined us in our recreational fighting... which was probably a good thing, given how strong he was.

But once inside, the three of us stood in a large opulent foyer not knowing which way to go. The long entry hall had two sets of double doors along the left side, two on the right and a single set of double doors at the far end. There was a desk in front of a single door, just inside and to the right, with a young woman and older man behind it. Only the man had looked up at our arrival and his eyes were now bulging, his expression filled with shock.

"You there," he said to us, then turned to his female companion and whispered. "Call nine-one-one." Then back to us. "You can't be here. Get out. We're calling the cops."

I got the feeling from his tone that these *cops* would be some sort of city guard or watchmen, which wouldn't be good.

"We don't want any trouble," I said, raising my hands, palms out to show I didn't have a weapon and meant him no harm.

"We don't keep money on site," the man replied, his shock shifting into fear.

"That's... good?" I took a step toward him not sure why he'd brought that up. "We're just looking for some friends who're at a... *wedding*?" Was that the right word? Annie had said it several times in relation to this event, so I was pretty sure that was the word I wanted. "They're in danger and we need to get them out of here."

"Yes," Aethan continued. "A goddess in a red dress with a tall man who has blond hair. Have you seen them?"

The man standing behind the desk seemed confused and was eyeing the set of double doors to his right, while the woman spoke softly on a small square device that she held to the side of her face. Goddess Annie had one of those things, and she'd spoken into it as well.

"I'll block the door," Keph said then stepped outside again, right in front of the large main double doors, and turned to stone.

I'd only seen the transformation a couple of times since it wasn't common for Keph to shift, and I still only partly sensed the change by how stiff he went, but there was also a tell-tale sound that came with the transformation, a sort of subtle grinding and cracking sound, like pebbles under the wheel of a particularly heavy wagon.

Blocking the door wasn't a bad idea, but it made the man behind the desk even more nervous. The blood drained from his face and he started to tremble.

"Where are they?" Aethan pressed.

The man shook his head and the woman's grip on her device tightened, turning her knuckles white.

Aethan waited for a response, but none came.

"Zeus's balls," Aethan huffed. "He's not going to help us." Then he vanished.

There was a grunt and the sounds of someone falling from farther into the large reception area to the right, and I glanced over to see Aethan tumbling across the floor, almost at the set of double doors at the far end of the foyer, cursing his man-legs for tripping him up.

"Holy mother of—" the man at the desk gasped and darted for the closest door to his right, quickly slipping into the room beyond. The woman ducked behind the desk, still urgently speaking to someone in a whispered voice.

This was not going well.

"Poseidon help me!" I didn't usually curse by the gods, but this seemed appropriate.

Aethan was up again. "I'll find her," he called back, then was off again at his incredible speed.

The doors at the far end of the hall burst open, then slammed shut and there was a crashing sound from the other side.

What was the word the goddess used when upset?

Fuck.

I didn't know what it meant, but is sure seemed appropriate now, and I really hoped we weren't about to make more trouble for her.

I went to the first set of double doors on the left side of the foyer and carefully opened one to glance inside.

The space was large with a second story balcony that ran around the circumference of the room leaving the center open to both floors, and there were a couple hundred people, all dressed like the goddess and Rion had been. A good number of them, somewhere between twelve and twenty, stood in a long line along the far right wall from where I'd entered. They were chatting with others, who moved past them in another line like some form of ritual conversation. The moving part of the line seemed to be coming out from a different room, through a door at the far end of the same wall as the door I was peeking through.

I slipped inside and hid behind one of the pillars supporting the second floor balcony to get a better look and search for the goddess.

The line of unmoving people had a woman in a white dress who stood out. Next to her were five other women in identical cream and purple dresses, and to the other side of her were six men in... what had Goddess Annie called them? *Suits.* Then there were five older people — a mix of men and woman who looked to be elders. Everyone seemed to have a quick conversation with the person in front of them, then the person in front would move to the next one in the line and have another similarly short chat.

What boggled my mind, however, wasn't the oddity of this strange ritual, but the number of people who seemed to be casually kissing other people as they moved down the line. One older woman embraced and kissed every member of the unmoving line fully on the lips be they man or woman — and all those people couldn't have been her bonded mates — while another older man also kissed his way along the line, though when he got to the men it was on both cheeks instead of the lips.

My thoughts tripped, the casual kissing was so different here than in my world. *Could it be that kissing means something different for these people?*

If so...

Then Goddess Annie may not have been claiming a bond with Rion as we'd all thought. If kissing was something much more casual here, then...

I needed to tell Rion immediately.

I turned to the double doors to go back into the foyer, but as I did, a couple who'd already left the strange ritual-line headed toward the doors as well. Hurrying, I tried to get there first, hoping they wouldn't notice me, and slammed into a metal bar between the two doors. The impact stunned me and I staggered back, half turning toward the couple, a hand on my face where I'd hit the bar.

The lady's eyes widened, her gaze swept down me, and she took a quick step back instead of going through the door, while the man stepped in front of the woman and glared at me.

"What are you doing here?" he demanded. "Who are you?"

Balls. I'd forgotten I wasn't supposed to draw attention to myself and with my clothes looking different than everyone else's, it was obvious I didn't belong.

Right. I hurried back — through just one of the doors — into the foyer, realizing too late that there was a blaring noise coming from outside, blue and red flashing lights, and four men in matching clothes trying to get past Keph to open the front doors.

"You there!" One of the men shouted at me. I could only just hear him through the glassed-in front of the foyer. "Halt, you're trespassing on private property."

He drew something from his hip, a metallic object and pointed it at me.

This... wasn't going well. So much for not drawing attention to ourselves.

But in the end it didn't really matter. Goddess Annie was in danger and I would do everything in my power to protect her... even if I did end up upsetting her.

I ran from the men in uniforms, toward the doors at the far end to find Aethan. Two sharp bangs and the sound of shattering glass rang out.

Sharp pain bit the side of my leg and I stumbled toward the door.

We needed to find the goddess and Rion. And we needed to find them now.

CHAPTER 18

HYPERION

I COULDN'T TAKE IT ANYMORE.

Annie kept trying to apologize for the kiss, saying she didn't know what it had meant, but how could she not? This ceremony she'd brought me too was obviously some elaborate bonding ritual for the people of this world — which I was starting to believe weren't gods at all — and it had ended with a kiss... on the lips.

It was clear that even here a kiss of that nature meant something similar to what it did in my world.

I had to get away, but the hallway seemed far too narrow with her standing in the middle of it, and it was hard to get past her without touching her. And that was a problem. As much as my heart was torn by her casual dismissal of our kiss, I still ached to grab her, push her up against one of these walls, and slip my hands under her dress. My lips burned to be on her skin once again, or even better, between her thighs.

She'd tasted exquisite, sweet and luscious, and my cock had been awkwardly hard nearly every moment we'd been together today despite my anger. Seeing her in that alluring and sensual red dress, covering what I knew to be a full and wonderous body, only made it more alluring. By Hades I was aroused and angry and so very confused.

Still I managed to brush past her. I couldn't look back once I had gotten around her.

I wouldn't.

So, I headed for the door leading back into the room we'd come from. At least from there I knew the way out, and that was exactly where I needed to be going. Out.

I'd had more than enough of this and I was leaving. As much as I knew she needed protection, the others could take care of that. I couldn't be near her anymore. I'd either take out all my fury on her or all my passion.

Pushing open the door, I strode into the other room, shouting back at Annie. "I'm leaving. You can't tease a man like that, promise him everything then tear it away!"

There were only a few people left and they were lined up at a door on the far side of the room, which led into another area. Many of them turned to look at me as I shouted, but I didn't care and headed straight for the doors leading back to the foyer.

Except before I reached them, the doors whipped open and slammed closed, and then Aethan appeared out of nowhere, stumbled into the last row of chairs, and bowled through three more before coming to a stop in a heap on the floor.

Now everyone was looking at *him*.

Good.

I reached him and, battered and bruised, he rose, unsteady on feet that had been shoved into human-looking boots. He wore some of the clothes Annie had bought for us, but it was clear he didn't fit in here. Everyone else who'd attended the ceremony was dressed as Annie and myself were, while Aethan had on mismatched bright green pants and a heavy yellow hooded shirt, and a blue jacket.

"*You* can protect her now," I snapped, heading for the double doors. "I'm done."

"Rion? What...? By Zeus!" This last was in a hushed, awed tone. I turned, curious what had caused it, but shouldn't have.

Annie had come out from the hall where we'd been arguing, tears in her eyes, cheeks flushed — actually all of her flushed — and that dress...

That's what Aethan had seen. The goddess in all her stunning glory. He was staring at her just like he'd stared at her in her residence, and now I was staring again too, captivated. I couldn't move.

By Hades! What was it about this woman that confounded me so?

She saw Aethan and her sorrowfully torn expression turned to confusion. "Aethan? What are you doing here?" Then horror. "Did something happen? Is my apartment—?"

"We needed to find you," Aethan said, shaking his head as if it took physical effort to take his attention off her and focus. Then he took a step forward, and, between one blink and the next, he crossed half the distance between them. "Keph had a vision. He saw the darkness coming for you. We need to get you out of here!"

The darkness?

Keph had visions?

Aethan glanced back at me.

"I'm sorry Rion," he said, voice torn, face contorted in sorrow and need before turning back to Annie. "But you can't send us back just yet. I need to be with you. I need you to heal me."

Heal him?

Okay none of this was making any sense.

I didn't think anything was wrong with him.

And what was he doing asking to be with her when—

Well, she'd torn out my heart, so what did I care?

Except I *did* care.

The thought of him with her, her body pressed to his while she moaned with pleasure—

Oddly wasn't as objectionable as I thought it would be.

Instead, I was aroused yet again by the thought of her taking her pleasure and it didn't seem to matter from who. Just the thought of her finding bliss was enough.

I blinked, not knowing where those thoughts came from.

My mind swept further still to a fantasy of myself and Aethan with Annie, and the heights of pleasure she might reach with both of us together.

I jerked away, my cock hard, straining the fabric at the front of my already too-tight pants.

How could I still wish to be with her after she'd—

But I did.

It didn't matter that she'd dismissed my bonding. It didn't matter if she wanted to be with others. I still wanted to be with her... desperately.

I tried to get myself under control, tried to push my thoughts to other things when loud, sharp bangs erupted on the other side of the double doors leading to the foyer.

A second later they flew open and Del rushed in. Blood stained the calf of his pantleg but not enough for the wound to be serious, and his eyes were hard with determination. "We need to get out of here."

CHAPTER 19

ANNIE

HOLY-WHAT-THE-FUCK!

I could hear the distant sirens and even more, had heard the sound of gun shots just before Del, looking like a hobo, had limped in as if he'd been the one who'd just been shot.

Add to that Rion marching out, and Aethan, looking like a punk with his dark red mohawk and standing before me with a very noticeable 'tent' in his bright green sweatpants, and I was overwhelmed.

I didn't want to know where Keph was.

The few other people left in this room were staring at the four of us and had been ever since Rion had shouted those words about me teasing men and promising them everything then tearing it away. It made me sound like some floozy.

And I was *not* a floozy.

But now everyone here thought I was. And I knew far too many of them. Luckily the bulk of the guests, including my immediate family, had gone into the adjacent hall for the reception, but still.

"What the hell is going on?" I shouted at Del. I didn't want to be yelling, but he was at the far end of the hall and there were sirens and people shouting behind him. None of which sounded good at all. "What are you doing here? And where's Keph?" The thought of him alone in my apartment trying to do the simplest thing and accidentally trashing the place leaped to mind. It shouldn't have. The chair had been an accident and he'd hardly moved since then, but I couldn't help myself.

"He's a statue, out there." Del pointed over his shoulder to the foyer.

"A what?"

Fuck.

I was about to ask why the cops were here, but then given that Del and Aethan looked like criminals — and had probably acted like ones too — I really didn't need to.

Fuck and double fuck.

"We need to go. Now." It was the only thing I could think of, but before I was able to turn and direct them back to the hallway Rion and I had just been in — which had had a door marked exit at the far end — Del sprinted toward the other door where the few other people in this room were leaving. Into the other reception hall. Where the wedding party — and everyone else — was.

No. Please. Not that way!

But I never got the words out.

Aethan blurred, moving unbelievably fast, wrapping strong arms around me and lifting me. Then the world blurred and my stomach lurched as he ran.

We stopped suddenly. My stomach heaved from the sudden halt and I desperately hoped I wasn't going to be sick, but with everything else that had happened — my life being turned upside down — and now having been shaken and stirred, I couldn't help myself.

I tried to avoid losing my lunch on Aethan, turned my head to the side... and threw up all over Lisa's pristine white wedding dress.

Oh no!

The sight was so shocking and disturbing, I threw up again.

Oh God!

This was the worst. The absolute possible worst. The shock and horror on Lisa's face and my brother's face was too much to bear. I needed to get out of there. Please.

Then everyone turned at a great noise from the far end of the hall. Thank God, a distraction from the horridness that was me.

But when I looked, I saw Keph crashing through the doors pursued by cops. The doors flew off their hinges, flying into the room with the force of Keph's desperate rush. Dressed like some practicing line-backer in sweat clothes that were skin tight on him, Keph seemed unaware of his surroundings and didn't even notice the marble pillar he ran right into... then through. That caused part of the balcony above him to collapse, which thankfully meant the cops were blocked from entering the room.

Except Keph continued his charge across the hall, through the table of gifts and, of course, the wedding cake, the impact tossing everything in all directions.

There weren't enough fucks to sum this moment up.

This was *the* roaring dumpster fire of all dumpster fires. And my whole family was watching.

Then I heard Rion's hushed voice. "Close your eyes."

Yep, I didn't want to see any more of this.

A great brightness erupted, momentarily blinding me even though my eyes were closed.

"Get her out of here," Rion said, and Aethan was moving again, making my stomach twist and lurch, threatening to expel what little I had left in it.

Next thing I knew, I was shivering and throwing up in an alley a few blocks from the wedding hall.

Somehow all the guys had gotten out and were crowded around me, and I collapsed to my knees, my vision swimming with the incredible shambles these men had made of my brother's wedding.

No, this was my fault. And puking was the only logical response to everything that had happened.

My vomiting turned to sobs. I squeezed my eyes shut, tears leaking beneath my lashes, and pressed my hands over my face. I couldn't bear to see the world right now.

None of the guys said anything. They had to know what a mess that had been. Even if they didn't know my world, they had to know how much they'd fucked up.

God! Fuck me. Fuck my life. Fuck these idiot guys!

They had to go.

And they had to go now.

CHAPTER 20

ANNIE

FURIOUS, ON THE VERGE OF TEARS, AND WITHOUT HESITATION OR A second thought, I marched the guys farther from the wedding hall. My goal was the alley where I'd tumbled into their world, and not home, because they had to go!

The Incident — because I couldn't think of what had happened at my brother's wedding in any other way than *the Incident* — was the last straw.

But I was in such a hurry to get them out of my now-completely-ruined life, that I forgot to get the coat and boots I'd warn to the hall and now found myself trudging and slipping through snow and slush in my best heels.

But I wasn't turning back no matter how cold I was. I couldn't let them stay in the wedding hall or anywhere near my family. I couldn't let them stay in my world. They didn't belong.

Aethan opened his mouth to say something, but I glared at him, and he snapped it shut and gave me his jacket, which would have been a sweet gesture if I wasn't so mad at him and if it hadn't smelled faintly of vomit, reminding me of what I'd done.

We reached the alley and I pointed to the brick wall where I'd fallen through.

Aethan cursed when he realized where I'd taken them and Del looked grim.

"Go," I said

"But we need to protect you," Del replied.

"No, you don't." I wasn't in danger. This *darkness* whatever the hell it was, came from their world, where they belonged and I didn't. I didn't care how sexy they were or that they thought I was a goddess. That had turned to shit like everything else in my life. Their hot-cold act made me so sexually frustrated I wanted to scream and I was never going to be able to show my face at a family dinner again because of what had just happened at the wedding.

"Goddess, please—" Aethan started.

"No! You've ruined my life. My family is never going to speak to me again and—" And my ex, Carter, had even more ammunition proving just how stupid and foolish I was. I couldn't even bring an *escort* to the wedding and not fuck it up. "Go."

They stared at me.

"I said go," I snapped, my teeth chattering from the cold. "This was a horrific cluster-fuck-shit-show-dumpster-fire and I don't want to see any of you ever again!"

Rion glanced at me for a second, then his gaze slid past me to the wall as if he couldn't even look at me.

"As you wish," he said, the same words he'd whispered to me during the most blissful moment of my life.

Warmth and yearning whispered, seductive and sultry, through my chest and I quickly froze it into a hard ball of ice. He'd said horrible things to me in front of my family, things that implied I was a floozy, and I was sure that was how they thought I'd managed to *land* him long enough to bring him to the wedding.

Then he stepped through the wall and was gone.

"By Zeus, I'm sorry," Aethan said, his gaze meeting mine for a second before he dropped it and stepped through.

Out of the corner of my eye, I saw Keph reach to touch my back, then pull away before making contact.

"Sorry," he said. "I know it was wrong. I didn't mean to destroy... so much. I just— There were people yelling and strange lights and really loud noises and something kept stinging me and..." He sighed then stepped through, leaving Del.

"I'm really sorry... for all of this." He ran a hand through his long blue-black hair, pushing it away from his face, and sighed. "I thought it was fate when you appeared from the stones on the beach. And how the others all felt for you, how you healed those people... I thought I'd finally found something that... that meant something in my life." He released another heavy sigh. "I can see that I've destroyed it now. I understand why you're sending us back. But... if you ever need us, know that we'll always be there for you, Annie" he said. His voice lowered and filled with reverence. "Our goddess."

Then he was gone as well.

Good riddance.

Except—

My chest hurt and my throat was tight, and it had nothing to do with the cold.

His last words, *our goddess*, whirled around and around in my head. I wanted to go through and call them back. It didn't make sense, but I wanted it so much I couldn't breathe.

I reached for the invisible portal—

No! I had to be stronger than that. I had to let them go. They'd made enough of a mess of my life.

I jerked back, my heel slipped on the ice, and I fell onto my butt.

They'd ruined my life.

I barely knew them.

Why did their leaving hurt so much?

Because I was silly and stupid and wanted things that weren't mine and would never be mine.

I forced myself to stand and walk out of the alley.

I was half frozen and shivering uncontrollably by the time I got back to my apartment, where I threw off the jacket and fell into bed with my dress still on, even though I knew to take better care of it. But I didn't care. I didn't care if my far-too-expensive dress was ruined and I didn't care about anything anymore.

For the next few days, I was sick, feverish, and sleeping most of the time, and when I wasn't asleep, I was crying.

My brother and sister showed up, worried. They thought I'd been kidnapped by the four strange men. Happy to find me safe, if a mess, they even stayed to take care of me, which was so much worse than just being alone.

I'd ruined Daniel's most important day and he was still kind enough to take care of me. I was torn and ashamed. I wanted to tell them to leave me alone, that everything had been my fault, but I was also very grateful that they didn't think the whole mess had been because of me. And I didn't have the courage to tell them the truth.

I demanded Daniel leave to go on his honeymoon, which left my sister to take care of me, but I avoided her when she wasn't bringing me food or water or a cold cloth. I didn't say anything. I couldn't. The *Incident* kept playing over and over again in my fevered dreams... as did my time with Rion in bed.

And in my delirious imaginings, I also pictured Aethan in Rion's place... and Del... even Keph. Though with Keph, I was riding him like some prized stallion. He was far too big and heavy to be on top.

Hot in all the wrong ways, feverish, dreaming, and crying, my week slipped by. It was Thursday before I felt better and my fever had fully cleared. I told my sister to go home, that I was well enough now, but that left the apartment empty. And though the heat was on, it felt... cold.

I felt cold.

Diane had been covering for me at work, and I knew I had to go back, but I couldn't bring myself to drag my life back together.

I couldn't.

I didn't want to.

But that wouldn't get the rent paid.

I was still a mess when I went into work on Friday. I did my job, half-heartedly, distracted and distant, and was glad nothing important was due. Again, Diane had saved me there. She'd done all the important items earlier in the week, which meant all I needed to do was put together a presentation for a future meeting.

On my way home, I stopped in front of that fated alley, my chest and throat once again too tight, and stood there, disrupting foot-traffic for some time, staring at the wall.

It was a normal looking wall.

And yet it had changed my life.

For the worse.

Except, I couldn't stop staring at it, couldn't return home, couldn't even move. I stood there until it was dark, then finally, exhausted, I forced myself to look away and plod back home.

That night, I sat on my couch, staring at the dark TV, knowing I should turn it on and distract myself, but unable to make myself do it. I'd picked up a slice of pizza from a little shop on the corner, but I stared at it too, unable to make myself eat it.

I went to bed hungry, feeling like crap.

My dreams were dark and confusing, like the fever-dreams earlier that week. More sick people were reaching for me, only this time the guys were sick as well. They were calling out for their goddess, begging for her help, and she never came.

With a jerk, I woke up, sweating, my heart racing.

I couldn't take it anymore. I needed to do something, get out, turn my life on its head, but in a good way this time. It had been thrown into such a shambles that I just couldn't get over it. I was still thinking about the guys. I'd hated them and screamed at them in my fever-dreams, but with a clearer head now, I hated myself for hating them.

I didn't know why they'd come to the wedding, but ultimately, it hadn't been their fault. Yes, they'd trashed the place, but they wouldn't have been able to do any of that if I hadn't brought them back to my world.

I'd been so enraptured with the fantasy they'd represented that I'd wanted more. I should have put my foot down and just left their world... alone. But they'd been so kind, so caring, so protective. They may not have known the ways of my world, but in many ways, they'd been more gentlemanly than any man I'd ever known. They'd treated me... well, like a goddess and I'd loved it.

Oh, how I'd loved it. That reverence in their eyes... and the desire. No one had ever looked at me like that before, not frumpy ol' Annie Chambers.

I should have spent more time teaching them the ways of my world and made them understand the norms and customs, and the technology before leaving them alone. They hadn't even known how to use a light switch! Maybe, if I'd done that, they wouldn't have come after me, wouldn't have made a mess of everything.

Except that would have required explaining that I wasn't a goddess.

I still didn't know how I'd been able to heal those people in their world.

And as I thought about it... they'd been able to do strange things here as well. Aethan had moved far too fast and Rion had created that blinding light at the wedding.

Perhaps it was something about people from one world being *special* when they were in the other world.

I didn't know. It was a wild theory. Though no wilder than the existence of another world.

Outside my window a faint light at the edge of the horizon said it was near dawn, so I dressed, getting ready for work, still thinking about my theory.

I was so caught up in thought, moving on autopilot, that I didn't realize until I looked up that I'd returned to the alley instead of my office *and* that it was Saturday and I hadn't needed to leave my apartment.

It had snowed overnight, a good three or four inches, and while most of it had been cleared from the sidewalk, the alley hadn't been shoveled. That meant I could clearly see the two sets of footprints which originated at that *special* part of the wall and walked out of the alley.

But that wasn't possible, no one could come through without me.

I stared at the footprints for a long moment then drew closer, drawing up to *the spot* and stared at it.

I needed to see the guys.

And I needed to confess to them that I wasn't a goddess. I was fairly certain once they knew I wasn't a goddess they'd be furious with me. They'd think I'd taken advantage of them, and in a way, I had. I was certain none of them would have wanted to have sex with me if I'd just been... me.

I shoved that thought back, reminding myself that even if they weren't angry. I didn't know if I wanted them back in my life. Their world and mine didn't mix.

Except that didn't matter. Whether I wanted them or they wanted me, they still deserved the truth. I'd feel better once they knew. Then this could all end and — I hoped to God — I could get on with my pathetic life.

I had no idea exactly what I'd say, but I had the walk from the stones to the village to figure that out.

And a walk on a gloriously warm beach seemed like exactly what I needed — and wanted — right now.

I reached out to touch the wall, my hand passing through into the unsettling nothingness that should have been brick, then stepped through the wall.

And there, lying in the early morning sunlight, less than a dozen feet from me, was Rion, face down in the sand, wings splayed out and limp. Black spots covered his skin, and even as I stared at him in horror, the diseased spots grew, consuming him. He'd be dead in a matter of minutes, if he wasn't already.

CHAPTER 21

ANNIE

My heart racing, I ran to Rion and placed my hands on his blistered and diseased skin. The sight of it was sickening, but I knew I could heal this even if no one in the camp had been this far gone... so long as he was still alive.

Please, let him still be alive.

I couldn't see him breathing and was too afraid to check his pulse to find out the truth, so, like I'd done before, I pushed energy into him instead, praying I wasn't too late.

For a terrifying second, I feared even if he was alive, it wouldn't work. My previous time here had felt like a dream, and if it had been a dream then it had turned into a nightmare and it wouldn't matter what I tried, I'd lose him.

But the horrible spots on his skin began to heal and fade and then he drew in a long, heavy breath.

Oh, thank God.

I sat back on my heels, exhausted and relieved and suddenly extremely warm.

Right, tropical world.

If I didn't want to pass out from heat exhaustion, I needed to shed some clothes. Luckily, I'd come prepared this time, with a light T-shirt and shorts under all my other things... which, if I'd been paying attention should have told me where my subconscious wanted me to go instead of thinking when I'd left my apartment that I was going to work.

I stripped down to my tropic-appropriate clothing as Rion dragged in another couple deep breaths before groaning and slowly rolling over into a sitting position

He stared at me, his expression stunned.

"Annie?" His gaze slid to the stones from which I'd emerged then returned to me. "I'd been coming to get you, or trying to get you, but I couldn't pass through the stones. How did you know?"

How had I known?

Had I known?

Certainly my dreams the night before now seemed prophetic if this was what had really happened to them, but I didn't put much stock in prophecies. This was just coincidence and good timing. Nothing more.

"It doesn't matter, I'm just glad you're well," I said. "Actually, this will probably work for the best. I don't know if I could face the others, but perhaps I can tell you and you can take it back to them."

"Annie, the others are—"

"Rion," I said, cutting him off even as I dropped my gaze to my feet. I needed to finish this and if I didn't say it now, I was afraid I'd lose my courage and never would. "I'm not a goddess. I don't know why I have powers here, but I don't in my world. I'm nothing special. I—"

"Annie," Rion said his voice strange and soft, but I couldn't tell what that meant. I didn't know him well enough to know if he was so furious he'd withdrawn and become quiet or if he wasn't furious.

And if he wasn't furious, would he still want me?

The thought shocked me even though I knew I still desired him and the others. I didn't think I'd ever stop desiring them.

But that wasn't the point. I'd lied to them, made them think I was a goddess and I couldn't have all four. That just didn't happen.

"Annie." He tucked a finger under my chin and urged me to meet his gaze. The look in his eyes was also strange, a mix of desire and longing and... fear.

He was afraid of me?

"I know."

My thoughts tripped. "What?" What were we talking about?

"I know you're not a goddess."

So he *was* mad.

Except he didn't look mad and wait—

He already knew?

But—

"We have to hurry. The others were infected too. The sickness came, but it wasn't just a sickness, it was a person, someone like you, with powers. He walked through town and infected everyone."

I gasped as my thoughts did another flipflop.

A person infected everyone just by walking through the town?

That didn't make any sense—

"The others...?"

"Need your healing."

"Take me to them."

I jerked toward the village and started to run, but Rion yanked me into his arms and with a *whoosh* that sent the sand sweeping around us, he leaped into the air.

His body was hard and hot, pressing into my back. I snuggled closer and his arms tightened around me. One arm was high, just below my breasts, the other low, on my hip, keeping me close, pulling me closer. My heart skipped and soared from the intimate contact and... from freaking flying! My breath hitched and I had trouble fully recovering it, because if I wasn't thinking about flying, or how good it felt to be close to him, I was thinking about the rest of my guys in pain.

Not my guys... *the* guys.

Fuck... whatever.

We spotted Keph just outside the village trudging through the sand in the direction of the rocks carrying Aethan under one arm and Del under the other. The disease covered all three of them, and I was surprised how well I could tell where it was on Keph, given his black skin. But then his natural skin was ever so slightly shiny and the diseased parts were dull and oozing.

Aethan and Del looked to be almost completely covered by the ichor, and my chest squeezed with fear.

Please, God. They had to still be alive.

"Set them down," I said as Rion landed in front of Keph.

Keph dragged his gaze up — he'd been staring at the ground just putting one foot in front of the next, trying to move forward.

"You came." Relief filled his large silver-lined black eyes, and he sagged to his knees and released the others onto the sand.

My chest squeezed even tighter at the sight of seeing the powerful man brought to his knees like that, his head bowed with exhaustion, but the others weren't even moving, and just like Rion, I couldn't tell if they were still alive.

I knelt in front of Keph and placed one hand on Aethan's head and the other on Del's, praying that I'd be able to split my energy and heal both of them at the same time.

Strength swept out of me, flooding into them, as if once I'd made the connection, their bodies had taken over and was sucking me dry. But I didn't fight it. My soul cried to save them even if I barely knew them, even if it didn't make sense to sacrifice myself for them if that's what it took.

The horrible black welts on their skin melted away and Del groaned, while Aethan sucked in a deep, gasping breath.

The pressure in my chest eased a bit, and I dragged my attention to Keph and raised a trembling hand to his head.

One more. That was all I needed to do.

"Annie, stop," Rion said. "You've done too much."

I ignored him and set my hand on the top of Keph's smooth head, and let my power flow into him. He wasn't as far gone, and didn't take as much from me, but light and dark spots surged and danced across my vision by the time I was done.

The rest of the pressure in my chest eased and the irrational fear that I'd lose even one of these men who I'd just met, faded. I drew in my own ragged, gasping breath.

My guys were safe... except they weren't *my* guys... and I didn't know if they were safe.

Rion had said everyone in the village had been infected, and I didn't know if this magical illness worked like a regular illness. Would the guys have antibodies? Were they now immune, or could they be infected over and over again?

And really, did that matter?

I still had some strength left. I could save a few more people.

I had to.

"The village," I said, my words slurred as I struggled to stand. "I need to heal as many as I can."

"No," Rion said, "you'll kill yourself."

"I don't think we can stop her," Del said, dragging himself up into a sitting position.

Rion huffed. "She can't even walk. Stopping her won't be a problem."

"I'll take you, Annie," Keph said, slowly standing up as he shot Rion a look filled with scorn. "We need to help as many as we can. This is our fault."

Which didn't make any sense, but I could barely focus and knew if I thought too hard about it, I'd lose my concentration and wouldn't be able to help anyone.

Keph leaned down and gently picked me up. His hands were huge, one under my back, the other under my butt, my legs hanging over his elbow, and he cradled me against his massive chest. I leaned my head against his large shoulder and struggled to stay conscious.

I just needed to hold out a little longer and save as many people as I could.

He carried me into the village. People lay in the street, gasping, moaning, and some not making any noise at all. It was the most horrific thing I'd ever seen, straight out of a horror movie, and a part of me was grateful that I was dizzy and exhausted and my mind was unable to fully register the complete terror of the situation.

Keph stopped at one person then the next, kneeling so I could reach them, but never letting go. In the back of my mind, I knew he was going to people who were alive. We never stopped at someone who I couldn't heal, and I was pretty sure my magic wouldn't work on someone who was dead.

I healed as many of the villagers as I could — more than I thought I would — before the darkness and exhaustion fully engulphed me and dragged me into unconsciousness.

There, I drifted in darkness. Far off, out of reach and barely audible, people cried. A part of me knew they were dying from the terrible illness and that I had to save them, but I couldn't reach them, and I couldn't make myself focus on them.

The darkness churned and swirled, sweeping me around and around, the voices always at the edge of my hearing, always crying for help. Help I couldn't give them.

I woke to hushed voices, arguing nearby.

I could barely move and couldn't get my eyes to open, but it was light enough behind my lids that I knew it had to still be daytime. Exhaustion still pulled at me, making me feel dizzy and heavy and slow.

"—her world. After she healed me, she told me she doesn't have powers in her world. As we'd suspected." This was Rion's sensual tenor, strong and commanding even though he was whispering. "I don't know how we'd stop him."

Who? What? My thoughts muddled and I tried to ask him what he was talking about but couldn't make my mouth move.

"Wouldn't it stand to reason that if she can't heal, then he can't infect?" Aethan asked, his tenor was higher pitched and his words quick and not quite as clear or commanding as Rion's.

"True, but what about the woman who was with him?" That was Keph's rumbling bass. Gods, I'd forgotten how much I loved that voice. I could lie there with my eyes closed and listen to him speak for an eternity and be happy.

"She's one of us, a naiad. So, yes, she might have powers in Annie's world, but how could we be certain she'd have the exact same disease powers as that man did?" Del asked in his smooth, resonate baritone.

And what was this about disease powers? Rion had mentioned it before? Maybe? Something about a man spreading this disease?

"No, Keph is right," Aethan said. "If she's spent any time around the man, she'd have to be infected, but she didn't look like it. There were no blemishes on her blue skin. But that might mean she's immune and a carrier of the disease. If she walks around that crowded city where Annie lives, that could be disastrous."

My pulse lurched. That didn't sound good at all. I needed to know what they were talking about, but I couldn't get my mouth or my eyes to open and only managed a strangled groan instead.

"Annie?" Rion asked.

I groaned again.

"We're working on it," he said, and an enormous, firm hand — it had to be Keph's — settled on my leg. He rubbed my thigh, his thick fingers gentle on my skin. "Don't you worry, rest for now."

"I'll keep you safe," Keph rumbled.

Some deep and smoldering part of me wanted more from those fingers. Instead of brushing the cuffs of my shorts, I wanted them under my shorts. But that part was drowned out by the vast, exhausted majority of me, who just felt comforted by Keph's presence.

I slipped back into the darkness and dreamed again of people screaming and crying and dying from a horrible, devouring illness. But this time instead of it being far off and just out of reach, I was in the middle of it, rushing from one person to the next desperate to save them.

But there were so many. Rows upon rows of people begged for help, begged for me to heal them, even as the exhaustion of having used all my power slowed me down. I had to save them all, but I couldn't. I was just one person and I wasn't strong enough to do it.

Gasping, I jerked awake, my throat tight with the horrible realization that my dream had been real.

Tears burned my eyes.

I hadn't been able to save everyone in the village. I'd barely been able to save a fraction of them.

I dragged myself into a sitting position, drawing my knees up and resting my chin on them as I stared at the last remains of what had to have been a stunning sunset.

All those people had died and this world just kept going as if nothing had happened, just like my world would. It didn't feel right that I was sitting on a tropical beach, looking at a cloudless sky dotted with stars, the dark velvet blue of nighttime sliding toward the crimson edge of the sun sinking behind the waves. It was so beautiful and it seemed so wrong.

So many people were dead... and I had the horrible feeling that, on some level, this had been my fault.

"Annie," Aethan exclaimed, from somewhere behind me. "You're awake."

I kept my gaze on the sunset, unable to look him in the eyes.

I'd failed so many people. I hadn't even known how much I'd wanted to save all of them until I'd failed so miserably.

Out of the corner of my eye, I saw Aethan's hoofed feet step up beside me, and then he sat close and pressed a warm hand against my back. His palm wasn't nearly as big as Keph's had been on my leg, but his touch was just a soothing.

"You saved us," he said softly. "You save so many."

But not everyone.

A tear leak from beneath my lashes.

"How many?" I asked my voice strained and hoarse. "How many died?"

"Only a few."

"No, Aethan, tell me the truth." As much as it hurt, I had to know. I didn't know why. It was stupid to punish myself for failing, but I couldn't stop myself from asking. "How many?"

He gave a soft chuckle, and I couldn't quite understand why he was so happy and relaxed. So many people were dead!

"No, truly," he said, cupping my cheek and drawing my gaze from the sunset to him and letting me see the earnestness and affection in his soft brown eyes.

He still looked at me like I was a goddess, even though I'd lied to him and had to be a mess from having exhausted myself and sleeping in the sand and crying.

"You saved most of them, if indirectly," he said. "One of those you healed was the healer woman for the village. She'd dealt with diseases similar to this one in the past and from those you'd healed she took blood to create a cure. It didn't work on everyone, and some she didn't get to in time, but most of the village is alive now, because of you."

So I hadn't failed.

I hadn't succeeded, either. I just gotten really lucky by healing the right person at the right time.

"And what about this disease man you and the others were talking about?"

His gaze dipped away from me and he stared out at the sunset. "You heard that, did you? We tried to stop him." He huffed a bitter laugh. "Keph nearly did, but it wasn't enough. He'd already infected us and most of the village with that foul illness, and we just didn't have the strength." The muscles in Aethan's jaw flexed. "He went into your world, Annie."

"But I thought I was the only one who could go back and forth on my own."

"It seems that's not the case, and..." He drew in a long breath, grimacing. "We think we know why."

"Oh?"

Aethan's soft brown eyes were intense as he looked at me. "He's not from this world at all, but from yours."

CHAPTER 22

AETHAN

"Mine?" Annie said, her eyes wide. The next moment they went wider still with realization. "That means he has powers. People from one world have powers in the other."

"Yeah." After we'd returned to our world, the guys and I had spent a lot of time talking about our adventure in the other world and our time with Annie and came to the same conclusion.

Which meant we knew Annie wasn't a goddess. Though oddly, all of us still thought of her in reverent terms. We'd spent a lot of time talking about her and I smiled as I looked at her now, sitting in the sand as the last light of day, an angry red line at the edge of the horizon that was mellowed to softer pinks and oranges and deep blues, faded from the west.

Despite the dimming light, I could see the same shade in Annie's hair, that pale red, fading to blond. Even if she wasn't a goddess, she was still unlike any woman any of us had ever known.

Something about her was special, unique. Perhaps it was that pale skin and those many dark spots over her face, chest, back, and arms. Perhaps it was her hair like the dying embers of a fire, or perhaps her form, taller than most women here and with more curves. Most likely it was all of it and more.

I was drawn to her, all of us were, and I knew in my heart that it went deeper than just physical attraction, and none of us had been able to put her from our minds.

And once Rion had learned that a kiss on the lips didn't mean the same thing for her as it did for us, all he'd wanted to do was apologize and try to win her back.

We all wanted her back.

I so desperately wanted her, but not just for sex. I had a deeper need that was more than my intense desire to be inside her, pleasuring her. I needed to simply be near her, make her laugh and smile and take away any fear or pain or heartache. I needed a connection with her that went beyond the physical.

The thought shocked me. I'd never felt that way for a woman before, and now I knew the other women I'd been with were inconsequential, meaningless sexual encounters, a way to bide my time while I'd unknowingly been waiting for Annie.

Of course, I wanted sex, too. And I was grateful that I was sitting at the moment, legs pulled up — mirroring her — and able to hide my raging erection.

I couldn't stop from glancing at her full breasts, straining against the fabric of her tight shirt, or slide my gaze down her body, past her slender waist. Those short pants were also an incredible tease, showing off her long legs while concealing what was most precious.

Gods! I didn't know why she wore so much clothing, but it drove me crazy.

Except now wasn't the time for that. There were other things to discuss, to take care of, before we got to what my body so desperately desired.

"I think it's time you heard the full story. I'll get the others and get you something to eat, I bet you're famished."

"I am," she said with a breathy bit of a laugh. "How long was I out?"

I rose, trying to turn to hide my stiff cock without making it obvious that I was hiding it. "Most of the day. You finished your healing by mid-morning and have been resting since."

"Only one day?" She frowned with confusion.

"You thought it was longer?"

"After healing those people I felt like I was going to sleep for a week. Except it hasn't even been a day and I'm feeling a lot better." She grimaced. "Okay, I wouldn't say I'm feeling good, but certainly far better than when I passed out."

I resisted the urge to wrap her in my arms and offer her more comfort. She needed to eat more than she needed my touch, not to mention I wasn't sure she wanted my touch. She'd seemed soothed when I'd rubbed her back, but that didn't mean she wanted more.

I ran the short distance to the edge of the village, always making sure to keep Annie in sight, spoke to a man there, and sent him running to get the others. They'd been helping with getting the village back to normal. Many were still weak and the day to day tasks like cooking, hunting, and such, still needed to be done.

I returned to Annie. But I took my time on the walk back. She was looking away, over the dunes as the first stars of night came out.

Something about that peaceful image of her caught in my soul. Yes, what I loved about her went far beyond her features. It was her soul. That fire within matched with a kindness and a heart that cared for all beings. She'd passionately fought to heal the villagers when we'd first met her, staggering, sometimes crawling, from body to body, growing weaker and weaker, but still seeking the next person to heal. It had been awe-inspiring to watch, and my heart swelled at the thought of her passion and generosity.

Oddly, by the time I'd returned to her, my erection was nearly gone.

Then she turned toward me. The light of the new moon caught in her eyes turning them from a light brown to molten gold, and smiled, stealing my breath and my heart.

My cock swelled again, painfully hard, and I bit back a curse.

Except she didn't seem embarrassed or look away. If anything, her smile grew, and she gave a mischievous laugh.

"I see," she said raising an eyebrow. "Well, there'll be time for that later. You said we needed to talk, right?"

Time for... for me?

As much as I — and all the guys — were still captivated by her, we knew we'd messed up — and immensely so — at her brother's bonding ceremony. That couldn't be undone. She'd been furious with us and rightly so. Had she so easily forgotten? Or more astonishing yet, had she so easily forgiven?

I stood there, stunned, for a long moment. "Annie, do you—"

"She's awake," Rion said, landing next to me with a whoosh of air. "Good. There's no time to lose. Annie," he said, rushing to her side and kneeling. "I'm sorry for how I acted. There was so much I didn't understand, and I know you can never forgive me, but we have to work together. We believe your world is in grave danger."

CHAPTER 23

ANNIE

I SAT IN FRONT OF A FIRE MADE FROM DRIFTWOOD, LETTING THE HEAT wash over me. The temperature had dropped when the sun had gone down and I was chilly in just my shorts and T-shirt.

Del and Keph had brought food and water with them and I felt even stronger than when I'd first woken, stronger than I should have for just eating and drinking. It made me wonder if I could heal myself as well as others and if I was doing so on an unconscious level. Certainly, after having been out in the sun for an entire day, I wasn't close to burned at all. Though my freckles were uber-visible.

"It was early in the morning, just as the sun was rising, as people were starting to go about their business," Del said, finally deciding that I was strong enough to listen — and worry about — what had happened.

His voice was low, his baritone closer to a soothing base, like Keph's, yet he retained his sing-song quality as if he was about to tell me a bedtime story or a fairy tale, not actual events.

"He came from the west, walking through town, a man in a

white cloak. Some thought him a healer because of his garb, but that was far from the truth."

"No, kidding," Aethan huffed, making Del glare at him for interrupting.

"At his side was a naiad, with skin the color of a summer's sky, as reflected in a still pool. Her hair was blue-white, like sea-foam. The man called out to the town, to bring him the healer who'd cured the sickness in the camp. He said he wanted to thank her for the work she'd done. That there was another such camp of the sick on the far side of the island who needed her aid."

A shiver swept through me. Whoever had infected the village knew about me and had been looking for me.

"But the villagers said the strange woman had left, perhaps returned to her godly realm, and the man grew furious," Del continued. "With each wave of his hand, he cast that dreaded sickness about the town. Those closest to him were more grievously infected."

"He spared no one," Rion said. "The only people he couldn't infect were those you'd already healed. And this time the illness developed much quicker."

"We were in the cantina," Aethan said, his voice lighter and quicker than Del's or Rion's, but still filled with the same grim frustration. "We came out and saw what was happening. I raced to the man to try to stop him, thinking that if I could stop his hands, that might stop the disease. I caught one hand, then the other, but..."

"I saw him fall," Keph rumbled. "The man seemed to push the darkness from himself into Aethan and Aethan screamed and—"

Aethan's gaze dropped to his hands and his shoulders slumped forward with defeat. "I blacked out. I don't even remember hitting the ground."

"I was furious," Keph said, his voice dark with a terrifying anger

I'd never heard from him before and one I hadn't thought the gentle giant was capable of. "I didn't think I could get the illness. Stone titans are resistant or immune to most diseases. Yet he pointed at me, and I felt it—" Keph shuddered. "It was horrible. But it didn't stop me. I hit him so hard he flew across the street, but it wasn't enough."

Holy smokes! Keph was strong. I wasn't sure anyone could survive being punched, full out, by him and yet this man had.

"The damage had been done. The disease had already been spread to everyone," Del said. A pain filled his blue-green eyes, and I couldn't help feeling that same pain. We'd both seen something we'd never forget, something that would haunt our nightmares for years, possibly forever. "The naiad helped the man escape and all of us fell deathly ill."

"I flew after them," Rion said. "They were headed for the rocks. That's when I knew he had to be from your world. I'd hoped to get to the gate first, to block their way out, but the infection moved too quickly through me. I blacked out and landed where you found me."

"We assume he made it to your world," Del said. "But we can't be certain of that."

"He did," I said, recalling the footprints in the snow I'd seen coming out from the wall.

"And if he did, then we fear he'll spread his disease in your world as well." Aethan was somber, the most serious I'd ever seen him.

"But he won't have powers," I said.

"No," Del said, his expression grim, his voice dark.

I didn't like the way he said that, like they already had an answer to that.

"But the woman with him, the naiad, we fear she was immune to his disease and may be a carrier. If so, she could have taken it to your world with her."

My pulse stuttered. I didn't have magic in my world, which

meant I couldn't heal anyone, and even if I did, the man and the naiad were a day ahead of me. They could have come in contact with any number of people who then would have contact with more, and I had no idea how contagious this disease was.

"Fuck."

Rion frowned. "You use that word a lot. What does it mean?"

"Well it..." How could I explain it? "It means..." My face heated, likely turning red with my blush. Jeez, and now, for no apparent reason, I was embarrassed to say sex in front of these guys. "It's the act you and I did, in my bedroom."

All of them raised their eyebrows in surprise.

"But it's ah... it's taken on more meaning than that. It's hard to explain, but it's also a curse we use."

Aethan eyes widened in shock. "You curse on the act of mating?"

When he put it that way, it didn't really make much sense. "I guess so, but I really don't have anything against the act. It's just the perfect sounding word for so many occasions."

They all nodded at that with seemingly varying degrees of understanding.

"Fuck," Aethan said, trying out the word. He nodded to himself. "It does have a good sound to it for cursing."

"Exactly," I said with a small laugh. I really couldn't believe this was where our conversation had gone.

But as much as I'd rather talk about whether fuck was a good word for cursing or not, I couldn't let myself get distracted from what was important.

The thought soured my mood. A potential carrier of a deadly disease was walking around Chicago and had been all day. "So what are we going to do about the carrier in my world?"

What could we do?

Maybe she wasn't a carrier. Maybe she was just Disease Man's friend?

Except I wasn't willing to bet the lives of everyone in Chicago — hell, the whole world on that. I had to assume she was infected and going to infect others.

"We have to stop them," Del said vehemently. "Whatever it takes. They could kill thousands in that well-populated city of yours."

"More like millions," I whispered.

That got a few surprised looks.

"There are that many people living there?" Keph asked in awe.

"Yep."

"Fuuuuck," Aethan said, drawing the word out.

I couldn't agree more.

CHAPTER 24

ANNIE

"IF WE'RE GOING TO DO THIS RIGHT, WE NEED TO GET YOU DIFFERENT clothes," I said, surveying the guys. We'd stopped at the stones before entering my world and I'd donned all my winter things again.

The guys had kept what they'd worn the day of *The Incident* and were now standing in front of me wearing them and looking ridiculous... well, everyone but Rion looked ridiculous. Rion looked hot in his slightly-too-tight borrowed suit — that, oh my God! Margie was going to kill me for not returning.

But the others were going to be a problem. Aethan looked like a punk who'd jumped into a vat of primary colors with his red mohawk, bright green pants, yellow hoodie, and blue and purple coat. And Del looked like a lazy goth with black sweatpants — with a rip in the thigh that I was sure hadn't been there when I'd bought them — a black long-sleeved T-shirt, black jacket, and his long blue-black hair.

And Keph... well, was Keph. Just by his sheer size, he'd ripped open both shoulders on his skin-tight five-times-extra-large football jersey. But given how tight the sleeves were, clinging to his massive muscles, they weren't going to fall off any time soon.

Which was so damned sexy... if a little intimidating. I still couldn't quite imagine sex with the stone titan. He was just... so... big. And yet I couldn't deny the shiver of desire that always rushed down my spine when I thought of him.

I shoved those thoughts aside and drew in a long breath. "Here's the plan. There's a big and tall store not too far from the alley. We'll go there and get you all outfitted so you don't look like thugs—"

"Thugs?" Del asked.

"Ruffians? Thieves? Criminals?"

His eyes widened. "Is that why we caused so much trouble at the wedding?"

I sighed. "Probably, yes."

"Oh."

"That's why, if you're going to help out in my world, you need better clothes, otherwise people won't take you seriously. Once we get you outfitted... well..." That was really as far as I'd gotten.

I wasn't some mastermind planning genius. I had no clue what Disease Man and his accomplice would be up to in my world. But that thought did bring something to mind: powers.

"The woman— What did you call her, a *nyad*?" I asked.

"Naiad," Rion said. "A river nymph, yes."

"She'll have powers in my world, like you did. Do you think it'll be something to do with water?" I asked, wondering if they got magic in my world connected to who they were in this world... although if the opposite was the case, it didn't make sense that I'd be able to heal people. That wasn't really something that was fundamental to me in my world. Still, maybe if I knew what they could do, I'd be able to figure out what she could do. "What were your powers?"

"I could run really fast." Aethan flashed a grin which quickly faded into a grimace. "And I always ended up crashing into things." His grimace grew even darker. "Fuck." He was really getting the hang of the word. "I'm going to need man-legs again, aren't I? I hate man-legs."

I gave him an apologetic smile. "It's for the best."

The guys were big, muscular, and gorgeous. They stood out enough and Aethan's horse-legs would only draw more attention. Even if he hid them under pants, they bent the wrong way and people would know something was wrong the second they saw him walking.

"I was able to emit light in varying intensities," Rion said.

"And I can feel and manipulate water," Del added. "Or, I think so. I didn't get much of a chance to try it out while I was there."

"I think I'm stronger, tougher too, maybe," Keph said. "When those uniformed men used their weapons on me, they seemed surprised. To me it felt like I was being bitten by something tiny, but I think they expected more of a reaction."

I raised my eyebrows. "Those weapons are called guns, and they're deadly to most people. So yeah, you'd be super tough if they didn't slow you down at all."

"He also picked up one of those cars when we were on our way to see you," Aethan said. "I'm assuming they're heavy. They look really heavy."

My jaw dropped. "You picked up a car?"

Keph nodded.

"Holy fuck. Yeah, they're heavy. That's really strong!" And I'd thought he was strong in his world.

Well, it was an interesting mix of abilities. Though none of them seemed to be much help in figuring out what the naiad's power might be or in stopping her and Disease Man from spreading the plague. At least she'd be easy to spot.

"You said she had blue skin? That will stand out. So, once we have clothes... I guess we start looking for a blue woman."

There were nods all around.

"If any of you have better ideas, I'm all ears. I don't need to be the leader here." I didn't really *want* to be the leader, but they all still looked at me with that same reverence and respect as before, even if they'd stopped calling me a goddess.

"You know your world better than we do," Aethan said. "Is there a good place for these people to go to spread the disease?"

"There are lots of places," I said, a little terrified at the options. "Malls, the airport, hotels, the hospital." That last one reminded me. "You said the man was hurt... he'd probably need a hospital." I grimaced. "But he's not the one we're really after at the moment. Fuck. Well, let's get moving, we can talk as we walk. The sooner we get you guys outfitted the better." I put my hand to the portal and the guys moved through.

Once on the other side, I pulled out my phone. "This way, follow me," I said and began walking. As I did, I searched the internet for the CDC and called their number.

"CDC," the guy on the other end said, his tone brusque and sharp.

"I wanted to call and report an outbreak of the plague in Chicago," I said. I didn't really know what to call this disease. The plague seemed like the closest thing to me. I figured it couldn't hurt to get the CDC here as soon as possible.

"The plague?" the person on the other end said, clearly disbelieving. "The bubonic plague?"

"Yeah, sure, that one, or something like it. How am I supposed to know? I'm just a civilian. But it doesn't look good and it's everywhere, and you should get someone here to check it out."

"Listen lady—" I could tell this guy was about to give me an earful, but I didn't let him.

"You can call me crazy if you like and ignore this warning, but I wouldn't want to be you when the reports start coming in and people find out you knew and didn't do anything. So just investigate this disgusting thing, damnit!"

I hung up.

That didn't go quite like it had in my head, but at least I'd done something.

We reached the big and tall store and outfitted everyone but Rion — I didn't have a lot of extra spending money and even though his suit was too tight, it would do. Aethan probably could have done with normal sized clothes, but we didn't have time for a trip to multiple locations. It would have been cheaper — God these specialty clothes were expensive — but Disease Man was already a day ahead of us and I could pay off my credit card later.

While the guys were getting measured and trying things on, I slipped out to a convenience store and bought a burner cell. I made sure it had my number in it, and put its number on my cell before returning to see how the guys had done.

I walked through the door and the guys were lined up for my inspection. They now looked like government operatives, in dark suits and white shirts. All they needed were dark glasses, but they didn't sell those here.

The well-tailored suits on their muscular bodies was so God-damned hot, I got more than a little wet as I looked them over. I wanted them to rip off those clothes nice and slow in a strip-tease, then... I was getting off track.

Even Keph, who was still too big for anything here, looked sexy. He'd tried the largest they had and still ended up ripping the shoulders out of the shirt. So, he'd just ripped the arms off entirely, wearing just the white shirt, now sleeveless. Luckily, they did have some oversized shoes that had fit him, which was a minor miracle.

I paid, not looking at the total, stuffed the receipt in my bag and headed out. "Come on, let's go."

Then we retraced our steps back to the alley.

This had been Rion's idea. Start where the woman had come out and see if we could find a trail of people with the disease. I wasn't sure how quickly it would set in, but it was the best idea we had, and better than Rion's other idea of breaking out his wings to do an aerial view of the city.

The guys spread out a little to look around, now much more respectable-looking... and gorgeous. I had trouble keeping my eyes off Keph, in just that thin white shirt, the buttons straining, his massive shoulders exposed.

Thankfully he, Rion, and Aethan spread out while I stayed with Del in the alley as he crouched next to the wall-portal.

"This white stuff," he said, picking up a handful of snow. "It's... water?" He seemed uncertain. It only occurred to me then that he'd probably never seen snow before.

"Yes. It's called snow. It's frozen water that falls from the sky like rain and accumulates in winter."

"Winter?"

I didn't have time to go into the seasons. "Don't worry about it. Why do you ask about the snow?"

"I hadn't been certain, but I'd... felt it. I hadn't realized it was water. If it is then... give me a moment." He held out a hand, palm down, hovering over the footprints coming out from the wall. He muttered, "There is a bit of... memory in this solid water. I may be able to read it."

I watched, fascinated and clueless as he crouched there, concentrating, eyes closed. Finally, he nodded to himself.

"I know where they went," he said, opening his eyes to look up at me. I didn't know how he'd come to that conclusion, but I was thankful for it.

Rising quickly, he moved to the mouth of the alley, and I followed.

"That way," he called out to the others as he pointed down the street toward the lake and downtown.

Of course that's where Disease Man and his naiad went.

Fuck.

CHAPTER 25

ANNIE

WE HURRIED DOWN THE STREET FOLLOWING DEL, UNTIL RION HAD called out, stopping us. He pointed into an alley at a homeless man, curled up inside serval sleeping bags with a wool hat pulled low. But even with the hat and his dull gray beard — the only indication I had that he was actually a man and not a woman — I could still see the heavy black spots forming on his cheeks.

I rushed over, knelt beside him, praying he was still alive and could tell us where the naiad and Disease Man had gone, and his eyes cracked open.

He wasn't dead.

"Hello? Can I help you, miss?" He seemed kind enough, smiling faintly through his beard, and it broke my heart. There was no way he was going to get proper medical attention. This disease would kill him... probably slowly, and there wasn't anything I could do.

The muscles in my jaw were so tight they hurt. I didn't know what to say, but I forced myself to ask him what we needed to know. "Did you see a strange woman with blue skin come through here?"

He frowned and for a moment I was worried he didn't know what I was talking about and thought I was crazy. "Now that you mention it, I did. Really strange."

Oh, thank God. "I need you to tell me everything that happened. Please, it's important. I reached for my wallet and pulled out—

Damn. I only had three singles. That wasn't enough. This man was going to die. He deserved to be comfortable before that happened.

"I, ah... If you tell me everything you can, I'll... let you stay in my apartment tonight." Which was the stupidest thing I could have said, but I wasn't going to take it back.

I took out my keys and held them up to him. Hell, if I needed to, I could sleep on a warm tropical beach just on the other side of that portal. I'd be cozy enough. And something told me I wouldn't lack for bodies to warm me further if I asked for it.

The man's eyes went wide. "That important?" He levered himself up to a sitting position. "Let me see..."

I glanced back over my shoulder at my guys. Rion stood nearby, watching me, while the other three were asking around — Del doing most of the talking — on the other side of the street.

"Ah, well, I was asleep when I felt someone touching my face. That woke me pretty quick. Not many people want to touch me." His face lit up with a dazed smile. "Two pretty women approaching me in one day is odd enough." His smile deepened and his gaze grew unfocused. "And she was odd. Blue skin and a weird white cape and hood. I'd never seen anything like it. Well there was this time—"

"Did she say anything to you?" I asked, before he got completely off track.

He blinked, his attention refocusing on me, and frowned. "She apologized for waking me, but said she was desperate. Her friend, this man with her, needed help. He didn't have a coat and looked cold, and he was holding his side and leaning on the wall."

So we'd been right. Keph had hurt Disease Man.

"The woman said they were in town for a convention downtown, had gotten lost, and her friend had been beat up. They needed to know where the nearest hospital was." His frown deepened. "Which was odd, because before I'd even said anything, there was an ambulance pulling up." He shrugged. "I guess someone else had already called nine-one-one?"

Although I couldn't see how... unless Disease Man had a phone and had called himself. Except if he had, why would he bother stumbling five blocks to this alley before doing so?

The man before me continued. "She helped the man into the ambulance, getting pretty familiar with the paramedics, touching their faces, too."

And infecting them. Swell. I glanced at Rion but didn't see recognition in his face. Of course, he didn't know what an ambulance was and didn't know that as soon as those paramedics walked into the hospital they could end up infecting thousands of people.

"The ambulance left with the man, but she stayed, and I—" He glanced at me then Rion before dropping his gaze to his weathered hands. "I must have fallen asleep and had a weird dream." There was sweat on his brow. I didn't know if this was from the disease or some nervousness at his recollection.

"Why do you say that?" It was entirely possible he'd had a dream, but it was also possible he'd seen something that was a clue to this woman's powers.

"Well, I watched the woman meet up with four other women with blue skin, all wearing the same weird white cloaks, and they went around the corner over there." He pointed to the mouth of a narrow loading bay. "But you can see into it from the reflection of those windows across the street." He jerked his thumb to the large store windows sure enough offering a weak reflection of the empty driveway and closed loading bay door. "Then they sort of... merged into one person, and only one woman came out. Then she flagged down a taxi and left."

Which had to be her power... not flagging down taxies — although there were days when that definitely was a superpower — but cloning herself or splitting herself into multiple copies or something. I dropped my keys next to the man. "Thanks, you've been a big help. Get yourself warmed up at my place. It's three blocks down and over one, the Fleischmann Building. Unit ten. The door code is seven-zero-one-nine."

"Oh, well, thank you, young lady," he said, his expression filled with shock as if he hadn't believed I'd actually let him stay in my place.

But hell, it was the least I could do since I wasn't going to be able to cure his disease.

I rose and went to Rion.

"I think I know what ability our naiad has."

"Oh?"

"I think she can duplicate or replicate herself." Which, now that I thought of it, was going to be a problem. "That's going to be really useful for her spreading this disease, especially if all her copies are carriers."

Rion's expression turned grim. "Agreed." He glanced back over my shoulder and a hint of grief crept into his grim determination. "Are you... certain you can't heal him?"

Certain, no, but I was pretty damn sure. I thought I would have noticed if I had superpowers in my world... of course what if I'd just needed to go to my guys' world to awaken my powers?

Except if that was true, it brought up a whole other list of problems, the main one being that Disease Man, having been to both worlds now, would still have his powers in my world, too, and he was on his way to the hospital.

And that wasn't what we were talking about.

I glanced back at the homeless man, clutching his sleeping bags around him to fend off the cold, the ugly black spots on his face still small, the disease not spreading as quickly as it had when Disease Man had infected the guys and the village.

"I suppose it wouldn't hurt to try." But I wasn't going to hold my breath. "Excuse me, sir? Do you mind if I..." How was I going to ask this?

He staggered to his feet and offered me a gentle smile. "Look lady, you're letting me stay in your apartment. That's more than my own family has done. Whatever it is, you go right ahead."

"I need to touch you, is that okay?"

He shrugged. "Sure."

I touched his cheek above his beard, drew in a deep breath, and concentrated on pushing the energy into him like I'd done with so many others in the other world.

Nothing.

Then—

Something. A trickle? It could have been my imagination...

But the trickle grew stronger and my energy surged into him and consumed the disease.

He gasped as well, eyes going wide. "What is that?"

He hadn't been that far along, only just starting, and it had been easy to heal him, but I was too stunned to answer. I stepped back, trembling, staring at my hand.

That shouldn't be possible.

"I..."

And if I had my powers did that mean Disease Man did as well?

But if he did, then he wouldn't have needed the naiad to infect the paramedics. He could have done that himself.

So...

He didn't have powers in this world, but I did?

Rion's strong arms wrapped around me. "You did it?" he whispered.

"Yes."

"What was that?" the old man asked again. "I feel great."

I smiled, still stunned, but with the slow dawning that... I had powers... here in the real world.

I had powers!

How the hell did I have powers?

And really, that wasn't important. I could figure that out after I'd figured out how to stop a plague.

"I... you had an illness and I... I healed you." The words were faint, only for us, and the man's eyes got wider still.

"Are you an angel?" he whispered.

Rion answered, voice hushed, "No, my good man. She's a goddess."

CHAPTER 26

DELPHON

"So you can heal?" I asked, stunned, even though I'd just watched it happen. How was that possible?

"Perhaps she's a goddess after all," Rion said.

Annie seemed stunned herself. She'd healed everyone in the area who we could find who'd talked to the Blue Lady, and now the five of us were standing in a nearby alley, comparing notes on what we'd found out.

The consensus was that the naiad could indeed be several places at the same time, and was spreading the disease. Yet it was a slow thing. She couldn't seem to accelerate it, only spread it, and only by touching people. Which was good news... sort of.

"How?" Keph asked.

Annie shrugged. "I have no clue. I didn't think it was possible, but... it is!"

I took a long look at her then. It had been some time since I'd first seen her on the beach. She'd captivated me then, bundled as she was, even before she'd started stripping away the many layers of clothes. And I was still captivated. It was far more than her body that called to me.

I'd seen most of her luscious curves before and she was beautiful, no doubt, but even bundled up against the cold once again, only seeing that speckled face of hers — a few wisps of that red-gold hair peeking out from her hat — I was enraptured. I felt it in my gut, a pull, a call to be with her, near her.

There were other parts of me which yearned to be inside her, deep, truly connected. Those parts were more than a little uncomfortable in the confining clothes she'd bought us, but my desire was so much more than just physical. It was an intense need to be near her. I'd felt it the entire week she'd been gone from my life, like someone had severed a limb that I just couldn't live without. I'd been incomplete, not whole as I was now.

Whatever else happened with her, with this diseased naiad and her companion, I knew that I'd stay with Annie, no matter what. And from the conversations I'd had with the guys, they all felt the same way. We didn't yet know how that would work out, but we'd all agreed that if she came back into our lives, we'd make it work, somehow.

And she had.

"Was there anything else you learned?" Annie asked, perhaps trying to get the conversation away from her. Her inability to meet our gazes and the way she shifted made it clear that talking about her and her new power made her feel uncomfortable.

"The fellow in the alley over there," I said, pointing behind me, "said he asked the woman about her strange skin. She'd seemed confused for a moment, then mentioned a convergence of some sort."

"No, a convention," Aethan corrected me. "That was the word he'd used."

"Mine mentioned a convention as well. Said she was in town for one." Annie frowned but I couldn't tell if it was in confusion or thought. "But why would that explain the blue skin?"

I didn't know, and from the looks on the other guys, they didn't either.

Then her eyes went wide and she gasped. "Wait. I have a friend who's into sci-fi stuff." I had no clue what that was, but I let her go on without interrupting. "I think she said that there was a comic convention in town. It was going to be soon, but that was a couple weeks ago."

"Sci-fi stuff? Comic convention?" Aethan asked before I got there.

Annie opened her mouth then snapped it shut as if realizing that explaining might make things more confusing. "The details don't matter," she said instead. "What's important is that there will be a lot of people there and a blue-skinned woman won't be out of place. My people will be in all sorts of costumes and makeup. She'll fit right in."

"We need to get there quickly," Rion said. "Where is it?"

"I have no clue." Annie pulled out the device she called her *phone*. "Give me a sec and I'll call my friend." She tapped the luminescent pad with her finger then put it to her ear. "Hey, Lacey! — Yeah, really loud. — Are you at that sci-fi convention thingy?" Annie removed the phone from her ear and covered it, as she hissed, "Fuck." Then turned to us and said, "She's there, and I don't want to tell her to leave in case she might already be infected. I wouldn't want her to spread it." She didn't look happy, but put on a fake smile as she put the phone back to her ear as if her friend could actually see her as well as hear her. "Ah... no, cool. Remind me, where is it again? — McCormick Place? Thanks — Yeah, I'm coming. Maybe I'll see you. Gotta go. Bye!" She tapped the *phone* again before putting it away.

"McCormick Place?" I asked, sounding out the words. "Where's that?"

"Closer to downtown. We'll need a tax—" Annie's gaze swept

over us and her frown deepened. "We'll need two. You all won't fit in a single taxi. Fuck."

"I could fly there and take Annie," Rion suggested.

"No wings," Annie insisted. "Although, once we get there... you all might just fit in fine, even with your powers. They'll think it's special effects or something. She put her *phone* against her cheek again, turning away as she spoke to the person on the other end. I didn't know exactly how the device worked, but had figured out that somehow she was able to speak to people through it, which was absolutely amazing.

Annie turned back to us. "Okay. I'm just gonna run up my credit card today, but fuck it. We need to save the world, right?"

We all agreed to that.

A few minutes later, two of those self-propelled carts arrived. Apparently, that was what Annie had meant by a taxi... which led to our next hurdle: trying to get Keph into one.

He didn't quite fit well inside, but we eventually managed to squish him into the back of one — it's rear portion now scraping the ground, making the driver glare at us. Annie took the seat at the front of that one, ignoring the driver's dark look. The rest of us piled into the other, and we were off.

CHAPTER 27

KEPHAS

I WAS RELIEVED TO BE OUT OF THE METAL BEAST, WHICH HAD MADE the most horrible screeching sound the entire time I'd been in it. Except upon exiting the car, I was faced with a crowd larger than any I'd ever seen before. That made my heart race and cold fear slide down my spine.

"So many people," I breathed.

Annie, next to me, didn't seem bothered by this at all. "Lacey said these things can draw tens of thousands of people."

"Tens of... thousands? By the Hammer!" That was more people than I'd ever seen in my life. The stone titans were few, perhaps a few thousand in total, and I'd never met all of them. I knew only my clan, one of the largest, and it didn't even number a full thousand. The only other place I'd been was the town of Masia and it held no more than a few hundred people.

I drew in a long breath, trying to steady my nerves.

"You're not afraid, are you?" she asked. "You're bigger than anyone here. You can easily push through these people."

True.

And while I was a little afraid — afraid that the wrong move could hurt a lot of people — I was also awed and a bit stunned at the sheer number.

But this was where we had to be, so I was just going to have to deal with it.

I sucked in another breath and was feeling a bit better, by the time the other three had joined us.

"Zeus's balls, there's a lot of people here," Aethan said. I was glad I wasn't the only one who felt that way. "How are we ever going to find one woman... who can be several women. Gods, this is impossible!"

"We'll need to split up," Del said. "But we'll need some way to keep in contact."

"Oh, right!" Annie dug around inside the bag she carried and pulled out another device like the one she'd talked into. She handed it to Del. "Take this. I got it while you guys were getting fitted for your suits." She showed him how to use it. "It should come up to this screen when you press here. And I've programmed my number in. Just touch where it says Annie. Then we can talk to each other."

"Only one?" Del asked.

Annie gave him a dry look. "I'm not made of money, you know."

"Then two groups." Del looked around. "Rion with me, Aethan and Keph with Annie. How's that sound?"

"It sounds like this is still going to take forever," Aethan replied, his gaze sliding over the crowd. "Half of these people are dressed up in strange ways even for this world. There's another woman with blue skin, but she has red hair. We can't even ask around for a blue woman."

"Unless you can think of something better, this is the best plan we've got," Annie said. "You can call when you come up with that. Until then, let's start asking around and keep an eye out for any signs of the disease. That could lead us to her as well."

Del nodded and he and Rion set off into the crowd.

"Come on," Annie said, pushing forward into the sea of people.

Once inside the large building, things got worse. Luckily the halls and rooms were large with soaring ceilings that were more than big enough for me, but everywhere I looked there were people. And while Annie had been right and they got out of my way quickly, there were, however, lots of muttered comments.

"Who's that supposed to be?"

"Dude! He's huge!"

"That's got to be padding."

"Great costume, bro!"

We stepped into a narrow side hall which seemed to run between two of the larger rooms. Thankfully the smaller hallway was empty, and I didn't feel like I was accidentally going to crush someone — which had seem inevitable in most of the other packed rooms and halls.

"I'm going to check down here," Aethan said, pointing down the tight hallway. There were a few small doors off it farther away from the bustling crowds. "Back in a moment." Then he was a blur moving down the empty hall, checking doors. He was back to us quickly.

"I think I found her," he said excited. "Or at least one of her."

"Which room?" Annie asked.

"Second on the right."

"Okay, you two get your hands on her, make sure she can't get away," Annie commanded, looking sure of herself in a way I'd never seen from her before. It was a good look on her, and reminded me that goddess or not, she was an amazing woman. "I'll see if she's infected anyone and try to heal them."

"Aethan," I said, as we headed for the door. "Zip in and grab her if you can. I'll clear the room for you."

He raised a brow at that, but nodded, and I opened the door, ducked, and squeezed through the entrance.

A second later Aethan was a blur, rushing past me.

"Got her!" he shouted. He'd moved perhaps thirty feet in and had a woman in a white cloak by the arm.

"Everyone out!" I roared as loud as I could. I saw Annie jump beside me.

Then she muttered. "So much for finding any sick ones."

Oh... right.

Still, my plan had worked. People scattered in all directions, leaving a large area around Aethan and the woman. She was much smaller than Annie was, and I stalked forward and reached to grab her. But as I got there, the struggling woman seemed to dissipate. Her clothes fell in on themselves and Aethan was holding nothing but clothes and... water.

"Fuck," Aethan cursed, as I too recalled that naiads could shift into pure water, similar to how I could turn to stone.

The woman flowed out of Aethan's hands, reformed, now naked, behind Aethan and kicked him hard between his legs.

Aethan doubled over with a yelp and a thick groan.

I took one large step and reached for the woman, but she was quicker than me, dancing away, before turning to run. But Annie had gotten around behind her and slammed her fist into the woman's cheek.

The naiad reeled back toward me. I caught her this time, one hand easily holding her shoulder, and the thumb and finger of my other hand clamped around her neck.

She huffed in disgust and turned to water again, slipping from my grip.

"Fuck!" Annie said. "That's getting annoying."

I had to agree.

I turned, following the moving puddle as it slid across the floor to reform on the other side of me. The woman kicked again, perhaps thinking I'd go down as easily as Aethan.

Her foot landed hard against my groin. I hardly felt anything, but she shrieked in pain and hopped back, probably with a broken foot. Stone titans were tough to begin with. And in this world, I was tougher still.

I stepped in and swung, remembering at the last minute how much stronger I was in this world, and pulled the punch.

Still the small woman lifted from the ground, flew a few feet away, hit the floor, and slid a dozen feet across the polished tiles. She collapsed in a blue, naked heap and lay still.

Annie ran to her, checking at the woman's neck. Except even as she did, the woman melted into nothing.

I rushed over, checking for water. "Did she shift?" I asked.

"To water?" Annie patted the floor. "No, it's not wet at all. She just vanished." She looked up at me surprised. I was just as astonished and shrugged my ignorance of what had happened.

"Perhaps that's what happens when you kill one of her duplicates?" Aethan said, voice strained, as he staggered over to us.

That made sense.

"So, this wasn't the real one then," I said, then huffed out a sigh. What was that word? Oh Right. "Fuck."

CHAPTER 28

HYPERION

"There!" I spotted a woman in white and caught a glimpse of blue skin, and pointed across the massive hall filled with people milling about. "She's there."

"I don't have eagle's eyes like you do. All I see is people everywhere," Del muttered. "You'll have to get us closer."

I grabbed his arm and began pushing through the crowd. People were packed in tightly among booths which seemed to be selling all manner of strange items. I threaded my way through them, Del in tow, but progress wasn't quick.

I debated using my blinding light like I had at the wedding, but that would be a beacon to our quarry in addition to blinding everyone here. And I wasn't certain that would actually get people out of our way.

Once closer, perhaps fifty feet away, I pointed again. "There, in the white."

"I see now, yes. Any ideas?"

"Remember, she's a naiad. That means she can turn to water and slip out of here, if she wishes." If we still had our other shifting powers, then she would as well.

Del laughed. "Well that sounds like a plan to me."

I frowned at him and he flashed me a wide grin.

"I can control water, remember?"

Right! He could. "So I get her to shift and you—"

"Do what I do," he finished.

We moved closer. The naiad was at a booth, looking over items, but also subtly touching peoples' hands as they reached for things under the guise of reaching for the same one.

"I'll get around the other side," I whispered and slipped off into the crowd, finding a slow-moving flow of people and threading my way around. Once close, on the other side of the woman, I caught Del's eye and nodded.

He nodded in return, closing in a bit more.

I reached out and grabbed the naiad's wrist.

Startled, that hooded head turned to me. It was her, blue face, shimmering blue eyes. I lowered my voice. "Come with me, naiad." Her eyes widened a bit more.

I made sure my grip was iron around her wrist. Her only way to escape would be to shift.

And, as expected, my fist clamped closed around the woman's sleeve as she turned to water.

"Del!" I called out.

"Got her," he replied, pushing through the crowd to the booth. "Under the table."

I knelt and lifted the skirt around the booth's table, to see a frozen glob of ice.

I looked up at Del as he arrived. "Frozen?"

He smiled. "I was inspired by the snow outside. I've been toying with freezing and unfreezing water while we were outside talking to people. It seems to have worked."

But then, as I looked back at the ice, it simply vanished. "What did you do?"

"Nothing," he replied. "The water just... went away."

I rose. "I'm guessing this wasn't the original woman then. I—" I caught sight of another woman with blue skin and a white cloak, staring at us from across the hall.

Her eyes flashed wide and she turned and ran.

It would take us forever to get to where she'd been if we tried to push our way through the crowd.

"By Hades!" I cursed.

I'd be able to get there a lot faster if I shifted. My mind warred as to the best option, but then I remembered Annie's words: *You all might just fit in fine, even with your powers.*

"Prepare to fly," I said to Del. It would be easiest to carry him in my full eagle form, but that would tear up the suit Annie had borrowed for me.

I shrugged out of my jacket and tossed it to Del. There wasn't time to undo all the buttons on the shirt, so I unleashed my wings, which ripped through the back of the fabric, and I tore the rest of the ruined shirt away. Then I grabbed Del under the arms, leaped into the air, and flapped my wings to gain some height in the — thankfully — high-ceilinged hall.

Del started cursing and went rigid in my grip. Guess he didn't like flying. But this was our only option. I soared across the room reached the door the woman had just exited through, and landed, setting us both down lightly.

People all around us gasped and clapped as I set us down and shed my wings. They vanished before they'd even hit the ground, drawing even more gasps and a louder round of applause.

As Annie had suspected, people were surprised, but not overly so, nor terrified. Strange folk.

I grabbed my jacket back from Del and we pushed through the doorway out into the hall. But I couldn't see the woman among the crowd. Then I caught sight of Annie — I'd never be able to miss her — and Keph, who was also hard to miss. They were moving toward us down the hall.

Which meant the woman probably wouldn't have gone that way.

I flagged down the others, then began pushing through the crowd in the opposite direction — hopefully the direction the naiad had gone.

"This way," I called over the roar of voices around us.

I caught sight of the white cloak again. The naiad was about a hundred feet away, talking to two burly men guarding a closed set of doors.

Then the cloak fell limp. She'd turned to water, and the guards hadn't even blinked an eye. I had no idea why they hadn't reacted to her suddenly disappearing and I didn't have time to worry about it. Without a doubt she was slipping into that guarded room, which made things more difficult

But Keph would be there soon. He'd convince the guards to move... or he'd make them.

CHAPTER 29

ANNIE

RION POINTED TO A DOOR WITH TWO LARGE SECURITY GUARDS AND I hurried up to them.

"We have to get in there," I said.

"You and everyone else," the guy on the left said.

"Look I don't have time to explain." And even if I did, I doubted either of them would believe me. *'Hi, yeah, a blue-skinned-woman is spreading a disease by touching people and now she's in that room because she turned to water.'* A not-so plausible story, even if the evidence — the woman's clothes — still sat in a lump in front of these guys. They'd watched her melt, but still didn't look willing to talk and I had no idea why—

Okay, I had a pretty good idea. Magic. Magic was the reason they hadn't seemed to notice— why no one had noticed that a woman had just turned into a puddle.

"I'll make this simple. Move or my friend here will make you move." I jerked my thumb at Keph.

On cue, he slammed one massive fist into his other palm. The resulting *crack* made both security guards start and stare.

"Fuck, it's not worth it," the one on the right said and stepped aside. The other quickly followed.

"Thank you, gentlemen," I said and pushed through the double doors they were guarding.

Beyond was a massive hall being set up with chairs with about half of them set up so far. Men and women worked to place more chairs in long rows, quickly taking from piles stacked on trollies and moving them into position. At the far end sat a stage with a long table and half a dozen chairs most likely for a panel of some sort.

I searched for the woman, but the only people in the room were the people setting up, and I was sure a naked blue woman would have been easy to spot.

"Do you sense any water?" I asked Del.

He concentrated for a moment then nodded. "There."

He pointed to... nothing, at least nothing I could see, and surged ahead of us, leading the way.

Rion, who was now bare-chested for some reason, his shirt gone, and carrying his jacket, leaped into the air and was suddenly winged, flying above us. He tossed his jacket aside.

I guessed that was how he'd lost his shirt the first time.

Gods, he was amazing when he flew. My mind flashed to us hovering above my bed as we climaxed together. I shuddered at the memory, desire sliding warm and low within me then shoved the thought back. Now wasn't the time.

With a frustrated sigh, I ran to catch up to the others.

Keph was plowing through the chairs, heedless of the damage he was causing, while Aethan was a blur, zipping forward to the door on the far side of the hall.

"I need to get a bit closer to freeze her," Del said.

But then the woman appeared and reformed next to a terrified worker who was staring at Keph barreling down on him.

"Help me. Please," the woman begged, clutching the man, one

hand going to his face, infecting him even as she asked him for help.

The man turned to her, eyes going wide as he took in the naked all blue woman, and didn't move, too stunned to do anything.

"You're useless," she hissed and she pushed the man toward Keph and ran toward the door at the back of the room.

The hapless worker stumbled and collapsed in front of Keph, who deftly leaped over him, sending a resounding *thud* booming through the room as he hit the floor and kept running.

She reached the door Aethan was guarding and hesitated for just a moment before turning to water. But Del had drawn close enough to use his magic and the puddle instantly froze.

I reached the men, assembled around the frozen blob, gasping for breath, knowing I really needed to do more cardio. Like a lot more cardio if this was the way things were going to be with the guys.

"Is that her, the real one?" I asked.

"The ice hasn't vanished yet, so I'd guess it is," Del said. "I'm going to release her."

The ice melted to the pool once again, but it reformed quickly into the naiad, who was hugging herself and shivering.

"I give up," she hissed, but instead of looking upset, she looked wickedly victorious. "You've got me," she purred. "But I've already spread the disease to hundreds, if not thousands of people and they'll spread it farther. There's no way you can stop it now. As my god wills it, this world shall fall to his decay."

Perhaps, but there was at least one person I could help. The guys had the woman covered and I wasn't afraid of her escaping. As soon as she turned to water, Del would freeze her. So, I turned and went to the poor man the naiad had begged for help, infected, then thrown in Keph's way. He still lay on the floor, stunned, and he flinched when I touched his elbow.

"Hey," I said softly, kneeling beside him.

He turned to me, blinking. "I... The woman, I didn't... She was all... That man had wings!"

"Yes, I know, don't worry. It was all a show. You got the preview. Amazing isn't it?" I said as I held his hand in both of mine and sent my healing energy into him. It didn't take much. He'd only just been infected. He wasn't even showing signs yet.

"Uh... yeah. Wow," he muttered, before climbing to his feet and staggering away to sit in one of the still-standing chairs. "Wow."

I looked around the room. Keph had done an amazing job at smashing through the chairs, some were thrown dozens of feet away, others were crushed or bent beyond recognition. That would take a bit of time to clean up, and without a doubt, we'd have to explain this to someone, although I had no idea who. Already men with vests saying "security" were heading our way.

The trouble was, I couldn't let them touch the woman or they'd be infected too. Only my guys were immune since I'd cured them. We were the only ones who could safely secure the woman.

Which meant, for now, we needed to get her out of there, but I also needed to try to heal as many people as I could before they left the convention center and infected the rest of Chicago... although I had no way of knowing who might be infected.

We'd captured the carrier, but there was still a lot of clean-up to do, and I had no idea how we were going to do any of it.

Though... there was one thing I could do. If I healed the naiad, she'd no longer be a carrier. I rushed back over to her before security got there and grabbed her arm.

"What are you doing?" she hissed. I didn't respond and pushed my healing into her. Her eyes went wide. "What...?"

It was done quickly. She wasn't infected deeply, just carrying the disease, which was easily cleansed from her system.

"Now you can't hurt any more people," I said as I released her.

Except—

Damn it. We still couldn't hand her over to the authorities. She'd just turn to water and escape.

"We need to get her out of here," I said. "Del and Aethan, get her somewhere safe and call me when you're secure and alone. Keph and Rion with me. We'll slow down the guards while you escape, and hopefully by then I'll have figured out a way to heal the people here."

The men acted instantly, following my instructions without question or hesitation. Aethan and Del ushered the woman out the far set of doors, while Keph, Rion, and I turned to the guards.

Keph growled at them.

They stopped, terrified.

I approached them. "Sorry for all the fuss, gentlemen. Let me see if I can explain what happened here." If I could explain it.

It was certainly going to be an interesting story, and for any of it to make sense, it was mostly going to be complete fiction.

POWER OF THE GODDESS

GRECIAN GODDESS: BOOK 2

CHAPTER 1

ANNIE

Half a dozen, big, tough, no-nonsense security men from the convention center looked at me, although none of them were as big or tough as the two guys, Keph and Rion, who flanked me.

We stood in the middle of a large room with a stage that had a long table on it, waiting for a panel to present at the comic convention. Half of the chairs had been set out for the audience, and half of those chairs had been crushed or tossed aside. And there was no way the security guards hadn't noticed.

Except I couldn't let that distract them. The *naiad* had infected who-knew-how-many people at this convention, and I couldn't let anyone leave without figuring out how to heal them with magical powers that I shouldn't have in my world and yet still did. That, and I wouldn't be able to do that if the security men took me into custody.

Which meant I had to take control of this situation.

The trouble was. I wasn't that sort of woman. I was quiet and reserved. I didn't face things head on. There was a reason I wanted to live alone in some tropical paradise.

But I'd gotten myself into this mess. I'd chosen to chase after the *naiad* and Disease Man and try to save as many people as I could, and I needed to do something about it now.

I just had to figure out what powerful Annie Chambers looked like.

"Listen up!" I shouted, just a little too loud. The men before me started and from the side of my vision I caught Rion twitch as well. "We have an emergency situation here, and I'm going to need all of your help with this."

The security guards stared at me with a mix of surprise, confusion, and disbelief.

Swell.

"That woman my men just apprehended is a bio-terrorist," I said before they could question me. "She's been releasing a nasty disease on the premises. I've stopped her, but there's no clue how many people she's infected. I need a level three quarantine set up on this facility, all exits closed, and everyone ready for my inspection."

"Who are you?" one of the men managed to say. He stepped forward, perhaps a leader, not the largest of the men, but seeming less confused than the others.

"Annie Chambers." That much was true.

And now time for some confident lies.

"Special Agent in Charge of the FBI's Bio-Terrorism team. These are my men—" I hadn't shown ID and the man who'd spoken up frowned with skepticism. I turned to Rion. "This is Ryan—" I needed a last name quick, and seeing him shirtless reminded me of our time in bed which made my lips quirk in a smile that I hoped no one saw and a single word jump to mind.

Jeez I had a dirty mind.

"Long," I said. "Agent Ryan Long." I turned to Keph. "This is —" Keph...? No. His name, like Rion's, was too weird and would draw suspicion. "Kevin." My mind jumped to Keph's *member* and my dirty mind couldn't stop coming up with descriptive names for them. If Rion was long, then Keph was... "Thicke."

"Can I see some ID?"

"There's no time for this," I said, pushing on as if I hadn't heard him and praying he'd give up and get to saving people. "People are infected out there and the longer you stand here, the worse things are going to get."

I stalked up to the lead security guy. He was half a foot taller than me, but I met him gaze-for-gaze, eyes hard, with all the certainty and urgency I could muster.

He took a step back.

Ha! Yeah!

Oh... Wait.

That was probably because Keph had just stepped up close behind me.

"Move! Now!" I shouted.

At the same time Keph growled, "You heard her."

"Yes, ma'am." The security man turned to the others. "You heard her, go."

They hurried from the room and the guy in charge took two big steps away from me — or rather away from Keph — and shot me a dark look. "I'm calling the FBI, though. Confirming your story."

"Good," I said with a spark of fire in my voice. "And while you're at it, call the police. Your men will probably need help here to keep this contained."

He huffed, but thankfully didn't put up more of a fight and rushed out of the room.

Once he was out of earshot all the bluster drained out of me. "Holy-fucking-wow! I can't believe that worked!" A cold sweat trickled down the insides of my arms and another pool was forming between my breasts.

Fuck, that had been too close. I was sure the only reason those men had listened to me was because I'd had Keph backing me up. Speaking of which...

I turned to the guys.

"Thanks," I said, blowing out a huff of air, my body starting to tremble with the shock of fighting and capturing the *naiad* and then lying to the security guard. But I couldn't lose it now. There were people here who needed healing, far too many people, possibly thousands of them. This was going to be a long day.

"I'm exhausted, but we need to heal as many people here as possible."

"Those men are corralling everyone. There'll be time to heal them, though I fear what that will do to you," Rion said as he put his jacket back on, the dark material accentuating his bronzed skin, pale blond hair, and blue eyes. God he was sexy and the open jacket instantly drew my eyes to his naked, chiseled chest and hard abs.

I wanted to rip that jacket right off and—

No not the jacket. He could leave that on while his pants came off and he pushed that incredible cock of his into me once again. I shuddered, growing hot, and the look in his eyes grew just as hungry as I felt.

Suddenly I had lots of energy.

I laughed, was sex the answer? After the last time with him, I'd been a pool of jelly with no strength at all. So, perhaps not.

But the intensity of my desire swelled. There was no way I'd be able to concentrate without relieving the pressure.

And if I kept it to a tease, maybe that would give me the energy or in the least the motivation to push through and wrap this mess up quickly.

That, and Rion was right. It would take a moment or two for those guys to lock down this place and I wasn't going to be able to stand there and wait. Not while I was suddenly aware of Rion and how I knew — because of amazing firsthand experience — how he could make me feel.

Then my gaze flicked to Keph.

The heat in my chest sunk deeper, my breath catching as the flash of the three of us together came to mind. Keph with his huge... well... everything.

Oh, yes, please!

I grabbed their hands and began leading them to the doors at the other end of the room, in the opposite direction the security guards had gone. "I have a plan to get me some more energy." Not to mention get me thinking straight, because now having sex— No, just a tease. Having a tease was all I could think about, even though I *knew* I should be thinking about the mess at hand. "And it involves the both of you."

"Whatever you need," Keph said softly, his deep voice rumbling through me, bringing a smile to my face. I'd hoped he'd say something like that.

"Annie, what's this plan?" Rion asked, his tone more hesitant than Keph's.

"We need to find some place to be alone. Then you two are going to get me all worked up so I have the energy to heal ten thousand people."

"I, ah..." Rion frowned, looking pained, clearly wanting to say yes but questioning the efficacy of the plan. "I can't say I'm not... intrigued, but are you certain that will give you energy and not take it from you?"

"As long as I don't get off, then sure... I think so." I shrugged off my doubt. "Either way, I'll feel a whole lot better." Or so I hoped. I couldn't see how I'd feel bad after sex with these two. Sore maybe, but not bad. And this wasn't sex. This was just a really good tease to get me all worked up and get me motivated. That was all.

The trick would be stopping there.

There were two sets of doors at the back of the room that led to a hall, the direction Del and Aethan had gone with the naiad, and another single door next to it, leading to a storage room. It was probably going to be the most private place I could find. It was dark inside and there wasn't anyone there. A large, floor to ceiling metal shelf ran along the right wall close to the door filled with cleaning supplies, toilet paper, paper towels, linens, and other stuff, while stacks of tables and chairs filled the rest of the room. I flicked the light on and looked around. No other entrances.

Even better.

I pulled the guys inside. "Keph, close that door and keep your back to it, so we're not interrupted," I ordered. My body thrummed with need, and I was suddenly jittery, excited, and apparently back in command mode.

Keph did as I'd asked, leaning his massive back against the door, and my pulse leaped into a quick tattoo.

Oh, God.

This was really going to happen.

Was I crazy?

Probably. But I knew I'd be even more crazy trying to concentrate past my sudden, aching desire. I wouldn't be able to fight it along with my exhaustion and worry, so I might as well get my desire out of the way.

"How would you like us to... work you up?" Rion asked.

I glanced at him then Keph. The three of us were standing there, awkward. This was all a bit staged... but screw it.

This was definitely what I wanted and I wasn't going to get anywhere with my clothes on so I pulled off my jacket and shoved it onto the rack beside me. I reached to pull off my sweater but Rion stepped close and captured my wrists in his hands.

"Let me," he murmured, his smooth tenor sending a shiver rushing down my spine.

I lifted my gaze to meet his. His pupils were dilated with

desire, turning his blue eyes into bottomless dark blue depths that made my pulse pound.

"Okay," I breathed and he slid his hands to my shoulders and turned me away from him to face Keph.

A moment of disappointment flashed through me at the loss of eye contact, but he pressed his hard body against my back, and I could feel his erection, large and hard against my rear through my thick skirt.

Oh, yes. That was what I wanted—

No.

Not what I wanted... at least not right now.

The plan was for just a tease, to get worked up enough and be motivated enough to heal everyone here and *then* come back for more.

He grabbed the bottom of my sweater and slowly lifted it, the action so simple and yet, so damn sexy.

I raised my arms and he drew the sweater off and set it on the shelf beside my coat then slid his hands back down my arms, skimming the edge of my breasts sending a thrill rushing through me despite the fact that I was still wearing a T-shirt and bra.

My pulse roared in my ears and my breath picked up. Was it me or was the storeroom getting really hot, really quickly?

Maybe asking for just a tease was a bad idea.

But even as I thought that, I locked gazes with Keph, who watched Rion slowly undress me.

Desire filled his silver-rimmed black eyes, and while I wasn't sure I'd be able to tell if he was flushed given his glistening onyx skin, just that look in his eyes and seeing the hungry, aching need there was more than enough to tell he was aroused. And that made something in my chest swell. It was a matching need, except it felt deeper than just a desire for physical release. It was like I craved a connection with him, which was crazy because I didn't know Keph or any of the guys well enough to crave a deep connection with them. *Want* maybe, but not *crave*. Not yet.

Rion grabbed the hem of my long-sleeved T-shirt, leaned close, and brushed his lips against the sensitive skin behind my ear.

A soft moan escaped my lips and I tilted my head to the side to give him better access, but didn't take my gaze off Keph. The big man's chest rose and fell, his breath getting faster too, each inhalation expanding his bulky muscles and straining his white dress shirt. The sleeves had been too tight so he'd ripped those off and now all I could think about was ripping off the rest of it.

God! This was taking forever.

But then... it was supposed to be a tease wasn't it?

The muscles in Keph's jaw tightened and the big man fumbled with the tiny-to-him zipper on his pants, trying to free his erection. The fabric bulged, reminding me of just how large he was. I'd seen him and the others naked since clothing was optional in their world and had dreamed about what it would be like to have sex with him.

Oh yes, break that beast out.

Rion's breath came faster as well now, his desire clearly rising like mine and Keph's. He pulled off my T-shirt, his pace, like his breath, no longer slow, as if he was losing control as well.

Keph finally found the zipper and pulled it down, but hadn't undone the button, and wasn't free.

He grunted, as Rion undid the clasp on my bra and let the lacy fabric fall away, then Keph gasped as if the sight of my breasts had stollen his breath.

Heat pooled between my thighs and my core ached. I was so very ready for one of these men to be inside me— Well I was ready for Rion. I wasn't so sure about Keph yet, but I had no doubt with a little more attention from them, I would be.

Except this was just supposed to be a tease.

If I was smart. I'd stop things where we were. I was certainly full of energy for *something* right now, and that something was supposed to be healing everyone in the convention center. But I couldn't bring myself to say it. I wanted more. I wanted to feel Rion's hands on my skin, wanted to see how large and dark Keph's eyes would get with his need.

The large man finally succeeded in popping the button at the top of his pants without ripping it off and freed his monster erection, breathing a heavy sigh of relief.

Rion's hands found my breasts, clutching them greedily, and I gasped at the hard grip, a sudden contrast to the slow, soft, and sensual touch he'd used to undress me. He sucked on the skin behind my ear and kneaded my girls, tightening my nipples into stiff, aching buds with an onslaught of passionate sensation.

My legs grew weak and I leaned back into him. My breath was ragged and I moaned my pleasure, my body throbbing with need.

"Too much?" Rion asked, his lips against my skin, his hands still working my breasts.

Oh, hell yes. We were beyond teasing now, and it was exactly what I wanted.

"No," I gasped.

And that was it. I'd fully committed. To hell with this being just a tease. I'd lose my mind if he stopped now.

CHAPTER 2

KEPHAS

I'D NEVER BEEN THIS AROUSED IN MY LIFE.

Oh, I'd been aroused and been with women a few times. Oddly, I'd never been with another stone titan. Being a secluded and private people, mating was saved for after the bonding ceremony. But in my adventures to Masia to see my fellow emissaries, I'd had a few women.

Few.

There hadn't been many who'd wanted to be with me after seeing my full size, but a brave few had tried, while even fewer had succeeded.

They'd required a lot of 'working up' as Annie seemed to call it, before they were ready for me. They'd ride me, carefully, and leave happy, but I'd never truly been able to fully be with a woman. None would be able to take the full force of my thrusts, and Annie probably wouldn't be able to either

Except right now, watching Rion strip and fondle her, I was so ready to try.

I wouldn't, not without her say-so, which I was certain she wouldn't give, not now, since she'd made it clear she only wished to be aroused. But I couldn't help being turned on and the pain in my cock as it strained against my pants, had been so intense, I feared I'd have ripped the fragile fabric if I hadn't released it.

Except now that it was free, it was so much harder to remember I couldn't go any further.

It took everything I had to just stay put, keep my hands to myself, and let Annie see how amazingly sexy I found her without touching her. Her intense gaze never left me, moving from my eyes to my cock and back again, and she licked her lips, making my pulse stutter in an anticipation I shouldn't have.

Soft moans escaped her lips and she moved against Rion as if she was fully aroused even though she'd assured him that what he was doing wasn't too much yet.

Rion's hands left her gorgeous, full breasts, sliding down to her hips and drew her back hard. She tensed with a gasp, her eyes starting to roll back, her long eyelashes fluttering.

This certainly seemed like too much. It was almost too much for me and from the dark need in Rion's eyes, it was almost too much for him, too.

I waited for her command to stop, but it didn't come.

Apparently, it took a lot to tease our little goddess.

Rion slid his thumbs under the waistband of her skirt and ran his hands to her back where her garment was secured, his next action clear: remove the rest of her clothes.

"Are you sure you want more?" he whispered.

She nodded as if she couldn't find her voice, and he knelt and pushed her skirt, skin-tight pants — she'd called them leggings — and her underthings down her legs. My breath stalled, watching her flesh being revealed.

He helped her step out of her boots and the clothes, one foot, then the other, which left her standing beautiful and naked before me.

It took all my willpower to keep from coming at the sight of her. She was unlike any woman I'd ever seen before and I'd been mesmerized from the moment I'd seen her. Her pale fiery hair, her full round hips and ample bust and those odd, but somehow enticing, spots all over her face, arms, and chest. Gods above she was stunning.

"It's your turn Keph," Rion said, and as he rose, he put one hand behind each of her thighs, and lifted her from her feet.

"Oh, yes," she breathed, as he stepped closer to me and opened her legs in invitation.

"Are you sure?" I glanced from her to Rion and back again. Her gaze was simmering with desire... and so was Rion's. "You two are bonded."

"Bonds aren't the same in this world," Rion said. "Even if they were, this doesn't feel wrong, and if I hadn't been a fool that night, I would have realized that." He teased his lips along her jaw, drawing her gaze to him. "I don't know if it's because you're from a different world or if you really are a goddess, but I know you'll never be mine alone and I'm fine with that. I want you to have anything and everything that makes you happy. Keph," he turned his attention back to me. "It's your turn... if that's what the goddess wishes."

She half huffed half moaned as if a mix of emotions had swept through her. "I'm not a goddess."

"You are to me," he replied. "And is it?"

She frowned at him. "Is it what?"

"Is it your wish for Keph to work you up, too?"

"Oh, yes." Her gaze jumped to me, her eyes filled with sexual hunger, making my cock throbbed even more.

Except I couldn't give her that, not without breaking the rules that we should just tease her. Also she'd need more 'working up' for her to be ready for me.

Instead, I sank to my knees, making sure one foot was still on the door behind me to keep it closed, and ran my hands along the inside of her thighs.

Her breath hitched the closer I got to her folds, and left her altogether on a low, sensual groan, when I teased my thumb along her opening, feeling her wetness and desire for us.

"Oh, yes," she said again, and I gently probed her opening, slowly sliding in one finger.

It filled her, not completely, but close. I began a slow rhythmic stroke of that tender flesh and leaned closer, teasing my lips over the top of her left thigh and inching closer to where my finger filled her.

She moaned her pleasure and captured my cheeks between her tiny, delicate hands, figuring out what I intended with my lips. Except instead of pushing me away, she urged me closer, giving me permission.

Rion lifted her slightly to meet my lips, and I swept my tongue from my finger up to the hardened sensitive nub that I knew drew the most amazing sounds from women.

Annie was no exception. She gasped, her body tensing, her eyes rolling back with pleasure before she released a low sensual moan.

My cock ached, desperate for a release, but I kept my gaze locked on hers, waiting for the moment when she said stop.

Except I was starting to get the impression she wasn't going to say the word, and a part of me really liked the idea that she desired Rion and I so much she couldn't help herself.

I slid my finger in deeper, in and out, in and out, as I kissed and sucked around it, always coming back to the sensitive nub.

Her breath turned ragged and little whimpers and gasping moans fell from her lips.

"This is too much," Rion groaned, his breath just as fast, his body trembling, but not with the effort to hold her. She was so small I had no doubt he could hold her for hours. Which meant he had to be fighting his own need.

"No," she begged. "More."

"Any more and you'll come," Rion said.

"I don't care." She squirmed against him, her hips rocking forward — as much as they could in his grip — to meet my finger and mouth. "This is what I want."

And she did.

It hadn't struck me right away, but I could see now that she was glowing. Her skin gave off a faint luminescence similar to Rion's glow when he'd first made love to her, similar to the light emanating from his face now.

"You're both glowing," I said, stopping my work between Annie's legs for a moment. This seemed significant.

Annie glanced down at herself. "Holy fuck."

Rion moved her away from me and gently set her on her feet, but she trembled and clung to him as if her legs wouldn't hold her, and he held her tight to help her stay standing.

"What is this?" Annie asked.

I didn't know, but it made her look even more amazing, certainly more like the goddess we'd all thought her to be initially. Perhaps...?

"Can't you feel it?" Rion said softly. "Our bond."

She looked him in his sky-blue eyes and then her own golden eyes widened. "I... do."

"What are you feeling?" I asked, as I stood. It seemed the pleasuring was done for now.

"I felt a connection when we bonded," Rion said. "Something... magical that was truly tying us together. That kiss we shared was far more powerful than just a bond kiss. There was magic to it in this world or..." He looked at Annie. "Or in you."

"In me?" Annie's eyes widened even more. "No. I'm not spe—" Her expression turned sad and I didn't have to wonder what she was thinking. It had been obvious in how embarrassed she'd been when it had come out that she wasn't really a goddess.

"Special?" I finished for her. She looked at me, those gold eyes literally shining, and nodded. "But you can heal in your world," I continued. Another nod. That's what she'd been pondering as well that had made her reconsider her words.

"So?" I prompted.

"Perhaps I am...?" She couldn't finish and it broke my heart.

"You *are* special. Even if you didn't have magic in your world, you'd still be special," Rion said, his voice filled with devotion and love. "You're magical."

She tangled her fingers in his hair and drew her lips to his in a long, deep, impassioned kiss. Both of their bodies began to glow brighter. It was going to be blinding in here soon.

She broke off from him, breathing hard, her gaze locked on her glowing arm.

"I'm magical," she whispered, then a stunned, giddy expression flooded her face. "I'm magical!"

In the next moment, her expression changed to a wide-eyed realization of some sort. Then she slowly turned to me. "And I know exactly how to get the strength I need to heal thousands of people."

I was confused. She was looking at me so intently

She stepped away from Rion, her legs steadier now, and reached out to me. "Keph, get those lips down here, so I can kiss you."

My heart skipped a beat, my own realization flooding me. She wanted to bond with me.

CHAPTER 3

ANNIE

KEPH'S EYES WENT WIDE AS HE KNELT AGAIN. REMEMBERING WHY he'd knelt the first time made my knees wobble even more. He was certainly a master with his fingers and lips—

His lips, yes, back to the task at hand.

I didn't really know how the fuck I was magical, but I couldn't deny it was happening. Apparently sex with Rion— no *kissing* Rion had created an actual bond between us. Enough of one that I seemed to have access to his light powers. And if that was the case, and if Keph was super-strong in my world, then I could kiss him to share his strength.

While kneeling, his face was at the perfect height, ever-so-slightly below mine. I put my hands to either side of his large head and leaned in.

Then stopped, pulling back.

Kissing on the lips meant so much more to them than it did to me, and I had no idea if this bonding thing was permanent.

Except... that didn't matter. I might barely know these guys and the idea of being magically bound to a stranger should have terrified me, but it didn't. Being with them felt, as Rion had said a moment earlier, right. Still, just because it felt right to me didn't mean it felt right to them.

"Keph—" I didn't know how to ask this.

Will you bond with me?

Can I kiss you?

I want to bond with you. How do you feel about that?

"Yes," he whispered. "Yes, Annie, I will bond with you." His gaze moved past mine and over my shoulder. "If Rion is also well with this?"

Right! I'd already bonded with Rion.

And while he'd said he was fine with Keph teasing me, I didn't know if that made him fine with me also bonding with Keph.

Except it was the only way I was going to be able to save everyone infected in the convention center, hell, the world if I didn't stop this plague here... or in the very least heal as many as I could and get the rest into quarantine before they spread it.

I turned to Rion. "I, ah...."

Jeez. Just rip off the bandage.

"Sorry, but I need to bond with Keph and get his strength," I blurted out. Wow that sounded really utilitarian and was certainly a slap in the face to both of them.

I spun back to Keph, but he didn't seem offended.

Back to Rion.

He seemed fine as well. *Oh, thank God.*

"Sorry, that came out wrong, what I meant was—"

Rion drew close to me — I hadn't really gone that far, there hadn't been much space between him and Rion for me to go — and pressed a finger to my lips to hush me.

"Annie. I know my bond can never claim you, not fully, and I don't expect it to." His look was intense, his body still glowing faintly, though it had faded a bit from earlier. "It's clear this bond between us is more than usual. It's magical. But I know that magic isn't coming from me. It's you, Annie, who've claimed me, taking what's mine."

God, that sounded horrible.

He seemed to see my distress and smiled as he gently brushed a lock of hair away from my cheek. "I want you to take it. I *know* you should. Everything I have is yours if you want it." He knelt as well.

I flushed with the sudden realization that two men were kneeling before me, and we were talking about bonding. Was I about to marry two men? I had no clue. I didn't particularly mind given the men in question. They were kind and generous, if a little strange — although I'm sure I seemed strange to them as well — and it didn't hurt that they were hot as hell.

God, what would everyone say? What would *my family* say?

I didn't care.

"Our bond is forever," Rion continued, his words not striking the kind of fear I'd have expected. "My heart is yours and yours alone, but I can see now, your heart is larger than mine. It can accept more than one bond. I ask only to remain in your heart and in your thoughts."

I stared at him. That sounded a lot like vows.

Fuck.

This was really happening.

I needed to say something in return. "Thank you, Rion. You'll always have a place in my heart and soul." There was little chance I was ever going to forget him, nor our time together.

My dirty mind added another vow: *there will always be a place for you in my pussy, too.*

It wasn't like it wasn't true. And thinking about it only made me more wet down there.

"I formally accept your bond. I know what I did before hurt you, and I'm sorry. You'll always be—" I needed to say something significant here. Oooh! "My first bonded."

I smiled at him and leaned down to kiss him again. His lips were soft and warm and wonderful. As I pulled away, I said, "And I think you're right. I think I can have this sort of bond with more than just one man." Certainly, I didn't feel the sort of singular devotion to him he seemed to feel toward me. Sure, in past relationships I had been singularly devoted to the guy I'd been dating, but this felt different. I felt like there could be— No, that there *should* be more bonds.

He nodded, smiling. "And if it is to be with another, then I couldn't think of a better, truer, more honest and caring man then Keph."

My heart fluttered with joy and desire and certainty, and I turned to Keph. Time for my second set of vows.

Keph was beaming, smiling with acceptance from Rion's words, and that smile grew as he looked at me.

"I, Annie Chambers, would like to bond with you, Kephas... do you have a last name?"

He shrugged. "My clan is Vathia Spiti."

"Kephas Vathia Spiti," I said, letting the name slide over my tongue.

"You make it sound beautiful." His whole being seemed to soften. I could tell he was touched and all I'd done was say his name. "And yes, I will bond with you, Annie Chambers—" His grin deepened. "Goddess extraordinaire."

That brought back some awkward memories. But I still smiled back at him, cupped his face in my hands again, and drew close to kiss him. I had to step to either side of his still-aroused cock, and it brushed against the insides of my thighs and ever-so-faintly against my opening.

All of a sudden, this kiss was making me really, really hot again.

He didn't lean in, didn't force his lips on mine, but was gentle like he always was. Which was good, because where Rion had soft and warm lips, Keph's were firm and unyielding.

The kiss was chaste at first — other than the fact that I was naked and his cock was poised and ready to fill me — but I wanted more from this significant moment, felt it needed to be more, so I brushed my tongue over his lips, teasing them open.

He sighed softly, the sound a low rumble that shivered through my body turning me on even more and wrapped a massive arm around my back and carefully pulled me closer. Even so, I felt the latent strength there, the immense power of which only a meager fraction was used.

His tongue met mine and the kiss deepened, lengthened. I pressed my body to his, savoring the feel of his enormous, hard muscular chest through his sleeveless dress shirt, and a spark snapped through my lips.

I gasped and warmth flooded me, reigniting desire that had been simmering within me since our first encounter.

Oh hell, I wasn't going to be satisfied with just a tease.

I was already wet and ready from Keph's work earlier and he was right there, ready and waiting.

Our lips still locked, I relaxed my legs a little and brushed myself against the massive head of his hard cock. A shudder of need rushed through me, and Keph gasped in a sharp breath. His erection, amazingly, got larger, longer, and harder, and forced me onto my tip-toes to avoid getting impaled.

Holy fuck!

I shifted position, rolling my hips and rubbing myself over his tip. There was no way he'd fit inside me right now — I'd need to be wetter, or have a bottle of lube standing by. But just feeling that impossibly large cock pressed against me, so hard, was enough to tease my opening and hit my clit. I pressed down on it, throwing my arms around Keph's neck to help me keep my balance, while continuing to kiss him.

Keph's breath quickened and he shifted his hand on my back a little higher and pressed the other one against my butt, offering me support but not taking control.

I reached a mini-orgasm just rubbing myself on his tip. My body trembled and I pressed my forehead to his and released a soft groan. The climax relaxed my muscles and got me even more wet. With a small shudder, which echoed through both of us, his cock inched inside me.

My breath hitched. The promise of another climax quivered through me at him stretching me, promising to fill me completely — hell beyond my limit — and oh-my-fucking-God, it felt incredible.

I slowly tipped my hips forward, inching him in just a little farther, igniting hypersensitive nerves already on the edge and setting off a bigger orgasm. It wasn't the fuck-my-brains-out, stars-flashing-behind-my-lids orgasm I'd had with Rion the other day, but it was still so much more than I'd had in the past.

A long, throaty moan escaped my lips this time and Keph tensed. His tip swelled inside me and he groaned his own soft release, sending more blissful waves washing over me.

Except the waves didn't diminish, they blossomed into a surprising full-body orgasm, that tore out of me with a shuddering scream as his heat and the initial magical heat from our kiss surged inside me.

"Oh, God!" I breathed, when I found my voice again. "That's a kiss I'll never forget."

Keph nodded and shuddered with another surge of his release then finally gasped, "I am yours, Goddess."

And I was his... and Rion's.

Time to see about that. I punched the door behind him, but not very hard — I didn't want to hurt myself — and was shocked when it didn't even sting, even though I'd left an impression of my knuckles in the metal.

Well, damn. I could live with this.

With a groan, Keph carefully withdrew from me, leaving me feeling hollow and unsteady. I glanced around to find my clothes and my gaze landed on Rion.

Fuck! I'd forgotten he was there while lost in the passionate moment with Keph.

But Rion didn't seem put off by our quickie at all. He'd dropped his pants, pulled out his cock, and was stroking it with long, firm strokes. It seemed harsh to leave him there literally with his cock in his hand, so, gripping the shelf beside me to keep my balance, I wobbled the two steps over to him.

I'd just had a mind-blowing kiss. Perhaps I'd give him one as well.

"It's well, Annie, you don't need to—"

I sagged to my knees before him, slid my hand over his hand holding his cock, and wrapped my mouth around the end.

"Oh," he gasped and I grinned up at him. His eyes had grown wide, his pupils fully dilated while his breath had jumped to ragged and fast and his body trembled.

I nudged his hand away so I could fully take over, running my hand down his length to his base while swirling my tongue over his tip.

"Oh, Hermes!" He grabbed the shelf beside him, his cock growing harder in my grip.

I drew my hand up his length and back down, mindful of my newly found strength, and took more of him in my mouth.

"Annie, I—"

Another stroke and this time my lips followed my hand, taking him fully into my mouth.

"Annie," he groaned and his body stiffened as his salty release rushed into my mouth. Oh, yeah, he'd been well primed.

I bit back a silly grin. Now, we'd all had something.

And I felt strong enough to take on the world.

CHAPTER 4

ANNIE

My body thrummed with energy as I used a wad of paper towels — stollen from the shelf beside Rion — to clean up then started to get dressed. I felt like... there wasn't a comparison. I'd never felt so self-assured and confident. Being with these two men, at the same time, seeing how much they wanted me, had filled me with so much love and certainty. I was on top of the world... which was good, because I still had a convention center full of people to cure.

I finished dressing, feeling refreshed and ready to work. Turning to the guys, they too were ready to go, and looked God-damned sexy.

Another thrill rushed through me. They were bonded to me. Both of them. And had shown me just how much they desired me. And the best part was that I knew this wasn't a dream!

"Ready to go?" I asked.

"Are you?" Rion replied.

I nodded. "Let's do this."

We left the storage room in time to find one of the security men running toward us. "Everything's been shut down," he called out. "People are being kept in the larger rooms and a few hallways. The police have arrived and are taking care of things outside." The man actually looked worried. It wasn't the leader from before, just some poor young man in the wrong place.

With all the poise of my newfound energy I smiled reassuringly as I approached him. Reaching up I cupped his cheek to check to see if he was infected. He didn't have the disease.

I blinked.

I shouldn't have known that right away. Before, I'd had to actively search for the disease in someone, but I'd known the second I'd touched him that he wasn't infected.

Guess my new found ability was growing.

"Everything is well," I said calmly. I made a show of looking in his eyes and opening his mouth to look inside. "You're well and haven't contracted anything. Keep away from people for the moment if you can. It's spread through skin contact and the onset is quick." I didn't know if it was quick, but if it wasn't, there was no logical way I'd know if he was infected or not by just looking at him.

He seemed to relax a little, thankfully not questioning how my explanation didn't really make sense, medically speaking. "Thank you, ma'am."

I'd never really been a 'ma'am' before and wasn't sure how I felt about that. I wasn't old enough to be a ma'am, but ma'am's were in charge and that's what I needed to be right now.

"Take me to where the people are gathered so I can take a look at them."

He nodded, turned on his heel, and led us out of the large room and into the hall.

"You calmed him down quickly," Rion said.

"It helps when I feel calm myself." I stopped and let the two men flanking me pass me a little. They turned back. "Thank you, both of you." I met the level gaze of each of them in turn. "Rion,

Keph, I know this is going to sound crazy, but I love you." It felt right in my soul to say it even though I barely knew these men. "I don't know how this is all going to work out once we're finished here, but I know I love you."

All my life I'd thought true love was something between two people, and a fairy tale at that. Yet I had a new certainty now. True love was something that could be shared and was completely real. I had no clue what that really meant, but I needed to let them know how I felt.

Both men smiled, then simultaneously glanced at each other. Something, some unsaid notion passed between them and they both nodded.

"I love you too, Annie," Keph said softly.

"As do I," Rion added. "We'll... work out the details of this odd relationship later. Know that we are with you, for whatever you need."

Whatever I needed. Oh, I was well aware of that. They'd just shown me. And I was looking forward to *more* later.

"Good," I said, and hurried after the security guard while the guys fell in a step slightly behind me and to either side.

The guard led us to a large hall filled with stalls where security had done a good job organizing people. They were lined up around the outside wall, then in a single file row down each of the aisles between stalls.

Stopping, I turned to Keph and reached for his hand. That large, hard, yet gentle hand engulfed mine, and I felt his power fill me once again. This bond thing was amazing.

"Let's do this!" I said and turned to the first row of people.

Time blurred and I focused solely on checking people. One person then the next. I couldn't look at how many I'd checked or how many were left. I just had to keep going. One foot in front of the other.

When I grew weary, Keph was there for another surge of

energy, and I kept going until I stepped away from a tall, skinny man in some kind of plastic, homemade body armor, and realized there wasn't anyone else.

There'd been close to two hundred people infected, but thankfully they'd all been in the initial stages and were easily healed. Still, healing two hundred people had been exhausting even with Keph's help.

With a heavy sigh, I turned to find the lead security guard in my face flanked by men with FBI in big bold letters on their jackets.

Well, fuck.

"Special Agent Annie Chambers was it?" the security guard said with a sneer. "Seems the FBI has no record of an agent by that name."

"Great, you can arrest me now." I held my hands out, wrists together. Even without looking, I could tell Rion and Keph were confused. Perhaps it was some effect of our bond that let me know what they were feeling. "But I wasn't wrong about the bio-terrorist attack. Luckily those here are clean, but you take an infectious disease specialist through the other halls and check for people with small black spots on their skin. They'd be hard to find at this early stage, but those people are still highly contagious and should be quarantined from everyone else and anyone else should be checked hourly to see if such spots develop."

The man's bluster deflated just a little at my calm confidence. "Who are you?"

"Annie Chambers, goddess." I tilted my head just a little to the right and offered him a dazzling smile. I knew that line would probably land me in a loony-bin, but I couldn't help myself. Besides Keph and Rion would protect me. Just to be really messed-up, I made myself glow.

The security guard's eyes bulged just a little.

"Now, are you going to have someone look at the other halls, or are you going to let me through so I can heal them?"

I didn't think the guard or the two FBI agents quite knew what to do with a self-assured, glowing woman flanked by two guys: one who looked like a model and the other like a small mountain.

I walked forward, and the security guard moved aside. The FBI agents, looked at each other, shrugged then also moved aside.

"Thanks, boys," I said casually, my heart racing a mile a minute, my entire being filled with bravado and justified bluster. I could get used to this.

Behind me I heard one of the FBI-guys probably on a phone. "Ah... yeah... can we get an infectious disease specialist out here?" A pause. "Also, maybe someone from the paranormal division."

That was a thing?

Cool.

"What do we do now?" Keph asked. "Stay and heal more or let them deal with it?"

"I'm going to stay until someone kicks me out." Or I collapsed from exhaustion. Whichever came first. "On to the next room." I indicated our way with an assured straight-arm point.

Rion chuckled. "I take it people in your world aren't used to seeing a goddess."

"Nope."

"Those men looked like they were going to run when you started glowing." His laughter deepened and I joined him. For the moment at least, I felt good.

I began examining the people who'd been lined up in the next hall, but about a third of the way through, more people in FBI uniforms arrived, three of whom — two burly men and a lean woman in a lab coat — came to me.

The woman, with sharp green eyes, pale brown hair pulled back in a professional bun, and carrying a bag with the strap slung over her shoulder, cleared her throat. "Uh, excuse me?"

I smiled at her as I moved on from one person to the next. "Yes?"

"You're the uh... healer?"

"Yep."

"Might I... watch?"

"As long as you don't get in my way."

The woman nodded.

True to her word, she, and the two larger men with her, simply watched me for a while. The next seven people I inspected weren't infected, but the one after that was.

"Hey," I called over to her. "What's your name?"

"Janice," she said moving a little closer. "Yours?"

"Annie Chambers." She looked like she was about to ask more, but I cut her off. "See these spots?" I said indicating the small black dots on the face of the young man in front of me.

"Yes." Janice looked closer. "This is the disease?"

"Yes."

"Might I take a sample?" she asked.

I didn't know if that was a good idea, but if the authorities came across someone who was infected without me, they'd need to know everything they could about it. "Just be really careful with it."

"I will." She pulled a long swab from her bag, broke open the packaging and took a sample from the man's mouth. Then, with another swab, took a sample from one of the black spots. Once done, she put the swabs in sealable plastic bags that then went in another bio-hazard pouch.

I turned to the man, whose eyes were now wide with fear.

"Don't worry," I said. "I'm going to heal you."

Which, if I really thought about it, was crazy. If I didn't know what I knew, I would have thought I was crazy.

But I touched his face and let my power seep into him, and the fear in his eyes changed to awe as he felt my power flow into him.

It didn't take much energy, either that or I was getting used to this, and the small spots faded from the man's skin.

"Oh, wow. I didn't think I felt bad, but... wow. I feel great now!" he gasped.

I turned to Janice, who was also wide-eyed with awe.

"All gone," I said.

"How...?" Janice opened her mouth then closed it as if she were at a loss for words.

I shrugged. "I don't really know. I shouldn't be able to do this, but I can. If you ask either of these two," I said, indicating Rion and Keph, "they'll tell you I'm a goddess. Right now, I can't refute them."

"Uh-hunh." Janice looked at me like I had two heads... sort of. It was a strange look, as if she didn't want to believe what she was seeing, but was also coming to terms with my 'two heads.'

She shrugged after a moment. "Go about your work then," she said and turned to the two bewildered men behind her. "I can't explain it," she whispered. "Faith healer maybe?"

I went back to work, and Janice and her crew kept watch from a distance.

When I was done, I stepped back into the hall to go to the next room only to find a squad of men wearing black body armor pointing their guns at me. They looked like they were staring down a rabid rhino.

Keph laid a heavy, reassuring hand on my shoulder, his thumb rubbing gentle circles on the back of my neck. It was a comforting touch and made me just a little warm, but also renewed my connection with him, giving me more strength.

"Annie?" Rion asked.

I was about to ask these men what they wanted... when my phone rang.

The FBI guys all flinched and tensed, and, with my hands

open, palms up to show I wasn't armed, I slowly reached into my pocket and drew out my phone.

I swiped to activate the call and put it to my ear. "Yes?"

"We have a problem," Del said.

A squad of FBI guys had their guns pointed at me. That... was a bit of an understatement.

CHAPTER 5

HYPERION

ANNIE WAS VERY STILL, BUT ALSO SMILING. I WASN'T SURE HOW MUCH of Keph's abilities she might have taken from their bond, just as I was uncertain how bright she could become using my light. There were a lot of unknowns floating around, but I didn't want to risk her getting hurt. And right now, with these men pointing their weapons at us there was a good chance she would be.

I edged a little closer to her. I didn't know how those strange looking weapons worked, but I'd put myself between her and danger. My vow — my *bond* — demanded it.

"Yes?" Annie said into the device she held against her cheek. What had she called it again? A *phone*?

"Oh? Really? So do I. What's yours?"

No one moved. Apparently, these men with the letters F B I on their strange, padded armor were willing to let Annie talk.

"Well, fuckity-fuck-fuck!" Annie hissed, too quiet for the men to hear and without losing her smile. "And we have no idea where they are? ... Of course. Well, stay with her and stay hidden. ... My problem? Oh, just some men with guns. ... Yes, those things that hurt you from a distance. No! Del, stay where you are with the *naiad*. She can't be set free. Maybe we can get more information out of her. ... Yeah, bye." She removed the *phone* from her ear and sighed as she slowly put it away. Turning to the men with the guns she asked, "How can I help you?"

"Annie Chambers?" someone called out.

"That would be me."

"You're under arrest for impersonating a federal agent and inciting chaos."

"Sounds fair," she whispered.

"Wait!" the woman who'd been watching Annie work said as she hurried out of the room we'd just been in. "Put those guns down and don't arrest her. Who's in charge here?"

This began a heated conversation in hushed voices between that woman — also with the F B I letters on her uniform, half hidden under her long white coat — and another man.

The man's voice rose enough for me to hear a derisive scoff, then, "Yeah, right, and I'm the president."

Janice spoke louder. "I saw it with my own eyes."

"Then your eyes are failing."

"Ah... excuse me?" Annie said. She had her hands up and out in front of her and slowly inched toward them even though a few of the men still had their weapons pointed at her.

Keph and I moved with her, and I knew he was just as ready to protect her as I was.

"What?" the man snapped, his voice thick with exasperation.

"If you're looking for proof that I'm some supernatural entity, I can give that to you." Annie's smile deepened. She seemed so confident, different than when we'd met her. Well, no, she'd seemed confident when we'd first met her, but she'd thought everything was a dream. Once she'd realized the truth, she'd seemed so small and uncertain and it had broken my heart.

"A supernatural what?" the man asked.

"Entity. Goddess to be exact."

"Yeah, right!" he huffed.

"Okay, here goes." She began to glow.

The man's eyes widened with shock. "Fuck me!" he gasped then his expression snapped back to hard skepticism. "That's just some trick of the light."

Annie shrugged. "Fine, just remember, you asked for this."

She stepped in and punched the man in the stomach, hitting him square in the middle of his armored chest. He flew back a dozen feet, hit the slick, shiny floor, and skidded another dozen feet before stopping.

A loud crack exploded around us and Annie flinched and grabbed her forehead. "Ow! Hey!"

My pulse froze and I grabbed her arm to pull her to safety, but she glanced at me, looking fine, and the rest of me froze.

I didn't know what had happened. She had a wound on her forehead smaller than my smallest fingernail, that wept a small trickle of blood, and her gaze had dropped to a small deformed ball of metal in her hand. Even as I watched, the wound stopped bleeding and faded to nothing.

"Well, if I didn't believe it before, I do now," Janice said in awe, as Keph jerked in front of Annie, shielding her with his massive body from any more attacks.

Annie used that distraction to turn to me. "Bring out your wings," she whispered.

I did.

I felt the familiar rush of power and whispered pain as my wings sprung from my shoulder blades and flared out on either side of me. Except, too late, I remembered I still wore the jacket Annie had borrowed for me, and they tore through the fabric. So much for that.

"I also come with an angel," Annie said jovially. She'd called me that before. I didn't know what that was, but everyone else seemed to. There were gasps and exclamations from the group.

"Now, Janice," Annie said, turning to the woman. "You seem reasonable. Is it okay if I go and heal some more people?"

The woman stammered for a moment, eyes wide, staring at me before she nodded. "Ah, yes, go ahead. I'll take care of this."

"You're such a dear, thank you!" Annie headed down the hall to go to the next room and Keph and I followed.

When she got to the FBI man she'd punched, who was still lying on the floor, she knelt next to him. He seemed stunned still and struggled to catch his breath.

"Sorry about that," Annie said, and laid a hand on his cheek. His eyes went wide with fear. "Oooh, really sorry, wow, so many broken ribs! I don't know my own strength yet. Here—" The man's fear changed to awe and he drew in a full, deep breath. "Better?"

He nodded.

Annie patted his cheek. "Great! Gotta go heal some other people." She rose and moved off.

Keph glared down at the still prone man and offered a low threatening growl that frightened even me.

I looked back as we moved on. The man was staring at us, his expression a mix of shock and confusion and awe. It seemed we were getting a lot of those looks. I waved, and released my wings, letting them melt into nothing as we continued on.

"What did Del say?" Keph asked as we entered yet another large room filled with people. I wasn't sure how many Annie had checked and healed so far, I'd lost count. At least a few hundred if not a thousand or more, and while she looked in good health, I was still worried that she was going to keep going until she collapsed, just like the last time.

"Apparently the *naiad* let slip that two of her duplicates are still out there, spreading disease," Annie said. "I'm betting they've already fled the convention center, but just in case, keep an eye out for her. There isn't much we can do about it now, though." She glanced out the door into the hall and frowned.

I shrugged out of my ruined jacket and turned to see what concerned her. Janice was running to catch up with us. Her two escorts flanking her, but thankfully the men in the strange black fabric armor had dispersed.

Janice stopped, a bit out of breath. "Ah, miss— Annie— Goddess?" she said, stumbling over her own words.

"Yes, Janice?" Annie said.

"I'm to be your liaison for now."

"That's great, and while you're here, can you put out an A.P.B. — or whatever you call them?"

Janice frowned. "Ah... sure. For who?"

"The woman who caused all this. She's ahh... triplets! Yes, triplets. We caught one of them, but the other two are still out there. They shouldn't be too hard to find. They have blue skin. Light blue, like a summer sky."

"What if they take off their make-up?" Janice asked.

"It's not make-up. They actually have blue skin." Annie laughed. "Actually, we'd need to be worried if they *found* make-up and knew what to do with it. Oh, and be careful, she can turn to water and slip away at will."

"Turn to..." Janice's frown deepened and I could see questions form in her eyes before she gave a tight nod of acceptance and forced a smile. "Right, will do, thanks Goddess Annie." She turned to one of the men behind her. "Call it in."

"I can't—" the man said. "No one will believe me."

"Just call it in," Janice pressed.

The man reached for his *phone,* his expression clear that he thought it was pointless and Janice turned back to us.

"Anything else?" she asked.

"That's it for now, thank you."

"Whatever you need," Janice said, though she sounded just a little less certain than she had a few moments ago.

Annie moved through the next room, taking energy from Keph

more and more often. By the time she was done, Keph was looking weary, something I'd never seen before. It was a testament to the massive amount of work Annie was doing and the energy she was expending.

The two of them rested for a bit in the next hall, Keph gathering Annie in his arms and holding her close while they sat on the floor, and I took Janice aside to speak to her.

"Do you know how many more people there are to heal?" I asked.

Janice stared at my bare chest for a long time before blinking, as if she'd just realized I'd asked her a question.

"Ah... what? People? Oh, right, sorry." She pulled out her *phone* and activated it, scrolling through some images. "It looks like there were a total of twenty-three thousand, seven-hundred-and-forty-three people here when we quarantined the place."

It was my turn to stare at her like she'd stared at me with my wings out. "That's— That's so many! How many have we looked at so far?"

"About seven thousand."

My jaw dropped again. I knew it was a lot, but that was more than I'd expected. And at the same time still only about a third of what needed to be done. This was going to take forever.

"I know," Janice said softly. She looked back at Annie resting in Keph's arms. "I don't know how she's come this far, doing what she's doing. Not that I have any clue what she's doing, but even just following her, watching her, staying on my feet for this long, is exhausting."

"Thank you, Janice," I said and slowly returned to the other two.

"What was that about?" Annie asked. She was recovering quickly, but I couldn't say the same for Keph, who still looked weary.

"I asked how many people there were left to see."

"And?"

I did the math quickly. "Roughly sixteen thousand."

Annie nodded slowly. "Fuck."

"Yeah."

"How many have we gone through?" she asked.

"About seven thousand."

"Ah, okay, good, good." She nodded again as if that was the only action she could think of doing then released a heavy sigh. "This is going to take forever."

"That's what I was thinking."

Annie forced a smile and slowly rose. "Better get to it then."

Gods, she was amazing.

CHAPTER 6

ANNIE

I HURT IN PLACES WHERE I'D NEVER HURT BEFORE. SOMEONE HAD brought me food several times, one of them a breakfast, and I assumed that meant I'd worked through the night. There were windows somewhere in the building, but I'd long since stopped paying attention and had no clue what time it was. All I knew was... I was finally done!

I slumped in a hallway, sitting against a wall, staring at the opposite wall but not really seeing it. With an earth-shaking *thud*, Keph sagged to the floor next to me. He was in rough shape.

I'd pulled everything I dared from him, and I knew he'd have given more if I'd asked, but I was worried what that might do to him. I recovered quickly with my healing ability, but Keph... he was much more sluggish than usual and I didn't know how long it would take for his energy to come back.

"Done," Keph said heavily.

"As if you did anything," I said, softly elbowing him and trying to be playful. With the power I took from him, he actually swayed a little from my nudge... or maybe I was just that strong and hadn't fully realized it.

He turned to me, one brow raised. "Really?"

"It was a joke."

He smiled faintly, then thumped his head back against the wall so hard the wall cracked.

Rion glanced at us. He was pacing, full of nervous energy, but I didn't know if I could take strength from him the way I did with Keph. I'd assumed I could only take the ability associated with the man, nothing more. And while I was curious, I didn't have the energy to try. I'd have to experiment with that later.

Everything would come later.

Which reminded me. I needed to check in with Del and Aethan.

I took out my phone, swiped it on, and hit the last number called. It rang for a while then Del answered.

"Annie? Is that you?" he asked, his voice filled with concern. "Are you well?"

"Well enough, yes. Thought I'd check in with you. How's the *naiad*?"

"Thank the gods," Del said, relief flooding his voice. "The *naiad* hasn't said much in... it's been a long time. We're getting hungry here."

Right. Fuck. They were hiding somewhere in this complex of buildings, waiting while I'd healed all those people. And even if they'd tried to go out and find some food, they had no money.

"Aethan stole us some food yesterday, but we don't want to push our luck."

"Stole?" I didn't want to know from where. "Where are you guys. I'll come to you. I'm tired, but we should regroup and figure out our next steps."

"I honestly have no clue where we are. Some closet deep in the bowels of one of the many buildings here."

Great. Well, they were well hidden at least.

"Do you remember how you got there?"

"Aethan says he does."

I rose, slowly, leaning against the wall to keep my balance. "Okay. Let me make my way back to where we left you, then you can guide us. We'll come to you and—"

Agent Janice walked around the corner at the end of the hall and headed toward us. A small exhausted part of me said I should probably ask what her last name was, but the rest of me was too tired to care. And really, it wasn't that important at the moment.

"I'll call you back when we're ready." I hung up to some clipped reply from Del that I didn't quite catch.

"Does the FBI need more from Amazing Goddess Annie?" I asked, my voice weak and wobbly, like the rest of me.

"Once we track down the last blue-woman you told us about, we may need you to heal more of the city. If that's... possible? You look tired."

"Little known fact, gods have their limits, and I've reached mine."

"Ah. Well, can we call you when we—?"

My brain finally caught up with what she'd said a moment ago. "The last woman? You found one of them?"

"Yes, and we have her in custody."

Wow. "You actually managed to capture her, even when she can turn to water." I was surprised and impressed. I figured they might find her, but I hadn't expected them to actually capture her.

"Indeed." Janice smirked. "No one believed me when I told them that. But they tracked one down and that's exactly what she did. But I guess she didn't count on how cold it was outside and she didn't get far, nearly freezing, so she turned back into a person. The agents then deployed some... ah... innovative techniques to capture her."

"Innovative techniques?" This, I had to hear.

"A... ah... fish tank. They've restrained her in a large fish tank and are carrying her around in it." Janice shrugged. "Things I'd never thought I'd say. If you'd told me a week ago this was how today would go, I wouldn't have believed you."

"I have that effect." I gave my winningest smile. It was probably wobbly too. "I have to go. If you need to reach me, call me." I told her my number then turned away to go meet Del and Aethan.

"I'll text you my number in case you need it," Janice said.

I wobbled a few steps farther and Rion rushed forward to help me, while Keph staggered to his feet.

"Annie?" Janice said, her voice soft.

I glanced back at her.

"Thank you." She bowed her head as if I really was a goddess... and well, maybe I actually was. I didn't know, but the reverence made me slightly uncomfortable. "I don't know about anyone else, but I'll say a prayer to Goddess Annie every night for a while. What you did today... and yesterday... was a miracle."

I smiled again, not sure what to say to that then continued walking away, with Rion helping and Keph, looking like he wanted to also help but needing the wall to stay upright.

We moved slowly and eventually found our way back to the room where we'd captured the *naiad*. I called Del and he led us — with only a few dead-ends and wrong turns — to them. They were indeed in a storage room with shelves and stacked chairs. Just looking at it made my face heat. After my escapades — I guess it was yesterday now — I had a completely different view of storage rooms.

"Save us some time and just tell me where your duplicates are," I said to the *naiad*, too tired to beat around the bush. "I'm sure you have some way of knowing their location."

"I don't." She flashed a victorious smile even though she'd been captured and was probably hungry. "They know where I am and can return to me whenever they wish or if I call them."

Call them, hunh? That was a slip, and from the sudden crack in her smile, she knew it as soon as she'd said it.

"Then call them. 'Cause I'm tired and if you don't, I'll have one of my big friends here crack your head open like a melon. Do you have melons in your world?" I asked Del.

He nodded.

"Yep, like a melon," I said to her. "I'm sure that would deal with your duplicates, too."

Her eyes widened and Keph growled on cue.

Good Keph.

"Fine! Yes, I'll call them in." Her smile returned. "But they've been out there for over a day. The damage is done."

Which I already knew. But I'd deal with that later... if I could deal with it—

No. I *would*. I was a goddess after all.

But the first thing to take care of was stopping the duplicates from continuing to actively spread the disease.

The *naiad's* smile weakened then slid into a frown and a few minutes later she hissed a sharp curse. "Akheloios! One of my duplicates has died."

That wasn't too much of a surprise. I wasn't sure what her 'return call' was like, but if the duplicates couldn't resist it, then the one in custody probably had tried to escape and been shot and killed.

"The other one is coming," the *naiad* huffed. "It might take a while."

Great. I didn't want to keep standing around, I wanted to go home to bed, but I also wasn't going to leave until the duplicates weren't running around creating more problems. Sure, the disease was likely already being spread by humans now, but they weren't actively trying to spread it like the *naiad* and her duplicates had.

While we waited, I tried to figure out what the hell I was going to do with her. My initial thought was to hand her over to Janice but I had a feeling that would create more problems. I felt like I could trust Janice — don't ask me why — but that didn't mean everyone Janice worked with and everyone the *naiad* might come in contact with could be trusted.

It was bad enough one evil man from my world had learned about having powers in my guys' world. I couldn't risk more people finding out. That had disaster written all over it. Even if they didn't have a power that they could manipulate to influence my world like Disease Man had, they'd still have power in the other world and could terrorize those people.

No. The only safe answer for everyone was for the *naiad* to return to her world and then hope Janice wouldn't think it smart to question the decision of a goddess.

I really wanted to be able to hand the *naiad* over to whatever authorities there were in the guys' world, but I didn't really have the energy to make that happen and what energy I managed to recover after getting some rest should be put toward figuring out how to deal with the plague in my world.

Not to mention the second we stepped through the alley wall the *naiad* would be able to turn to water — since the other world's natural shifting abilities worked in both worlds — but Del would lose his ability to control her.

And I wasn't going to hope that Disease Man hadn't mentioned the fact that people only had powers in the other world and not their own. I had to assume that she knew and the second we crossed over, the guys would lose their magic and she'd be able to escape.

Crap. I wished I'd been thinking about this when I'd first told Janice to catch the duplicates. But I'd been so focused on containing the disease and healing everyone, I hadn't been thinking about what would happen afterward.

While I thought, Rion told Del and Aethan what had happened with the security guards, the FBI, Janice, and about healing everyone in the convention center who'd been infected — the last part making the *naiad* deflate even more and glare at me.

An hour later, the last remaining duplicate staggered in, looking exhausted and wearing rags. The *naiad* held out her hand as if to hug her and the duplicate stepped into her embrace and the two merged into one.

"It's done," the *naiad* said. "Now what?"

"Now we put you back in your world."

She scowled. Guess she didn't like that idea. I didn't care.

Rion met my gaze and I could see the question in his eyes, but I didn't want to say anything about what I'd decided in that last hour while in front of the *naiad*. But then he gave a tight nod, all question vanishing from his gaze, as if he'd come to the same conclusion I had — and in a fraction of the time. Well, I was exhausted from having healed *thousands* of people.

We covered her up in some of my layers, snuck out the closest exit, headed away from where the FBI guys had been, and hailed a cab.

Luckily this one was a mini-van and big enough to take all six of us. It still groaned under Keph's weight, but it got us to the alley across town.

I got to the wall, put my hand on it, and Keph pushed the *naiad* through.

And that was that.

It wasn't great or perfect, but it was the best I could come up with.

Now I needed to sleep.

Then we'd find the man behind all of this, the one with disease powers who could cross worlds like I could, and then I'd somehow heal an entire city.

Sure. Easy.

CHAPTER 7

DELPHON

W E'D ARRIVED BACK AT ANNIE'S RESIDENCE TIRED AND HUNGRY. THE man who Annie had healed in the alley when we'd first been searching for the *naiad* and who she'd said could stay in her residence for a couple of nights had been there. But he hadn't wanted to stay with a group of strangers, and Annie had given the man some green papers and wished him well before sending him off.

While we'd been waiting for the naiad's duplicate to return, we'd gotten the whole story about what had happened to Annie, Rion, and Keph after Aethan and I had taken and hidden with the *naiad*. It was... mind-boggling and there was still a lot left to do before the whole situation was over.

The trouble was, neither Aethan nor I knew this place well enough to go anywhere or do anything to help out while Annie recovered from healing all those people, so, we waited.

Luckily Annie had bought some food on our way back to her home, so at least we weren't starving any longer.

Now Keph was asleep, sprawled on Annie's common room floor, and Annie was in her bed, also slumbering, while Rion slept on the floor next to her. Aethan and I had slept in shifts, watching the *naiad* in turns while we'd waited for Annie and the others to deal with the guards and then the infected people. So we weren't that tired now. I tried to think, while Aethan paced, moving normally for a few steps then zipping forward, hard to see before reappearing somewhere else still just pacing. I didn't know if it was helping him to calm down or not.

I, too, tried to find some calm, but alas, it was fleeting, slipping from my mental grip the second I thought I had some, my thoughts constantly jumping back to what had happened and about Keph and Rion and their new relationship with Annie.

She'd mentioned — glossing over the details — that she'd bonded with Keph, and how she was able to borrow abilities from those she'd bonded with.

Which was amazing and unheard of and made her look more and more like the goddess we'd all initially thought her to be.

And no matter what I tried, I couldn't help but imagine her kiss, those soft lips on mine, her body pressed close, arms and legs entwined—

I tried to shove those thoughts aside. They weren't helping. They only made me more uncomfortable... although not as uncomfortable as I could have been if I still had my pants on. We'd disrobed as soon as we'd returned to Annie's place, feeling much more at home with nothing on — which, given the customs of Annie's world might have also explained why the old man hadn't wanted to stay with us.

With a heavy sigh, I changed positions on the long couch from sitting and watching Aethan's fast-slow stuttering movements, to putting my feet up on one end and resting my head on the other and—

I started awake. Someone had called my name.

Apparently, I'd fallen asleep and had been dreaming of Annie and me, unencumbered by clothes, frolicking in the sea.

I rubbed my hands over my face, disappointed that I'd been

woken and glanced at Aethan who was looking at me with a wide grin.

"Sleep well?" He jerked his chin toward a tired looking Rion coming out of Annie's room, which sent a spike of jealousy twisting in my gut even though I knew he'd slept on the floor. "The goddess wants to see us."

My jealousy snapped to hope for a moment, but I quickly shoved the feelings down. This was most likely *not* what I hoped it would be.

I stood and Rion took my place on the couch, falling asleep before I'd even closed the door to Annie's room behind me.

She sat in bed with a glint of something — mischief perhaps? — in her eyes, looking mostly refreshed. It stunned me to see how fast she recovered, but then she was a goddess, or as close to a goddess as someone could be, and it made sense that she recovered faster than normal.

She'd pulled the blankets high on her chest, but I could tell from her bare arms and shoulders that she wasn't wearing anything beneath them... or maybe that's what I wanted to think. And even if it wasn't true, the idea was a strong enough tease that my already semi-hard erection from my dream grew harder, which was strange and amazing and wonderful. Women in my world didn't wear much clothing if any and while I'd been attracted to and had reacted to many women, I had never reacted like this with anyone but Annie. Gods, she was beautiful with her gold eyes, red-blond hair, and the mysterious spots on her face and arms.

"We need to... talk," she said with a coy little smile that made my heart skip a beat.

Was I right? Were my dreams about to come true?

I glanced at Aethan. He'd caught her smile too and was trying to hide a hopeful grin and doing a terrible job at it.

"Yes, Annie?" Aethan said. "We're here for whatever you need."

"That," she said softly, "is exactly what I was hoping you'd say."

She let the covers fall away from her, and, as I'd suspected, was wearing nothing, giving us a stunning view of her full, inviting breasts.

She slid her legs out from under the blankets over the side of the bed, and they too were bare. Then she rose, letting the coverings fall away and stood before us nude and proud and beautiful. Gods, but she was amazing!

Her gaze locked onto mine and seemed to hold my very soul. Then, she slid her attention to Aethan, capturing him for a moment as well. Finally, she let out a heavy sigh. Her coy smile slipped away and she lost a hint of her glory.

"I'm afraid," she said softly, "that what we faced these last few days is only the beginning. Disease Man is still out there and I can't shake the feeling that he's not the only one like me who can travel between worlds. That, and there are more people, most likely a lot more people, who'll need to be healed."

The memory of her healing the people of Masia until she passed out and her gray-skinned, exhausted look after healing everyone in the convention center flashed through me. She didn't know when to stop and would hurt herself trying to heal everyone.

"Annie, this isn't your responsibility," I said. "You— All of us, we're not heroes. We're normal people who happen to know of a way to cross between two worlds. I don't think—"

"You're wrong, Del." Her stunning gold eyes grew hard with determination. "One of my boyfriends dragged me along to a superhero movie a long time ago. I don't remember much of it, but there's one line that keeps coming back to me. Something about 'having power means having a responsibility.' And I have power. I might be the only one with the power to stop this before it turns into a disaster. Or—" Her gaze dipped down and a soft flush colored her pale cheeks. "Or I could have the power if..."

She could have the power?

My thoughts stuttered. She'd mentioned she'd gained the

powers that both Rion and Keph had gained in this world after she'd bonded with them. Something I'd never heard of happening before. Bonding, as much as it was a significant thing in my world, wasn't anything magical. It was highly symbolic, but not actually binding.

A warmth blossomed in my chest and I realized what she was trying to say and why she stood before us naked.

"You wish to bond with us, to gain greater power," I said.

"Not just power," she said, her voice soft. "Yes, I think I'll need to be stronger to face what's coming, but also—" Her flush deepened and seeped down her neck, making the spots on her skin stand out. "I don't know how to explain it. It doesn't make sense. I barely know you four, but I *know* I'm supposed to bond with you." She took two long strides to stand before me, so close her nipples brushed across my chest. My erect cock pressed against her belly and she stared up into my eyes.

I'd thought myself fully aroused before, but my cock grew harder and my balls tightened. Annie's eyes darted down and she bit her lip. Her breath picked up and she leaned closer, pressing her breasts to my chest.

"I don't know how or why you four came into my life, but my soul hurt when I sent you back to your world. I didn't realize the truth until I bonded with Keph, but I'm supposed to be bonded with you. I don't want to imagine my life without you. All of you." Her voice grew husky and desire burned in her eyes.

The urge to take her right there, lift her onto my cock, bring her pleasure as she claimed me with her kiss, surged through me, but Aethan shifted beside me, reminding me that we weren't alone.

Judging from his full erection, he was probably having similar thoughts. And as I thought that, the image of Annie in my arms, riding my cock returned, except this time Aethan was there, entering her from behind as we thrust into her together.

The vision was gone in an instant, but I was only more aroused at the thought of sharing Annie with the man who was like a brother to me, which made me realize just how true her words were.

I didn't particularly like the idea of sharing a woman, particularly a bonded mate. And yet the idea of Annie bonding with the others didn't bother me at all. In fact, crazy as it was, the idea of her *not* bonding with them felt wrong.

Annie's gaze dipped to Aethan's cock and she gave a light laugh. "I see you're ready. Give me a moment and I'll be with you shortly. But first—" She looked back to me, capturing me with her golden gaze. "There's a process to this. Delphon of Galniosia, will you accept a bond with me? There's no going back from this. I don't know how your bonds usually work, but this one, I believe, is truly binding. I won't do that to you unless it's what you want."

My heart skipped a beat.

"I—"

Did I want this?

I mean, by Hades, yes, I wanted Annie. She was the most wonderous woman I'd ever met: enigmatic and powerful yet still somehow vulnerable. She was so very different, in nearly every way, from the women I'd known before. The trouble was... I really liked being with women.

I'd shared a lot about myself with my friends, these three men, but I'd kept one big secret from them. I spoke often of the 'great prince' of my kingdom in my reports, but had never mentioned that *I* was that prince.

I'd never wanted the responsibility of being a king. I'd loved my position of privilege, but didn't want the responsibilities that came with it. I knew that was selfish and irresponsible, but for the longest time, I'd just accepted that was who I was: a selfish and irresponsible prince, who loved how women flocked to my position of power in the hopes of winning me and becoming the next queen.

I'd loved that life... and hated it.

I'd loved the many trysts with triton noblewomen, but hated that I always felt I was lying to them. It was one of the reasons I'd waylaid our emissary to these meetings in Masia and taken his place. I wanted to be free. I wanted to have a moment in my life where I wasn't a prince, to see what that was like. And it turned out I loved it. I was still a bounder who loved to dally with any woman who'd have me, but there were no perceived promises to them. I wasn't a prince, just a man.

If I accepted this bond with Annie, I'd have to give up all that. Everything. The women, and probably my title. The title would be easy to leave, though the privilege that came with it would be tough to abandon. But I'd live. I liked being just Delphon the triton.

Yet the women...

Didn't matter. They'd been a way to bide my time while I'd been waiting for Annie. I just hadn't realized that until now and I knew, without a doubt, I'd give up all the women in two worlds— in all the worlds, for the one in front of me.

"Yes. I want this."

Her smile grew and she brought her arms up behind my head to urge me down as she rose on her toes to press her lips to mine.

The kiss was everything I thought and hoped it would be, soft and yielding, yet hot and passionate. Teeth nipped, lips pressed, tongues dueled. And she claimed me. I felt it deep in my soul, like a powerful wave sweeping through me as an incredible magic bound me to her with an unbreakable connection. It, along with her kiss, stole my breath.

I grabbed her waist, lifting her, so she wouldn't need to crane her neck back. She wrapped her legs around me and deepened the kiss. Her hips rocked and swayed, and she ground herself against my cock captured between us, making my pulse roar in my ears.

Then she drew back, her golden eyes shining. "I accept your bond," she whispered.

I couldn't move, mesmerized by her eyes and her glorious smile. "And I accept yours." I kept her there, close, my desire growing until her smile turned playful.

"You need to put me down, Del, so I can talk with Aethan."

Oh... right. It wouldn't be fair to Aethan for him to have his moment with her while she was still in my arms. That would be awkward in so many ways. He'd let me have her to myself for our binding, I could give him the same consideration.

I set her down, but she didn't move away quickly. Instead, she grabbed the base of my erection, hard, squeezing as she roughly slid her hand up to the tip, then off.

I shuddered with a minor orgasm, barely keeping myself from bursting with my release.

"I'll be back, for more," she said running a finger over the tip of my cock, before finally stepping away.

By the gods! That had been one of the most sensual and arousing moments of my life. I couldn't wait for her return.

My mind played with images of us together, not really watching as she went to Aethan and had her moment with him. Her words with him were lost to me. I saw them kiss and my heart only swelled for my friend, confirming what my soul said was true: that the four of us belong with Annie.

But something else was swelling too and if I didn't have her now, I was going to explode.

She finished with Aethan, returned to the bed, and laid back, her legs inching open just a hint and her smile turning coy again. "Some time ago, you all promised to ravish me..."

I didn't need any more permission—

Except despite my near-to-bursting erection, I wasn't a small man and I didn't know if she'd be ready for me.

I knelt next to the bed and, sliding my hands up the insides of her thighs, I leaned down to help ensure she would be ready.

She drew in a sharp breath of pleasure as I brushed my lips against her folds, teased my tongue into her, then swept it up her opening and flicked the tip across her clit.

She was wet, and getting more so, and would be ready soon enough, and I guessed her anticipation to join with us had been as aching as mine to join with her.

I kissed and licked, adding my moisture to the mix and drawing soft sighs and making her hips start a slow rocking against my mouth.

"Oh, yes," she sighed, and I flicked my tongue against her clit over and over again, feeling it swell, then sucked on it hard and was rewarded with a deeper sigh of pleasure.

Gods I loved that sound, and I loved it even more coming from Annie.

Lifting my lips away, I slid two fingers into her to test if she was wet and relaxed enough for me. She was close, so I reached deep within her, curling my fingers up to find the magic spot that would heighten her pleasure. With my thumb on her clit, I rocked my hand back and forth, fingers pressing inside, thumb on the outside, working her up until her legs tensed, closing around my head a little and she groaned. Her muscles contracted around my fingers as she shuddered, and she released a loud, breathy moan, as her wetness rushed around my fingers and her body relaxed further.

Now she was ready.

I climbed onto the bed, sitting back on my heels, pulled her closer, and began a slow, teasing thrust into her fully aroused opening.

CHAPTER 8

ANNIE

I LET OUT A SERIES OF QUICK GASPS AS DEL PUSHED INTO ME. HE WAS big, but thanks to the man's exquisite work with his lips, tongue, and fingers I was more than ready for him. Still, just because I could accommodate his large cock, didn't mean I was prepared for the sensation of it slowly filling me. I felt every rigid inch, every bulging vein. It was a blissful agony as I waited for him to bury himself fully, but Del was going so... very... slowly.

I moaned and rolled my head to the side.

It was only then that I saw Aethan, standing at the foot of the bed, erect and ready, his expression pinched as he waited patiently.

My body warmed and tingled with its newly acquired connection to him. "You don't need to wait," I breathed. "There are many parts of me a man can love."

God, where had that come from?

I'd never have said anything like that a few weeks ago. I hadn't thought any part of me was particularly lovable. I knew men were drawn to my full breasts, but I figured once they saw the freckles covering my girls that would be a turn-off.

"Of course, my goddess." Aethan climbed onto the bed.

That was something else I'd never have imagined a few weeks ago. Not only were men calling me a goddess, but... I felt like one. I was worshiped and adored, but more than that, I now possessed more power than I'd ever imagined. I could feel all of their abilities thrumming through me, strength, light, speed, and water. It was amazing. Nearly as amazing as what Del was doing.

He finished his tantalizingly slow thrust, my legs falling wide to accommodate his body. He wasn't as long as Rion, nor as massive as Keph, but that didn't matter. He still felt amazing inside me.

Aethan crawled up the bed next to me, resting on one arm as he leaned down to kiss the oh-so-sensitive nipple of my right breast. His other hand reached out to cup my other breast, and began to massage it, working both of my nipples into tight, aching buds.

Oh, yes! This was just fine with me. To reward the man for his dedicated work, I reached down and wrapped my hand around his cock. He grunted. He must have taken that as a sign I wanted things a little rougher, and he raked his teeth over my nipple.

Oh, wow. His lips formed a seal and he sucked hard, his teeth running roughly over the area again. I cried out in pleasure, in part because of the sensation shooting straight to my core and because Del was finishing the slow withdrawal from his first thrust and I wanted him back, deep inside me again.

Del's next thrust was hard, fast, and surprising. I yelped again, and Aethan growled low as his whole body tensed. Crap. I'd squeezed his cock at Del's sudden thrust.

Except it didn't feel as if Aethan was upset, more like he was trying not to come. He trembled and sucked in sharp breaths and I was sure he *was* going to come, but somehow he managed to hold himself together. God, the man had an incredible control.

He moved his lips from my breast to my mouth, and kissed

with a ferocious, urgent passion. It was far different than the deep, soft and lingering kiss we'd had when I'd claimed him. That had been precious and lasting, lips and tongues mingling in a long, sensual union. This was rough and fierce, and I returned the kiss in kind, tangling my hands in his red mohawk and holding him close.

After a wild, breathtaking moment, he jerked away, and his soft brown eyes were not-so-soft anymore. Fiery passion filled them and his chest heaved with deep, rapid breaths. "I need you."

I felt the same. I wanted him inside me and was about to pull that cock of his up to my lips, when Del said, "Aethan, move away."

The *satyr* looked down at the triton with fire and death in his eyes. He didn't want to move, didn't want to leave being so close to me.

"No," Aethan growled.

"Trust me," Del said with a smile and a wink, "you're going to like this."

Aethan frowned, confusion seeping into his passion, but he eased back as ordered.

I was a little confused as well. What was Del thinking?

He didn't say, but, fully inside me, he reached down, hands under my butt and back and lifted me. I did my fair share of planking, but never really thought I had the 'firm and solid' core of most of the girls at the gym. But with Keph's strength lingering in me, I lifted myself up, wrapping my arms around Del's neck to help support me. With a moan, I wrapped my legs around his hips and pulled myself closer to him, pushing him deeper inside me.

"What are you—" I tried to ask, but with his hands on my butt he had a lot of control and used it to grind me down into him for a moment, which drew more gasps, stopping whatever I was going to say.

He turned and shifted, swiveling around to lay back. I

unwrapped my legs from him, straddling his hips, my full weight pressing down onto that amazing cock.

Del pulled me down, my breasts pressed against his wide hard chest. "How would you feel about both of us inside you at once?" he asked with a mischievous glint in those sea-green eyes. His blue-black hair splayed over my pillow.

Oh?

Aethan moved behind me, straddling Del's legs, and realization kicked in.

Oh!

Aethan pressed his cock against my other entrance, teasing around the sensitive area, letting me know what he intended while waiting for permission.

"Oh, yes!" I exclaimed. I'd never done anything like that before, but I so desperately wanted both of them in me, and Aethan deserved a reward for his incredible patience. "Oh, yes. There's lube in the table beside the bed."

"Lube?" Aethan asked.

"It makes things slide better. I've heard you need it for—" My pulse skipped a beat in anticipation. "For that."

"Oh, like oil!" Aethan's eyes lit up and out of the corner of my eye I watched him open my night table drawer and pull out the lube — thankfully even if he wasn't familiar with tubes of lube, the container was the only thing in my nightstand that looked like it might hold a liquid.

He poured a liberal amount into his palm and pumped his hand up and down his length a few times, before drawing close again, his heavy, shuddering breath washing over my back.

This time, he grabbed my hips, pressing himself at my entrance again, then, pushed slowly past the tight ring of muscle, filling me with a seductive fiery sensation, pleasure mixed with a lick of pain.

He entered inch by inch, pacing himself and giving me time to adjust to him— to both of them filling me. His body trembled—

No. He wasn't trembling so much as... vibrating. The rapid micro-movements of his cock were like nothing I'd ever felt before, heightening my pleasure, twisting me tighter, and relaxing my muscles so he could fully sheath himself within me. And while I had a vibrator, I'd never used it there. God, I was an idiot for not even imagining that this might be something I'd love, because man, this was incredible!

He sank in all the way, his breath heavy, my breath and Del's heavy as well. Need thrummed through me. With my hands on Del's shoulders, I pushed myself up to arm's length and started to slowly rock my hips, unable to stay still.

Aethan slid his hands, also now vibrating in the same way — perhaps all of him was — from my hips, up my belly to my breasts. This was another sensitive area where I'd never thought to use a vibrator, but the way he gripped, pulsating as he was, nearly made me come. Certainly, I was on the verge now.

Shivering lips pressed against my shoulder and neck as he leaned forward. His whole body was vibrating. Oh, God!

Del's hands replaced Aethan's on my hips, urging me quicker in my rocking movement atop him. I knew he was close. I could feel his cock swelling inside me, his head pressed back into the sheets, his gorgeous long blue-black hair splayed around him, but I didn't want him to come yet.

On instinct, I used his water powers, reached into his body and clasped shut the flow of his release at the base of his cock.

He grunted, back lifting from the bed, gasping in — what looked like — exquisite, blissful pain.

I opened my mouth to apologize and release him, but his gaze locked with mine, desire burning in his eyes.

"Don't you dare release me," he said. "I want you to come first."

Gasping, I mentally held him on the precipice as Aethan pumped harder and harder into me, building me up.

I was ready, oh so ready, and a wave of ecstasy so powerful and encompassing I thought I might drown in it, crashed over me with a violent shudder. That was all Aethan needed to find his release and I let go of Del so he'd come at the same time.

The three of us cried out in a series of grunts, wordless screams, and low moans. Yet I got the best of the three of us. Feeling their twin release within me was the most powerful and bliss-inducing thing I'd ever felt and my orgasm simply kept going as the two men pulsed inside me.

Slowly they relaxed, spent, but I remained rigid and trembling in my climax, clamped onto each of their cocks, unwilling to let go.

Aethan began massaging my back, his hand no longer vibrating, just soft and relaxing, while Del messaged my front... which had a whole other, opposite reaction.

When I finally released them, Aethan sighed and withdrew, and I slowly lifted myself off Del and flopped onto my back in the bed, tired for the moment, but still buzzed, my body hypersensitive. And with the two men, one on either side of me now — a little cramped on my double-bed — caressing various parts of me, I was quickly trembling with renewed anticipation.

Aethan slowly slid his hand, vibrating yet again, down my body, and teased the insides of my thigh. That vibration ability of his, moving himself so incredibly quickly, was really quite the trick. Del, on his side, traced lazy fingers over my face, shoulders, arms, and breasts. Where he touched, he left lines of fiery pleasure whispering through my skin, and I finally couldn't take it anymore. The barest of touches was too much, I needed hard and firm. I grabbed his hand and pressed it to a breast.

"Harder," I whispered to him.

He gave a nod, his strong hands gripping and pressing on my flesh as he leaned down and kissed my shoulder. Here again, he began soft and tender. I fixed that quickly, reaching around his neck and head, to pull his lips to mine. I was quickly building to another peak, feeling feral, needing things rough.

My body shuddered as Aethan's pressing fingers brought me to a small climax. Except it wasn't a climax at all, just a ridge on my way to a much higher peak.

Del was all in now, hands and lips hard and demanding. He kissed his way down to where his hand was working on my breast and, as Aethan had earlier, nipped at my hypersensitive nipple. That elevated the wave of bliss I was riding, drawing a gasping, shuddering moan.

"Harder," I whispered again.

He grunted and bit me. I yelped as pleasure spiked hard in my core. Oh, yes! That was exactly what I wanted. A little pain, a whole lot of pleasure.

He plucked my peaked nipple, drawing another delicious spike of pain. Moaning, I arched my back, my body begging for more.

Oh yes, yes, yes.

I'd never wanted anything like this before, never been interested in pain adding to pleasure, but in this instant, it was exactly what I wanted.

Aethan moved, settling on the bed between my legs, resting my calves on his shoulders. He cupped his hands under my butt to raise my hips, pulling me close. With his shivering cock aligned with my opening, he stared down at me, his gaze filled with breathtaking desire and love.

Never before had I felt so wonderful, powerful, and confident with my legs up in the air. Then Aethan pushed into my more-than-ready opening, his vibrating cock sliding against my uber-sensitive channel, making me nearly come with just a single thrust. Shuddering again, I found a new peak and rode that, sensing that I hadn't yet reached the top.

CHAPTER 9

AETHAN

I COULD SEE THE EFFECT I WAS HAVING ON ANNIE. THE WAY HER body trembled, her muscles contracting on the verge of release as my vibrating cock found every sensitive inch of her.

She groaned, the sound muffled against Del's mouth, the man kissing her with a ferocity I didn't realize he was capable of.

It took everything I had not to give in and start thrusting with a matching wildness. But this wasn't about me. It was about Annie and her pleasure, and I shifted her hips a little until she moaned low, bucking in my hands, telling me I'd hit the right spot.

Then I slowly withdrew and pushed back in, hitting the spot again. She clung to Del's head, her fingers tangled in his hair, their lips battling, her breath quick, her gorgeous breasts heaving with each rapid breath.

Another withdrawal and push, this time faster, and her hips rose to meet me, sending a tremor through me that I shoved aside.

I wouldn't come before her. I. Would. Not. It was actually astounding that I was ready to come again so soon after the first time, but I could feel my balls tightening, on the verge of another release.

I shifted forward a little, resting her hips on the top of my thighs, and swept my vibrating hands over her belly, sending one up toward those incredible breasts and the other to her mound, where I messaged her clit with my thumb.

Her hips jerked again.

"Oh, God yes. Please, Aethan, please," she begged, her voice filled with undeniable pleasure.

It astounded me and filled me with such awe. I'd never felt this confident with a woman before or this in control and powerful

But then, no woman had claimed me like Annie had.

That kiss, the moment of our bonding, had been the most inspirational, astounding kiss of my entire life. I'd felt the bond form, my soul locked with hers as our lips had played and roamed. But the true joy had come from simply knowing that she'd wanted to claim me.

Me.

Aethan, the sexual outcast, the uncontrolled 'lusty' *satyr*.

Just knowing that had been enough. Then she *had* claimed me, the magic of our bonding flooding me with strength and power. It was more than I could have ever expected. And from that had come this newfound confidence and control in my love-making.

Even now, I was exceptionally aroused, and seeing Annie's multiple orgasms and knowing I was causing that was enough to make me burst. But I wouldn't. I'd keep my release back, giving Annie so many orgasms she melted into a pool of quivering flesh before I gave myself any kind of release.

And I was well on my way to that goal.

She seemed to have no control over her hips now, the way they were writhing from my ministrations, and she mewled and begged into Del's mouth, no longer kissing him, just holding on for dear life.

"Enough!" she gasped, pushing Del aside and sliding her legs off my shoulders, to sit up. She grabbed my head and — riding so high upon me — pressed my face into the softness of her breasts and ground down on me. "Come, damn you!"

Her hips thrust down hard, and she screamed, her whole body tensing with her release.

I let myself go in that instant as well, my mouth pressed to the top of one of her breasts.

She stayed there for some time, her body jerking with pleasure, her breath hard and fast, as my own release crashed through me.

"Holy fucking-fuck," she gasped. "With guys like you around, I might never leave my bedroom again!" She kissed the top of my head then leaned back a little, which meant my face was no longer pressed into her bosom, giving me a perfect view of her amazing speckled breasts. It was hard to take my eyes off them, but I managed to drag my gaze away and look up at her.

"I thought nothing would beat that first round, with both of you inside me—" She squirmed as if just the thought turned her on again. "But gods! This second time was entirely different and just as amazing!" She squirmed again, pulling herself up a little to rub her breasts against my chest, her soft skin sending tingles rushing through me. If she squirmed much more, I'd be ready for a third round in no time.

But alas, she moved off me and flopped down on the bed. "I don't know how, but I'm both exhausted and more alive and energized than I've ever been before. I feel like I could take on the world."

"I believe," Del said with a satisfied grin, "that was the point."

I'd never shared a woman before, but with him it seemed almost natural. We were close enough as friends that it hadn't been awkward. Instead it had been— Well, it had been the best sex I'd had in my entire life. I, too, felt powerful and ready to take on the world — and also just a little exhausted.

"Let's see if the others are awake. I think it's time to make some plans," Annie said sliding over to the edge of the bed. She tried to stand but couldn't, sitting back down on the bed heavily, laughing.

"My legs don't work," she giggled. "You two have fucked me so hard my legs don't work." She turned back to us. "I guess one of you will have to carry me into the other room."

With my super-speed, I was up and beside her, standing next to the bed with my hand extended in an instant.

Annie started at my sudden arrival next to her. "I'm going to have to get used to that," she murmured. "Hand me that robe." She pointed behind me to the heavy, fuzzy garment on the floor.

I did as asked, and she put it on while sitting, then smiled up at me. "Okay, now I'm ready, let's go."

I rushed her first to the bathroom where we cleaned up a bit, then into her common area and set her in a chair at her dining table. Thankfully, unlike the first time I'd used my speed with her in my arms, she wasn't sick. Instead she was giggling again.

"I think now that I have access to your ability, I'm good with being whisked around like that."

Well that was good, because I wanted to whisk her anywhere and everywhere.

"Any time," I said with a bow.

"You sure made a lot of noise in there," Rion said, sitting up on the couch. "Could hardly get a wink of sleep out here." Yet he was smiling and looked refreshed enough.

Del strode out of Annie's bathroom, also cleaned up, and joined Rion on the couch, while Keph sat up from his spot on the floor, but stayed where he was.

"Good," Annie said. "We're all ready. Time to get down to business."

CHAPTER 10

ANNIE

"WELL... FUCK," I HISSED, MUTING THE TV.

With the *naiad*'s duplicates having been out in the world while I'd been healing everyone in the convention center — yeah... I'd done that... wow! — I'd wondered if there'd been anything on the news about a spreading disease. And it hadn't been good news.

I'd forgotten about Disease Man. I mean I hadn't really forgotten about him, I just hadn't thought about the implications of him also being able to spread the disease. He'd been sent to the hospital because Keph had seriously hurt him in his world, and I'd assumed when the *naiad* had infected the paramedics instead of him that he hadn't kept his powers in this world.

Except Mercy Hospital was reporting a massive outbreak of a nasty disease, one with black spots and terrible death, and it was looking like he — just like I had — had kept his powers. The disease wouldn't have spread as rapidly or killed as quickly if it had only come from those two paramedics.

"Fuck, fuck, fuck."

The guys sat around me, Aethan to my left, Rion on my right, while Del leaned on the back of the couch behind me and Keph sat on the floor by my feet. They were tense. I could feel it even without looking at them.

"He's kept his powers too, it seems," Rion said.

"Yeah, and now I have a lot more people to heal." I wasn't happy about that at all. From the soaring heights of magnificent sex... to that. It made a girl want to gather up her little harem and go get her brains fucked out all over again... preferably some place warm and tropical.

But that silly line from that movie kept repeating in my head. It was my responsibility to help because I could. In fact, with my healing magic I was uniquely suited to do so.

"And we need to deal with this fucker," I said, standing. "I won't let him infect any more—"

"Ah... Annie?" Aethan said.

I looked at him. He pointed at the TV. The story had turned from the outbreak to a murder at the same hospital and was showing a picture of the man who'd been murdered.

"That's him," Aethan said softly. "That's the man who spread the disease."

I blinked. I hadn't actually seen Disease Man so I had no idea what he looked like.

"Wait, what?" I'd automatically assumed the murder victim had been killed by Disease Man for getting in his way as he'd tried to leave the hospital or something, but if the victim was the man spreading the disease...

My head spun. This didn't make any sense... and yet... my words to Del from earlier came back to me: Disease Man is still out there and I can't shake the feeling that he's not the only one like me who can travel between worlds.

I don't know how I knew that, but I was sure that Disease Man hadn't been killed by any normal person. In fact, I was certain it had been someone special like him and me.

But fuck! I didn't know what that meant.

I slumped back onto the couch.

"Annie?" Keph asked, concerned. "What is it?"

Aethan shifted closer, while Rion laid a hand on my thigh and Del placed his on my shoulder. Keph turned, kneeling before me and looked at me — our eyes were level when he sat like that. His gaze was filled with love and certainty, but it was clear he was still worried. They all were. But with just a shift of their body language and a determined look in their eyes, they were telling me that they had my back, whatever I chose to do.

I looked at each of them in turn.

"How did I get so lucky?" I hadn't really meant to say that out loud. But hearing my voice say those words, and seeing the concerned looks of the men around me, gorgeous, powerful men who loved me... my emotions broke and with a smile that trembled with a sad mix of joy and gratitude, a tear traced down my cheek.

"You were just you," Rion said softly.

Those were the exact right words I needed to hear.

I wiped away that tear and drew myself up. "Well boys, it seems we have a mystery to solve and some people to heal. Get dressed. We're going out again."

They all dispersed at my words to find their discarded clothes. I pulled out my phone to call Janice from the FBI. I wasn't sure what I was going to say if she asked me about the *naiad* — and a part of me hoped she wouldn't say anything — but I doubted that. She knew we'd had one of the *triplets* in custody and it was her job to apprehend those responsible for this bio-terrorist attack.

Except there wasn't anyone else who might be able to help us. Janice already knew that I, and the people we were after, had powers.

I pulled up her text and was about to dial her number when my phone rang. I was so surprised I dropped it onto my lap.

Picking it up again, I looked at the name: Diane Jenkins.

Work.

Fuck!

What day was it? I had no clue. I'd been healing the convention center for what felt like a week, but I knew it hadn't been that long. Still, it had been longer than a weekend from when I'd first gone back to find the guys infected with the terrible disease. Which meant it was sometime in the work week and I hadn't gone in to work at all.

I answered. At least it was Diane and not my boss.

"Where the fuck are you?" she snapped. "I've been holding down the fort here, but Jake is starting to get antsy. I've told him your bad flu acted up again, but I don't think he believes me anymore. If you want to keep this job, you need to get in here!"

Jake was my boss. The trouble was, I didn't have time for my mundane job anymore. I had a more important job to do.

"Oh God, thank you Diane, but... I can't. And I can't explain why either. Trust me, you won't believe me and neither will Jake. I'm sorry." Time to make a decision. One I didn't like at all. "I'm sorry Diane, but... I think I need to quit. I'll tell Jake in person... well, I'll call him. My life has just been turned upside down these last few weeks and..." And I had other priorities now. Like saving a city from the outbreak of a nasty disease. Then finding out who else was like me and what they wanted. But I couldn't tell her any of that. "And... yeah, sorry."

"Annie, I hope you're okay," she said, sounding concerned and not upset or angry like I expected. "It won't be the same here without you. I'll miss you. We really need to have a coffee some time and you can tell me all about the things no one will believe."

"I will," I said, lying. Not that I didn't want to have coffee with her. I enjoyed her company. But because I wasn't sure where I'd be when all of this was said and done.

We hung up and I quickly dialed my boss. He answered with a harsh, "Annie, where have you been? Are you okay?"

"I am, and I can't explain all the details. But a lot has come up in my life and I can't keep this job anymore. I'm sorry. You've been good to me, and I wish I could stay on until you found someone else, but I just can't. Sorry."

He harrumphed. "I figured it might be something like that. Sad to lose you. Take care." And he hung up. He'd had that 'I'm not angry, I'm disappointed' tone of voice, which was always worse than just being angry, but there wasn't anything I could do about that.

I clenched my jaw for a long moment, wondering how in the hell I was going to pay my rent then quickly dialed Janice before the pressure of the responsibility and panic over the situation took over. I needed to just keep moving, keep focusing on what was important, and that was stopping an 'evil someone' with powers like me.

Janice didn't sound surprised to hear from me — and she didn't sound angry that I'd just up and left the convention center without handing over the *naiad*. Of course maybe she had more important things to worry about, like a rapidly spreading plague.

"Oh, thank God," Janice said. "Have you heard about the hospital?"

"Just saw it on TV, yeah. I'm on my way there."

"I'll send a car. It can get you here faster," she replied.

"A van would be better. With really good rear suspension. I have big friends."

She chuckled. "Yeah, I remember. Lucky you. Car'll be there in five. I'll meet you out front when you get here."

And that was it.

Hunh. Maybe I worked for the FBI now. I'd have to ask Janice if I could get paid to do this healing stuff.

Me. Working for the FBI. Now there was something I'd never expected to think about.

I bet they had an amazing health plan—

The thought made me snort.

I didn't need to have a health plan anymore. I *was* my health plan.

The guys were ready well before I was. Though their suits were all looking a little wrinkled and rough and Rion had lost both his shirt and jacket—

And shit, that was the suit I'd borrowed from Margie for my brother's wedding... which also reminded me that I'd have to explain the guys to my brother and family at some point.

Which would be... awkward, to say the least.

And really, it could wait. It wasn't a priority.

Thankfully I still had the secondhand long-sleeved T-shirt I'd originally bought him when I'd first bought them clothes. It didn't fit the FBI vibe of the others, but it was black and at least matched his pants. That and Keph didn't exactly fit the FBI vibe, either. There hadn't been a suit jacket big enough for him and he'd ripped out the sleeves of his dress shirt.

I had the world's quickest shower and dressed in comfortable slacks and a merino wool pull-over shirt I loved. It was warm, but also form fitting. I was comfortable and looked hot. Odd... I wouldn't have used that word before. I would have said I looked "good", but not "hot." Perhaps having four hot guys who'd devoted their lives to me had changed how I saw myself, but I didn't have a lot of time to mull it over before the car arrived.

It was your standard black government SUV, and it didn't completely give way when Keph got in. So that was good. Although the driver did seem a bit shaken at how the car rocked as Keph settled into his seat.

I sat up front next to the driver and smiled. "He's big boned."

God! That brought up thoughts of his 'bone' which made me giggle. The man looked at me strangely, and I snapped my mouth shut, swallowing my laughter. Government workers shouldn't giggle. But then I thought of all of the guys' 'bones' and how they were all commando under those suits. That was just a little too sexy a thought for being on my way to heal hundreds of people and I pressed my legs together and thought of diseases. Yeah, that dried me up real quick.

The car had a hidden set of flashing lights and a siren, so, we blasted through traffic and were at the hospital in record time.

All the entrances to the hospital had heavy plastic quarantine entrances set up in front of the actual entrances with men standing guard from preventing anyone from entering or exiting the building.

Janice stood out front in a black coat, huddled against the strong wind coming off the lake. Flurries blasted sideways around us as the guys and I went over to meet her. When this was all over, I was going to join the guys in their world for a while. I deserved a vacation... with four sexy cabana boys serving my every whim. Oh yeah, that was happening.

For now, though...

"What do we know?" I asked as we got close.

She led us to a temporary structure a couple dozen feet away from the hospital. The temporary structure wasn't what I'd call comfortable. Even though there were heaters blasting, it was still a bit chilly. At least it was out of the wind. Perhaps it hadn't been here long enough for those heaters to do their job. Inside FBI agents and doctors bustled about and consulted with people wearing CDC jackets.

Perhaps someone at the CDC had actually listened to my warning call.

Janice stopped at a small table near the back with piles of papers scattered on it. "The numbers we're getting at the moment are roughly five hundred infected, with over a dozen fatalities so far and a few more on the brink." She looked up. "Are you recovered now? It's only been about a day since I saw you last." She squinted at me. "You certainly look recovered. In fact, you look great. God—!" Her mouth quirked. "Perhaps I should be saying *goddess*?"

"I'm feeling well enough to tackle this. Five hundred doesn't seem like that many."

"Really?" Janice asked, her eyes widening. "It seems like a whole lot to me. And they're far more infected here than they were at the convention center."

"Right, good point," I replied. "That will take more out of me, but I still think I can do it." I turned to Keph. "Ready to help me with some strength?"

He nodded, though he didn't look as refreshed as I felt after a day away from this slogging work.

"You can have strength from all of us," Aethan said. "I know we're not as strong as Keph is, but we can help."

I held out my hand to him and Keph. "Then help you shall, let's do this."

"Here? Now?" Janice said. "I thought you had to touch the person."

Oh, right... and yet...

That had been true yesterday, but I hadn't possessed Del's powers over water. I hadn't even realized it, but I was sensing all of those 'bodies' of water around me. And even at a distance, in the hospital, I felt the various people in there. More than that, combined with my own healing ability and knowledge of this disease, I knew who was infected and who wasn't. I could heal them from where I was. It would take more effort, but it would save time and with lives on the line, that was what was most important right now.

"Yes, here."

"You continue to amaze me," Janice whispered in awe.

"I continue to amaze myself," I mumbled, then I closed my eyes and reached out. I sought the most infected first, some with the very last of their lives ebbing from them. Those I healed first.

There were perhaps twenty in such need, and another fifty or so not far off.

Aethan gasped, releasing my hand and staggering back. Oops, I must have drawn too much from him.

"Sorry," I said, returning to myself. I looked over at him. He was pale, his eyes wide.

"I'm fine," he gasped, clearly not fine. But I knew he'd recover without any additional healing from me, he just needed time.

Rion stepped in to replace him, taking my hand.

"You sure?" I asked.

He nodded.

"Here we go again." I felt back to those in the hospital. Now, with the dire cases taken care of, I could take a bit more time. And time it took. Somewhere along the line Rion let go and Del stepped in.

I finished with those at the hospital and still had power to spare, though I was exhausted and felt Del and Keph were too, but still… There were people out in the city who could be spreading the disease. I needed to heal everyone, and I might as well do it now before there were twice as many infected.

So I reached out past the hospital, growing my awareness of 'infected-water' to the entire city. It strained my new-found powers with water to do so, but I felt I had a good enough radius to hope-fully catch everyone now. I pushed healing out to the hundreds— No thousands of infected bodies. Luckily, most of the infections were mild and easy to heal.

Del fell away. Even Keph released me and — as if through distant ears — I'd heard a thud and a shake of the earth. My pulse stuttered for a moment and I prayed he was well, but I had to finish what I started or everything I'd done so far would have been a waste.

Time expanded, drawn out, as I moved from body to body, water to water, healing… so very many.

Then... it was done! The city was cleansed.

I drew in a long breath, my head spinning, and opened my eyes to find the guys resting around me and myself sitting in a chair that hadn't been near me before.

"I'm done," I said, though it came out as a croak, my voice hoarse.

It was dark outside. At some point the sun had set and I hadn't noticed.

Janice looked over from some papers she was reviewing. "You've healed the entire hospital?"

"I've healed the entire city."

Her jaw dropped and her eyes flashed wide. Then her expression turned serious. "Was that worth it? We still haven't found the final triplet. She could still be out there infecting people. The one we had in custody died. Or at least we think she died, then she disappeared, but we never found the last one." She glanced around the tent then drew closer. "And you never handed over the one you caught."

Crap. I knew it would happen, but I'd been seriously hoping she'd have forgotten about that.

My pulse tried to pick up with fear that she was going to arrest me and my guys, but I was just too exhausted.

"We've taken care of the one we caught and her... sister," I said, praying she'd accept that and not force me to outright lie to her. Then I realized that 'take care of' could mean we'd killed her. "She's— They're not dead, but they won't cause any more trouble. Our prisons wouldn't really be able to hold her and—"

"And the fewer people who know, the better," Janice said with a tight nod. "I'm not sure how I'm going to explain any of this to my boss. I'm not even sure I completely get what's going on, but we owe you and I'd rather not make trouble for a goddess."

I released the breath I hadn't realized I'd been holding. "Thank you."

"I'll let people know the hospital and the city are disease free. They'll want to do their own verification of course, but..." Janice shook her head as if she still couldn't believe I'd just healed the entire city and headed to the front of the tent to speak to two women standing over another table.

I slumped in my chair, exhausted.

"How're you guys doing?" I asked.

Keph was out cold and snoring, but I got nods from the others. Good.

"I can't believe you did that," Aethan said, his voice filled with awe. He looked the most recovered out of all of them. "You exhausted us all, even Keph and then kept going for hours!"

"That's me," I said, eyes drooping, exhaustion pulling at me. "Annie Chambers, Goddess extraordinaire!" Then I fell into a black pit of unconsciousness.

CHAPTER 11

KEPHAS

I BLINKED MY EYES OPEN. THE HARSH LIGHT OF ONE OF THE MIRACLE lanterns of Annie's world pierced my eyes, and I sat up so I wouldn't be looking directly at it.

We were still in the strange tent outside the hospital and I was still tired and drained, but I had no idea how much time had passed. I'd given Annie everything I could, then I'd simply sat down, fell back, and slept on the spot. When you're used to sleeping on stone, everywhere was comfortable.

"Look who's up," Del said with a nod in my direction. "I didn't think we'd see you for a while."

"I'm tougher than *you* look." It was a joke, but it came out dry and harsher than I wanted.

Del looked a bit offended at first, then shrugged and nodded. "Well... yeah, you are."

Annie was asleep, draped in a chair, her legs splayed out in front of her, not looking comfortable at all.

"We should lay her down," I said.

The other guys all looked over and then looked to each other. "Why didn't any of us think of that?" Rion asked.

"We're all tired," Del said, gently picking Annie up and moving her to a small bed, which looked to be little more than fabric pulled taut over a metal frame.

Then we all simply stared at her for a long moment.

I didn't know what the others were thinking so I figured I might as well say my thoughts. "She's truly amazing."

The other three nodded solemnly.

"She kept going long after you collapsed," Aethan said. "I didn't think..." He shook his head. "Yes, amazing." I could sense his awe and wonder... and love. I felt it from all of them.

"So... is this our life now?" Rion asked.

It was the same question I'd been thinking, and from Del's grunt and Aethan's nod, I could tell they'd been thinking the same thing. We'd all bonded with Annie, dedicating our lives to hers, but... I didn't think any of us had truly thought about what that would mean for us.

"It is," Del said softly. "And speaking of our lives, there's something I need to tell you all."

"You're the 'great prince' of Galniosia you're always talking about?" Aethan said. It was a question, but he already knew the answer.

Del's eyes widened with surprise and it was Aethan's turn to grunt.

"Yeah, we know," he said. "Figured it out a long time ago."

I hadn't figured it out, but then I wasn't as quick witted as Aethan was. But he had told me the last time our group had met, so I wasn't surprised by the announcement.

"You do? You did?" Del asked.

We all nodded.

"But... you let me go on..." Del, frowned, his expression turning a little pained. "I must have looked like such a fool."

"Yeah, but we love you anyway." Aethan punched him lightly on the shoulder and chuckled and Del released a heavy sigh.

"Well anyway, I considered what it would mean to devote myself to Annie and I'm ready to give up my title. I'd give up anything for her." I could see the truth of that in his blue-green eyes, his devotion and dedication the same as mine.

"I'll be giving up my position as well," Rion said, sounding like he was just making the decision as he spoke. "I can't be in the sky navy of my people and here with Annie. I can't have divided loyalties, and frankly, I didn't want the promotion I was about to get anyway. This life will be much... simpler. Though I suspect it won't always be easy. Like today."

That was true.

And I was glad for Rion. He'd seemed so torn when he'd told us about his promotion. He hadn't talked much about his life back in the Phyllidian Forest, except to say it hadn't been easy. Yet, I got the sense there was far more behind those few words. I got the sense he felt driven to prove himself, but to who or why I didn't know, and I'd never asked. Yet, now that he'd given his life over to Annie, he seemed much happier.

"I have little to leave behind," I said. "I have no title or position. The only reason I was selected as emissary was because I had an interest to see the rest of the world, which is an anomaly among my people." Warm contentment seeped into me, my words making me feel steady and certain. This was where I belonged and who I belonged with. "I, too, have accepted this new life. Even if I'm going to spend most of it sitting, it seems. But then again, that's nothing new. I've had to do that everywhere outside the stone halls of my people."

We all looked at Aethan.

He shrugged. "I have little to give up. I wasn't anyone important and most of my people were glad to have me go off and be our emissary. I'm like you Keph, I just wanted to see other places. I guess I'm doing that by Annie's side now." But there was far more behind his casual words. I sensed his new-found confidence and inner-strength and was glad he'd found that.

"Then we're in accord?" Del asked. "All together? All for Annie?"

We all nodded.

"So..." Rion cleared his throat, his expression turning uncomfortable. "Are we all set on... sharing her?"

"I don't see any issues with it," Del said. "Aethan and I were together with her and it was..." His brow furrowed. "Well, if you'd told me before all this that I'd be sharing a woman in bed with another man, I'd have scoffed at you. That idea didn't appeal to me at all, but..." A soft, silly grin tugged at his lips. "With Annie, it's different. I want her to have everything, the highest heights of joy, and if that means another man is with her when I am, I can accept that." He shrugged, his smile growing. "And frankly, you're all like brothers to me. There's no one I'd rather share her with."

"Exactly," Aethan said. "We've all dedicated ourselves to her, we're all hers, and that brings us even closer now. I think we also need to be dedicated to each other, and to our mutual... worship of our shared goddess."

Rion nodded and glanced at me. There was a hunger in his eyes, but I knew it wasn't for me, he was remembering something, and I think I knew what.

"When Annie was bonding with Keph, I found that incredibly —" He drew in a sharp breath. "I think this could work. We're not so much sharing as we're all dedicated to making her happy any way we can."

I nodded. "Agreed." Looking around at this odd structure of canvas and metal, I shook my head. "Even if that means living in her world, strange as it is."

"I would like to learn to operate one of those *cars*!" Aethan said excited.

"I would like to get back to some water once this is all over... with all of you, and Annie of course," Del's said wistfully.

"And I to the skies," Rion added. "I fear that I may need to find some secluded place for that in this world."

I didn't really have a grand desire. Well I guess I did. I just wanted to be able to stand up inside and not break anything. But that was unlikely in most places I went, not just here in Annie's world.

"I don't know about the rest of you, but I'm looking forward to what comes next," Aethan said, which was obvious from his pent-up energy.

"Careful, you might just get something you didn't want at all," I advised.

His gaze darted out the opening to the hospital and he grimaced. "I suppose."

Annie stirred and we all turned to her, but she didn't wake, just adjusted herself on the small bed.

When Del turned back to the group, he, too, was frowning. "What if the old gods were like her? From her world?"

"You mean the ancient gods?" Aethan asked. "I guess that could be possible. If they had powers because they weren't from our world, *and* also acquired power from others like Annie has acquired ours, they'd certainly seem like gods to a more primitive culture than ours."

"Look around you, Aethan." Rion motioned to the tent we were in. "Our world, our culture is more primitive compared to this."

"I know, but I meant... *more* primitive. And we're not the only ones who think Annie is kin to gods. That other woman seems to believe it as well. So even in this advanced culture people are willing to believe someone with such powers is... god-like. Imagine what people thousands of years ago would have thought?"

Rion nodded. "True." He cocked his head. "But then, why weren't there more like Annie in the intervening times? What made the old gods disappear and why haven't there been others since?"

That was indeed a good question.

"Perhaps the portals, the ways to cross over from one world to another were somehow destroyed or limited?" I suggested. "If no one could find them then...?" I shrugged.

"That's very possible," Del said. "It seems likely. It would take just the right person to come in contact with just the right place."

Everyone nodded.

"If it is indeed that hard to cross over, then..." I looked over at Annie's slumbering form, my heart filled with desire and love for her. "What happened to us with Annie must have been fate."

CHAPTER 12

ANNIE

I WOKE FEELING REFRESHED AND SAT UP, SWINGING MY LEG OVER THE side of the army cot that was tucked against the wall of the shelter outside the hospital. My guys were all close and looked over at me, their expressions warm and relaxed. There was something different about them, something... united?

"How long was I out?" I asked.

"Pretty much a full day," Aethan said with a soft smile.

Before I could ask about it, Janice came over.

"Good you're up. We've done a sweep of the hospital and everyone has been cured. They're calling it a miracle. Even though I know it was you, I still think it's a miracle." She shook her head. "If there's ever anything I can do for you, just let me know."

I grinned. "Actually, do you think I could be hired on as a contractor or something? All this running off to heal people in the middle of the day means I've lost my job."

"I don't know why it surprises me that you had a normal job. I'm assuming it *was* a normal job?"

"Yeah, admin guru at a software company. Then this whole god thing sort of got in the way."

"I bet," she said. "I'll see what I can do. I have no clue what I'd put down as your skill-set, but I'll figure something out. Maybe Immunologist? Anyway, thank you for everything. The car is ready to take you back to your place whenever you're ready." She nodded, then hurried off on other business.

So, perhaps I *could* get a job with the FBI. That would be... interesting.

I turned to the guys. "Shall we go?"

They nodded and stood with me. As we left, they formed up around me in a protective square. It was done without words, as if on instinct, and it made me shiver just a little with the precision and decisiveness, knowing this was all for me.

The large black SUV was parked at the side of the road, the driver outside. He nodded to us as we got near, but what drew my eye was the sleek white limousine parked a few feet in front of the SUV. A large man stood next to it as well, and as we drew close, he called out, "Annie Chambers?"

I stopped and all the guys tensed, ready for danger. Again, I got a thrill at the intense sense of protection and well-being I felt with the guys around.

"It's okay guys," I whispered. I didn't know if it was okay at all, but I felt reassured with them close by.

"Yes?" I called out to the man.

He motioned to the rear door of the limousine. "My employer would like a word with you."

A sense of foreboding whispered down my spine and I fought a shudder. If this were a movie, it would mean I was about to speak with a benefactor or a baddie, and the benefactor was the least likely of the two options.

Except... I was curious. I'd been wondering if there was more going on and I had a sense this was the only way to find out.

"Sure." I headed for the limousine and without needing to tell the guys, they headed with me.

"I don't like this," Del muttered as the others made noises of agreement.

I was about to call to the driver of the SUV and tell him he wouldn't be needed when the man next to the limo called back, "Just you, not the men."

My heart froze.

Yeah, this wasn't going to be a warm and fuzzy meeting. Instantly I was on alert. I liked having the guys around me. It made me feel whole, loved, protected, and warm.

"Not going to happen," Rion said.

The limo driver shrugged. "If you want to find out what's going on, you'll come, alone," he replied to me.

And damn it. I *did* want to know what was happening. With Disease Man dead, I was pretty sure there was someone else with powers out there, and I couldn't risk that they weren't behind trying to infect the world.

Well, fuck.

"Annie, you can't go with them. I have a bad fee—" Del said, but I turned to him, cutting him off.

"Listen." I lowered my voice and spoke quickly. "Whoever this is might be behind the plot to infect everyone. Just because Disease Man is dead and we've healed everyone, doesn't necessarily mean this mess is over. We need more information and this is the only way to get it. Tell the SUV driver to follow us and that if he loses us, you'll tear off his head. Sound reasonable? That way you'll always be nearby."

They frowned at me, their expressions clear that they didn't like my plan and needed more. Frankly I wanted more assurance as well, but there wasn't much else we could do.

"Del, take out the phone I gave you." He did. "Turn it on."

I did the same with mine. The guys were huddled close, with Keph on the side facing the limo, and I was fairly certain no one would see me playing with my phone.

I quickly called the other phone then shoved my phone back into my pocket. "Leave your phone on. You'll be able to hear what's happening with me. If things go bad, have the driver ram the limo and stop us."

From their expressions, the guys still didn't like the plan, but this option seemed acceptable.

"Be careful," Aethan whispered.

"Always," I said, and flashed him a grin — though I wasn't feeling nearly as cocky as that grin let on.

The guys broke away from me, and moved toward the SUV. Suddenly I felt exposed and vulnerable... and normal. I knew that wasn't the case, that I still had powers. But I'd felt safe with the guys close.

The large man opened the limo door, and I slipped inside and sat on the rear seat of the large back passenger area.

I wasn't sure what I'd expected, but the immaculately attired and stunningly gorgeous woman sitting on the rear-facing seat at the front wasn't it. Her face was lean, but her lips were full. Large silver-blue eyes peered out from under perfectly tended lashes and brows and raven black hair framed her face, falling to her shoulders in lustrous waves.

There was no one else in the vehicle and I felt a bit better with it being just her and I, especially with all of the guy's powers tingling within me. I could be over to her in an instant with super speed, or blind her with Rion's light and be out of the car just as fast.

"So, who are you?" I asked as the driver closed the door, sealing me in with her.

The woman smiled, but it wasn't a friendly smile. Something about the predatory nature behind her eyes made the smile more like that of a tiger about to have lunch, and I was the lunch.

"Annie Chambers, I—"

"No, that's me, who are *you*?" I couldn't help the jab. It might not have been the smartest choice, but I couldn't help myself.

She blinked. "Impertinent, aren't we?"

"Just curious. You're the one who invited me in. Thought you should at least introduce yourself."

The driver got back into the driver's seat, started the car, and pulled away from the hospital.

"To the rest of the world I'm June Olympios," the woman said. "But you can call me by my real name. Hera."

One of the guys — Aethan, I think — swore so loud I could hear it faintly from the phone in my pocket.

June... or Hera, cocked her head to one side as if listening. She looked at me... then directly at my pocket.

"Do we have others listening in?" she asked, her tone darkening with annoyance, before raising a delicately sculpted eyebrow. "I suppose I can understand the precaution. But understand this, Annie, I'm not here to hurt you. I don't want to be your enemy. I want us to be friends."

Hera... That was Greek. My mind spun back to my one college class on mythology. Hera was the queen of the gods? Married to Zeus? I didn't know much more than that. It certainly wasn't a common name these days.

Also, I'd barely heard Aethan's voice over my phone and she was ten feet away. How had she heard?

Of course!

I'd already guessed there was someone else with powers involved in this, so I shouldn't have been surprised. The bigger question was: how much power did she have and was she the big boss or another henchman like Disease Guy? Also, was she on my side and not involved in trying to spread the plague—

No. From that evil look in her eyes, I doubted she was one of the good guys.

And I wouldn't really know anything unless I asked.

Well, she wanted to be friends... *Let's see how friendly she wants to be.*

"Your man said you'd explain what's going on. While you're at it, you can also tell me how you heard my phone from over there and... well if you want to be friends so bad, you might as well tell me everything about yourself." I sat back, hoping I looked over confident and had made her think that I hadn't already figured out she had powers. Hopefully if she thought I was stupid she'd tell me more.

"That's fair." She leaned back as well, at ease, mirroring or mocking my position. "My story begins around three thousand years ago."

I tried not to gape.

Three *thousand* years? I hadn't expected that.

"You look good for your age," I said, hoping I sounded calm and not completely shocked.

"I do, don't I?" She smiled, that same predatory smile. Perhaps it was her only smile. "If you know anything about Greek mythology, then you'll know the name Hera."

"Queen of the gods?"

"Indeed, yes."

"And that was you?"

"It was."

Holy fuck. Three thousand years! "Your powers— You— How —" I stammered all attempts to play it cool vanishing.

I didn't know how that was possible. Could her magic— could *my* magic let me live that long?

She chuckled at me as I opened my mouth and closed it again.

"I was the first," she said, "But I was foolish enough to share the knowledge with my friends. They too became known as gods. Zeus, Athena, Ares, Poseidon, Demeter, and so on."

The first? I couldn't help my eyes going a little wide at that.

"Really?" I tried to sound interested and not stunned and knew I was failing miserably.

"I assume the four men with you are from Eytheron, the other world?"

She knew the name of the other world? That was a first. I wasn't even sure if the guys knew its name. I also didn't know how much to give away and hoped a simple: "Yes," wouldn't be too much information.

She nodded. "In my time, our two worlds were closer, the gateways much more numerous. Their kind came and went from our world and ours from theirs. Yet I was the first to forge a bond with one of them. And as you've done, I followed that up with others. I shared the bonding ability with my friends and as they gained powers, they rose to rule over our small corner of the world."

Of course they did. Because it couldn't have been kind, benevolent people who gained superpowers... and even if they had been kind, would they have eventually taken over? Would I? I was bulletproof thanks to Keph. It would take more than just a cop or FBI agent with a gun to stop me if I wanted to take over Chicago or even the world.

"As I'm sure you've discovered, you take their powers and keep your own. That was always how the bonds were meant to work, granting us greater powers and taking them from their kind."

"Taking?" I'd felt like it was more along the lines of borrowing. The way Hera spoke of it, it sounded like she could take their powers completely away from them.

"Little at first, but ultimately, yes, you can completely take their powers from them. That's how I've come to be who I am, with no others around me to hinder my progress. I was a goddess after all. I took what I needed or wanted and others... accepted it," she said casually.

Too casually. I could almost feel the frosted-mist rolling off her. This queen was made of ice.

"I have powers of immortality, hence why I've stayed so young, and you saw my enhanced senses at work a moment ago. I have other powers as well, but a woman needs her secrets. I don't even know your powers yet." She waved that off with a lazy sweep of her hand. "That can come later. For now, I'll finish my side of the tale."

Because this is all about you.

I bit back my words. Right now this *was* about her. I needed to know as much as I could about her. That, and she was the first person I'd come across who knew what was going on with me.

"As time passed, our worlds grew apart, the portals became fewer and harder to find. They began to shift and scatter, their locations not set, at least in our world. Most of those from the other world returned there. It was their home after all. My fellow gods and I moved on with our lives. Most of them died eventually, not having my true immortality. I used the time over the many ages to start amassing a fortune. As I saw the dawn of the modern age, I began to use that fortune, funding many projects and inventions. Some... did not do well. Alas, Tesla was just too temperamental a genius to be productive. Edison, was a much better bet. And some of my investments did very well. I'm the wealthiest person on the planet by far."

That didn't seem likely. "I think I'd have heard of you, if that were the case."

"In a way, you have." That tiger-smile returned. "I grew to like my anonymity, so I found men to play the part of princes and coal barons, the super-wealthy of their day. But they were doing it with my money. I funded them, gave them a lavish life, and in return, all they had to do was be visible. In the background, I managed their companies and properties. I'm six of the top ten wealthiest people in the world. They all work for me. Either I've bought the company they created — allowing them to keep running it as normal — or they're just actors in my employ."

Holy-fuck.

My thoughts jerked back to something she'd said earlier. "So, you stole powers from men who came from this other world—"

"And women."

Well, that was interesting. "You stole from men and women of this other world, then used them to amass wealth and power? And you want to be friends with me?"

"You make it sound like I'm some villainess. It's not like the beings from their world are truly human. They're beasts and abominations for the most part. Few of them were truly civilized. And trust me, they were well *satisfied* with our arrangement. And yes, I figured if I was going to live forever, I might as well live in luxury. What's so wrong with that?"

Nothing... and everything.

This woman was crazy. I could see that now. There was nothing wrong with living forever in comfort, but she'd taken things well beyond comfort.

And the way she talked about the people from the other world was cold and distant. They were feeling, loving, thinking beings, not abominations. I got the feeling she'd lived with unlimited power for too long.

How did that saying go? Absolute power corrupts absolutely? I was fairly certain I was seeing that personified in front of me.

"I'm always on the lookout for more like me. You slipped under my radar for a while. Until you completely and royally fucked with my plans... twice." The vehemence in her voice was terrifying.

I leaned a little further back into the cushioned seat. Where was the door? How far away? Could I run — with Aethan's speed — to match the car so I wouldn't be tossed out onto the street? Did it matter? I could heal myself.

Her demeanor changed in an instant to flashing geniality with a harmless smile — so she did have another kind of smile.

"But I forgive you," she purred. "You didn't know of my plans.

That's why I wanted to meet you, to let you know who I am, and bring you into the fold."

That sounded less like being friends and more like being her lacky.

"So that disease guy," I said. "He was one of yours?"

"Yes. He was a critical part of my plans. He created the disease and I had the cure. Once the sickness had spread around and everyone was terrified of it, I'd release the cure, and make sure everyone had a dose. I wouldn't charge much, you don't need to when you're selling it to the entire world. It was a glorious plan." She sighed. "But alas, you came along. And since he wasn't of use any more, I retired him."

One of my brows shot up. Retired? "You *killed* him?"

"Of course not. I simply let him go. I don't know who killed him. I assume he'd made enemies along the way. Perhaps one of them did him in." She flashed that genial smile again, but I didn't believe her. If she hadn't killed him, she knew who had and didn't care.

"And what do you want from me?" I asked carefully.

"Simple," she said, all disarming smiles now. "I want you to join me. I already rule this world. I figured I'd let you in on it, if you'd like. Who wouldn't want that?"

I bit back a huff. *No way in hell.*

It was the innocent and charming way she said she 'ruled the world' which let me know she was truly mad.

The question now was... what was I going to do about it?

CHAPTER 13

ANNIE

"A ND JUST OUT OF CURIOSITY, IF I DON'T JOIN YOU, WHAT HAPPENS then?" I asked.

"Well, I'd let you go back to your mundane life, of course." She frowned. "Why? What did you think? I'd kill you if you didn't join me?"

Yeah, a little. "No, of course not," I lied.

She laughed, and that was just a bit terrifying.

"Annie, there's no way you can ever compete on my level. You're an inconvenience at best." That didn't seem to match with how I'd 'royally fucked with her plans.' "If you don't want to be a part of greatness, that's your choice." She leaned forward then, and all the niceties were gone from her face, the tiger returning. "Just one warning, though. Don't act against me again. That would make you my enemy. Then... I'd have to destroy you."

"And what would 'acting against you' entail?" A small part of me was tempted to do just that while the rest of me wanted to run screaming.

"To answer that, I'd have to know the complete extent of your powers. I know you can heal. What else can you do?"

Like I was going to tell her that now. Still I needed to say something. So, I lied. But that meant quickly recalling any and all superhero movies that ex-boyfriend had dragged me to, or what was common knowledge. "I can... fly, and walk up walls... also I'm super tough and strong." Fuck, that last one was the truth. Oh well, couldn't take it back now.

"And do you plan on 'fighting crime' in any other ways in the future with these powers? Now that I know you can heal, I'll stay away from that, at least locally. You shouldn't be called out by the FBI again."

"Crime fighting? Ahhh, no, not really. I just want to live a normal life." With my four hunky roommates. Yeah... because that was *normal.*

"Then I think we'll be fine." She leaned back, the tigress gone once again and glanced out the window as the car pulled up to the curb and stopped.

"I think we're at your place," she said softly. "You can leave now." She motioned to the door.

"Ah... thanks?" I didn't know what to say exactly. I let myself out, seeing the guys piling out of the SUV behind me.

It was disconcerting that this woman knew where I lived, but she was uber-rich, so I wasn't actually surprised.

I waved to the limo as it drove away, though the windows were tinted black and I couldn't see in.

"Are you well?" Aethan asked, zipping to my side in an instant.

"I will be," I said. "Let's get upstairs."

I was a bit shaken, but felt a lot better with the guys around me. All of this was too much to take in and I needed time to digest it all.

I walked up to my apartment in a daze. I was so out of it, I just stood staring at my front door for a minute before remembering I needed keys to get in.

"You seem distracted," Rion said once we were all inside. The guys, as they did, disrobed quickly, not used to being dressed all the time.

"Yeah, I guess I am," I said, looking around at my amazing troop of guys. This caused a whole new distraction. Maybe I needed some life-altering sex to make sense of all this. And if that didn't work, at least I'd have had some life-altering sex.

The question was, with who?

That's when it hit me: Did I have to choose? If they were interested in it, could I have all of them... together... at once? My time with Del and Aethan had been my first threesome. I'd certainly never been a part of a five-some before. It felt more like some sinful orgy. Yeah, that would definitely be the distraction I needed.

"Ah..." I didn't know how to ask for it, though. "Guys... Would you all consider...?"

It was Del who saved me. "You want to be with us, *all* of us, at once?" He smiled. "You sure you'd be up for that?" He'd been serious, a bit concerned, but Aethan dispelled all of that with his next words.

"Yeah, we might just be too much for you. What's that saying of yours? 'Blow your world?'"

I giggled just a little. "It's 'blow your mind' or 'rock your world.' But I think, right now, what I need is to have my world blown."

The guys all shared a look, then nodded. They didn't seem bothered by this at all. Something had definitely changed between them while I'd been asleep.

Keph came over and easily lifted me off my feet, cradling me in his arms. He turned toward my bedroom.

"No," I said softly. I didn't know if my bed could take all five of us and I really wanted this to be special. "We can stay out here."

Keph set me down. They all drew close then, very close. More than one of their erections brushed against me.

They helped me out of my clothes, slowly, patiently. I shivered a little once I was naked, but it wasn't from the cold. With four guys so close I wasn't cold at all. No, I was quite warm and getting hotter. The shiver was the thrill of anticipation, except I had no clue how this was going to work with the four of them.

"What would you like?" Rion asked. "Soft and slow, rough and hard?"

I wanted to savor this moment. "Let's start soft and slow. I'll let you know when I want things to change."

They moved in, hands reaching, caressing. So many hands, warm and rough, teasing over nearly every part of me.

Aethan, standing beside me, turned my face to his. Of all the men, he was closest to my height and our lips met easily. His one hand roamed over my left butt-cheek, while his other cupped my face as we tenderly kissed.

I felt him tremble, whether with anticipation or something else, I wasn't sure, and I opened my eyes to look at him. His eyes were closed and his expression was filled with reverence, reminding me of how we bonded and how much a kiss on the lips meant to them.

I closed my eyes again, giving in to the moment, savoring the feel of Aethan's mouth on mine, and the others standing close, their bodies brushing against mine, their hands caressing and teasing me.

Long fingers slid down my belly, into my curls, and teased my opening, making heat blossom low within me but vanished just as I was getting wet.

They were quickly replaced by thicker, harder fingers: Keph. He was careful at first, then he probed deeper, searching for that magic spot. His thumb maintained a consistent gentle pressure on my clit, rubbing slow, wonderfully torturous circles, and the heat inside me grew.

Large, softer hands — Del — firmly slid up my hips and sides before wrapping around from behind and capturing my breasts.

He slowly started to knead them, working my nipples into tight buds.

I released a breathy moan of pleasure and he shifted closer, pressing his hard cock against my back. The memory of both him and Aethan inside me twisted my desire tighter, and sent a shudder rushing through me.

Rion, kneeling on my other side, hummed with pleasure at my moan, his lips teasing the sensitive skin near my navel, his slender-fingered hands messaging my right thigh, inching higher and higher, closer to where Keph's fingers were starting to drive me crazy.

Gods, this was glorious. I could see how cooperation between them could be a very *very* good thing. And it didn't seem confusing for them at all. There was no jockeying for position or awkwardness. They were working as one to tantalize and stimulate me, and it was breathtaking.

"Aethan," Keph rumbled.

I opened my eyes as Aethan's lips left mine and Keph's fingers slid away from tormenting me.

The guys were all moving, changing positions. Now Aethan was in front of me, Keph behind, and Del on my left, while Rion stayed on my right.

Keph's large fingers slid over my ass to my thighs. He grasped them, his hands easily holding me, making me look tiny and fragile, and lifted me. I leaned back against his massive, muscular chest, and he opened my legs to Aethan, who stepped close and pressed his cock against my more-than-ready opening. Then he began to vibrate.

My breath hitched and my mouth went dry with anticipation. I knew exactly what he could do with his vibrating cock, and I had to have him inside me.

But he teased me instead, brushing around my opening instead of pushing inside me.

The tremor of a climax whispered through me, and my eyelids fluttered shut as my head fell back against Keph's chest.

Oh, God, yes! And he hadn't even entered me yet.

"Annie," Rion murmured, cupping my cheek and turning my head toward him.

I opened my eyes and met his bright blue gaze. With Keph holding me, I was level with him, and he looked at me with the same awe and reverence Aethan had. A soft glow radiated from his skin and even without his wings he looked like an angel.

"You're so beautiful," he breathed and he dipped in and captured my lips in a slow, sensual kiss.

I tangled my fingers into his hair, pulling him closer, deepening his kiss and letting him see how much I loved him — how much I loved all of them.

Rion match my intensity, one hand finding my breast while Del flicked his tongue over my other nipple then sucked on it. I gasped at the sudden sting of delicious pain and Rion slipped his tongue into my mouth, any restraint he might have had, now gone.

Then Aethan finally — thank the gods, finally! — pushed inside me, scattering what little thoughts I had left.

Oh wow. Even after having experience it before, the sensation of his vibrating cock moving inside me was surprising and incredible. He worked me up even further, making me pant and moan with pleasure, before hitting that miracle spot inside me.

I came in a gasping, moaning rush as Del and Rion were both firmly grasping a breast each, hands kneading my flesh, hard and insistent.

We'd moved on from slow and soft, but I didn't care. My muscles contracted with a stunning, shuddering, trembling wave of pleasure.

"I've done my bit," Aethan said, pulling out of me. "Who's next?"

My thoughts stuttered at that. I hadn't even had a chance to give him his own release.

I didn't see what must have passed between them, and they didn't say anything, but before I could protest Aethan stepping aside, they were changing positions again.

Now Del stepped between my legs and pushed into me with one smooth, quick thrust. Even as worked up as I was, his cock felt huge, and just that single thrust nearly made me come again.

He buried himself fully inside me and Keph nudged me forward, pressing me against Del's chest. Instinctually, I wrapped my legs around his waist and my arms around his neck, and Keph moved out from behind me and Rion took his place.

God, I hope they're going to both be inside me at the same time.

Rion boxed me in, his sculpted chest pushing me up against Del's muscled body, and teased my other opening with fingers slick with lube — Aethan must have zipped to my bedroom and gotten it while I was distracted.

I moaned louder, the sound coming out stuttering, my breath coming faster, my desire building again.

Slowly at first, Rion worked one finger then two into me, stretching me, getting me ready, and I ground down on Del, needing more, needing all of it. The anticipation was driving me crazy. I wanted them both, ached to be filled completely.

"Oh yes," I begged and Del captured my hips in an iron grip and held me steady as Rion withdrew his fingers and pushed his slickened tip inside me.

Sensation swept through me, fiery and delicious and full. It was almost more than I could handle and my body heaved, needing to move, aching to be fulfilled. But Del held tight, keeping me still as Rion inched slowly, so damned slowly, into me until he was fully buried inside me.

"Yes," I gasped. "Oh, yes yes yes." I couldn't stop repeating the word. They were perfect like this. Rion's more slender cock fit so well in behind, with Del's thicker erection in front.

Then they started moving, finding a rhythm that spiraled my need tighter and tighter, until another, small orgasm crashed through me.

But they weren't done, and even as I trembled with my orgasm, they picked up their pace. Once again I found that I hadn't reached a peak so much as a plateau on the way to incredible bliss. It felt like I just kept orgasming over and over and even still, knew some greater ecstasy awaited me.

Holy Fuck!

I gasped and moaned and tried to writhe against Del's hold, the urge to move screaming through me. But he and Rion had control of my body and unless I told them to stop — which I sure as hell wasn't — my pleasure was fully within their control.

Then large hands reached from... somewhere to cup my breasts. I didn't even know where Keph was and didn't care as he fondled my already sensitive skin. A few seconds later, his hand began to vibrate, shooting me up to my next peak with another fast shuddering orgasm that made me cry out in pleasure and left me gasping. I didn't know what Aethan was doing to help Keph, but it was working and it was wonderful.

My cry set off Rion and Del, and they came nearly at the same time, swelling and releasing inside me, making my muscles contract in another stunning orgasm.

God, there were no words for the incredible sensation that crashed over me. It swept through every cell of my body, making fireworks explode behind my lids, and sent me spinning. I spun around and around and around among flashes of light— No I *was* the light, blazing bright, fluttering, sparking, trembling with sensation.

When I returned to myself, I was still in the throes of the most amazing, shuddering orgasm of my life, floating, moving, and carefully lowered down to straddle... Oh!

My eyes popped open — had they been closed? — and I met Keph's dark gaze.

He lay on the floor, watching me as the others helped me slide onto his massive, fully-erect, cock. My body shuddered with orgasmic aftershocks as he stretched me and rubbed against hypersensitive nerves.

I took him as deeply as I could, and he still wasn't fully sheathed, but he captured my waist with his large, strong hands and helped me keep my balance.

Another set of hands, swept around me from behind, capturing my breasts as one of the others drew close behind me, and pressed his cock against my other entrance.

My pulse stuttered and I wasn't sure how much more I could take.

Then the cock began to vibrate, and my need jerked so taut it stole my breath. All I could think about, all I craved, was to feel Aethan pushing his vibrating cock into me again.

"I love that sound," Aethan said, his breath feathering across the back of my neck, and I realized I'd released a long, low, throaty moan as he pushed deeper inside me.

He swept a hand down my belly, and teased my clit with his fingers, but instead of staying there, he grasped the base of Keph's cock and made it vibrate as well. The two vibrating erections inside me, one so very very large, the other nowhere near as big, but in a very sensitive area, was just too much.

I cried out as I rocked slowly, back and forth, releasing wave after wave of bliss, each hitting me harder than the last, each fueled by their vibrating cocks.

Aethan slowly pulled halfway out and pushed back in, sending more waves of twitching, contracting bliss rushing through me, the sensation stealing my muscle control.

Oh God, it was incredible and too much. I was going to shake myself apart.

"Please," I begged. "Oh, please." But I didn't know what I was asking for. To stop? To finish? To keep going until I died with a silly, dazed smile on my face?

As one, Keph and Aethan, carefully moved inside me, finding their release with a few quick, shattering thrusts as if they knew I wouldn't be able to take much more. Their bodies tensed and Keph's eyes rolled back with pleasure, and a final, wave slammed over me with spinning stars and whirling darkness.

I didn't realize I'd passed out until I was coming to.

I lay on the couch, bathed in a sheen of sweat with my body aching in all the right and wonderful ways. My nerves were still hypersensitive and whispers of the most amazing climax I'd had in my life trembled through me.

The guys had all cleaned up and sat nearby, but had kindly given me space. Which was good, because I wasn't sure if just being in contact with one of them would send me spinning again.

Del brought me water and I drank thirstily. Even with that, my voice still croaked when I said, "You guys are amazing!" An aftershock swept through me, stealing my breath and making me moan in pleasure.

"We're here—" Aethan began.

"For whatever you need," Rion finished

"Always," Keph added.

And just the thought of more mind-blowing— No that had been so much more than mind-blowing. It had been world-shattering. Just the thought of more sex like that was enough to make me giggle and send another aftershock sweeping through me.

CHAPTER 14

AETHAN

Two days had passed since Annie had met Hera.

Hera. I still couldn't believe that. If there was one overarching villain in most of the tales I knew, it was her. Admittedly, she was justified in her rage most of the time since her husband, Zeus, hadn't been a faithful fellow. Though, if what she'd said in the car had been true, then Zeus may not have been her husband at all. I wasn't certain of anything anymore.

And the thought of her being out there made my skin crawl.

So, I'd been very happy to keep Annie distracted. She'd been insatiable the last few days. She'd sleep for some time, then wake, eat, and want more from us. It was clear she didn't want to think, didn't want to face what she'd learned. And the rest of us were in the same place. So, we'd kept her... busy. Not like it had been any hardship for us.

But now, after waking and having a shower, she was different, serious, pensive.

"Aethan and Keph, put on your clothes, we're going for a walk," she said, her casual command not bothering me or any of the others. Our bond with her was complete and we wanted to serve her. Which didn't surprise me. I was actually more surprised about how unsurprised I was.

"Do you need us?" Rion asked, motioning to Del.

Annie smiled, cupped Rion's cheek and kissed him then turned to Del and kissed him, too. "I will always need you. Both of you. But for this, I'll be fine with Aethan and Keph. Thank you." She looked around. "This place is a mess, though. Could you clean it up a little? I hate to ask that, but—"

"No, don't worry, we'll do it," Del replied, the words easy and quick, a demonstration of our devotion to her. I was sure as a prince he'd never cleaned a day in his life. Also, he lived in a kingdom underwater, so did that mean everything was clean all the time? I didn't know about that. Yet, he hadn't even hesitated to agree to the chore.

Once Keph and I were ready, we were out the door. Annie wore tight leggings, which really showed off every curve of her gorgeous legs and ass. Over this was a tight short-sleeved shirt, again form fitting, but unfortunately hidden by a bulky sweater which hung down to the middle of her thighs. Then she'd added her jacket as well, but even fully covered, I couldn't help seeing her naked and radiant body in my mind's eye.

Just thinking about her made me ache for her, and yet not uncontrollably. I'd had so much amazing sex recently that the thought of her didn't send me into an instant erection.

Sure, I was aroused, but I was also very satisfied at the moment. Being with Annie had helped heal my overly "lusty" nature. Of course it helped that Annie was also fairly lusty and had done her best to tire us all out these past couple days. Still, having more control and restraint with my arousal felt empowering.

"Where are we going?" Keph rumbled.

"Shopping. We need food and you all need more clothes before you destroy those nice ones I bought you. Also, I just wanted to get out and get some fresh air. I need to think." She turned to me. "Do you mind if I pick your brain?"

I was honored. "Not at all. What do you need?"

"I just need to talk. I need a sounding board and your mind is probably the quickest of the group."

I beamed at the compliment. "I'm all yours." And I was.

She was silent for a bit as we walked down the cold, slushy city street, and I could tell she was trying to figure out what she wanted to say.

Keph let us walk a few steps ahead of him. I wasn't sure if I wanted to call him up and tell him to walk on Annie's other side and join us or not. He pondered things a bit longer than the rest of us, but was very insightful at times. However the three of us walking abreast would have taken up all of the walking path — Annie had called it a sidewalk — and other people wouldn't be able to get past us.

That, and I doubted Keph would say much of anything. If he did make a comment, he'd likely make it much later once he'd had time to really think about things.

"What do you think of Hera?" Annie finally asked, her breath misting around her head.

"She's dangerous," I replied without having to think about it. "That much I know from legend. When you were speaking with her, I couldn't see her, but I felt as if... she wanted to somehow devour you."

Annie laughed. "Yeah, she had this look. I called it her tiger-face. It was this predatory look in her eyes and a smile that made me think she wanted to eat me." She was silent for a moment. When she spoke again, her voice was much softer. Annie had been much more assertive and commanding since the events at the convention center, but this tone was subdued, even timid, making my chest tighten. "I'm terrified of her."

I reached out and clasped her hand, squeezing it as we walked. Our joined hands swung between us and she squeezed back.

"We're here for you," I said to reassure her.

She looked at me, concern in her eyes. "But you heard what she said about the people from your world? How she thought of you? It was disgusting. It's like she doesn't see you as real people." She bit her lip, her golden eyes filled with worry. "I'm afraid for all of you as well, of what she might do to you."

"We can take care of ourselves. She'd have to catch me first." I grinned, hoping it was cocky and confident. Certainly, I felt fairly self-assured in that moment. I was pretty fast after all.

"Yeah... but..." She released a heavy sigh. "I lied about my powers. She could have lied about hers, too, or not told me everything. In fact, I *know* she didn't tell me everything. Maybe she has some way to counter your speed? She's three fucking-thousand years old! She has to have ways to protect herself and deal with threats."

I didn't like where those thoughts were going. But there was something deeper going on that I wanted to address. "Annie, she said she'd leave you alone as long as you didn't go against her. Are you thinking of confronting her?"

Her gaze swept over the *cars* stopped at the intersection ahead of us, waiting for the light to turn green. "I think that's what I'm trying to figure out."

"Oh?"

"I mean, yeah, I've got everything I need right now... well except money. That's another problem I'll need to solve, but not right now. I've got some savings. So, why would I even entertain trying to go against someone like her? It's stupid. It's certainly not safe, so why am I even considering it?"

"Why *are* you considering it?" I thought I knew, but it would be more impactful if she came to the realization on her own.

"I..." Now her gaze drifted up to the tall buildings around us as if she couldn't bring herself to focus on me. "I just..."

She sucked in a heavy breath and turned her attention to me. I could see the knowing in her eyes, but also that she didn't want to put it into words. If she did, it would be real and then she knew she'd have to act on it.

"I can't... It would be stupid. I'm not... I mean I am, I guess sort of, but really... I'm just Annie, aren't I? I know you all think I'm a goddess and all, and I did heal all those people but..." She trailed off and my chest squeezed tighter at her worry and self-doubt.

I stopped, and she stopped with me. Turning to her, I grasped her other hand to hold both of them, and locked my gaze with hers. "Just say it. You're talking around it right now, trying to avoid it. Just say it."

Her gaze went from curious to confused to solemn.

"She's evil," she said softly.

I nodded.

"And..." She grimaced. "Aethan we can't... can we?"

"Can't what? Say it Annie." I knew what she wanted to say, knew that deep inside she wanted to fight Hera because she'd been determined to heal all those people. She had a huge heart and knew Hera wouldn't stop her schemes unless someone stood up to her and stopped her.

"We can't stop her, can we? It would be silly to even try. She's so powerful. She's had three thousand years to prepare for this and I've had three weeks!"

I kept my gaze on her as Keph drew closer, a silent, steadfast guardian.

"Aethan, I know she's evil and... well, that's just it... I *know*. And the way she was speaking, I don't know if anyone else knows or cares! She's evil and powerful and she used that other guy to make thousands of people sick. She doesn't care about anyone. She's... an apex predator and she knows it. She can't be hurt by anyone except..."

I nodded. "Exactly."

In a tiny, mousy, terrified voice she said, "Except me."

"So, you're the only one who knows what she is, and you're the only one potentially with the power to stop her. So..."

Annie's eyes were a little too wide, her breath a little too fast. Even just thinking about taking on Hera terrified her.

"I have to try," she whispered. "I can't let her do what she's going to do. I don't even know what it is, but I know it's going to be evil. Well, maybe not evil but definitely self-serving and probably at someone else's expense. She was going to casually kill thousands of people, probably more! I... you're right... I'm the only one." But she didn't sound confident at all.

"You're not alone," Keph said, pressing one of his massive hands against her back.

"Exactly. You have us," I added. "She's gotten rid of her Bonded. She didn't value them. But you do, and that strength, that... love is stronger than anything she can throw at us. Together, we can defeat her."

Annie drew herself up slowly. "Gods, I can't believe I'm going to do this." Her smile was manic, the fear in her eyes shifting to a wild uncertainty.

"Do what? Go shopping?" I asked innocently.

She laughed, liked I'd hoped she would, and all her tension seemed to release. "Yeah, how could I ever go shopping!" She let go of my hands to throw her arms up in the air in mock defeat. "But I will! Gods damnit. I will go shopping!"

She laughed a bit more, smiling. It had been a joke, but I knew what she'd really meant with those words. She'd made her choice.

It seemed she and I, and the rest of our little group, would be taking a stand against a powerful force of evil.

Now this... This was like the stories of legend.

And I was finally feeling like I might just be a hero.

CHAPTER 15

DELPHON

I SAT DOWN HEAVILY ON THE COUCH, ANNIE'S ANNOUNCEMENT weighing on me even though I knew it was the right thing to do.

"Well..." What was that word Annie used so often that even Aethan had taken to using it? Oh right. "Fuck."

Annie, Aethan and Keph had returned from their excursion, laden with clothes and food. Then they'd told us the realization Annie had come to and what it would mean. We were going to face off against a powerful ancient goddess.

"Indeed," Rion said, sitting beside me. He seemed just as surprised and stunned as I was.

"But how do we even find her?" Annie asked softly.

I pointed at Keph. "Tell her."

"Oh, right," Aethan said, realizing what I meant before the stone titan did.

Keph looked confused for a moment as everyone looked at him, then his eyes widened with understanding. "I have the sight. I may be able to divine her location."

"The sight?" Annie asked.

"It's how we knew where to find you for—" Aethan snapped his mouth shut, realizing too late he was about to mention the mess we'd made of her brother's bonding ceremony.

"The wedding?" Annie finished. "That explains a lot." She sighed. "Don't worry too much about what happened that day. It was everyone's fault, even mine. Someday I'm going to have to tell my brother the truth, but that's not today." She turned to Keph. "How does this 'sight' work?"

He shrugged his massive round shoulders. "Usually I don't want it to happen and it just comes upon me. But... I was able to draw upon it once before when needed. I'll need to concentrate for a while." He looked around. "It would help if I could have the scent of earth and stone around me."

I looked around. Annie's home had several dead plants, but that was it.

"Ah... yeah..." she said, drawing the words out in thought.

"I've got this." Aethan was gone in a flash, the door slamming shut behind him, though none of us saw him leave.

It was so sudden, we all just stared at the door for a long moment.

"I wonder what he's doing?" Rion finally asked.

"I'd guess he's going to find some earth and stone?" I replied.

"He's going to have trouble with that around here, especially with snow covering everything. I don't know—"

The door slammed open and shut again, cutting Annie off, and Aethan appeared before us. He was huffing and sweating as he put down several buckets, then took off his jacket.

"Got it," he said.

Indeed, there were two buckets of dark loamy earth and one with small to fist sized stones.

"Where—?" Annie asked.

"When we were out for our walk, I noticed a store which had

some—" He frowned. "What did they call it? Right! Gardening supplies. I went back there. I didn't have any of your little bits of plastic to pay for it, so I'm afraid I stole it, but I figured we're saving the world so..." He shrugged.

"Gardening supplies?" Annie frowned. "Hunh. Right. I don't pay any attention to it much, but yeah, we did pass a hardware store didn't we." She smiled. "Glad you're so observant."

He beamed.

I turned to Keph. "What's next?"

"Bring it here," Keph said, reaching out to Aethan before turning his attention to Annie. "This may get messy, do you mind?" He sat in the middle of her living area on the bare wooden floors.

"We're saving the world. As long as I don't have to clean it up," she said with a chuckle as if she only half meant the last part.

"I can get it done in a flash," Aethan volunteered. I was about to offer, and, from the way Rion opened his mouth, he was too.

The cleaning we'd done around her place while she'd been out hadn't been as bad as I'd thought it might be. Handling a broom was easy, and with my powers over water, I'd summoned small streams from the bathing room to further clean the floors and some of the surfaces while Rion had worked in the kitchen, wiping and tidying the counters. Overall, it had been easy. I could get used to this simple domestic life.

"What do we need to do?" Annie asked Keph.

"Make a circle with the earth, as close as you can around me. Leave a little to put in my hands. Then do the same with the stones, placing them atop the earth."

Yeah, that was going to make a mess of Annie's nice wooden floors. We made sure any rugs were moved then did as instructed. It was done quick enough, and when we were finished, Keph sat in a stone and earth circle with his large hands cupped together before him, holding a small pile of earth and stones.

He drew in a long, heavy breath and released it, then did so again, this time lifting his hands up before his face, and closed his eyes. "This may take some time. Do as you wish, though try to be as quiet as possible please."

I looked at the others.

Yeah, we weren't going to do anything. We were all curious about this process and were going to be watching this, at least for now.

But... there wasn't much to watch. Keph sat perfectly still, his massive chest rising and falling with slow even breaths... and that was it.

After a few long, boring minutes, Aethan slipped silently over to Annie, whispering to her. She nodded and the two of them came to Rion and I.

"Once we find her, we'll need to figure out what we're going to do about it," Annie whispered to me, her breath hot on my ear, as Aethan presumably did the same to Rion. She motioned to her bedroom.

I instantly felt a stir of arousal, though I was more than satisfied at the moment. Annie's desperation to not deal with reality these past few days had been... tiring if extremely pleasant and oh so very stimulating. But I knew she didn't want to use the bedroom like that, just wanted to be away from Keph so we didn't disturb him.

I nodded and we headed into the room. It seemed smaller with the four of us crowded in there. Annie sat on the bed, pulling herself up to the top, leaning against the wall, while Rion sat at the foot, the farthest from her. Aethan sat on the top corner beside her and I took a spot in the middle.

"Soooo?" she asked, drawing the one word out. "Any thoughts?"

"What did Hera say her powers were?" Rion asked.

Yes, that would be a good place to start.

"Immortality and heightened senses," Annie said. "But I don't really know what that means. Does immortality mean she can't be killed at all or just that she doesn't grow old and die? If she can't be killed at all— Well, actually I'm not sure I want to kill her. I just want to... remove her from power."

"That can be very hard to do with tyrants," I replied. I'd read enough history of the triton people to know that much. We'd had a sordid past and there'd been a number of tyrants that had been overthrown. "Even if we remove Hera from power there may be a network of people around her that can keep her activities going without her."

"Right, so we need to stop her, then dismantle her organization." Annie frowned in frustration. "That'll take forever."

"We'll do what we can," Aethan said softly, reaching over to lay a hand on her shoulder. She smiled at that, her gold eyes twinkling just a little brighter.

"We have to assume she has more powers," Rion said stoically. "In fact, we have to assume that whatever we can do, she'll have some tactic to defend against it. She's been alive long enough to know how to protect herself."

"So, all our powers mean nothing?" Annie asked, her overwhelmed and discouraged expression returning.

"No, they mean something," Aethan said. "We'll just have to have plans to counter her plans. Luckily where she has age and experience, we have five heads to put together to figure out a way to defeat her."

"Right... Okay... Good," Annie replied, but she still seemed uncertain as if she didn't know where to start. "Gods, this is just so overwhelming!"

"I think the best plan is to try to catch her when she's alone," I said, having thought about this from the moment Annie had stepped out of Hera's *car*. "She'll have lots of lackies and guards, like that man who was outside her *car*. The weapons of this world are... violent and effective even at long range. So, we'll want to eliminate that factor since her powers will probably be more than enough for us to deal with. We won't want any other distractions while fighting her."

"That makes sense," Annie said, nodding. "Assuming that works and we can capture her. What do we do then? Where do we take her? How do we get her there? I doubt any prison on this world could hold her, and that's assuming any judge would try her."

"Our world?" Rion asked.

"No," Aethan responded quickly. "If she can bond with others from our world, that would just give her more power."

I'd had the same thought, just not gotten it out as quickly.

"Then where?" Annie asked.

"Are there any remote, secluded places on your world?" Aethan asked. "It seems there are people everywhere here."

She laughed. "No, not everywhere. Just in the cities. There are still some secluded places. So we... bury her somewhere? Drop her in the deepest part of the ocean?"

"Ocean? You have oceans?" I couldn't wait to see them, but that also meant that with my powers over water, I'd probably be able to fashion some sort of prison for her. "I could probably use my water powers to imprison her."

"So, we go in while she's alone and grab her, then take her to an ocean and trap her there?" Aethan summed up.

"That's a bit... simple, but for the basics of a plan, I think that works," Rion said.

"Without food or drinkable water, won't she just die, trapped like that, though?" Annie asked. "Maybe her immortality keeps her alive no matter what, but maybe it doesn't. We just don't know."

"Which means if we want to capture her, we'd need to commit to tending to her," Rion said. "But we will all eventually die and then what?"

Annie sighed. "You're right. I hate to say it, I don't want to kill anyone, but that may be our only option. Gods, that's horrible!"

It was and yet what did you do with a goddess who you couldn't control, couldn't contain, and couldn't make powerless?

I sighed. "We can take that burden from you, Annie. If it's our only choice, then one of us will do it."

"Thank you," Annie said, shaking her head. "It's still horrible."

Silence hung between us for a long time as we all tried to think of an alternate solution. Except even with our combined thoughts, we couldn't come up with anything. A heaviness settled over us as we came to the silent conclusion that in order to end this, we'd have to eliminate Hera for good. As Annie said, it was horrible.

"It's settled, then," Aethan said, his expression grim. "We'll discuss the details of that later without you," he said to Annie, "so you don't have to know."

She nodded, her expression just as grim as his.

"We're missing how we're going to get to and from wherever she is, though," I said. "It's not like we can just appear there by magic."

"Actually, I think we can," Aethan said slowly. "With your powers over water, can you sense where people are?"

"Yes," I replied. "In general, at least. If it's a specific person, I'd need to... have a sense for them, I think."

"Which means Annie can too."

She nodded.

"And with my speed, Annie and I can move around faster than most people can see. With Keph's strength Annie can carry each of us around. So theoretically, Annie can quickly get to wherever this woman may be, moving around people, avoiding them, and moving fast enough to otherwise not be seen while carrying the rest of you. It would have to be one at a time, but I think that could work."

That made a lot of sense. Though my pride was stung just a little at the thought of my bonded mate carrying me around like a sack of seaweed. But I'd get over it.

"Depending on where it is, I could also fly myself and someone else up there," Rion said.

"Not me!" I said quickly. Gods, flying was *not* something I wished to ever do again. That one time he'd carried me across the hall at the convention center had been enough for a lifetime. I was meant for water, not sky.

Rion grimaced. "I don't think I could carry Keph, and everyone else can move quickly."

Still, I shook my head vigorously. "Never going to happen," I ground out.

"Suit yourself." He shrugged. "Just myself then."

"So, we have ways in and out. What about actually fighting her?" Annie asked. "Alone is all well and good, but she still might be uber-powerful on her own."

"I'd like to think that a swift punch from Keph would take her out, no matter how powerful she is," Aethan said.

Annie didn't seem convinced. "What if that doesn't do it. What if she's immune to punches? The trouble is that we just don't know. She could do anything!" Annie threw her hands up and sagged back against the wall.

"That's just it," I said slowly. "I think we have to make the assumption that she can do almost anything. And from that point try to still figure out some way to kill her. I know it seems impossible, but I don't think it is. Perhaps that means having several options on the table and going through them until one works, I don't know. But Annie is right. We have to assume that she can do pretty much anything. Because it will be the one thing we didn't account for which stops us."

From everyone's expressions, it was obvious no one liked that much, but accepted that it was the truth.

"Hey, guys," Keph called out from the next room. "I found her!"

CHAPTER 16

ANNIE

I HURRIED OUT OF MY BEDROOM WITH THE OTHERS, BUT BEFORE WE could get to Keph and ask him what he'd found, my phone rang.

"One sec," I called to the others and went to my coat and pulled my phone out from a pocket to check the number. The caller was blocked. I was about to cancel the call when some instinct told me to take it. I swiped my thumb over the answer button and lifted it to my ear.

"Hello, Annie," Hera purred over the line.

I froze, my mind whirling.

"I thought I'd call and follow up on our conversation," she said, her voice was the 'tiger' tone from earlier.

I quickly tapped the mute button and called out to the guys. "Quiet, it's her!" Then unmuted and lifted the phone again.

"Uh, yeah? What do you want?" I asked, trying to sound nonchalant.

"I want you to be smart, Annie. I know you're planning to come after me. This call is a friendly reminder that that would be a very stupid idea. If you persist, my next interaction with you won't be so pleasant." A razor's edge to her voice made her already dangerous tone down right deadly. "I hope we understand each other, Annie. I'd hate to have to kill you and your precious minions. But don't mistake my one-time kindness for mercy. I have no mercy. If you go any further with your plans, you, and those savages from Eytheron, will be dead before you know it."

Fuckity-fuck-fuck!

"Ah, yeah, right, sure, I understand."

"Say the words."

"What words?"

"Say, 'I know you are far more powerful than I am, Hera, and I know if I try to stop you, I will die, probably slowly, watching my precious lovers die first.' Say that."

Holy fuck this woman was pure evil.

"Ah, yeah, sure. I know you are far more powerful than I am, and—"

"Hera. More powerful than I am, *Hera*."

"Right. You are far more powerful than I am, Hera, and if I go after you, you'll kill me slowly and my guys first. Close enough?"

I could almost hear her sinister smile. "Yes. Good. I trust you now know I can tell if you're lying." A faint chuckle. "Goodbye, Annie. Have a pleasant day." Hera hung up.

I nearly dropped my phone trying to set it on the counter, my hands were shaking so hard.

"What was that?" Aethan asked. "Why did you say...?"

"She knows," I said slowly, not knowing how that was possible, but it was. Perhaps it was one of her powers, one we hadn't considered, just... knowing everything... apparently. "Fuck. She knew and she told me to stop."

The four of them just stared at me.

"That wasn't a power I'd considered," Aethan said softly. "Long distance mind reading, or some sort of omniscience?"

"So," Keph rumbled. "What do we do now? Do you want to know where she is?"

Hell, no!

I didn't want to die. Worse, I didn't want my reckless actions to kill these four wonderful men who I loved and who loved me. I'd only just begun our relationship, complex as it was.

"Fuck," I hissed again. I didn't know what else to say.

The others slowly found seats, Rion and Del on the couch, and Aethan at my small kitchen table while Keph remained where he was. A mix of fear and frustration colored all of their expressions.

I couldn't think. Mindlessly I hit the power button on my phone to put it to sleep. The screen went dark, then almost instantly lit up again. I hit the button a second time, the same thing happened.

"What the..." I held the power button until the phone turned off completely.

A moment later it was chiming back to life.

I blinked.

My phone had a life of its own.

No...

Realization hit me. That was how Hera had known what we were doing! She'd been listening in on my phone just like I'd let the guys listen in on our conversation in the limo.

I didn't know what power that was, or whether it was just mundane hacking skills or something, but it seemed clear enough to me now that that's how she'd been spying on us. At least, it was one possible way.

Except I couldn't tell the guys, not with the phone listening.

And... I couldn't destroy the phone. That would also let her know I knew she was listening and she'd probably assume that such an action would indicate I was still going against her.

So...

Crap. Del had a phone, too.

I needed to say something, do something. "I guess that's it, guys. Sorry. We're giving up playing heroes. I guess we'll just have to go back to fucking all day." That hadn't exactly come out as I'd hoped. I left my phone on the counter and zipped — with Aethan's speed — into the kitchen where I kept my pen and pads for a shopping list. I quickly wrote down 'we're not giving up, but stay quiet' on one pad, then on another 'where's your phone?'

I zipped around to each of the guys, showing them the first note. When I got to Del, I showed him the second one as well.

His brow furrowed, then he pointed at his suit jacket, which was slung over the arm of the couch. I went over and rummaged through it, finding the phone and laying it on the couch, so it hopefully wouldn't be seen to be moving — this was assuming that whatever it was Hera was doing was also linked into the device's GPS and would know if it was going anywhere.

I nodded for the guys to follow me... quietly... into the bedroom.

Keph had trouble doing anything quietly, but managed well enough, squeezing himself through the small doorway without too much noise.

"Okay guys, time to fuck my brains out!" I called out, then closed the bedroom door.

My heart pounded, my blood rushing in my ears. If Hera had any other way of knowing what we were doing, I was about to put all of our lives at risk with my next move. I considered it for a long moment as the guys, arrayed around the room, stared at me with confused looks.

Well, fuck it.

I went to Aethan and got close, really close, my lips brushing his ear. He shivered with what could only be sexual anticipation even though it was obvious we weren't going to have sex. Man, I knew how it felt, the intensity of a breathy whisper in your ear. It made my heart race with need just thinking about it.

"I think she was listening in on our phones." I kept my voice as low as possible, barely a breath since I also knew she had enhanced hearing. "Nod, if you understand."

He nodded, his ear moving against my lips.

I waited, looking around, though I didn't know what I was looking for, nothing really. Just waiting to be struck down by lightning if she had been listening in some other way.

Nothing so far.

"We need to get everyone back to your world for a bit. I don't think she can do anything to listen in on us there."

Everything within me screamed that we should run there as fast as possible, but if she had someone watching us, that would look suspicious.

Except if I announced we were going back to the guys' world then Hera would just place someone to watch the alley for our return.

No, we had to sneak there— Or rather, zip there and hope no one noticed. Better to completely disappear. It would make Hera suspicious, but hopefully we'd be able to return unnoticed.

Except even if we did just disappear, Hera would be smart enough to have someone watching the portal which meant it didn't matter what we did, so I gave in to my desire to just run away as fast as possible.

"Can you take Del?" I whispered to Aethan.

He nodded again.

"Give me a moment to tell the others what's happening."

I went to each, whispering my plans. Aethan would take Del, Rion would fly and hopefully loose anyone watching us before meeting us in the alley. I'd take Keph, carrying him. It would be awkward, but since I possessed the same supernatural strength he did, I'd make it work.

Once everyone knew, I waited for a long moment once again.

Still no strike of lightning.

With a nod, everyone sprang into action. Aethan was gone

with Del. Rion was out the window, and I sped to Keph and picked him up, not easily, but with his strength, it was doable.

It was incredibly awkward moving with Keph. I had to set him down and manually maneuver him through doorways, but once outside, things were a lot quicker. We reconvened at the alley wall and the invisible portal to their world that only people like me and Hera could open.

It was only once we were on the other side, that I allowed myself to release a huge sigh of relief.

CHAPTER 17

HYPERION

IT WAS HARD TO RELAX. I LAY ON THE WARM SAND AS DAY DWINDLED and the shadows grew long. We all did, but we were also restless. We'd gone to our world to escape prying eyes and ears, but once we'd gotten here, we hadn't known what to do.

We assumed that as soon as we returned to Annie's world, we'd be targets. If this Hera was as cunning as we suspected, she had to know about the portal in the alley. She'd have someone watching it.

So then...

We had no idea. We'd all tried to think of some course of action as the day had waned, but in the end, we'd all ended up just lying there on the sand. Annie had discarded most of her clothes, while the others had already been either naked or wearing very little and had stripped down the moment we'd returned.

"I could go to my kingdom and gather us an army," Del said, though he didn't sound certain. "I'd need to speak to my parents and that might not go well, but I might be able to convince them."

I could also potentially rally some of my people. I'd been away far too long, more than a week overdue to be back, but I could make excuses. I had a rank and privileges. I'd thought to give that all up for Annie, but perhaps I could still use them, except would they be able to stand against Hera?

"I don't think that would matter," Aethan said, responding to Del, echoing my unspoken thoughts. "We'd have to assume Hera has an army as well, all armed with the weapons of Annie's world. I don't think our people would do well against that. We'd only be sending them to their deaths for a cause they probably don't believe in, on a world that isn't theirs."

Exactly.

So then... What could we do?

I suddenly needed to move. I rose and began pacing. Summoning my wings, I stretched them out, arching my back and rolling my shoulders. Gods, I just wanted to fly. I always thought better riding a thermal.

"Are you going to fly?" Annie asked excitedly. She rose and came to me. The bits of cloth across her breasts and loins were alluring, hiding her treasures — even though I'd seen those treasures before — and I felt my cock start to harden

"Yes." I shook out my wings, ready to launch.

"Take me with you?" she asked drawing close, a soft hand on my chest, her light red-blonde hair catching some of the last rays of sunlight turning it into a stunning pink-gold.

Her eyes were hungry, excited, and she wrapped Keph-strengthened arms around my neck and pulled herself up to wrap her legs around my waist. Her gold eyes were level with mine, and I dipped forward to brush my lips against hers.

"Fly me," she murmured. "Please. I just need to get away." Her 'please' had been soft, urgent, heartbreaking, and accompanied by a small rock of her hips, pressing her barely covered loins against my now full erection captured between us.

Wrapping my arms around her to keep her close, I leapt and flapped my wings hard, lifting us. *Erinai* mated in flight. It was a beautiful, sensual dance, high above the earth, and while I wanted to share that with Annie, I was afraid for her. She didn't have wings and if either one of us let go or slipped—

Gods, I couldn't have her fall.

She leaned close, pressing her body against mine, our cheeks touching. "Don't worry about me. I can lift myself," she said as if she'd been reading my thoughts.

When she pulled back, she was smiling mischievously, but must have seen my scowl of confusion.

I still wasn't that high, perhaps a hundred feet up from the beach, and she released my neck and leaned back. I held onto her still, but there seemed to be little weight in my hands. When she unwrapped her legs from around me, she was... floating.

"How?" I gasped. I didn't think it was possible for her to have acquired my flight ability. That wasn't a power I'd gained by going through the portal. I'd always had it. And yet...

She laughed, lightly. "I can manipulate water, lift it. And people are mostly water."

Del's ability?

Were people mostly water?

They had lots of blood, which was a liquid. I'd never thought about it. Yet I couldn't deny she was floating in front of me.

But her smile melted away. "It's not comfortable, though. It feels like my insides want to come out, but I wanted you to know that nothing would happen if you dropped me. I can save myself."

She slid off her loin covering and drew herself back to me, wrapping her legs around my waist again and sliding her wet heat against my cock. Gods I loved that feeling, loved her heat, her soft skin, and how she completely relaxed and trusted me when we made love.

Then she reached back and removed her upper covering as well, freeing her breasts.

She wrapped her strong arms around my neck again, allowing

enough space between us so I could caress her body, kneading her breasts and teasing her nipples, and building up her arousal.

With a soft, seductive moan, she leaned in and pressed her lips against mine, connecting us in the most delicious, sacred way, fueling my own desire.

We were both in too much need to play around for long, and I slipped my grip down to her hips, easing her away from me until I was poised at her opening.

Her body trembled, but from her too-fast breath and her moans of desire, I knew she shook with the same anticipation and need that blazed through me.

"Hard," she murmured against my mouth, and in one fluid motion I thrust into her, pulling her hips down to grind against mine.

"Oh, yes!" she cried out, making my balls tighten at her pleasure.

I flew higher, thrusting in and out of her quickly, building my release. I wanted to be as far away from everything as possible and be truly alone with the woman who made me feel like I was complete. She made my heart skip a beat when I saw her, and my soul ached with longing when she wasn't there.

She rocked into each thrust, crashing our bodies together, the impact almost too much with her Keph-enhanced strength. Then she tensed, legs tightening around me, with a fast and hard release.

"Oh, yes, yes, yes," she moaned, her voice thick with satisfaction.

Her muscle clenched around my cock and I gave her a second to ride the wave, sucking in my breath and fighting my own release. I knew from our three days of making love that this first one was only just a prelude to stronger, more satisfying orgasms, and I wanted to give her that.

Her release started to ebb and I slowly pulled halfway out then pushed back in again, drawing a groan of pleasure.

"More," she begged, rocking her hips into me, urging me to pick up the pace again.

Behind her, the sunset blazed with brilliant reds, oranges, and yellow, almost as beautiful as Annie, the color full and intense, like our passion.

I quickly picked up our pace again, and she threw her head back, her eyes closed, a look of pure abandon, and a little bit of desperation, on her face as if she was trying to lose herself in this moment, lose her fear and the crushing responsibility of wanting to stop a goddess.

It twisted my heart that she had to feel such fear, but I also knew that despite the fear she wasn't going to give up. My mate was strong and determined and compassionate, and if she needed to forget for just a moment, I'd give that to her.

She came again, harder than the first time, as expected, and she cried my name, pulling me over the edge with her.

We clung to each other, shuddering in the sky, high and serene, our breaths fast, our hearts pounding, our muscles locked in our release, my body barely able to keep us aloft in the most incredible way.

I managed to regain control of my flight and spun us slowly as we went through the last, glorious throes of finishing, not wanting the moment to end, but knowing it eventually would.

"The sunset is almost as beautiful as you are," I murmured against her lips, telling her the thought that had come to me while we were making love. "But nothing can truly match you."

She glanced over her shoulder to look at it. "It is beautiful. So beautiful." Then she laid her head on my shoulder and cried.

I held her close, knowing she needed this emotional release, letting her have the time she needed. There was too much at stake and it seemed no matter what we chose there was a good chance people would die.

CHAPTER 18

ANNIE

"WE CAN'T STAY HERE FOREVER." I'D SAID THOSE WORDS, BUT IT didn't feel like me. I didn't feel anything like me at the moment. The 'normal' me — the one from before I'd met these amazing guys — wouldn't be standing, hands on hips, buck naked and not caring, before four hot men demanding a plan of action.

I'd come to accept being naked. It helped that when I'd discarded my underwear in a fit of passion while flying with Rion, I hadn't been able to find them afterward.

This power, this *confidence,* was a strange thing. I'd possessed it while healing the people at the convention center and the hospital, but then I'd met Hera. I'd seen her power and been terrified of it. I'd returned to my old, shrinking-violet self, and it had taken that amazing flying-sex with Rion — and some time up there to release my fears and doubts — to find this power again.

Now, I'd had a night to sleep on it and, as the sun rose, I challenged my guys.

"There has to be a way to fight Hera." It had been a statement, though part of me wanted to make it a question, adding 'right?' to the end. "Sure, she has powers we don't know about, and is probably super strong, and she has an army, but so what?" I glared at each of the guys. "Are we just going to stay here and pout about it?"

It was Aethan who said what I still feared. "We could die. *You* could die, Annie. None of us wants that."

"You're right. I don't want to die," I replied, looking Aethan straight in the eye. "What you have to ask yourself is, what would a hero do? Do they sit and do nothing in the face of danger, or do they risk death to defeat the villain?" My heart was pounding. Had I really just said that? Was I ready to die for this cause?

I could see the same question in the eyes of each of my guys.

We all thought about that for a long moment.

Was I willing to die for this?

Except could I live with myself if I didn't do it?

That answer was clear to me. No.

We were the only ones with any kind of chance of stopping Hera and there was no telling how many people she'd already murdered and how many more would die.

"I'm willing to die for this," I said. "Because I couldn't live with myself if I didn't try to do something."

Del nodded. "You're right, neither could I. I'll do it."

"As will I," Rion said, his expression somber.

"And I," Aethan added.

"And that means I have to go to keep you all from dying," Keph said so seriously it took me a moment to realize it was a joke.

I laughed, as did the others, but it didn't last. Too much was at stake.

"Good, now that that's settled, what's the plan? Same as before? Something tells me Hera's going to be expecting us now. That and she may not be alone that often, if at all."

"I think the plan is the same," Aethan said considering, eyes downcast, staring at the sand. "She may not be alone, but she can't be surrounded by an army at all times, not too closely anyway. There has to be moments when she's at least minimally guarded."

Rion huffed out a sigh. "Still."

"Still?" I asked.

"We just don't know enough. How did she know what we were planning? What are her powers? If she just *knows* things, then how will we ever hope to surprise her?"

Del sat up a little straighter suddenly. "There might be a way to know."

We all looked at him. He himself seemed a bit surprised. "I don't know why I didn't think of it before." His expression of enlightenment shifted to one of chagrin. "Perhaps because I'd accepted I was never going home again."

"Just because you're bonded to me, doesn't mean you can't go home. I'd never do that to any of you," I said, wondering where this strange thought from Del had come from.

Everyone looked at me now.

What had I said?

"We never told her, did we?" Rion said slowly.

"I'd meant to," Del replied sheepishly.

"Tell me what?"

Del stood and gave a very formal bow. "Annie, I am Delphon of Galniosia, Prince of the Realm and heir to the Pearl Throne."

I gaped.

Fuck me! And he had... several times. And it had been wonderful. I shuddered blissfully with the memories. I was bonded to a prince!

Suddenly, every girlish fantasy I'd ever had of being swept off my feet by 'prince charming' returned to me and I was that giddy school-girl again. "A... prince? My very own prince?"

"Well, yes and no."

"No?" My school-girl hopes sputtered out.

"By bonding with you, I've dedicated myself to you and I can't accept my responsibilities back home. I have to abdicate. That's why I can't return. If I do, I'll have to have a very awkward conversation with my parents. My little brother will be happy though, he gets to be the next king." He blew out a long breath. "So, I'm sorry, but I have to give up being a prince."

Oh... I was okay with that. A prince who'd give up his position of power for a girl like me? That was among several of those girlish fantasies.

"I can accept that," I said. "Going back, though. You said there might be a way to know Hera's powers? I'm guessing it involves going home? What is it?"

He nodded. "Right. Ah... well, my old tutor was also the curator of the library of Galniosia. That old woman knew everything there was to know about... well, everything, including the ancients. And if she didn't know it, she knew a book where she could find out about it. There has to be something in that library. It's the largest in all of Nikandra."

"He's right," Aethan said. "Anything my people have pales in comparison. We don't even have books, just an oral tradition handed down by elders."

There was something about the words 'oral tradition' that made me think of Aethan's face between my legs, and I fought to hide my expression at the thought. Gods, but I had a dirty mind!

"Then let's go!" I said, struggling to stay on topic. "Del, lead us to your library and this tutor of yours."

Again, everyone was looking at me.

"What?"

"Can you breathe water?" Keph asked.

"What? No. Why?"

"Neither can the rest of us, except Del," Aethan said.

"And?"

"And, my kingdom and this library are underwater, Annie. I'm a triton remember. I live in the seas."

Oh.

I searched my memory. Had he told me that? If so, I'd forgotten with everything else that had happened. I knew he was a merfolk, but I'd never made the connection that his home might be underwater. I guess I'd assumed it was on an island somewhere since he could easily turn his fishtail into legs.

"So, how do we get there?" I asked. "Is there a way?"

Everyone turned their attention from me to Del.

"There is, but it's not particularly pleasant."

Aethan's eyes suddenly went wide. "You don't mean huphelopoids?"

"I do."

"Fuck." Aethan drew out the word. Whatever this 'Hufflepuff' was, apparently Aethan agreed that it was unpleasant. The look on his face was one of disgust mixed with morbid curiosity.

"What's a huphelopoid?" Keph asked as Rion frowned, his expression making it clear that he didn't know what it was, either.

Del gave a grimace. "Follow me." He began walking toward the town of Masia. "We'll need to catch a boat. There's only one island in the archipelago where you can find them. I'll... explain along the way."

Somehow, I didn't think I was going to like this explanation.

CHAPTER 19

ANNIE

"THAT'S DISGUSTING!"

Del had just fully explained the 'Hufflepuffs' and yes, they were really called huphelopoids, but my mind really wanted to call them Hufflepuffs. Too much Harry Potter as a kid, I guess. And now that I knew what they were and what they did, the "puff" seemed more than adequate to describe them.

"On your face?" Rion asked, looking as disgusted as I felt.

We all stood on the docks, waiting for the small ship we'd hired as it prepared for departure. I was still naked and unashamed about it. It helped that all the guys were too, as was everyone else in the village, and no one made a big deal about it. It was strange, but that was the way of this place. When you lived in a tropical climate, you didn't really need clothes, especially if the idea of physical modesty just didn't exist in the culture. And to be honest, it was kind of liberating.

"Yep," Aethan said, also looking a bit sick at the prospect.

"And they breathe air and water and carbon dioxide?" I asked. It seemed the understanding of the elements here wasn't as clear as on my world. My use — and then explanation — of the words 'carbon dioxide' had stunned all the guys.

"I don't know all the details," Del said. "I've never had to use one. But whatever we breathe in and out, they seem to be fine with. From what I've heard, they live happily on shorelines, half in and half out of the water. It was some adventurous nymph who tried them first and found out if you allowed them to latch to your face, covering your mouth and nose, both you and the huphelopoid would survive just fine. It's a symbolic relationship."

"I think you mean symbiotic," Aethan corrected him with a chuckle.

Del rolled his eyes at him. "Whatever, yes."

"And they have tentacles, like squid?" I asked.

"Yes. That's how they clasp onto your head. You may have little suction marks on your face for a while afterward, though. I've heard that happens if you wear them for a long time."

"Great." I was going to have to stick a squid to my face and breathe into it to go underwater. That was a wonderful fashion statement. Especially going to see the parents of one of my guys. *Royal* parents at that.

Yeah. That would be a meeting of the in-laws I'd not soon forget. *Uh, yeah, hi your highnesses, pardon the squid on my face.*

Just the thought was making me queasy, though that could have also been the soft rise and fall of the floating dock we were standing on, too. I wasn't much looking forward to this boat ride. I'd been out on Lake Michigan all of once on a boat that belonged to my ex's parents. That had not gone well. I'd had my head over the side, losing my lunch, for most of it. Another wonderful interaction with potential in-laws. At least I was consistent.

The captain waved at us, indicating the boat was ready and we boarded. The crew, all minotaurs, big and brawny, were all larger than my guys except for Keph — no one was larger than Keph...

well, no one I'd met yet — and they rowed us out a bit, then unfurled the sails and we were off, skipping across the water.

Surprisingly, my stomach was fine.

But then, I did have healing powers and powers over water now. Perhaps that was what was saving me.

It turned out, sailing was quite lovely when you weren't puking over the side of the boat. Aethan, however, turned a bit green, and I used my powers to calm his uneasy stomach. We sat on the benches off to one side at the rear of the boat, and he curled close to me, laying his head in my lap as I stroked his temple. It was intimate and endearing without being sexy, and it only really occurred to me then that I'd bonded with these four guys without really knowing them. Most of the time we'd spent together had been either dealing with a crisis or... bumping like bunnies.

"I know this may sound weird after all we've been through," I said to them. "But I know very little about all of you. I didn't know Del was a prince. That feels like something I should have known. Tell me about yourselves."

"To be fair," Del said, "I only just told the guys I was a prince a few days ago."

"But we already knew," Aethan said from my lap. "It was easy to tell from how he always glorified tales of 'his prince' when he spoke to us. There was a gleam in his eye. An 'I'm talking about me' sort of gleam."

Del sighed. "Well, there's one thing about me, apparently I can't keep a secret or tell a lie convincingly."

"Not to people who know you anyway," Rion said.

They were all quiet for a moment after that.

Finally, Rion sighed. "Where to start..."

"Tell me about your families," I said softly. But then... they didn't know about mine. This whole 'get to know you' thing would have to go both ways.

"Mine are good folk in general," I said, willing to start us off.

"They just never really understood me or what I wanted. My dad's a doctor." Rion frowned, reminding me that they didn't use the same words I did for certain things. "That's a healer, but without powers. I think you have those here, right?"

The guys nodded their understanding.

"My mother was the same." I had no clue how to make the distinction between a doctor and a nurse to them so... yeah. "And in my world, you make a lot of money doing that. But I didn't want to make money, well I do, but I didn't need to be rich like they were. I wanted to live a simple life, somewhere warm."

"It's warm here," Keph said, turning his face to the sun, his eyes closed, soaking it in.

"It is. It's wonderful here. I'm tempted to stay here... when this whole Hera thing is over, that is," I replied.

"Not your world? I thought we'd live there," Rion said.

"I'd rather live here, if you're all good with that."

The guys exchanged odd looks and I had no idea what it meant.

"That would require a lot of explaining to our various families and clans," Rion said.

"I'd have to explain why I'm living with four guys to my friends and family in my world." I shrugged. "We'll all have to explain it eventually to everyone."

From their reluctant nods, it was clear that was a truth none of us wanted to face anytime soon.

"Anyway, my family. My brother is—" Did they have accountant's here? "He works with numbers and my sister is a florist. She works with flowers. They're all very successful at what they do. And I... well, I had a job where I was doing well, before you all came along. Now that's gone." I held up my hand to stop them, their apology for me losing my job clear in their expressions. "I'm fine with it. It just means I'll have to start my own business all the sooner. It's what I'd planned on doing."

"If you do stay here, a healer with powers like yours would be welcome in any society. People would be happy to pay, those that could. You'd do very well," Keph said, his eyes still closed, his face to the sun.

Hunh. That was an interesting option I hadn't thought of.

"That's my family. I love them and they love me, but we've never really understood each other. As for friends... I have a few." The sad truth, though, was that none of them were close. I was an introvert. I liked snuggling on the couch in my apartment and watching a good rom-com.

I'd had a few acquaintances through work, but if I was honest, I probably wouldn't keep up with them, now that I'd left.

There were a few other friends from childhood, but they lived across town or in different states now and that group had moved apart, growing into their new lives as adults. We met up, one-on-one, every now and then, but we very rarely met as a full group anymore. Some of us might get together around the holidays, but it had been years since everyone had been there.

"I'm not really close to any of my friends." A wave of melancholy swept through me as I realized that my distance from my family and how they'd treated me and my dreams meant I'd never really felt comfortable sharing myself with others. I'd kept things light and fun with my friends, not letting them see the real me. Now, I was alone and no one really knew me.

Well, no, I wasn't alone. I was surrounded by four hunky guys, and they were far more than just man-meat. I could see in their faces a reflection of my own sadness as I spoke. I was getting the feeling they were all like me, distant from the family and friends who were supposed to know them.

Gods, how had I gotten so lucky to find others who were so much like me.

I smiled. "Now I have you four though, and that's all I really need."

CHAPTER 20

HYPERION

"Now I have you four though, and that's all I really need."

Annie's words sank into my soul, a balm on all the pain I'd bound deep within me. I could see the pain in her expression as she'd spoken of her family and friends and it had echoed that same ache in my soul. We were kindred spirits, fated, meant to be. How else could her words speak to me so deeply?

"I feel the same," I said softly. I looked around at my three best friends and my bonded love. "I don't think I've known anyone as well as I've known you three. I don't know how you feel, but you're like brothers to me."

They all nodded. Keph did so without opening his eyes or adjusting the relaxed, upward position of his head.

"Brothers," Aethan said. I felt a touch of envy for the man, his head resting on Annie's thigh, though I understood his sickness and dislike of water. I was used to the high buffeting currents of air, much like the waves over which we now crashed, but he was from the plains and wouldn't have had a lot of experience with either wind or water.

"The others know some of this, but not all. Perhaps it's time I spoke about my life," I said.

Annie smiled a smile that brought so much warmth and peace to the layers of turmoil within me. It always did.

"I was raised with a certain amount of privilege. The *erinai* don't have much in the way of poverty, all people are integrated and work is found for everyone that best suits their abilities." I frowned. "Well, there are some who are looked down upon: the aged and infirm, who we literally look down upon because they can't fly. They're well-tended, but we all feel that their lives must be torture, to be born to the skies but not able to reach them anymore."

Del shuddered. "I can't imagine how horrible it would be to not be able to swim in the sea."

"Another reason I think it would be better if we lived here," Annie said.

"Anyway, my father is the Sky General, the leader of the *erinai* military. I was trained well, though not by him. He was always away on missions or in meetings with the Sky King. Even when he was at home, he was aloof, and hard to know. Hard in general."

I fought a shudder thinking about the cold, distant way he looked at me... at everyone. I wasn't even important enough to be looked at differently than anyone else.

"He's a stern man, even with my mother and my sister: rigid, no room for question, and old fashioned in his thinking. A woman's place is in the home, married, tending children. Yet my sister, Ehlana, wished to be in the military." Gods, that had been a terrible fight. And worse when he'd discovered the truth. "Father forbade it. So, I trained her. When Father found out he was furious. He sent her away to a school for girls and arranged a marriage for her as soon as she was old enough."

"That's horrible," Annie gasped.

And it got worse. "She died a husk of her former joyous self a few years later." My throat tightened. I'd never told anyone that, not even the guys, mostly because just thinking about it always infuriated me and tore at my insides. I clenched my jaw, trying to keep my emotions in check, but a tear escaped my control and rolled down my cheek. A part of me wanted to just weep openly, but that was another thing that had been — literally — beaten out of me. Men didn't cry.

"Oh, Rion," Annie murmured, reaching out to me.

I accepted her hand, savoring the feel of her soft skin and firm grip, knowing in just that simple gesture that she'd always support me. We might not agree on everything, but she'd never be cruel like my father and she'd always listen to my opinion.

Del placed a hand on my shoulder. "I don't know the pain you must carry from this, but—" He glanced at the others who all, even Keph, looked at me. "I know this, we've all been cast out from the places that raised us. Our pain may be different, but this is the same."

I knew enough of the tales of the others to know this was true.

Annie gave a soft, sad laugh. "So, we're *all* outcast then?"

"We are," Keph rumbled, his voice solemn.

"My troop of outcasts," she replied, giving each of us a tender, loving smile.

"Bound to you, bound as brothers, bound by our banishment, self-imposed as it may be," Del said. The poetry of his words caught like a bur in my mind and soul. I nodded. Looking at him, I put a hand on his shoulder as well.

"Bound as brothers," I repeated.

"Brothers," Keph and Aethan said as one.

After a long moment, Annie asked, "Is there more to your tale Rion?"

I sighed. "That's the bulk of it. My mother is always compliant with my father's wishes. She's... worn, aged beyond her years from dealing with him. I—" My emotions swelled again. This was the truth that frustrated and hurt the most. "I might wish to go back and free her from his grasp, but I honestly don't know if she'd go. She's been under his influence for so long, I think she's accepted her fate. It pains me to say it, but if I tried to take her away, she'd probably run right back to him. I don't know if there's anything I can say to reach her."

"Some women, even though they know they're in a bad place, fear leaving. They may even live with it for so long that it seems more painful to leave than to stay. All we can do is try to help, understand that it's a difficult situation, and be patient with them." She squeezed my fingers and offered me a soft smile.

"As for friends, I had few, and most were in the military," I said. "They revered my father and I'm afraid they wanted to get close to me so they could get close to him. Either that or they knew I might someday replace him and were seeking positions of power when that day came. Those sorts sicken me. The one true friend I had growing up, Eordal, was injured during a battle with some wild griffins. He lost the ability to fly and that broke his spirit. He died about five years ago now."

"More tragedy," Annie said. "I hope that's not all you've ever known."

I smiled, even if it was a wan, sad thing. "It's not." I glanced at Del. "Eight years ago, I met my brothers and that has been a joy in my life ever since."

Keph grunted his agreement and Aethan and Del smiled and nodded.

I let out a long, heavy breath. "That's my tale. Who's next?"

"Perhaps, since we're headed there," Del said. "I should tell you more of Galniosia."

CHAPTER 21

DELPHON

I'D MADE THE DECISION TO STAY WITH ANNIE AND GIVE UP MY LIFE AS a prince, and the thought of returning to the beautiful city of Galniosia filled me with conflict. I wished to see it, even if only one last time, but I knew there would be some hard conversations to come. I kept telling myself 'better now than later,' but that wasn't helping much.

"In my opinion, there isn't a more beautiful city in the world," I said wistfully. "Especially when the midday light filters down and washes over the towers and swaying stands of giant kelp." I sighed, closing my eyes to bring the sight to mind.

"How far down is it?" Annie asked.

"The lagoon here in the archipelago isn't that deep. Galniosia is at the center of it. There's a trench that runs through the west side of the city which falls to about two hundred feet, but the city itself isn't much more than a hundred feet down."

Opening my eyes to look around, I peered down into the waters. "On a clear day you can see it. We're not far away now. The path to the island we're going to won't take us directly over it though."

The waters were a bit choppy today as well, a stiff wind helping to make the sailing journey that much faster.

I turned back to the others. "My people aren't perfect. There are some tritons who live with little. They hunt for their food and live off the kelp and algae when hunting isn't so good. There's food aplenty, that's not the problem. There are simply few opportunities for those not born to power or wealth. Trade routes with the surface have been established and contracts are rarely broken. There aren't many raw resources to mine or work with, so crafters are generally scarce. The few there are, are generational now, passing down their craft from father to son or mother to daughter. New blood is rarely introduced. It's... static. Things rarely change beneath the waves."

That was one of the things that frustrated me the most about my people, and I knew any kind of change would be slow, take an enormous effort, and a powerful leader. And while I wasn't opposed to the effort and could be patient with things that were important to me, I knew enough about myself that I wasn't a charismatic enough leader to evoke meaningful change.

"We're perhaps a bit more progressive than the *erinai*," I said, glancing at Rion. "Though that's only because we had a queen as a ruler before our current king and she did much to progress the rights and liberties of women."

The previous queen — my grandmother — had been a true force to be reckoned with and whenever I thought about a true leader, I thought of her, someone with whom I'd never be able to compare.

"Yet, there was little that could be done for those who didn't have some form of power already," I continued. "There just aren't positions to give them. It's like a picture, beautiful, but unchanging." And nothing I could do about it.

I pushed aside my melancholy. It was what it was. "But, all that aside, we do care for our people. There's no rent or need to purchase land. People live for free. There are no taxes on those who aren't making a certain amount, so they can at least remain where they are. And where we're going, you'll see the Palace of Pearls and the Hall of Light." Which brought me to the not-so-fun part. "And you'll meet my family."

Annie let go of Rion's hand and reached out for me in silent support.

I took it, savoring the feel of her soft, delicate fingers interlaced with mine. A part of me was still amazed that she'd picked me, even though a stronger part of me deep within my soul, knew we belonged together, we all did, and us bonding was destiny. Maybe that was why I'd never felt like I belonged on the throne.

"Despite being king, my father is nothing like yours, Rion. He's a jovial, easy-going fellow. It's been over a hundred years since there was any strife or war among my people. He's a fair ruler, but in truth it's my mother that's the true power on the throne. She was handpicked by the previous queen to marry her son. She was tutored and trained to be a woman of power." I grimaced. "If I have trouble with anyone in my family, it's her. She expects a lot from all her children. She says that 'because we're royals, we have a duty to be and do more than those we serve.' I've never quite lived up to that for her."

"I don't know if that's better than having no expectations of yourself or not," Aethan said, reminding me that his exile was self-imposed. His people didn't understand him, nor he them.

"My mild-mannered brother is intelligent and artistic. He took to governance the same way he took to sculpting. He's taken to everything put before him and remains quiet and humble. That's the son my mother wanted. She smiles when she looks at him."

"I'm pretty sure that's the son every mother wants," Rion said.

"Or daughter," Annie added, and from what she'd said, I knew she understood how much it hurt not living up to her family's expectations.

My jaw tightened. It had been a long time since my mother had smiled when she looked at me.

"My sister is also another near-perfect child," I said. "Despite being ten years younger than I, she's already exceeded me in every way that counts to my mother. She's poised and strong, knowledgeable and quick of mind. She loves playing games of strategy and regularly beats our own generals. She'll probably lead our army one day, small as it is. If she has a fault, it's that she's strong willed and challenges my mother on occasion... or did, when she was a youth, not so much anymore."

And I wasn't sure if that was because she'd given up challenging our mother or realized it was smarter to just step around the confrontation and do what she wanted anyway.

I blew out a long, heavy breath. "I just..." I shrugged. "I didn't want any of that! I wanted to be free! It's not like I'm not-responsible or willing to put in the work, I just hadn't found anything I wanted to put work into until I met you guys. And you, Annie." The entire reason I was returning home was so we could research a goddess we were about to fight. "I never saw myself as a hero or warrior, but I'll fight for all of you. I'll do what needs to be done to rid your world of this Hera."

And there it was. I'd fled from responsibility and rulership, only to find myself dedicated to freeing a whole other world. I wondered if that would please my mother or disappoint her more?

"I never doubted your nobility," Annie said, her gaze soft yet still determined.

"I did. Often," Aethan said from her lap, but he smiled kindly, his words clearly a joke, and the others laughed with us.

"Will they help us?" Annie asked.

That was the question. "I have no idea. They'll certainly be upset with me, expect that much. I've been gone far longer than I should have been. They don't get many outsiders in Galniosia so I'd expect the rest of you would be more... curiosities than points of contention. They're good people, so I suspect they'll help *you*." I made sure I put emphasis on the *you*.

"And what will happen to you?" Annie asked concerned.

"I'll renounce my title." I shrugged. It was a whole lot easier to say than it would be to do. Well, that wasn't true. All I had to do was say those words again formally, but there would probably be a lot more of a discussion with my parents — specifically my mother — around it.

"And will that cause any problems?" Annie asked, although I suspected she'd already figured out the answer.

"For me, no, not in the long run. For my mother, it will be a huge problem. Well, maybe not a problem so much as it will confirm her problem child is an irredeemable lost cause." I gave a fake smile. A part of me thought of myself that way still, a part which had been ground into me by my mother.

"She can't really see you that way. You're her son," Annie said.

"I'm her biggest failure. It's a sore spot for her, I think."

Annie frowned. I guess she didn't much like that, but didn't know what to say. I couldn't blame her. I'd felt that way most of my life.

I shrugged again. It was all I could really do. "Don't worry about it. It's my burden to bear, and it will all be over and done with soon. Then we can get back to defeating an immortal goddess."

That thought brought everyone back on track, drawing us into a grim silence. No one said much after that.

When we arrived at the island, Keph hopped out of the boat first and instantly sunk a good foot into the soft sands. He looked down at the shallow water lapping around his knees then back up to us. "Is now a bad time to mention I can't swim?"

CHAPTER 22

ANNIE

I JUMPED OVER THE SIDE OF THE BOAT EVEN BEFORE IT HAD COME TO a full stop. The waters lapped around the top of my hips, warm and refreshing, and for a second I was awed at how amazing this island was. It was a tropical paradise with turquoise water and pale sand, matching the picture I had in my head of where I wanted to live.

I dove beneath the shallow water and swam around for a moment, noticing the many small to medium sized fish as well as several odd-looking octopus like things. Perhaps these were Hufflepuffs?

I surfaced a short distance down the beach, in time to hear Keph say, "Is now a bad time to mention I can't swim?"

I swam over to him as he trudged heavily out of the water.

"It's easy," I said, "I can teach you."

Rion laughed and shook his head as if he'd just realized the obvious and couldn't believe he'd missed it. "I don't think Keph is saying he doesn't know how to swim, though I suspect that's also the case. Look at him. He physically *can't* swim. He's not buoyant enough. I don't know why none of us thought of it until now."

Oh... yeah, right. He was heavy as a brick wall and build like one too. He'd sink like a stone.

"Well, is that a problem?" I asked. "Can't he just walk there?"

"He could," Del said, "but there's a lot of uneven ground underwater and it would take him some time to get there."

"We could have the boat go back and drop him in closer to the city," Aethan suggested.

"That *could* work," Del said then frowned. "Ah, no. Not a good idea. He'd have to walk out. None of us would be able to carry him while swimming, and that would also take a long time. No, sorry Keph, but you're right, I don't think you can come."

The large, onyx skinned man, shrugged and rubbed his hand over his bald head. "Oh well. I'll visit your city some other time. Although the thought of being under water, always... worried me just a bit anyway. If that thing came off my face, I'd just... well I'd have nothing I could do. So, it's probably for the best. I'll meet you all back at the rocks on the beach near Masia," he said, signaling the boat to come back and get him.

"We'll miss you," I said, swimming to his side and hugging him as best I could, since my arms couldn't reach around his massive body.

He knelt and we shared a kiss, as soft and tender as was possible with Keph. I lingered with him for a long moment, letting him know just how much I'd miss him, and was breathless when we finally drew apart.

"Stay safe," I murmured.

"And you," he replied, sliding a large hand down my naked back and cradling my butt, making me more than just a little hot.

He quickly kissed me again, then turned to the boat, as if he wouldn't be able to stop himself from going farther with me if he didn't leave right away.

I blew out a long, warm breath, trying to bring myself down from this new, aching heat as I watched Keph climb aboard. That was a show in itself, his heavy form nearly capsized the small craft. The minotaurs were experts at their trade, however, and managed to help him aboard while keeping the boat afloat.

He waved as the boat sailed away, and I felt like a part of me was being slowly pulled away with him. I sagged to my knees in the shallow water for a long moment, simply trying to breathe against the tightness in my chest. Since we'd bonded, I'd never been that far from any of my guys. I hadn't expected such a physical reaction and yet it made sense. They shared their powers with me, which meant our connection was deeper than just being in love. It was a soul to soul connection, bound by magic, and it squeezed tight with the fear that I didn't know how long we'd be in Del's kingdom or when I'd see Keph again.

Gods, Hera must be one cold-hearted bitch to have killed those she'd bonded with. Just being separated from Keph hurt. I couldn't imagine the agony of him dying or our bond being severed.

"Annie, are you all right?" Aethan asked.

I shoved up to my feet, rubbing my chest as if that would somehow ease the ache of Keph's absence. "Yeah."

I had to push onward even though it felt like I was missing a limb or something integral to my being. Keph couldn't come and we had to learn more about Hera. It was our only way to survive facing her — because I knew in my soul I wouldn't be able to let her continue killing people in my world or the guys' world.

Del offered me a soft smile and transformed into his merfolk form, flicking his massive tail out of the water and splashing Aethan, making the *satyr's* red mohawk flop in his eyes before diving under the water.

Those odd octopus-like things I'd seen were indeed the huphelopoids, and Del, lithe and quick in the water, caught three of the slippery things and handed one to each of us.

I stared at the squirming mass of goo and tentacles in my cupped hands, unable to make myself bring it to my face.

Rion was the bravest of the three of us, and just did it. The huphelopoid sent tentacles around behind his head and seem to snuggle close around his mouth and nose. He made a face, though I could only see his eyes, which still conveyed discomfort and disgust and didn't inspire much confidence.

Aethan glanced at me then down at the suction-cups and the weird sponge-like part which was supposed to go over his mouth and nose.

I glanced at mine. This was the only way. And while a small part of me said Del could go get this information himself or with Rion, a much larger part of me didn't want to be separated from another of my guys and didn't want Del to have to face his family alone.

"Ah, fuck it," I hissed and pressed the thing against my face before I could chicken out.

It smelled foul, and my eyes watered as my nose sank into its spongy body. It wrapped its tentacles around my head just like Rion's had done and pulled close and for a moment, panic seized me with the sudden fear that I wouldn't be able to breathe. But then I gasped in a full breath, a breath which reeked of salt and fish, and made me gag. I fought through the sensation, uncertain it I'd even be able to throw up with the thing on my face, and managed to draw in another, steadier breath, then another.

I turned to Aethan and—

Hunh. I didn't know if we could talk in these things. I could move my mouth and breathe in and out like normal, but I didn't know if that meant I could talk or if the others would be able to hear me.

"Can you hear me?" Rion asked, as if he'd known what I'd been trying to figure out. His voice was muffled, but I could hear him well enough.

"Yes," I said. The huphelopoid vibrated a little on my face as I spoke, making me wonder if they somehow amplified the sound, but I pushed that thought back. It wasn't really important. I had superpowers so it made perfect sense that I'd be able to talk and breathe underwater with an octopus thing on my face.

"I feel like I'm going to regret this," Aethan groaned as he drew the huphelopoid to his face. He sucked in a deep breath — that I knew smelled of fish — half coughed half gaged and jerked the creature away before its tentacles could latch onto him. "Oh gods, yes."

"You get used to it," Rion said, his expression perfectly normal as if the huphelopoid didn't bother him at all.

"*You* got used to it. I'm not sure I will," Aethan shot back.

Del rolled his eyes at him. "Just do it. We're wasting time."

Aethan tried again, this time lasting long enough for the thing to attach itself. He seemed to cough into it a few times, sounding like he was choking, his eyes wide, but eventually the coughing subsided and his eyes narrowed.

"This is disgusting," he groaned. "Come on, let's get this over with."

"What if one of these things just decides to detach itself and swim away while we're down there?" Rion asked, wading deeper into the water until it was chest high.

I had to admit, I hadn't thought of that, and now that I had, I didn't much like the thought.

"Remember, the city isn't that deep. At most we'll be perhaps a hundred feet down. That takes less than a minute to swim." Del was trying to be reassuring.

"For you maybe. You've got a fish tail. I don't," Aethan said, as Rion dipped below the water for a few seconds then popped back up.

"True. But don't worry," Del said. "I can help you to the surface and assist you in breathing while we go."

My pulse stuttered at that, and the image of our lips locked as he helped me breathe flashed through my mind's eye. Then the image jumped to Rion and Aethan lip-locked with Del, which turned me on and made me giggle.

I sank below the water like Rion had to try breathing with the creature on my face and to hide my laughter, and took a few unsteady breaths.

While the guys hadn't had a problem having sex with me at the same time, I had a feeling, they wouldn't be as excited as I was to be mouth to mouth with Del in order to breathe.

"—never heard of one of these things coming off without a bit of work, though," Del reassured us as I resurfaced. "You'll all be well enough."

And with that, a few false starts to get used to breathing with the things on, and just a bit of apprehension, we dove down, heading out into the lagoon.

It was amazing to watch Del swim in his triton form, so quick and powerful. He was literally swimming circles around us so as not to get too far ahead.

It was then I knew we would never be able to stay in my world, at least not in Chicago. Del needed to be where he could swim, and Rion where he could fly and Aethan where he could run. They wouldn't have that in my world.

No, if they were going to be their best selves, I'd have to live here with them.

And while I was a bit sad about that, I wasn't entirely heartbroken. Their world was a tropical paradise after all... if Hera didn't turn her attention to it, which, now that she was aware of me, seemed unlikely.

CHAPTER 23

AETHAN

THERE WAS A SAYING: LIKE A FISH OUT OF WATER. THERE SHOULD have been a similar one: like a horse in the ocean. I felt just as out of place in the water as I was sure a fish did on dry land.

We'd been swimming for what felt like forever before Del started to get agitated and excited. Then we reached a tall stand of sea-weed that rose dozens of feet high like an underwater forest.

"Just through here," Del said.

We swam through it and stopped just on the other side to stare in stunned silence at Galniosia.

Del had been right. The city was beautiful... I just wished it was on land.

Sunlight filtered from above in rippling waves, shimmering over the city. It gleamed off pearl-white towers, thin and tall, as well as the myriad of lower buildings. And not just the palace, but all of the buildings. They all sparkled in a spectacular fashion, and as we drew closer, I could see there were shells pressed into the sides and tops of the structures, catching the sunlight and shimmering in various colors.

"Oh, wow," Annie gasped, her voice muffled by the huph-elopoid on her face.

"Welcome to Galniosia," Del proclaimed brightly, before his expression fell into grim determination. "Time for me to face my family."

We swam to the palace, a towering complex structure, with large windows that were more like doors with people coming and going from them... or were they really doors and I just thought they were windows because there were so many of them and they weren't on the ground.

Although if I really thought about it, the function and design of a building could be quite different under water, where people could swim to any floor with ease.

The central part of the palace had a large landing with a garden of rocks and various colored corals with small, bright fish darting about.

We were met by guards, who stood before an opening larger than any of the openings I'd seen, and were quickly admitted inside.

There was a flurry of activity as soon as Del's arrival was announced with other guards called forward then sent off, quickly swimming to tell whoever was supposed to know that he'd returned and servants gathering in the corridor, waiting to be commanded.

A heavy-set man with a wide, blue-green tail and the air of someone who thought he was more important than he really was, darted down the hall to greet us like one of the fish I'd seen in the coral outside despite his girth.

"Welcome home, your highness," he said, his tone verging on condescension as his gaze slid over us then jerked back to Del. "Should I have rooms prepared for your guests?"

"No, I need to speak with Archivist Umandra as soon as she's available. I'm guessing my parents will also want to see me. Might as well get that out of the way as well." He looked at us and grimaced. "We won't be staying long."

Yeah, I didn't want to spend any more time with this squid attached to my face than was absolutely necessary. Sleeping with it on was out of the question. I was sure I'd never relax with it stuck to my face long enough to even doze.

"Their majesties are in the Hall of Light. I'll take you there." The man bowed then turned to a young boy waiting bright-eyed and expectant at the line of servants — a page? — and told him to tell the archivist that Del wanted to speak with her.

Then the heavy-set man led us down a long, wide hall to another grand archway, which opened into an enormous room. I wasn't certain, but I guessed most, if not all, of the city could gather within its walls.

The Hall of Light was aptly named, not because it was filled with blazing light, but because it had no roof, allowing the magical beams of rippling sunlight to fill the space, creating an airy — well watery — open feel to the space.

It only occurred to me then, that we had roofs on the surface to keep out the weather, and there wasn't any weather down here. Everything was full of water all the time, which allowed for a much different style of building. You'd still want a roof for privacy — since anyone could swim above your house — but in a hall like this, it made sense to keep it open.

The King and Queen sat at the far end of the hall on matching gleaming white thrones, but my attention was drawn to the young triton woman next to them. I guessed that was Del's sister, the princess. Long blue-black hair, just like Del's floated behind her, but her eyes, unlike Del's blue-green, were a shimmering pearl-blue. The rest of her didn't look like Del, either. Her face was slender, with a wide smile, and she gave off the impression of being delicate, almost translucent. As we drew closer, I could see it was clear that Del very much took after his father and the princess after their mother.

I glanced at Annie and was rewarded with her catching my gaze. Her cheeks lifted in what I assumed was a smile, though I couldn't see her lips to be sure. Even without a fish tail, which would allow for much greater mobility, Annie was full of grace as she swam down the length of the hall.

"The wayward son has finally returned. Shall we have a celebration?" the queen asked, her voice heavy and cutting with sarcasm. "And he's brought guests. This is new."

"Indeed it is, and a welcome change!" the king added, opening his arms in invitation. "Honored guests, welcome to our halls. Son, what brings you back to us with these surface folk?"

Del swam ahead of us to meet his parents and sister, and as he did, another triton entered. It was obvious at first glance that this was Del's younger brother. He had a mix of his parent's features, which made him delicately handsome, not rugged and large like his brother, but with the same striking blue-black hair and green-blue eyes that Del had.

"Mother. Father," Del began. I found it interesting that he addressed her first. "Luarnon. Poseia," he added, nodding to his brother and sister. "I've come here on a quick mission to do some research in the library. I've already called for Archivist Umandra, and I—"

"A quick mission?" the queen asked, cutting him off. Her eyes narrowed. "You're not staying?"

Del stiffened at the ice in her voice, and I fought back a shudder at the chill.

"No Mother, I'm not." He drew in a long breath and squared his shoulders. "And on that note, I'm renouncing my claim to the crown. I don't want it. Let Luarnon or Poseia rule in my place."

The queen's eyes flashed wide with surprise then snapped back to narrow and angry as her lips curled back in an unfriendly smile. "Of course, this is what we've come to. Running away from your responsibility permanently this time, are you?"

"I am," Del said, not even bothering to defend himself.

"Then go." She surged up out of her throne with a powerful swish of her tail, towering above everyone, her pale green hair billowing around her like a cloud. "But don't you dare return. And since you're no longer a prince, you have no right to call upon an Archivist of the Library of Galniosia!" Her smile turned into a full sneer of disgust, her face and shoulders flushing red with her fury. "I don't care why you've come. Leave now and never return!"

"No," the king roared.

Del jerked, the movement sending him back a foot, his expression shocked at his father's ferocious outburst. In fact, everyone in the hall looked stunned as if the king never raised his voice or countermanded an order from his queen.

The queen's gaze snapped to him. "I've given an order—"

"And we rule *together*. Hanea, you're my queen, my *equal*. I'm happy to let you make most of the decisions for this kingdom. When it comes to our people, you're a wise and thoughtful ruler, but not when it comes to our son. Even if Delphon wishes to give up his title, he'll always be welcome here."

"Not by me," the queen hissed. She jerked her attention back to Del, looking at him with a disgust that made me want to tell her off. It didn't matter that she was a queen. She was Del's mother. I didn't understand how she couldn't see what a strong and honorable man he was.

"I've said what I will," she snarled, then swept out of the room.

Ouch.

Yet as soon as she left, the entire feel of the room changed to one of welcome and acceptance. Del's family approached him, and he embraced each of them in turn, then they spoke quietly amongst themselves for a moment. I didn't know if they were talking about what they were going to do about the queen or not, but no one got upset and the tension from before didn't return.

"That was harsh," Annie said softly, floating up beside me, as Rion drifted closer as well.

"His mother and my father should get together," Rion said sourly. "They'd be perfect for each other."

"I apologize for my wife," the king said as Del, his father, and siblings swam toward us. The king's voice was low as if he didn't want it to carry throughout the room, which was something I could completely understand if I was the one who had to live with her. "She's... overworked with the cares of the kingdom."

I tried to not roll my eyes. That was a polite way of putting it.

"You're abdicating?" Del's brother said, with a look of not-completely-unexpected surprise mixed with a realization of how overwhelming his situation now was. "I'll be king?"

"The laws state it need not be the eldest who inherits," the princess said politely. There was a glint in her eye. I didn't think she was seeking power, but she certainly seemed more ready for it than her brother — who I presumed was older than her. She turned her attention to Del. "No offence Del, but I always assumed you'd not take the throne."

"Then perhaps you know me better than I do," he replied, not looking at all offended at her comment.

"And who are our guests?" the king asked, turning to the rest of us.

Del finally smiled. "These are my... close friends. Aethan of the Theophylian Plains, Hyperion of the Phyllidian Forest, and Annie Chambers of... Chicago," he finished awkwardly, as if he wasn't sure how to introduce Annie. And I completely understood the sentiment. How did one tell one's family that you'd fallen in love with a woman from another world and were sharing her with three other guys?

"I've not heard of this place, Chicago," the king said. "Is it far away?"

Very far, and yet not that far. I had to stop myself from laughing. It was on another world and you couldn't get there from here at all unless Annie took you. Though the rock on the shore which we travelled through was not too far from here. Again, hard to explain.

"Ah... yes," was Del's diplomatic answer.

"And what interesting coloring," the princess added, her gaze scrutinizing Annie, and I got the distinct impression — although I wasn't quite sure how, probably woman's intuition — that she already knew there was more between Del and Annie. "Dryad? *satyr*? *aurai*?"

"She's *heliai*, a Fire Titan," Rion said, saving the rest of us from having to come up with something, "and it is quite uncomfortable for her down here."

Annie nodded. "True."

The Princess' eyes widened. "Then you're from far away. Welcome to Galniosia." She gave a nod, and I got the feeling she still didn't believe us.

We were saved from further discussion by the arrival of an ancient Triton woman with silvered scales on her tail, some of which had been lost. Her hair was the same shimmering silver color, with eyes of steel-blue. There was a wiry strength in her form, denoting no lack of vigor in her old age, and my first guess was this was the Royal Archivist.

"Delphon? Finally returned and asking for me? Well that's something I thought I'd never see," she said. "You were never that interested in my studies."

"Alas, you're right, Umandra," Del said, bowing his head in apology. "And for that I'm sorry. It's because I was so lacking in my studies that I've come to you now. I seek information of the ancient gods, specifically Hera. I was hoping you'd be able to help me— *us* find out more about her."

Umandra's wispy, silvered brows rose. "Hera? In truth I'm not sure I taught you much about her. I can see why you might need to come to me."

"What's this for?" the princess asked.

"That's a long story," Del replied. "And we're in a bit of a hurry. As you can see, my friends aren't meant for the water. I'm hoping to get them back to the shore quickly." He turned to Umandra. "Is there much you can recall? Specifically, about her powers and what she could do?"

The elder Triton swayed in the water for a long moment, eyes half closed, as if falling asleep. Then she began to recite — what sounded like verbatim — text. "Hera, the reluctant bride of Zeus, and — some say — the first among the ancient gods. She held great power and import. Like Zeus she had many consorts: the healer Asclepius, Aeolus of the winds, Autolycus the thief, and even a few women, Theia and Echo." Umandra blinked, as if coming out of a trance. "There are some other vague references to binding these consorts to her and gaining their powers."

"Healing, winds, thievery, and senses?" Rion said.

Umandra shrugged. "The ancient texts and tales are never entirely correct. There may be some discrepancies, but Hera is depicted with some or all of these powers in most of them: heightened senses to spy on her husband's trysts, healing to recover from wounds quickly and rejuvenate herself, winds to bluster and blow about her enemies. Some tales tell of the few times she and Zeus worked together, she was the high winds and he the lightning of fury. As for thievery, that's more esoteric in its depictions. Often she seems to steal the very life or essence from a person. That's the least depicted of her powers. She was also known as the matron of the home, presiding over the bonding of mates, and childbirth."

That was a lot to take in. It sounded like Hera was going to be nearly impossible to defeat. Senses to see or hear us coming, healing to resist our attacks, winds to attack us with, and somehow also able to steal our very lives away?

Well... fuck.

The others didn't look that happy either.

"Why do you need this information?" Umandra asked as the entire royal family inched closer, clearly interested in the answer as well.

"Oh, no reason really," Del said, casually. "We just need to find Hera and remove her from power — probably kill her — as she's in a position of great power in another world, where she's plotting all manner of terrible things, or so we assume."

Luarnon laughed, clearly disbelieving.

It was the princess Poseia who cut him off. "By Poseidon, you're not joking, are you?" Oh, she was keen, something that would have turned me on a couple of weeks ago and now... the only woman for me was Annie.

The thought made my heart swell with joy.

"No, I'm not joking," Del said.

Luarnon stopped laughing and silence rippled through the currents around us as the shock of the situation sank in.

CHAPTER 24

ANNIE

AFTER DEL'S STUNNING REVELATION, IT HAD BEEN EASY FOR HIM TO make apologies and say a quick goodbye to his father and siblings and for us to hurry out of the Hall of Light to return to the surface.

We swam — slowly compared to Del and the other tritons — back down the long wide hall, but when we reached the edge of the palace grounds, the princess rushed out after us.

She was alone, so whatever she suspected, she hadn't wanted to share with her father or brother.

"Del, wait. You can't be serious. What's really going on?" She swam around in front of us, and her gaze landed on me. "I know you're not *heliai*. I've never seen one, and your hair is certainly red, but that one—" She jerked her chin at Rion. "He answered too quickly and you looked worried when my father asked about your heritage. Who are you?"

I bit the inside of my cheek. I didn't know how to begin to explain that I came from another world or that I'd bonded with Del, along with three others. That would just bring up more questions when we really needed to be coming up with a plan to stop Hera.

"We don't have time to explain," Del replied.

"Make time." A fire sparked in her pearl-blue eyes and it was clear she wasn't going to let us go without an explanation. "Are they compelling you somehow? You've never been this driven before about anything."

So that was it. She was suspicious because Del was taking action. It made my heart break a little for him. First his mother basically disowned him for refusing the crown, and now his sister was questioning him because he was actually trying to do something.

"They're not compelling me." Del frowned. "Well..."

"I knew it!" Poseia exclaimed.

I glanced at Del, uncertain why he'd hesitated. We weren't compelling him. At least I didn't think we were. I'd thought he'd wanted to bond with me. Was he having doubts?

His gaze met mine and his green-blue eyes filled with love. "I'm compelled by my heart." He turned his attention back to his sister. "I'm in love with Annie. And you're right, she isn't *heliai*. She's human. And I know that means nothing to you, but it would take too long to explain."

"She's from another world," Rion said with a shrug. "Easy to explain. Hard to understand."

"Human?" Poseia asked, but she didn't seem surprised. "There are legends of humans. They're the ones who drove us from the world of the gods."

Humans were legendary? Well that was unexpected.

Then Del's previous words must have hit home for Poseia and she frowned. "And you love her?"

Her frown deepened as if she couldn't understand what seemed so simple to me and probably everyone else, and her gaze swept over me. "You don't have a body made for water, but... you're not without strengths. Attractive... in an exotic and foreign way."

I snorted. Those words had never been said about me by

anyone, ever, until now. But I guess from her perspective, I was exotic and foreign.

"Thank you," I said, not sure what else I should say.

The princess turned back to Del and examined him. "You two truly are bound by something, aren't you?"

Del met her gaze head on, waiting for her to come to the realization that he hadn't lied about us being in love.

"You really are in love. You've bonded with her!" Her surprise blossomed into a brilliant smile. "By the gods, Del, I never thought you'd find *the* woman for you." Her gaze jumped to Rion and Aethan and she cocked an eyebrow. "And these others, the way they look at you and her— Oh!"

A mix of emotions flashed through her expression and I bit my tongue, watching her realize the truth, afraid of what her reaction would be.

"You're *all* in love with her." She nodded, her expression settling on understanding and... I wasn't quite sure. Was that pride?

"You've changed brother. Matured. You were never one for settling down, nor for sharing, but you've never looked more content." Her smile faded. "So, what's this talk of fighting Hera? A dead goddess? It makes no sense."

Del opened his mouth, closed it, then opened it and closed it again as if he couldn't figure out how to respond to his sister.

"Your highness," Aethan said to the princess. "If you can accept the strangeness of Annie's heritage and our... relationships with each other, perhaps there is another strangeness, a mystery you can accept as well. The world of the gods you mentioned isn't legend, it's real. But not many can travel between that world and ours. Annie is one who can. Hera is another. She lives in this other world and doesn't use her god-like abilities for the good of all people. She needs to be stopped."

The princess nodded, her gaze turning inward as if in thought.

"If only a select few can pass from one world to the other, that would explain why it's been lost to us for thousands of years. You're a group full of many wonders, not the least of which is my brother bonding with such strange folk and dedicating himself to a woman from another world." She swam over to Del, grasped his shoulders and looked deep into his sea-green eyes. "If you survive what's to come, we'll need to have a long talk."

He nodded. "Indeed."

She released him. "Father and Luarnon will have questions, but I'll make explanations for you," she said, motioning to the seaweed forest at the edge of the city. "Go."

"She's very perceptive," Rion said softly as we swam away.

"No kidding." I glanced back, but she was already swimming back to the palace.

"It was always hard to slip anything past her, even as a child," Del said. "And she's grown up a lot since then." He sounded a bit wistful. "Perhaps more than I have, even though she's the youngest."

"Facing off against your mother, renouncing your throne. I think you've grown up well," I said softly.

He smiled at me, glided over, and brushed his lips against my cheek. Then he led us onward to shore. We didn't return to Masia, but to the beach near the black rocks where we could travel between worlds. The boat with Keph would have travelled much faster than we had, and as expected, Keph was already at the stones waiting for us.

Once on dry land, after some struggling, we managed to get the huphelopoid off our faces. The three of us who'd worn them all took deep breaths of the fresh sea air, happy to be done with the stinky things. Then we told Keph everything we'd learned. He, like the rest of us, wasn't happy about the situation.

Now, after having discussed our options, we stood before the rocks, working up the nerve to go.

I looked at each one of my guys, making sure our eyes connected so I could show them with a look how much I loved them while trying not to show how much I was afraid I'd lose them.

"Are we ready for this?" I asked, tugging on my winter clothes.

We'd all gotten dressed again, ready for winter in Chicago, but after being comfortably naked for over a day, the clothes didn't feel right any more.

"I suspect Hera was listening to us through our phones, but just in case, we need to be ready for her as soon as we get through to the other side," I said.

The guys nodded, their expressions hard with determination.

The plan was simple, but I needed to go over it again to reassure myself. From Keph's vision, we already knew Hera was at the top of a building down town. We just needed to get there and hopefully surprise her.

"Aethan and Rion will flag down a cab, preferably two. Del, Keph, and I will head to a bar I know and use their phone to call my FBI friend. Hopefully Hera won't have every phone tapped. We'll need Janice's help for the next part. Then we meet up, get in the cabs, and off we go. Ready?"

Nods all around.

This was it.

I touched the stone, and we all stepped through returning to Chicago and to a fight I was less and less certain we could win.

CHAPTER 25

KEPHAS

THE ROAR OF THE *HELICOPTER*, AS ANNIE CALLED IT, WAS INTENSE even through the ear-muffling headgear we wore.

I'd never thought to experience flying. I was far too heavy to be lifted by Rion or any other winged race back home, yet in this world, there were machines that could lift many people. Funny enough, out of all of us, Del wasn't handling the flight well, his expression pinched and his complexion green. I, on the other hand, was loving it.

Annie had called her friend at the— *what is the name? Oh, right* — the FBI and arranged the flight, and now the city was flashing by below us.

My vision from before we'd left Annie's world had told me Hera lived at the top of a tall building at the center of the city, near the lake — the vision had even given me the name of the building.

But the building had presented us with a problem: how to get all of us past a building full of people to get to that top floor.

The solution was this flying craft. We'd be dropped off on the roof, right above Hera, although with the din of the machine, I suspected we'd lose any sense of surprise. Hopefully, however, that would be balanced out by our quick arrival on scene. And while Hera could call for help, if they were coming from elsewhere in the building, they'd need a little time to get there. With luck, we'd be in and out before that help could arrive.

It was a daring plan, but I believed in Annie and the rest of the guys. We could do this. Well, we could get in and out, but whether we could deal with Hera... that remained to be seen.

Del tapped my arm and pointed at the large building we were rapidly approaching. This was it. There was a large flat spot at the top of the building, though it didn't have an "H" like the place where we'd first gotten into the *helicopter*.

The craft swooped in and touched down deftly. The plan was that it would only wait for us for a few minutes, so we threw open the door and rushed out, determined to deal with Hera as quickly as possible.

Aethan was the first to the door. "I'll go scout things out as you all get down there!" he shouted over the roar of the *helicopter*, then he was off like a blur.

I got out next. Being the biggest and hardest to hurt, I was to act like a wall and protect them in case we were met right away with an attack.

No one came to stop us and we hurried to the narrow stairs — almost too narrow for me — and headed down to Hera's floor. Del followed behind me then Rion and finally Annie accompanied by the FBI woman, Janice.

We reached the first floor down, and met up with Aethan who was waiting for us in the stairwell.

"This place is huge," he said. "Her living quarters are two levels and it looks like we're in a private stairwell. There are guards outside Hera's main door, but I locked it on them and I hope they don't have a key. That should give us some time."

"Good," Annie said.

"I also think Hera is in there alone," Aethan added. "Which is a great stroke of luck!"

"That remains to be seen," Del said behind me, echoing my own thoughts.

"This way." Aethan led us out of the stairwell into an opulent hall with bright lights and a marble floor to a set of double doors.

"I think she's in here," Aethan whispered. "I caught sight of her from a balcony outside during my scouting."

"Indeed I am," Hera called from inside. "Come on in, Annie."

I huffed a heavy breath. We hadn't expected surprise, but it would have been nice.

Aethan pulled open the door, revealing a large room. It was lavishly decorated with thick carpets and many tables and cushioned chairs. Along the far wall stood a bank of floor-to-ceiling windows looking out over a large, sprawling balcony, and beyond that the lake.

Hera wore a silk wrap tied tight about her waist, accentuating her thin figure. It was colorful with flowers and birds depicted on it. She tossed her black hair back with a casual hand and peered at me, hungrily, as if she wanted to eat me, making my chest tighten with fear. The look was unnerving and she didn't seem worried about us at all. Something I didn't like.

And yet she seemed so small and defenseless. Maybe I could just grab her and be done with this.

I started forward and reached to grab her, but she seized one of my outstretched hands and I felt— I couldn't quite describe it. It was as if lightning shot through my entire being. Then the world was spinning and she casually tossed me across the room.

Annie called out my name and I landed hard, my breath knocked out of me.

"This was a mistake, Annie," Hera sneered. "You can't hope to win against me, and I can't be killed, so what was your plan?"

Aethan ran forward too fast for me to see. I was guessing he tried to grab her as well, but she blurred, as if she was moving as fast as he was, and he was flying through the air and crashing into a table beside me with a heavy grunt of pain.

"Unless, of course, you've come to hand over your men to me?" Hera purred. "That's very kind of you."

Annie's face had gone pale, the speckles on her cheeks dark in contrast, and her eyes were wide with fear.

I climbed to my feet as Rion and Del fanned out, looking at Hera warily, not sure what to do, while the FBI woman had her weapon out and pointed at Hera.

"June Olympios," Janice said, "come willingly and you won't be hurt."

Hera threw her head back and laughed. "Oh, Annie. You brought a poor civilian into this, too?" With a casual flick of her fingers, a wind gust swept through the room, knocking over a few chairs, and slammed into Janice. The woman flew back, crashing out the doors and tumbling into the hall.

"I don't know—" Hera groaned and dropped to one knee as her gaze jerked to Del and locked on him. "This is new. I haven't been attacked by a water-bearer in a while."

Grimacing, she slowly rose. Her body trembled, but her gaze never left Del, who was now also trembling and starting to curl in on himself.

His complexion started to turn gray and horrible realization hit me. "She's stealing our powers!"

It made sense. She'd thrown me like she had the same strength as me. Then she'd moved as quickly as Aethan, and was now using Del's powers against him.

"So that's what thievery meant," Aethan mumbled. "Well, fuck! How do we fight someone who has all of our powers plus her own?"

"Exactly," Hera sneered, her voice cold and deadly. She straightened and clenched her fist. Del screamed and collapsed, writhing on the floor in agony. "You don't have a chance against me. Give up now and I'll let you all live long enough to have a nice, sappy goodbye. Persist, and I'll kill you all in an instant."

A loud bang rang out and Hera screamed as blood sprayed out of her neck. She choked and clamped a hand over the wound, gasping for air, her eyes wide and stunned.

I rushed in, hoping the wound would disable her enough for me to knock her out. I swung a backhand at her temple with all my strength, and she caught it without even grunting with effort.

She glared at me with her silver-blue eyes and a feral smile, as the wound on her neck bled less and less, and closed up.

Then she squeezed and for the first time in a long time, I felt pain as her fingers dug into my hand. She seemed able to bypass my greater durability, nails digging in and drawing blood.

"This is your choice?" she hissed. "Big mistake."

She kicked between my legs and I nearly blacked out with pain and shock. I flew across the room, crashing through the furniture, but didn't really notice. That didn't hurt as much as her kick had.

The guys yelled and screamed, cries of pain and dismay filled the room, but my world was spinning on the edge of unconsciousness at the agony. I couldn't see, let alone stand up and fight, and I could only pray the others could succeed where I couldn't.

CHAPTER 26

ANNIE

NOTHING WAS WORKING AND EVERYTHING WAS GOING WRONG. I needed to do something and quick. I'd been stunned and uncertain so far, watching my guys get tossed about the room and tormented, but it had to stop.

Except what could I do? Hera had access to all my powers plus her own.

Rion was the only one of the guys still standing, since he hadn't acted yet. We glanced at each other and nodded, and I prayed he'd had the same idea I had.

I launched myself at Hera with Aethan's speed and closed my eyes, as Rion — on cue — blinded her with a flash of light.

Please work. Please, God.

The flashed dissipated, and I opened my eyes again to see Hera in front of me, stunned, blinking.

Good.

I hit her hard, tackling her to the ground. I didn't really know how to fight, but I hoped a super-strength slap, might just do her in. I reared back, sitting on her, and sent my hand flying, but she somehow caught it, even with her eyes closed.

"Bad girl!" she growled.

With a vise-like grip, she crushed my wrist, my bones shattering. Agony tore through me, drawing a scream as tears streamed down my cheeks.

A gust of wind slammed me into the ceiling, stealing my breath and making the world lurch, and I crashed back to the hard floor face-first, a dozen feet away from her. Pain sliced through my face and blood rushed from my nose.

Rion screamed, and he charged toward Hera, but she punched him with bone-crushing strength fueled by Keph's power. His ribs broke with a resounding *crack* and he flew across the room, slammed into the wall, and sagged to the floor, unconscious.

God, no!

My soul screamed. I was going to lose him. I was going to lose all of them.

I reached out to him with my healing powers. His pulse stuttered then stopped and my pulse lurched in fear as I flooded him with my magic. She'd almost killed him. If I'd been a second later, he would have died.

I pushed everything I could into Rion and watched his body convulse with the sudden healing. Strength returned to him, as it ebbed out of me. He was alive, but didn't regain consciousness.

I healed myself next, but only used enough power so my wounds wouldn't distract me, knitting my wrist back together so I could use my hand and easing the pain in my face. I didn't have a lot of power left after saving Rion and I couldn't afford to pass out from exhaustion. Not yet anyway.

Three more shots in quick succession roared through the room and Hera screamed again.

I forced myself to sit up as Janice hurried to my side and knelt next to me.

"You okay?"

"I'll be fine." But even as I said that, Hera rose from where she'd fallen, three bloody gunshot holes in her silk kimono showing her healing flesh beneath.

Del's Royal Archivist had said Hera could heal — so it didn't matter if she was using my power or not — but the gunshots were still knocking her down and forcing her to expend power. And if I had a limit, she had to have one, too.

"Keep firing at her!" I told Janice. So far that was the only thing that seemed to work.

We rose together and Janice fired three more shots. The first clipped a shoulder as Hera moved, zipping like Aethan, suddenly disappearing and reappearing right beside us.

"You've been a naughty girl, Annie. For that, you'll pay the dearest price!"

She grabbed the gun from Janice's hands and shoved the woman away. Janice tumbled across the floor, bumping to a stop at the windows overlooking the balcony.

"For your insolence, I'm going to take what you prize most," Hera sneered with the tigress grin, and she slapped a heavy hand over my heart.

I tried to jerk away, but something in her touch seized my muscles, freezing me in place, making it impossible for me to move. Then agony tore into me and I felt my life being ripped out.

I screamed, as her power sliced deep, reaching past my body, my cells, and tearing into my soul. Everything I was rushed out of me, and time stuttered into horrific slow motion, the horror and agony being drawn out while my mind and body howled.

Then she stepped back, and I sagged to my knees, gasping and empty... and not dead.

I didn't understand how I was still alive, how she could take everything from me and I was still—

My pulse stalled.

I couldn't feel their powers.

I couldn't feel *them*.

My connection with my guys was gone.

My bonds were gone!

Please. No.

I mentally clawed inside me, desperate to find our connection, desperate to rebuild the connection with them. But I was empty. Completely hollowed out, as if my heart and soul had been removed and I was now just a shell—

Except I wasn't empty. There was something deep within me, something small and strange, and it connected me to... Hera.

Oh, God.

Hera's eyes widened as if she, too, had just figured out we were connected, but her shock twisted into evil satisfaction and she shoved me back.

I stumbled and fell onto my butt. The impact jarred up my spine, but the pain was nothing compared to the empty agony of losing my bonds.

Hera laughed. "You were a fool to go up against the goddess of bonds, Annie. Who do you think made such things even possible? It was me! That is my ultimate power. To make and break bonds, and I've just taken yours."

"No." *Please no.* Except I knew the truth. I could *feel* it.

Her laugh rose to a crescendo. "What a wonderful look on your face. Such beautiful horror. I'd savor it, but I'm not that dumb. It's time for you to die."

She slapped her hands together and a blast of wind slammed into me, throwing me back and crashing me through the windows. Glass tore through my clothes and sliced into my back as I flew over the balcony. The backs of my legs hit the glass half-wall at the edge of the balcony, breaking bones — as well as the glass, which sliced into my calves — and sent me tumbling backwards around and around.

For a second, I was suspended in the air, time once again

slowing as I realized Janice had been caught up in the blast as well, thrown out over the edge like me.

Then time lurched back to normal and I fell. The world spun around and around, sky, ground, buildings, the wind from my fall stinging my skin.

I tried to control my water, make myself float like I had when I'd made love with Rion—

But I no longer had Del's powers.

Oh, God. They're gone.

And Rion was still unconscious and couldn't release his wings and rescue me.

There was nothing and no one who could help me.

Nothing.

Nothing but the ground rushing up to meet me.

BONDS OF THE GODDESS

GRECIAN GODDESS: BOOK 3

CHAPTER 1

ANNIE

I FELL, THE WORLD SPINNING: SKY, BUILDINGS, GROUND, SKY, buildings, ground, over and over, around and around.

My initial scream at having been flung out the window of Hera's high rise died as the aching emptiness of losing my bonds with my guys filled me and the certainty that this was it. I didn't have Del's powers anymore, I couldn't make myself float, and Rion was unconscious and couldn't fly out to save me.

Sky, buildings, Janice—

Janice!

She'd been caught up in Hera's gust as well, and just like me was spinning, her screams having died off too. What was the point? We were dead and there wasn't anything we could do about it.

She spun out of sight, then back into sight, then out, then—

Was way too close, swooping toward me with—

Holy-what-the-fuck!

Were those wings?

She seized my arm just before I hit the ground, and wrenched me up, making my stomach lurch at the sudden change of direction.

My heart pounded so hard it shook me with every throbbing beat, and my thoughts whirled.

I was just—

I jerked my gaze up to the top of the high rise where I'd fallen.

I was dead. I was sure I was going to die, then—

My attention jumped to Janice.

Then—

Then—

It was as if I couldn't comprehend that Janice had wings. She wasn't like me... was she?

She set me down, but between my shattered and sliced calves — from going over the balcony railing — and my own jelly-legs from thinking I was about to die, I simply sagged in a heap on the sidewalk.

Janice sat heavily next to me. One of her wings curled around before her and she stared at it, looking as stunned as I felt. Her feathers were large and long and a gorgeous golden-brown like hawk wings and not like Rion's white angel wings. Then her attention jerked to me.

"Did you do this?" she demanded.

Me?

"You're a goddess," she said. "Did you give me wings?"

Had I?

No. I couldn't have. Even if I'd been able to think past falling to my death, I couldn't give someone wings. I couldn't even give someone powers... could I?

No. I hadn't given the guys their powers. They gained their powers by entering my world, and when I bonded with them, I got their powers as well. And I was pretty sure I hadn't bonded with Janice.

My chest squeezed, my soul searching for the bonds with my guys that were no longer there.

I'd lost them—

But they were still alive and with Hera right this very minute. I had to save them, had to—

"Annie, did you give me wings?" Janice pressed, yanking my attention back to her.

"No," I said, but my voice was so shaky, I wasn't sure it had come out clear. "No," I repeated, trying to be firm, but too much was going on and I couldn't stop trembling.

"Then what the hell is this?" she asked, her voice also shaky.

She crossed her arms over her now bare breasts, covering herself in a weak attempt at modesty and an even weaker attempt to stay warm against the freezing temperature. It seemed an unfortunate side effect of the wings having sprout out her back was that they'd ripped off everything she'd been wearing above the waist.

People were gawking at us and a crowd was gathering nearby. Of course I couldn't blame them. Even if they hadn't seen us fall, Janice was topless and had wings.

Murmurs rippled around us.

"It's an angel!"

"That was some stunt. I don't even see the safety chute."

"I wonder what they're promoting?"

"We should get out of here," I forced out, my attention jumping back to the top of the building where my guys were as I tried to stagger to my feet.

Agony screamed through my body, reminding me I needed to heal myself, and that even if I could fix myself with what little magic I had left, I'd still be helpless against Hera.

Hell, me with all of my guys' powers and all of my guys, along with Janice and her gun hadn't been enough to bring down Hera.

I channeled my healing power to my legs, strengthening them

as I mended the broken bones and pushed out the glass shards. My back was cold and in pain. I'd gone through a window backward. My shirt was still mostly on, enough that I didn't care about the cold, but I healed the wounds there as well.

Standing — successfully this time — I helped Janice up as well.

Now that I was on my feet, I could see large men in tactical gear with automatic rifles, running toward us from Hera's building.

Well, fuck.

"We need to get out of here. Now," I said, my voice stronger this time. Looking around, I quickly got my bearings. We were across the street from Macy's downtown.

My mind spun into action as I recalled an article I'd read about the pedway, a series of tunnels creating a whole underground city below downtown. I'd never gone down there myself, but there was supposed to be an entrance from Macy's.

I grabbed Janice's arm and hustled her across the street, not caring about traffic. Luckily, we weren't hit, though there was a lot of honking and curses thrown our way.

Once inside Macy's, I instantly felt better. Who didn't feel better inside Macy's? The trouble was, Janice's feathery wings had barely gotten through the door and would be an issue now that we were inside.

"Can you get rid of those things?" I asked.

"I don't even know where they came from!"

"Well try," I snapped back.

That seemed to jolt some sense into her and she blinked as her gaze swept around the store as if she'd just realized where we were.

"Right, sorry." She frowned, then squeezed her eyes shut, then scrunched up her face, and for a second I was afraid she wouldn't be able to do it.

Then her wings vanished. One second they were there, the next they weren't, they didn't even melt away like Rion's did. Just poof.

She snagged a shirt from a nearby rack and pulled it on and we hurried deeper into the store.

"Hey!" a woman with the look of a store employee called out, racing toward us. "You can't just..."

"FBI!" Janice shouted a little too forcefully, her shock still evident as she held up her badge on the lanyard still around her neck.

The clerk stumbled to a stop, her expression shocked.

And because we didn't have time to waste, I took advantage of that shock. "Where's your entrance to the pedway? The under-ground thingy?" I asked, as assertively as possible.

"Over there." The clerk pointed toward a bank of escalators heading to the basement.

Right, of course. That should have been obvious, but I was running on pure adrenaline and was barely thinking. In fact, I was stunned I was thinking at all... which was just par for the course the last couple of weeks.

We ran from the still baffled clerk and hit the escalators as men stormed into the store behind us, and I prayed they'd have no clue about the pedway's layout, because I certainly didn't. My hope was to lose them and hide somewhere without getting lost myself. At least Janice was running on her own now, and I wasn't having to drag her along.

Everything became a blur. We ran from hall to hall, trying to avoid larger open areas. Finally, we came to the door of a service area. A janitor had just come out and was walking away, and I managed to stick my foot in the door before it closed and locked itself.

We slid in, pulling the door closed and leaned against the cinderblock walls trying to gasp for air as quietly as possible.

I was fairly certain we'd lost Hera's men, but I didn't want to risk it, and the second we had a little bit of breath back, we continued running.

I didn't know how long later it was when we finally rushed, out of breath, through a metal security door into a dimly lit, short hall. We sagged onto the floor, leaning against the wall behind the door so if it opened, we'd be hidden behind it, gasping and trembling.

"Holy fuck," Janice said, once she'd managed to catch her breath again. "Did that just happen?"

"Yep," I said, unable to stop myself from shaking. "But I couldn't explain it to you." All I really knew was that Hera had handed our asses to us and she still had my guys.

My chest squeezed again and I fought to breathe past the emptiness inside me.

"So ah..." Janice frowned, turned her back to me, and pulled up her newly acquired shirt, showing me her back. "Are there... markings or something? Am I bleeding?"

Her back was smooth and clear with no indication she'd ever grown wings.

"There's nothing."

She pulled her shirt down. "So just bam, I have wings? Then I don't? What sort of fucked up world is this?"

Except I had a sneaking suspicion that it wasn't *this* world that was the reason.

"I think... well, those guys I was with..." How did I put this without sounding crazy? Except Janice already knew about my magic and Hera, so hey, another world was just another detail.

"The guys are from another world where people have wings and can put them away when they're done. It's crazy, but it's true. I've seen it. I'm guessing you have some of that in your blood, probably from an ancient ancestor. It must have come out when you needed it most, I guess... maybe?"

"That's insane," she scoffed then frowned. "And yet... I have wings... so... what the fuck?" She snarled the last word, a mix of emotions rushing across her expression. She was upset and shocked and confused. I could understand that. Her world had just been turned upside down. I'd been there not that long ago.

"Someday I'll take you to this place and you can see for yourself. For now, we just need to survive." And I needed to get my guys back.

The pain in my chest clenched tight again, stealing my breath and a new realization hit me. Our bonds were gone and they'd watched me be thrown out a window. They probably thought I was dead.

For all I knew, *they* were dead.

I didn't know how everything had gone so wrong, and I could only hope Hera, being the sick fuck that she was, would want to savor my guys' suffering and keep them alive long enough for me to figure out how to save them.

Gods, please.

Except what else could I do? She was so damned powerful.

And yet, I couldn't just give up.

She had my guys!

"This is so messed up." *I* was messed up. I was stupid enough to think we stood a chance against a three-thousand-year-old goddess.

"At least you didn't sprout wings," Janice said, her voice thick with exhaustion and frustration as she tried to crane her neck and see her back.

No, but my bonds with the guys had been severed. I was so very alone and scared and I didn't know what to do. I should have never even considered going up against Hera. I wasn't a hero. Sure, I'd been given some powers, but... I didn't know how to fight crime. I was a quiet administrative professional. That's what I was good at. Not... trying to take down supervillains! What had I been thinking?

"We should probably go... somewhere," I said, my voice weak and uncertain. "Any ideas where?"

"Ah..." Janice still seemed distracted, as if she was stuck on the fact that she had wings. Which I could totally understand. "What? Sorry?"

"Where should we go? I can't go home and you shouldn't either. I'm guessing you can't go back to work. Hera will probably know if we go anywhere we'd usually go. We could try to get a hotel room somewhere, but I don't have a lot of cash on me and she can probably track credit cards and things. We need to stay off grid." But that left us with little to no options.

"I... uh... I think I might know a place." Janice dragged her gaze from staring off into space and back to me, but her eyes were still filled with shock. She hadn't fully come to grips with everything that had happened to us yet.

I wasn't sure I had either.

"There's this drug house," she said. "We took down some cartel guys there a couple weeks ago. It's empty now, and I can get us there if you have cab fare."

"Yeah, I think I have enough for that. Where is it?"

"Out in Oakbrook."

I raised my brows. "Swanky."

That was a nice neighborhood. My dad had doctor friends who lived out there, high-end surgeons who made a killing doing brain-stuff and heart-things.

I wasn't sure I had enough cash to get us there by taxi, but I could probably get us most of the way.

"Now we just need to get out of here and back to street level." I stood and looked around. There was the door we'd come through, next to where we'd collapsed, another at the end of the short hallway that said ELECTRICAL on it, and a third that said STOR-AGE. Our only way out was to go back into the hall we'd just come from.

And just as I thought that, the door started to open.

Crap. Hera's men had found us.

CHAPTER 2

ANNIE

PANIC SEIZED ME. THE ONLY SMALL CHANCE WE HAD TO ESCAPE WAS to fight and the best way to do that was to strike before they expected it, make an opening, and run like hell.

I jerked in front of the opening door and punched before I could lose my nerve. My fist slammed against a face dusted with stubble, but I no longer had Keph's strength and the impact jarred up my arm, probably hurting me more than the guy I'd just struck.

The man grunted and stumbled, his shoulder hitting the door-frame, and brilliant blue-green eyes widened with shock, capturing me.

My pulse lurched. "Del?"

He's alive. He's here. Thank God.

"Yeah," he said, rubbing his jaw. "You hit me."

I threw my arms around him and he easily plucked me up, lifting me from the ground in a tight embrace.

"Thank the gods you're alive and safe!" I said, though I didn't know if he heard it with my face buried in his chest.

"I'm the only one," he said, his voice grim as he set me on my feet but kept his arms tight around me.

The only one? Were the others dead? Had I killed them by insisting on confronting Hera?

"How did you find us?" Janice asked.

"I threw myself out the window after you, but my ability to manipulate the water within me is more like floating than flying. It took me a moment to reach the ground and when I did, I noticed you running into that building. At first, I didn't know where you'd gone, but then..." He hooked a finger under my chin and urged me to look up at him. Pain filled his stunning eyes, the same aching heartache I felt. "I can't feel you anymore... The bond...?"

I tried to swallow around the lump in my throat. "It's gone. Hera took it somehow."

"Gods," he breathed, the muscles in his jaw tightening. "I could *feel* your water. So I followed that and found you here."

"Feel her water?" Janice asked.

"It's his magic," I said, not looking away from Del. "What about the others?"

"Hera has them. I saw them all caught up in bubbles of wind, unable to move," he replied. "I was the only one who escaped."

But they were still alive.

Thank God. Thank any and all gods.

Except how long would Hera keep them alive? Would she drain them of their powers as she had her previous harem? Would she torment them? Or would she get bored and just kill them.

"We have to rescue them." But I was exhausted, Janice was rattled, and Hera would likely be on guard, expecting a rescue attempt. Even if we were at full power and unexpected, we still didn't stand a chance, not without one hell of a good plan. "Fuck!"

"We need to rest. We need help. We need..." Del ran a hand through his long, blue-black hair, pushing it out of his face. "Gods, I don't know. She was so much more powerful than I expected."

"We can go to my safe house for now," Janice said.

"Safe house?" Del frowned. "What's that?"

"Exactly what it sounds like," Janice said, rolling her eyes at him as if he was an idiot for not knowing — because she probably hadn't fully registered on the fact that he was from a different world. "A *safe* house."

He nodded with a grimace. Then, he looked at her, cocking his head in curiosity. "I saw you sprout wings, *aurai* wings."

"Or-eye?" Janice sounded out the word.

"Are they different from Rion?" I asked as Del glanced back into the hall we'd come from then motioned that it was clear.

"Yes. Rion is *erinai*. *Aurai* are nymphs of the high mountains," Del replied, confidently heading down the hall as if he knew where he was going. "Some spend all their time in the skies, rarely landing. Their wings are different, more like an eagle's. Whereas Rion's are more like a falcon's, built for speed and lower-level flight."

A falcon's wings were different from an eagle's? I had no clue... and really, I didn't want to get into it now. It wasn't really important.

"So I'm a nymph?" Janice said with a harrumphing laugh. "Some of my boyfriends would beg to differ."

"I don't know what you are," Del said. "You're of this world, so you shouldn't have wings at all... or so I thought. Although..." His frown deepened. "I suppose if my people came and went from this world in ages past, then perhaps some seed of my kind could still remain here. Very odd though."

"Lucky," I said with a shiver. If she hadn't sprouted wings, we'd both be dead.

"Very," Janice said in a similar tone, likely coming to the same realization.

Del led us to a wide set of stairs with a cold wind blowing down them and we climbed up onto a busy, snowy street where Janice flagged down a cab. We took it to Oakbrook, and I paid with the last of my cash, since I couldn't risk using my credit cards or going to a bank or ATM to withdraw more.

Luckily Janice's safe house was a fully furnished mansion set back on a large piece of property and there was even some food still in the fridge and pantry.

We picked through what wasn't expired or moldy, eating a meal in solemn silence around a table in the breakfast nook of an enormous luxury kitchen. I tried not to look like I was panicking, but my heart and thoughts had never stopped racing, even if the rest of me was starting to slow from exhaustion.

I had to rescue the others.

But I couldn't, not without an army. And even then, how would we do it?

Gods, I had no idea.

I only knew that I had to rescue them...

I had to—

Those thoughts just kept circling around and around in my mind, making me more frustrated and sad.

The food tasted like dust, but I didn't know if that was because it had come from boxes and had been sitting around, or because my soul hurt from the emptiness inside me.

Janice found a stash of liquor and we all had a tall glass to try to calm ourselves.

It didn't work. Now I was tipsy and panicking.

"Janice," Del said softly.

The woman turned to him. She still didn't look well. The realization that she was something other than human still pinched her expression. "Yes?"

"Might I have a moment alone with Annie?"

She looked from him to me a few times then topped up her glass with the amber liquid from the whiskey bottle and headed out of the kitchen, stopping at the large archway and half turning back to us. "It's a large house. I'll be... somewhere else... for as long as you need."

I didn't understand what she meant by that until she was gone and Del was suddenly very close, wrapping his arms around me in a comforting embrace.

"I'm sorry for all of this Annie," he said softly.

I melted into him, burying my face in his chest and sobbed, unable to hold my tears back. I was so lost and shaken. My body hurt, my soul hurt, and I couldn't hold it in and look strong anymore, especially with his arms around me.

He held me tight for a long moment then pressed his lips against the top of my head and murmured, "This is all my fault. Our fault. Us guys. We asked too much of you. You gave us so much and we just kept asking for more. We pushed you and ourselves beyond our limits and now..." His voice choked up and I thought I heard a faint sniffle.

I looked up at him then through the river flowing from my eyes, and he smiled softly. There was indeed a tear in his eye, just the one, but the hurt in his expression spoke of something deeper than just that single tear.

"Is it the same for you?" he asked, his voice heartbreakingly soft. "Like a limb has been cut off?"

I nodded.

"Only I imagine it must be worse for you. You lost all four of us and we only lost you."

I nodded again, unable to speak. The pain and the emptiness consumed me, threatening to drag me into darkness.

But then... I had Del. He was right here, and one kiss could fix everything.

Urgency flooded me, and I tangled my fingers in his hair, drawing him down to kiss me.

He caught on quickly, lifting me and meeting my lips halfway, and I kissed him with all the hunger born from the void inside me.

He matched my intensity, our kiss turning ferocious in our desperate desire to rekindle the bond between us that wasn't reforming.

My grip tightened in his hair and his embrace turned to steel. It had taken just one kiss on the lips before, but no matter how long or hard we mashed our mouths together, the bond didn't return.

No light. No warmth. Nothing.

Finally, with my heart breaking, Del released me and sagged back onto a chair. My soul and body throbbed with emptiness and unfulfilled desire, and I followed him, straddling him to stay close, unable to deal with the physical separation in the face of our spiritual one.

I needed him. Needed him in me, his soul, his body, anything, something, please. Even if it was just for a moment, even if it wasn't our permanent bond. I couldn't be without him. Not right now.

"Perhaps we need to do more than kiss this time," he said, a mix of hope and desolation in his sea-green eyes as he wrapped his arms around me, steadying me in his lap.

"Yes. Of course," I replied, realization snapping through me. I jerked to my feet and yanked off my shirt even as a part of me trembled with the fear that sex wouldn't be enough.

But it had to be. I didn't know how I'd live with the ache inside me.

I shoved my pants off as Del stood and started to strip as well.

He quickly unbuttoned his shirt and shrugged out of it, revealing his gorgeous, sculpted chest, arms, and abs, then stepped out of his slacks, his erection springing free, large and proud.

The first time I'd seen him, he'd been sitting on that rock, naked and erect, and I'd thought I'd been in a dream.

In a way it had been... and still was. His ridiculously wonderful cock was now mine. *He* was mine and I was his, and I was going to do whatever it took to claim him once again, to turn this nightmare back into the wonderful dream it had originally been.

We crashed back together, our lips hungry and desperate, and he sat back on the chair, drawing me down to straddle his lap as I wrapped my fingers around his cock. Not that he needed any working up. I was the one who needed help getting wet enough to take him inside me, but I had to have my hands on him, caressing him, feeling him, being connected with him in any small way that I could.

I stroked my hand from his base to his tip, squeezing hard, perhaps too hard, though at least I didn't have Keph's strength this time, and savored his shuddering groan into my mouth.

"Let me know when you want me," he said, his voice gruff with desire, his fingers roughly tormenting me, teasing through my folds and building up my own slick need.

"You'll come on command?" I gasped as he ground his thumb against my clit, the sensation just on the wrong side of painful.

But I didn't care. I was angry and empty and pain was something. Pain was what I needed, a way to release the furious heartache threatening to consume me.

"I'll come when you say."

He shoved two fingers inside me, his thumb still hard against my clit, and my body trembled at the invasion. I dug my nails into his shoulder as my grip on his erection tightened and rocked my hips against his hand, but it wasn't enough. I needed him inside me.

"Fuck me," I hissed. *Fuck me until I can't think straight, until I can't feel, until I've forgotten how terrified I am. Fuck me until our souls bond again. Please.*

I leaned back and aligned him with my opening. He pulled his fingers out, and I impaled myself on him in one hard stroke. He was too much, too large. I wasn't completely ready for him and I didn't care. I took him all the way to the hilt, crying out with pain and heartache, trembling with a small, pathetic orgasm.

My breath hitched with disappointment then Del rubbed his thumb over my clit, making my orgasm blossom into a soft full-body shudder. My release, still too small, swept through me, and for a flickering second I forgot my pain. We were connected, even if it was only in body, and I could lose myself in him... over and over again until I was too exhausted to cry.

Still trembling, I pressed a finger to his lips. "Remember, you don't come until I say so."

He nodded stiffly.

"Good."

Then I began to lose myself in the bliss of his amazing body, rocking myself to even greater heights, tears leaking from my eyes.

CHAPTER 3

DELPHON

BY ALL THE GODS, I WASN'T SURE I'D BE ABLE TO KEEP MY PROMISE. Annie was, by far, the most incredible and sexy woman I'd ever known, and she was lost in lust and heartache — the same heartache that threatened to consume me. Her eyes were semi-glazed as she took her pleasure from me, over and over again, working herself, hard and needful, until she stiffened and shuddered with yet another orgasm. Then she began again. Her nails dug into my skin, her head thrown back with the desperate, feral cries of a hunger she couldn't sate, a black pit inside her that she couldn't fill.

And through all this, I felt like I would explode within her. Yet somehow, by some miracle, I held myself back, tense and rigid. I was at the peak of my own bliss, but couldn't enjoy it, couldn't release, not just because I'd made a promise to her, but because watching her broke my heart.

Finally, she slumped forward onto me, her head on my shoulder, her body limp and weak even though her hips were still subtly grinding down on me.

With a hoarse voice, she whispered, "you're a miracle, Del. I can't believe—" She gasped and shuddered as another small orgasm rippled through her. "Through all that..." She lifted her head, her hair falling in a pale red curtain over her beautiful, speckled face, a thin veil, hiding nothing but making her all the more mysterious because of it.

"I've taken what I need," she murmured, even though I could tell from the desperate look in her eyes, she hadn't gotten what she truly needed: the return of our bond. "Your turn. Do what you will."

She moved in to press her lips to mine, her hair caught between us, but I didn't care. I kissed her all the same, wrapping my arms around her to press her amazing, lush body tight against me, savoring her hard, hungry lips against mine.

I was tempted to simply end this in that moment. Certainly, I was ready to, but now that it actually came to it, I hesitated. I'd let her take what she needed from me, let her use my body to distract her from the emptiness within her. Now I'd do a little taking of my own.

I carefully lifted her off me, making her gasp as I withdrew from her fully, and set her on the table beside us. She laid back, and I ran my hands up the insides of her thighs, opening her. Her entrance was swollen and wet, the perfect combination that would ensure a delicious, tight fit while still letting me push smoothly into her.

But instead of just plunging in, I teased her with my fingers, sweeping her wetness over her clit, flicking and rubbing it, making her twitch and moan, building up a desire she thought she'd sated.

I didn't think she'd been expecting this. Indeed, I was caught off guard that I wasn't cock-deep inside her, desperate for my release. But I didn't want to just find my own pleasure, I wanted to give her more, wanted to show her even if our bond hadn't reformed that I'd still be there for her, still go to the end of the world and beyond to support her and bring her pleasure.

I slid two fingers inside her, curling them up to hit that magic spot that always made her cry out with need, and rubbed my thumb over her clit. She gasped and shuddered, writhing on the table, her hair splayed out behind her, her skin radiant with sweat, making her look like the goddess that I knew she was.

Another orgasm crashed through her, drawing a desperate, hoarse, "Yes!" from her lips, making me chuckle.

"More?" I purred, unable to help myself.

"Yes," she begged as if she hadn't already had enough, as if we were just getting started.

Keeping my fingers inside her, I knelt and replaced my thumb with my lips, sucking on that sensitive nub. Her fingers tangled in my hair, drawing me closer, and she bucked into my mouth, gasping and mewling at my ministrations.

I made her come again, hard and fast, her cry making my balls tighten, threatening an explosive release. I needed to get inside her. Now.

Before she was done trembling, I roughly pulled her off the table, turned her around, and bent her forward, pressing her incredible breasts against the tabletop. Her legs were weak, so I held her hips, raising them until she was on her tip-toes. Even then I had to lower myself before I could find her opening with my cock.

She turned her head to the side, her golden gaze filled with a wild intensity meeting mine. "Yes, take me."

I thrust into her hard, stepping in as I brought her hips to mine. She cried her pleasure, her body already trembling again, another release building within her.

I withdrew and thrust again.

"Oh, yes," she cried, urging me on, and I thrust again and again. It was my turn to brand my heartache on her body, like she'd branded mine, and she was giving herself freely to me, like she always did.

I pounded into her, my strokes wild, frenzied and she heaved herself up on her arms and bucked her hips back, crashing our bodies together, trying to fill the emptiness inside us.

"Oh, gods!" Her head thrashed from side to side and her body started to tense with another orgasm.

I wrapped an arm under her chest and jerked her up, my pace frantic. I couldn't get deep enough, couldn't reach the part of her soul that would connect us again.

With a roar, I furiously thrust until I exploded inside her and her muscles clenched around me as she let out a wordless cry, shudders wracking her body just as shudders wracked mine.

We stayed that way, locked together in pleasure and soul-throbbing pain for a long moment. Then I released her, and she sagged on the table with a faint, tired smile.

I didn't want to take myself out of her. I wanted to stay within her forever and being connected like we were was our only way now. But eventually I withdrew from her, collapsed onto a chair, breathing hard, and pulled her into my arms.

My throat tightened with grief I refused to show her. Not after she so passionately made love to me. Gods, even with all of that the bond hadn't been restored. We'd shared a moment unlike anything I'd ever known and that hadn't done it.

Well, cursed crows! What was it going to take?

I held her, unwilling to let her go until she started shivering and had to get dressed. She took another long sip on the bottle of alcohol, then I helped her to a long, plush couch, where she collapsed and fell, almost instantly, into a fitful sleep.

I sighed, watching her, my chest aching. We were broken and neither of us knew how to put the pieces back together. At least not yet. Apparently, sex on a level beyond reason wasn't the answer.

I put my clothes back on and a little while later, Janice returned. I was leaning against the marble counters in the extravagantly large kitchen, not sure what to do, when she found me.

"You two have been quiet for a while, so I thought it safe to return," she said, pouring herself another drink.

"You could hear us? I thought you said this was a large house." It was certainly larger than most I'd seen in this world or my own — excluding the palace I'd grown up in.

"Oh, it is, but... wow. Annie is ungodly loud. I almost thought you were torturing her for some of that, except most torture victims aren't yelling out those sorts of things." She downed half of what was in her glass then lifted the bottle to look at it. "I eventually found the wine cellar and that worked to block you two out... mostly. I think once I'm done with this bottle, I'll grab a few bottles from down there."

"You're just going to drink yourself into oblivion?" I asked, a bit worried for her.

"Yep. Seems like the right thing to do after one sprouts wings." She nodded, pain and confusion swirling in her eyes.

I'd seen the moment when those expansive golden-hued wings had burst forth. Even I'd been surprised. This woman, who'd thought herself a normal person from this world, must have been even more shocked, and I couldn't imagine what she must have felt.

Well, actually, perhaps it was like me discovering my water powers. Though that had come as a slow revelation, a creeping feeling and testing of abilities. So, no, it probably wasn't the same.

"Perhaps your wings could be seen as a gift?" I offered tentatively. "Now you can fly. Isn't that... something..." I didn't quite know how to finish that since I hated the sensation of flying myself.

"Oh, it's something all right." She downed the rest of the amber liquid and filled her glass again. The bottle was nearly empty now. "Yeah, sure, flying would be great. Too bad I have to do it topless and flash my tits at the world when I do. That's an amazing side effect." She rolled her eyes at me, her expression and tone sour.

I hadn't noted anything wrong with her breasts, but then, it did seem like the people of this world were a lot more body-conscious than those of mine. They insisted on covering themselves. I knew that was partly because it was ungodly cold here, but even inside they covered up as well, which suggested a certain shame perhaps about their bodies? Something I didn't fully understand.

She took a sip from her glass. "You have powers, right? How did you feel when you got them?"

"Amazing, confused, curious," I said, thinking back. "But mine didn't show up as... forcefully as yours and aren't as visibly obvious either."

"Remind me what you can do?" she said.

I pointed at the bottle she held and made the little remaining liquid within stream up and into my mouth, then I drank it down, savoring the invigorating burn as it rushed down my throat. "I can manipulate water."

She nodded, looking at the empty bottle. "Neat." Then she emptied the rest of her glass.

I was a bit shocked when she then threw the empty bottle across the room to shatter against a bank of cabinets on the far wall.

She quirked a smile at the random violence, then pushed off from where she'd been leaning against the counter. "If you need me, follow the smell of wine and confused self-loathing." Then she was gone.

This day wasn't going well.

As much as I wanted to curl up on the couch with Annie, there wasn't a lot of room for the both of us and my soul ached at the thought of being so close to her and yet not having her bond, so I found a room with a large bed and fell onto it, instead.

Outside, darkness was closing in, while despair was closing in inside me, and I hoped a night's sleep would help.

But a part of me said nothing would be right until Annie and I were bonded again.

And I didn't even know if that was possible.

I slept fitfully and woke groggy, feeling like I'd barely slept at all. Annie had introduced me to a wonderful — if bitter — drink called coffee, and I staggered down to the kitchen to see if I could find and attempt to make some.

Annie was still asleep on the couch and Janice was nowhere to be seen.

In a moment of worry for Janice, and uncertain if perhaps she might have drunk herself to death, I put off making coffee and searched the house for a while.

I found her passed out on a couch in a large room on the lower of two subterranean levels. Next to her sat a table with several open bottles, some of which had only a little wine missing, others of which were near to empty.

Gods.

I checked her life-beat at her neck.

It was strong.

It seemed the woman had a significant tolerance for alcohol and was still alive. Although I suspected she'd regret that when she finally woke.

She shifted at my touch, but didn't wake, and began snoring, so I left her there. Until Annie was awake, we wouldn't need Janice to help us come up with a rescue plan, and I wasn't going to wake Annie. She'd looked as broken as I felt last night, and I hoped that sleep was a reprieve from that heartache.

Back in the kitchen, I fumbled around, finding supplies for

coffee, then making some. The first three attempts were awful, but the fourth was drinkable.

With that made, I stood with a steaming mug of the stuff, staring out a kitchen window at the frozen landscape beyond, and pondered what we should do next. We couldn't stay in this mansion forever, and we had to save the others — if they were even still alive. Gods, I hoped they were still alive. And once everyone was safe, we needed to find a way to get our bond with Annie back.

If that was possible.

A creeping doubt within me left black seeds of uncertainty that twisted around my heart.

We'd been as close as any two people could be last night and that hadn't done a thing. Though, to be fair, sex, even great sex, never was worthy of a bond in my world. It was only the intimacy of the touch of the lips that made it happen. Except that hadn't worked.

Perhaps we needed to return to my world to find out more about bonding? Someone had to know other ways to do it.

And the more I pondered that thought, the more going to my world made sense. Perhaps I could return to Galniosia and recruit some help to save the guys. My mother wouldn't like it, but to Hades with her.

Set on this course... I just had to wait for my companions to rouse themselves.

Annie was the first, sleepily and slowly swaying into the kitchen, her eyes still half closed. "Coffee?"

I nodded.

She held out her hands, her fingers making little grasping motions. "Coffee."

I poured her a cup and handed it over. She cradled the mug in both hands, sipping the dark liquid, then stumbled to a chair at the table and sagged down.

After another sip, she glanced at the table and the empty chair beside her — the chair where we'd made love — and a stunning blush seeped across her cheeks.

"Thank you for yesterday. That was…" Her face fell as she looked down at the floor. "It made me forget everything for a moment. A moment away from the horrid mess that's now my life."

"I had a thought," I said softly. She looked up, raising a brow in question. "We go back to my world. Perhaps there's someone there who knows more about how the bond works. Also, I might be able to recruit some of my people to return with us and help us get the others out of Hera's clutches."

Annie's face turned stony at the mention of Hera and she nodded stiffly.

"Good morning all!" Janice said, chipper and bright eyed as she strode into the kitchen. "I haven't slept— well passed out that well in ages!" She came over and poured herself some coffee, stunning me with her perky demeanor. I was expecting a half-alive half-awake mess of a woman that Annie would need to heal.

"You drink hard," I murmured.

She turned to me, sipping her coffee. "Yeah, my father got us started early and I had three brothers who liked to have drinking contests. I can drink any man under the table."

After last night, I had no doubt.

"We're going to go to my world," I said, and explained the plan I'd come up with.

She nodded, not even hesitating at the suggestion. "Wings yesterday, seeing a new world today, sure. Why the hell not?"

"You seem to have accepted the change… well?" I wasn't sure, given how she'd acted the previous day, if she had, or if she was on the verge of falling apart.

"A night of hard drinking often puts things in perspective for me. Well... first it puts things *way* out of perspective, but I think that helps to get it back to the right spot by the next day."

I supposed that made sense.

"Shall we be off then?" I looked at my two companions: Chipper Janice and hard, cold, heartbroken Annie. Gods, I wished there was something I could do to get Annie out of the depression she was in. But I suspected that wouldn't happen until she and I had bonded again, proving to both of us it was possible.

And I really hoped it was possible. It had to be.

CHAPTER 4

HYPERION

HERA KNEW THINGS. THINGS EVEN I DIDN'T KNOW ABOUT MYSELF and my species. Strapped, face down to some hard table, arms and legs outspread, she'd known some way to make my wings come out and keep them from disappearing. Now she was painfully plucking my feathers, gleefully giggling. She hadn't asked any questions, hadn't wanted to know anything about us or Annie. This was torture just for fun apparently.

I'd held out as long as I could before I'd started screaming. It wasn't even the pain — though that was part of it — it wasn't even the thought of not being able to fly. *Erinai* molted, like any bird, but it happened in a measured, symmetrical way so we could retain our balance. Hera seemed to know this and was tearing the feathers only from one side. I'd be horribly disfigured and unbalanced until they regrew, and that could take up to six months. But it was the thought I wouldn't be able to fly with Annie for that long, which made me terrified that maybe I wouldn't be able to be with Annie at all, ever again.

That she was already gone.

I'd seen Hera throw her out of the building and I couldn't feel her inside me. My soul was empty, missing Annie's, and I had no idea if our connection would grow back like my essential feathers would.

Finished with the wing, Hera went to a table and grabbed a small knife, then she returned and began running it lightly over my back. She was never consistent, never the same pressure or duration, but always enough to hurt, and she made me agonize over where she'd carve into next.

"I can't recall," she said casually. "In your world do they have such a thing as 'death by a thousand cuts?'"

I grunted in response, my teeth clenched. I hoped she'd take it as a curse against her, but she didn't even seem to notice.

"Oh, it doesn't matter. I think I'll still enjoy explaining it to you. I have a very steady hand, you see. Half these cuts haven't even completely broken the skin. They're just for the pain. But the rest, well, they are shallow enough that they'll only bleed a little. You won't lose copious amounts of blood and die quickly. No, the whole point of 'death by a thousand cuts' is to make it so deliciously slow. Just a little blood here and there, and a lot of pain in between." She laughed and began humming to herself.

It was a delirious amount of time later when she spoke again. "How's that wing feeling?"

The haze of pain, which seemed to be everywhere, suddenly blossomed specifically at the base of the tattered wing as she dug the knife into my back. "If you want, I can cut the whole thing off... Would you like that? It's going to take some time for those feathers to return. Perhaps it would be better if you didn't have the wing at all?"

Gods, no! I bit the inside of my mouth, before I cried out. That was what she wanted. If she cut off my wing it would be permanently gone. I wouldn't be able to shed it and regrow it, I'd be flightless forever.

"I'll take that as a yes," she said and began digging in around that area, still using that small knife, taking ages to finally rip it free, and making me black out...

I came to, agony screaming through my back, molten fire burning where my wing came from my back— where it *used* to come from my back. My throat tightened, my gaze landing on my wing lying on the floor, dropped in my line of sight no doubt on purpose. Tears pricked my eyes and I couldn't fight them. I was never going to fly again. I was never going to be with Annie.

Hera was nowhere to be seen and I thanked all the gods for that. She'd love to hear my whimpers and see my tears, and I just didn't have it in me to hold it back.

My throat tightened even more with self-loathing at my self-ishness. I was grateful Hera wasn't around, but that meant she was most likely with one of the others, and who knew what she was doing with them. I'd been raised in the military. I knew how to deal with pain. Admittedly what she'd done was well beyond anything I'd endured before, but still, I couldn't imagine her cutting on them and how they'd react, untrained and potentially less disciplined.

Except some soldier I was. I'd failed miserably in stopping Hera even with my power, and Annie and the others had paid a horrible price.

I heard a scream, faint in the distance and my jaw clenched harder.

I had to focus. While she wasn't around was my best chance to escape.

I heaved against my restraints, but they were too tight and I was weak from Hera's ministrations. My body — well everything on my back, except my other wing, pristine and untouched as it was — hurt beyond anything I'd ever felt before. Lines of fire criss-crossed all the way from my shoulders, over my buttocks and down my legs.

Still. I had to try. I couldn't think about the pain or about how tired I was, I had to keep trying to get away, for myself, for the others.

For Annie.

Oh gods, I couldn't think about that. I had to hope Del — who'd gone over the balcony after her — had saved her. She couldn't be dead. She just couldn't be!

Focus.

I was a soldier. I had to do something. I *could* do something.

I wrenched and twisted, sending agony through my body, making the thick leather straps dig into my wrists and ankles, and the one around my neck tighten, choking me.

Hera, whether out of ignorance or deliberate malice, hadn't told me what had happened to Annie. Out of all of Hera's tortures, that one hurt the most, eating at my heart as the emptiness of our missing bond sank deep and cold inside me.

I'd woken from my stupor in time to see her flying out the window. I'd leaped to my feet and tried to go after her, but Hera had seized me with her wind and howled with laughter as I heaved and screamed, knowing my mate was plummeting to her death.

Except I had to believe she was alive, no matter what the emptiness inside me was saying. Because if she wasn't, then I might as well just give into the pain and torture and die, too. I didn't want to live without her. I couldn't.

No. She couldn't be dead. She just couldn't be. And if she was alive, then she was out there, trying to figure out a way to free me and the others. With Del to help her, because he'd never leave her. And if she was alive and coming for me, then she'd be able to heal me. All the pain, the loss of the wing, it would mean nothing. I'd be whole again, in body and soul, as soon as she found us.

Agony screamed through my wing-socket and I jerked, my eyes snapping open, as someone — Hera — giggled. I wasn't sure when she'd returned and I had to assume I'd blacked out again.

"Fall asleep did we? Can't have that," Hera snarled, digging a finger around in the wound where my wing had been before grabbing her small knife and slicing into my skin again.

I gritted my teeth, fighting my scream and failing, panting through the agony.

I had to endure.

I would.

Annie was alive. The emptiness in my chest didn't mean she was dead.

She was alive.

She had to be.

Please.

CHAPTER 5

ANNIE

Janice watched Del and I strip off our clothes and raised her eyebrows at us. "You two aren't going to go at it like bunnies again, are you?" she asked.

We were in the other world, the one Hera had named... I couldn't remember what she'd named it and didn't want to think about her. I didn't want to think about anything to do with that woman right now or I knew I'd collapse into a puddle and wouldn't be able to stop sobbing.

I mentally focused on the wall I'd tried to build around my heart and concentrated on that. If I thought about anything else, about how the others could be dead, or how Hera could be torturing them — which, horrifically was the better of the two options — I'd break into a million pieces and wouldn't be able to save them.

And I *had* to save them.

Because they *were* alive.

"This is just the local dress," I said casually. "In that the local dress is nothing. Everyone is naked here, no religiously imposed moral sensibilities, just bodies of all shapes and sizes and everything hanging out. It's really quite liberating once you get used to it." Not that I was feeling particularly liberated at the moment, but I'd also been too warm in my winter clothes. "Also it's damn hot here and wearing nothing is a lot more comfortable."

"Aren't you afraid you'll burn?" Janice asked. "Isn't that a thing with redheads and all that pale skin of yours?"

"Ah, good point. You should probably keep something on. You might burn," I replied. "But I won't. Not with my healing powers. I guess, to that point, I can heal you if you burn too, so it's up to you what you want to wear.

I caught Janice's gaze drifting over to Del and his magnificent body. I had to smile just a bit at the remembrance of our oh-so-incredible sex yesterday, but the small happiness didn't last as the aching emptiness of my missing bonds flooded back in.

Del and I stashed our clothes in a cubby in the rocks near the large black rock where the gate to my world was, and Janice, after a moment, shrugged and stripped as well.

"When in Rome and all that..." she said.

"I'm going to head home," Del said. "There are no huphelopoids here so you can't come. Are you going to be all right alone... with Janice?"

"Don't worry about me." I pursed my lips, realizing how stupid an expression that was. "Fuck it, worry about me. I'm worried as hell about you and the other guys, so yeah, whatever. But, yes, I'll be fine. We'll head into Masia and see if we can't recruit some help from there as well. It's not like I didn't cure the entire town... however long ago." I'd lost track of time entirely and it oddly felt like both a lifetime ago and just yesterday that I'd saved most of the village.

"True," he replied. "Hopefully they'll be willing to help." He bent down and gave me a soft, tender kiss, his lips brushing mine and I felt...

My pulse skipped a beat.

I felt *something* at that contact, a stirring deep within me. Except if it was something to do with our bond, it didn't go further than that faint, aching stirring.

And perhaps it had been my imagination, my desperate desire to be with Del again, to fill the void within me.

"I'll be back as soon as I can," he said.

I nodded. "I know. I love you."

"I love you, too." He wrapped his arms around me, holding me instead of leaving, not moving for a long time.

"It's okay," I murmured against his chest. "I'm not going to break. Go."

He brushed his lips against mine again then turned and ran for the waves, splashing into the surf then diving in — suddenly having his fish's tail again — and was gone into the blue-green waters.

"And... he's a mermaid," Janice said. "Of course he is."

I turned back to her. She'd taken off everything except her underwear, including her bra — although if I recalled correctly, she'd lost her bra along with her shirt when her wings had appeared. She was a very fit woman with a beautiful tanned complexion that was all natural and meant she didn't burn in a heartbeat like I did... like I *used* to. Still, I was just a tad jealous of her sleek physique. But then, I was the one with a harem of hunky men, not her, so... yeah.

"Ready?" I asked.

"Yeah. Although I couldn't seem to make myself do the Full Monty, not on my first time."

"You didn't have to do that much, if you didn't want to," I said and started walking toward the town sitting almost out of sight at the end of the beach. "Last time I was here, I was in a t-shirt and shorts. No, that wasn't the last time, that was the time before... or was it? Well one time at least."

"Oh. Well I'd be fine with this and a bra, if I had one, but it got ruined when my wings came out. So... this will do."

I didn't even attempt to offer her my bra. I was larger than she was in that area and it wouldn't have worked well and I was afraid it would have just made the situation more awkward.

We hiked across the sand toward Masia, the sun, a wonderful heat, seeping into my skin, but it was unable to penetrate the dread for my guys and my missing bonds that churned in my gut and chilled my soul.

A part of me still didn't know how everything had gone so wrong, while the rest of me tried to shove those thoughts aside. I'd made a choice and even if it had turned into a disaster, I still knew in my heart it was the right decision... well, maybe not entirely right because we'd had our asses handed to us, but someone had to have done it. Someone had needed to stand up to Hera and stop her, and now that someone needed to pull up her big girl panties, get her guys back, and figure out how not to lose the next time.

And so long as I kept that thought in mind, maybe I wouldn't crumble into a sobbing heap.

About half an hour later, we reached Masia. The first time I saw the village, I hadn't thought it was much. The guys had called it a town, but it wasn't much more than a collection of shacks of varying sizes, and a dirt road that led from a long, narrow dock to a public square with a dozen vendors selling their wares.

On that first glance, I'd guess there were maybe a couple hundred people living in Masia and now it seemed like every one of them knew about me, if not by sight, then by name. People nodded their respect to me in passing, some even came up and gave me gifts of food or flowers, making me feel like I was some kind of hero.

It was a lot to take in, and from the size of Janice's eyes, it was even more for her to take in.

"The people are..." Janice whispered, her gaze jumping from a woman with horse legs like Aethan's to an enormous cyclops. "They're not..."

"Human? Yeah, you get used to it after a while." Well, to be fair, I still wasn't entirely used to it. Seeing a minotaur or centaur or a gaggle of girls with skin as brightly colored and varied as wildflowers was still just a bit odd for me.

"Why is everyone so— How do they know you?"

"I healed the village, well most of it, when that plague guy came through here."

"He was here too? Not just on earth?"

"Yep, he was from our world initially, but got his powers here. I think anyone who can travel between the worlds, like him and me, they get powers here."

"Ohhhhh..." she said, the word drawn out before fading away. "I feel like there's so much I don't know. There's so much everybody on earth doesn't know. There's a whole other world and no one knows about it. How's that possible?"

"I'm still a little fuzzy on that myself, but from what I understand, only certain people from our side can open the gates. Also, apparently, there are fewer gates then there used to be, and as you saw, they're well hidden. So, it would take an incredible coincidence for someone with the power to open a gate to find one and open it."

"Like you did?" she replied. "How did that happen anyway?"

"I..." I grimaced. I'd just said it would take an incredible coincidence, and it had. What were the chances I'd slip on some ice and fall through that wall? What were the chances I'd have dropped my phone and it would have been kicked into that alley?

Perhaps me going through the gate had been somehow fated. "Hunh..."

"What?"

"Ah... nothing. Yeah, it was very coincidental. I dropped my phone, and someone kicked it into that alley. I followed it in there, slipped on a patch of ice, and fell through the wall."

"Wow, really?"

"Yeah."

"That's some next level coincidence. If I didn't know better, I'd say it was meant to be," Janice said.

Which was exactly what I'd been thinking.

I pushed open the door to the cantina and we entered the dark, slightly cooler interior. There was still a crowd inside of — now that I wasn't suffering from heat stroke and could get a better look at them — people who looked rough around the edges, like this was the seediest bar in Masia... even though I had a feeling it was the *only* bar in Masia. But the crowd wasn't nearly as large as before, reminding me that while I'd saved much of the village, I hadn't saved everyone.

The man behind the bar had large horns curling out the side of his head, like a ram, squarish eyes, and I assumed his legs were goat like. He was like the healer-woman who'd been tending the sick-camp that first time I'd been here.

"Hello good sir, do you know who I am?" I asked, leaning on the bar.

"You are Anichambers, the healer woman, savior of Masia." The way he said my name, all running together like one word, was odd, but it was how most of the people in the village had already addressed me so I didn't correct him — trying to change an entire village was a battle I didn't want to bother with, not right now.

"Yep, I am, and now I need some assistance. Do you think some of the people here in the cantina, or the village in general, would be willing to help me?"

He bobbed his head vigorously. "Of course. You only have to ask."

"Good. I'll start with the people here. Mind if I stand on your bar?"

He quirked a brow, but waved a hand for me to go ahead, and I hopped up on the bar.

"Hey," I shouted to the assembled crowd.

All eyes turned to me and a part of me was suddenly acutely aware that I was naked and standing on a bar for everyone to see. It seemed like something a younger — and very drunk — version of myself might have done, but here I was, and I didn't feel particularly ashamed or self-conscious. I was even feeling a little liberated.

"I'm Annie Chambers." I separated the words just enough to satisfy me, but also made it sound like the name these people knew me by. "And I need some help. I'm a great healer, but there are some things I can't do, and I'm going to need some strong and willing people to assist me."

A chorus of shouts and cries went up, people offering to help without even knowing what I was asking. Hands shot up in the air, waving at me, and a small part of me heaved a sigh of relief. Sure, I'd helped save the village and my welcome back to Masia had been warm, but that didn't mean they'd want to help me.

But then guilt twisted in my stomach. I had to say more, had to make the situation clear. I didn't want to be responsible for more people getting hurt, but I wasn't going to be able to free my guys — because they were alive, God damn it — without help.

"Now you should know, this is a very, *very* dangerous mission." I stressed these words and the cries quieted down and some of the hands withdrew. "In fact, I won't lie to you. You'll be going to save some of your own people who've been taken prisoner by a god. Well a goddess, actually. Hera."

Silence fell over the crowd. There were a few gasps and whispered words. The ones I heard the most were: 'goddess' and 'Hera.'

"Three of my friends, men who used to frequent this very cantina from time to time, are in trouble." *Please, gods, let them just be in trouble and not dead.* "They are being held in a..." High rise wasn't a word they'd know. "Fortress?" That seemed to get some recognition. "A well-fortified tower. There will be many people with weapons, very advanced... god weapons." How else could I explain guns?

"God weapons?" Janice asked, whispering.

"These people have no idea what a gun is," I whispered back to her.

"Ah, right. Okay."

"There's a good chance those who come with me will be hurt, perhaps killed," I said, turning back to the crowd. "I can heal wounds, but I can't bring someone back from the dead."

Although... I'd never actually tried to bring someone back from the dead. Maybe I could? Wouldn't that be something! Fuck. Best to keep things limited and scary for this group though. As much as I wanted their help, *needed* it, I didn't want any of them agreeing to go with us without knowing all the risks.

"I'm a healer, not a warrior. I don't want to send anyone into danger," I continued. "But I'm going either way and I could really use some help. If you're willing, meet me down by the docks at sunset today. And spread the word around the town if you think anyone might be interested." I took a long moment then to scan the crowd, moving from face to face of as many as I could see. Such a variety of people. A part of me hoped they wouldn't come. They didn't deserve to be hurt for my crazy quest, but another part prayed they would. Because I wouldn't be able to free my guys without help. Lots of help.

I drew in another breath, uncertain how to finish and decided, "Thank you," was simple and probably all I needed. Then I hopped down off the bar.

"Wow, that was impressive." Janice said, seeming a bit star-struck herself. "Where did you learn to speak like that?"

"Like what?"

"So... moving."

"Really? That was moving?"

"Yeah."

"Oh..." Hunh. "I just said what I wanted to." But it occurred to me then that I was riled up. I was vibrating with energy. I desperately needed to get my guys back and find some way to rebond with them. It was imperative for me. Perhaps that had come out through my words.

"So," Janice asked, as we stepped out of the cantina onto the dusty, hard-packed dirt street in the center of the village. "What now?"

"We wait for sunset. Care to walk along the beach and get a tan?"

She smiled and gave a slight nod. There was an odd look in her eyes, a reappraisal of me perhaps? I couldn't quite tell. She didn't elaborate, and it didn't look like she wanted to talk about it. It didn't look like she wanted to talk at all, like she had as many fearful and confused thoughts rushing through her head as I did.

CHAPTER 6

DELPHON

MY FAMILY HAD BEEN SURPRISED TO SEE ME BACK SO SOON, AND MY sister, Poseia, had had a lot of questions. I'd told her they'd all be answered at the formal hearing, then I'd requested that hearing, and now stood once again before my whole family. My mother and father were on their thrones, flanked by Poseia and Luarnon, and Mother didn't look happy at all. Of course, the last time I'd been there, she'd disowned me and kicked me out of the kingdom, so I was already prepared for a less than warm welcome from her.

"You renounce your throne then return so quickly to ask something of us?" my mother demanded. "Of course you have. You could never do anything on your own."

I tried to ignore her bitter tone, but it struck a nerve I'd been trying to not think about. Even with my closest friends and my mate who was as powerful as a goddess, we still hadn't been able to stand up against Hera. That failure was just more proof that I was hopeless at everything.

But I couldn't leave the others to Hera. Even if we hadn't all bonded with Annie, I wouldn't have left them behind. I'd do anything to save them and if that meant humbling myself to my mother, then so be it.

"Hanea, stop it," my father said sternly. I wasn't used to him standing up to her like that. It was a new side of him that I was grateful was making an appearance. Hopefully with his help, I'd be able to convince my mother to give us an army. "Let the boy speak." He nodded at me, indicating I should make my request.

I sucked in a steadying breath, trying to still my whirling thoughts and fears. I had to word this just right or my mother and everyone else wouldn't listen.

"Your majesties," I said with a stiff and formal bow to both of them. That got a raised brow from my mother. Like always, I couldn't tell if that was good: curiosity, or bad: on the verge of a tongue-lashing. "I've come as a citizen of Galniosia, who was once a royal. I gave up my right to the crown and with it any power I might hold over this kingdom. I know that I have little or no power here."

"No power is right," my mother huffed.

I nodded to her, acknowledging this. "As you say." Here came the hard part... the truth. I turned my attention to Poseia who knew about our plans to defeat Hera with a look that I hoped said: I may need your help now, sister. "To fully explain my request of the crown, I need to give a little history. It may be hard to understand, as it involves things I, and all of us, once thought impossible. I hope you'll listen with an open mind."

Poseia shook her head, her eyes sad, telling me I'd already erred somewhere, and I slid my gaze back to my mother who wore a haughty look of 'he's going to make up some story.' Damn, I'd already lost her.

But I still had my father. He still looked interested, if concerned, and maybe with his new found command, he'd be enough to give me the help I needed.

"As you know, eight years ago, I took the place of the functionary you were sending as emissary to the lands above as part of The Treaty of Eronatus. Since then, I have happily taken on that duty and represented Galniosia in the meeting of emissaries." Everyone seemed to be following so far. "Those three men, with whom I met, became good friends of mine. In many ways they are like a second family to me." I looked long and hard at my mother for this next bit. Since I'd already lost her, it wouldn't hurt to get in a jab. "They accepted me for who I was, no conditions, just brotherly love."

Mother scowled and Father shot her a dark look, stopping whatever jab she was going to send back.

"At our last meeting of emissaries, there was an interruption. A strange woman came to Masia and used powers of healing, true healing, to eradicate a plague the town had been suffering." That was an amalgamation of several events into one, but it seemed a reasonable summary for the sake of expediency. Everyone except my mother looked surprised, raising eyebrows or sitting forward. "That woman was the one I brought to visit the last time I was here."

"The *heliai*?" Luarnon said.

I nodded. "Yes... but she's not *heliai*. And here begins the more... fantastical part of my tale, though I swear to you that every word is true."

A scoff from my mother. The others — except Poseia — looked dubious.

"Annie, this healer-woman, is from another world. She isn't *heliai*. She's human."

"Human!" Mother shot up from her throne, suddenly and shockingly enraged, which was something I hadn't expected at all.

I didn't think anyone knew what a human was. But I'd forgotten that my mother was raised from childhood to be the perfect queen. She'd been taken in by my grandmother, my father's mother, and trained in every way. She was well educated, perhaps more so than my father.

"Humans are what drove us from the paradise oceans. They multiplied rapidly and when there was no room for them and our kind, they and the gods drove us from paradise!"

They drove us from paradise? From Annie's world?

But then, I did recall hearing something like that... but where...?

Hera! I tried not to tense my jaw at the memory of listening to Annie and Hera talk over the *fone* while returning from the hospital. It had been when Annie had first met that horrid woman, going with her in that odd stretched out car, while us guys had followed behind. Hera had mentioned something — though we'd barely been able to hear her — about how in her time people had moved freely between the two worlds.

It seemed that most in this world didn't remember or believed it to be a myth, but my mother still knew the truth.

Although, if I really thought about it, while Annie's world seemed more advanced, I wouldn't have called it paradise. My world was much more like a paradise. Annie had even said as much.

"Annie is a good person. She healed the entire town of Masia even though it brought her to the brink of death." That might have been a bit of an exaggeration, but not by much. She'd worked until she'd passed out and had remained unconscious for hours. "Yes, humans can be petty and cruel and evil, but they certainly aren't the only ones."

I shot a hard look at my mother. I knew it was foolish. I shouldn't have baited her any more than I already had, but I couldn't help myself.

Poseia raised a hand to her forehead and gave me a look which said, 'you've messed up. Good luck getting help now.'

Yeah, that might have been a bit heavy handed.

"Annie's heritage is beside the point," I continued. "It's my friends—"

"She's human. That's not beside the point!" My mother proclaimed. "She's—"

"A good woman!" I yelled back. I could yell over her just as easily. "And if you want to condemn me or her, that's fine, but by all the gods, sit down and listen to my whole story first. Then you can banish me, if that's what you want!"

Mother's eyes went wide with the shock that I'd spoke back to her so forcefully, something I'd never done before. I'd been snide, sullen, and just plain ignored her, but I'd never spoken back before.

She blinked, an odd look on her face. I had no idea what she was thinking, but some of the tension left her shoulders and she drifted back down onto her throne.

"Tell your story then," she replied, her tone soft and filled with malice.

By Hades, it looked like I'd done it now.

Except my friends were in danger — if they were still alive — and I couldn't back down. I needed help.

I bit the inside of my cheek. I shouldn't have lost my temper. I wasn't sure why I had. My mother just made me so angry sometimes.

I drew in a long breath, fighting to calm myself.

"My friends, those I consider to be like a second family. They are in paradise, as you call Annie's world. They went there with myself and Annie to try to get rid of Hera, a human— yes a *human*, not a god, although she has many powers which makes her akin to one," I said. "We failed in our first attempt and my friends were captured. I've come to ask for the assistance of Galniosia to free them from the hold of this horrible woman and to liberate our people and the people of the paradise world."

"Is that all?" mother asked sharply.

It wasn't, but I wasn't going to ask mother about rebonding with Annie. That would be a question for Umandra, the Royal Archivist, assuming I wasn't run out of the palace first. I didn't think my father would let that happen, but given my mother's temper, who knew. "Yes."

Mother rose again, this time stately and calm. "You seek the aid of our people, our soldiers, to free your friends?"

"Yes." And here came the refusal.

"You, who have no say here, who have shirked all responsibility? You want our people to go and die for some land-dwellers? Do you think I care anything for your friends? They're not tritons!" Her voice had risen with each word to a culminating yell by the end.

I looked at my father, whose expression was tired and worn.

"Don't look at him! We rule this kingdom together. A call to war such as this would need the unity of the king and queen. If I say no, then that's the end of it," she snarled.

My father nodded slowly, but then he, too, rose. "I think perhaps there may be more to consider, my queen," he said stoically.

"There isn't," she huffed.

"Just sit down and listen, Hanea!" my father snapped, shocking me.

He'd never taken that tone with my mother before and she looked at him, her jaw tense, muscles twitching, and sat down slowly. "Listen? To what?"

My father turned to me. "Tell us of this Hera? What is she like? Why did you try to get rid of her?"

"She infected hundreds of people in this world and the other world with a horrible plague, a disease that could have scoured both our worlds. And it's only because of Annie that both worlds were cleansed of it."

My father frowned. "Why did Hera do this?"

"That I do not know." I saw the wicked smile starting to spread on my mother's face as if she thought she'd won. "But that's exactly what makes her truly dangerous," I added.

My mother's eyes narrowed.

"In the other world she's powerful, more powerful than all of the kings and rulers of our islands combined. She's beyond the laws of both worlds and can do anything she likes," I said. "We don't know what she's planning, but someone who would casually infect thousands of people for any reason, is someone I wouldn't want around. Yes, she's in the other world right now, but what if she decided to turn her attention here? What would we do then? Our kingdoms are divided. She'd easily walk over each of our territories and take us one by one."

"We're beneath the waves, she wouldn't be able to—"

"Are you certain of that mother?" I countered quickly.

My mother opened her mouth then snapped it shut. She wasn't a pleasant woman, but she wasn't foolish, and I could practically see her mind going over all the possibilities, coming to the realization that she didn't know if our kingdom was safe or not.

"What makes her dangerous is that she's powerful and unchecked, and we have no clue what she's going to do with all that power. She tried to start a plague in both our worlds just because she could. We were lucky that Annie managed to stop it, but we have to stop Hera before she does something worse, something we can't protect against."

My mother's expression grew even more grim, and Poseia gave me a slight nod, telling me my argument was good and I might have actually won.

"We wouldn't be able to lend you many men," my father said, turning his attention to my mother.

Her scowl deepened. "A dozen. If Hera is going to attack, we need to be able to protect ourselves."

"A score," Father offered. "Better to stop her in paradise than on our boarder."

"Fine, a score, no more," my mother huffed as she turned her hard gaze on me. "And for every one of them that falls, you will owe this kingdom fifty pearls."

I raised my brows at that. That was a steep price. If only a couple men died, I'd be paying that off for years. If they all didn't make it back, my children's children would be repaying that debt.

"Hanea," my father said. "That's—"

"My final offer," she interrupted, turning her glare back to him. "Take it or leave it."

My father sighed and both he and my mother returned their attention to me.

"Well?" my father asked.

"Agreed," I said. I didn't have much choice. Hera needed to be stopped and I could only hope my mother's selfishness didn't put our kingdom and the rest of our world in danger.

Poseia raised a brow, her expression a mix of surprise and worry. Me agreeing to such horrible terms told her just how serious this situation was.

"Come, brother," she said. "I'll escort you to the courtyard to wait for your men."

"I'll gather your men," said my brother, Luarnon, who'd been silently watching the exchange.

He swam out the door behind the throne, while Poseia led me back out of the Hall of Light.

"Do you think we can go to the courtyard by way of the library?" I asked, keeping my voice low. "I need to ask Umandra a few questions."

"I'm not sure if she has more information about Hera," Poseia said, even as she turned down the hallway that would lead us to the library and the Royal Archivist.

I doubted Umandra would, and even if she did, all we had was legend and Hera was so much more than our legends. "I need information on bonds."

Poseia swished to a stop and grabbed my arm. "What's happened?"

My chest tightened. Everything had happened. The worst thing possible. And I was grateful my sister didn't immediately accuse me of being immature and trying to get out of my bond with Annie — not that I would have needed Umandra's help to leave a normal mating bond.

"My bond with Annie is— *was* deeper than just a normal bond. There was some kind of magic involved in our joining."

Poseia's eyes narrowed. "Was? Is Annie okay?"

No. None of us were. "She's alive and unharmed, but Hera broke our bond." I pressed a hand against my chest. The emptiness inside me was overwhelming, and I'd only lost one bond. I couldn't imagine how much Annie hurt.

And yet she was still pushing forward, still willing to fight. Which only proved how strong she was.

"I have to get our bond back," I said. I'd never leave Annie, and I knew the others, once we'd rescued them, wouldn't either even without the bond, but I didn't want her to spend the rest of her life with a constant reminder that there should have been more between us.

"If anyone knows about this magical bond, Umandra would," Poseia said, resuming her course to the library.

Unfortunately, the aged librarian hadn't read anything about a bond being more than just a kiss on the lips that sealed a lifelong promise to be together. She knew nothing about the magic that had joined me and Annie and there was little in the library about something so mundane as non-magical mating bonds.

And if the information wasn't in the Library of Galniosia then it likely wasn't anywhere.

Which meant I didn't know how to fix our bond and I wasn't looking forward to telling Annie that.

CHAPTER 7

ANNIE

IT WAS AN ODD ASSORTMENT OF CREATURES WHO'D COME TO JOIN Janice and I on the sand near the long docks of Masia. There were three minotaurs, tall and broad, with their odd, bull-like horned heads and shaggy hooved feet, and two *panai*, which I'd come to know was the name for the people with the goat-like eyes, horns, and legs. A few feet away stood a satyr, with features like Aethan, and the same sort of horse-like mohawk mane of hair, and next to them a large woman — half a head taller than the minotaurs, but not as large as Keph — with only one central eye, a cyclops.

The five others were a variety of nymphs, two *epimelidai* with skin of mottled browns and greens, and an *oreadai* with skin of pale gray and soft white. The last two both had wings, but I was told weren't *erinai* like Rion. The one was a *nephelai*, with wings of gleaming silver, similar to Rion's snowy white wings, but the man's skin was also a pale silver-white, and the other winged man was an *aurai*, with wings of dappled gold.

Aurai was what Del had called Janice, and she kept glancing at the *aurai* man as if she wanted to talk to him but didn't have the courage. Which was kind of silly. A shy FBI agent. Who knew?

"Go talk to him," I said softly.

"What would I say? 'Hey there, I'm from another world, but I just found out I have wings like yours, we should talk?'"

"Those aren't the worst words. Why not try it?"

"He's from another world!" she insisted.

"So are the four men I fell in love with."

She glanced back at the *aurai* man who caught her look and gave him an awkward wave.

He smiled at her and nodded in return.

"An excellent start," I said, trying not to giggle. "Now how about trying words?"

"Maybe later," she huffed.

I snorted at her. For a tough FBI agent, it seemed Janice wasn't so aggressive in relationships. But I wasn't going to push. It was ultimately up to her, even if she just wanted to find out more about herself.

We had a full dozen men waiting — well ten men and two women, the cyclops and one of the minotaurs were female — and I had no clue how we were going to get them across Chicago to Hera's tower, looking like they did. But that was a problem for later.

"Thank you all for coming," I called out, and the group quieted, the soft hubbub of chatter dropping away. "Let me say again, this mission we're going on isn't going to be easy and your lives may be in danger. Are you sure you're willing to come with us?"

"We heard there may be pay in this for us?" the female minotaur said. "The three of us are mercenaries. We fight for gold."

Several others muttered similar things which seemed to suggest more than half the group thought they might get paid for this.

Hunh.

"I don't have anything to give you," I said honestly, because lying to a bunch of minotaurs was a terrible idea, and I could see that didn't go over well. "But we're going to fight a goddess. Any loot you can find is yours once the battle is done." I didn't know what Hera might have that these people would want, but it couldn't hurt to let them root around and take whatever they wanted. She was uber-rich after all and her apartment had been filled with expensive looking art and things.

That did catch their attention, both the part about fighting a god and the part about loot. A small group, including the minotaurs, still seemed hesitant however.

"There was mention of a god," the female minotaur huffed as if she didn't believe that. Guess she was the spokesperson for their party. "Tell us more. Which one?"

More? Well, that was fair.

"As you may know, I'm not like those here. I can heal, and that ability comes from the fact that I'm from another world. That world has many people, some of whom have abilities which make them like gods. Apparently, some of your gods may have come from my world long ago." I wasn't entirely sure about that part, but Hera had implied that all the Greek gods and goddesses had been her friends from my world. "We'll travel to my world to face one of these people with powers, who I believe you see as a god. Her name is Hera."

More muttering, but oddly not in fear as I might have thought. Instead it seemed eager.

"We're in," the minotaur called over. "It'll be good to test our mettle against a god, especially Hera. She was never good to our people."

Oh. Interesting. Well, that was fortunate.

"And the rest of you?"

The two *panai* were arguing with each other and the satyr looked hesitant. After a moment one of the *panai* stalked away with some words thrown back at us in a language I didn't understand. After a tremulous moment, the satyr followed, running off.

That brought us down to ten, but still more than I'd thought would have been willing.

Not bad.

But I'd give them one more out... because I wasn't sure my conscience could handle it if I was responsible for getting them killed.

"Are you certain you wish to come with us?" I pressed. "This is a very powerful woman, and she has many men guarding her. Their weapons are unlike anything you've seen before. I say again, this will be rough, some of you may be injured or die."

"You're doing a great job of selling this," Janice whispered, rolling her eyes at me.

"They need to know what they're getting into," I whispered back. "I want the risk to be clear."

There were a few more mutters, but no one else left.

Thank goodness.

"Then gather anything you might need for a long trip and meet back here. We're waiting on possibly some more support from the tritons."

Someone, the cyclops woman, scoffed at that, but I wasn't sure why she'd have that reaction.

A few left, but most stayed. It seemed they had everything they needed already. Perhaps they travelled light, though, I had to admit, this group was wearing more clothes than I'd seen in one place in this world. Although to be fair, it wasn't so much clothes as armor.

Then there was nothing else to do, so I sat on the edge of the dock. "Now we wait for Del and his reinforcements... hopefully."

Janice sank to the dock beside me, her gaze still on the group, her expression still shocked. I watched her eyeing them for a long moment, before she tilted her head curiously to one side and realization hit me.

"You're undressing them in your mind, aren't you?"

Her lips quirked in a smile. "It's strange. I've seen most of these folks in town — either this particular person or someone like them — and they were naked. But now that they're wearing things, I can't stop... It's fascinating."

It certainly was.

Though it lent credence to something one of the guys had said to me, that I got more alluring whenever I was dressed. Something about being a mystery, a tease. This new world was turning everything I thought on its head.

"And that *aurai* fellow, are you undressing him too?"

"Of course." Her gaze flicked to me, her smile increasing. "You've already got four hunky guys, leave me to my fantasies."

That was fair.

And that *aurai* man was handsome enough to spawn a few daydreams. He wasn't tall like my guys, though not small or short either. For my world, he'd have been average height, though in this crowd, he was taller than most except the minotaurs and the cyclops. And he was well filled out, with a thick, muscular chest under his heavy-looking plates of armor.

His shoulders were covered, but his upper arms were not and they were thick, the muscles bunching as he settled down, chatting with the *nephelai* next to him. He had a square jaw, piercing blue eyes, and long — yet somehow light and billowing — blond hair. He was Fabio, but with wings, which were folded behind him for the moment.

Hopefully he wasn't a complete jerk.

He glanced over at us again and smiled. I was fairly certain his eyes were more on Janice than me, and I gave a slight head tilt, indicating Janice. The man raised a brow, then nodded and rose, making his way over to us.

"Ah..." Janice said, stiffening as he approached.

"Just be yourself," I whispered, patting her shoulder and getting up to leave to give the two of them some privacy.

"Wait," she said, reaching for me.

I evaded her grasp. "He's not an enemy. Talk to him."

Except her eyes were wide as if she was actually panicking over talking with him.

"Hello?" the man said. "My name is Athanasios, though most call me Nasios or just Naz."

"I'm, ah... Janice."

"A pleasure," he said, and I turned away and walked down the long pier.

The dock stretched far into the water, as the shore was shallow here and I guessed larger boats wouldn't be able to get too close. There weren't any boats docked at the moment, and I strode out to the end, marveling at the beautiful teal waters. Soon, the sea would grow darker, changing color and reflecting the many vibrant hues of the imminent sunset, and while I knew it would be beautiful, I couldn't seem to feel excited for it. I wasn't sure I could be excited for anything, not with the emptiness in my soul.

"I hope you're having as much luck down there, as I am up here," I whispered.

"It wasn't easy, but I think I was lucky enough," Del said behind me.

Surprised, I spun, and there he was. He was wet, perhaps having just come out of the water, his blue-black hair, somehow still sexy, swept back and dripping. Just seeing those broad shoulders and wide chest, the strong arms, and sculpted abs leading down to that oh-my-gods-sized cock, made me weak in the knees. I leaped into his waiting arms. Even just having been away from him for one day had been far too long.

It was only once I was plastered to his wet body that I noticed his sister, Poseia, in the periphery of my vision, standing next to him.

Oh...

My initial awkwardness at seeing her was overridden by my desire and love for Del. With my legs and arms wrapped around him, I pressed close and kissed him long and full. Let his sister see us. There was equal passion in his kiss, and once again I felt something stir deep within me. I hoped, prayed, pleaded that it would turn into more, but it didn't, and I drew my lips away, curious and caught up in this odd sensation.

Del must have seen my curious confusion, and he set me down. "What is it?"

"Did you feel something just now when we kissed?"

Poseia gave a short laugh. "It sure looked like he was feeling most of you."

"Nothing other than all the wonderful things I'd expect to feel with you in my arms," he said, his eyes roaming over me and warming my insides. Suddenly I wanted to get him somewhere much more private.

But still... Odd.

He wasn't feeling anything special.

"What did you feel?" he asked.

I shrugged. "I don't know really. Something... deep within me. Something stirring."

"Do I need to leave you two alone for a while?" Poseia asked with a chuckle.

"No," we both said quickly. Then, once again speaking over each other, "Well, yes. But—"

All three of us laughed at that.

"But I was feeling more than just... that," I said to Del. "I mean, I do want to get you somewhere private and do all manner of unspeakable things with you, but this was something more, something deeper."

His expression darkened. "I wish I could say I felt the same, but I don't think I feel what you're feeling."

Yeah, this was more than just my love or lust for him, but if it was something related to bonding, I'd expect Del to be feeling it too. I knew — or maybe I just hoped — there was more to this feeling, but for now, I had no clue what it was.

A spike of laughter from down the docks caught my attention. I looked around Del to see Janice laughing at something Naz had said. She seemed much more relaxed with him now.

Good.

If only I was feeling so relaxed. This strange sensation within me had me perplexed and unsettled and worried that I'd never get my bonds back.

"I managed to get twenty men," Del said, changing the subject. "It seems you've had a bit of luck as well."

"Yes, ten men and women from the village."

"Women?" he asked.

Poseia slapped him. "We can fight as well as any man."

"Uh, yes, of course."

"And we strategize better than most men. That's why he brought me along," she added.

"That's why she insisted on coming," he said. "She thought we could use some help in figuring out our next step."

"We could, thank you," I said with a nod to the keen young woman. "Are you going to fight with us?"

"I'm flattered that you assumed I could, and I can, but no," she replied. "I'm terrified of what you two are about to do and not stupid enough to try it."

"That makes you smarter than both of us, I think."

She smiled at that, but there was a look of concern in her eyes, like she didn't want to lose her older brother.

Well, I didn't want to lose him either.

"We'd very much appreciate your help," I said. "I want to make sure we all come back alive and well."

"Indeed." Del released a heavy breath and grimaced.

I quirked a brow at that.

"Long story," he replied.

"Not really," Poseia said. "He agreed to pay an exorbitant sum back to my mother for every triton who falls in battle."

I raised my other brow.

He shrugged. "We needed the help. I had to agree."

Which was true. "Then, let's go have a chat and see if we can't ensure we all stay safe."

CHAPTER 8

ANNIE

AFTER JUST ONE EVENING WITH HER, I WAS FAIRLY CERTAIN POSEIA was smarter than everyone else in our small army combined. The sheer amount of tactical knowledge in her head, and the ease with which she recalled it, was amazing. She also quickly assimilated what Janice told everyone about our human world and adapted plans on the fly when I was having trouble keeping up. Not that I was a tactical genius, or a tactical anything, really, but still, it was astounding.

Eventually it was just Janice and Poseia chatting away like old friends, planning our attack on Hera's tower in Chicago while of the rest of us tuned them out and settled down for the night.

"Your sister is amazing," I said, as Del gesture toward the beach, indicating he wanted to go for a walk. "So smart and friendly."

He laughed and I took his arm, letting him lead me away. "She got the best qualities of both my parents. Unlike me."

"Oh, I very much like your qualities," I said suggestively, waggling my eyebrows at him.

"And I yours," he purred back, echoing my innuendo.

After that, we walked in silence, hand in hand, wading through warm, soothing, ankle-deep water until we were a good distance from the others. Then, away from eyes and ears, standing in the pale light of a full moon and under a brilliant expanse of stars, he turned me to face him and stepped in close.

My heart pounded. I'd hoped he'd had more of a reason for wanting to get away than just stretching his legs and clearing his mind, and his hard erection, captured between us told me clearly I hadn't been wrong.

"I feel guilty doing this," he breathed, "having you all to myself, while the others..."

My heart lurched at the thought of my other guys being held by Hera — because, God damn it, they were alive. I wasn't even going to consider that they were dead. The trouble was, if they were alive, then they were probably in agony, and I wasn't sure if that was better.

"No," I said, my voice catching with those horrible thoughts. "We'll get them back and then they'll have all the time in the world with me. I'll take them for long walks on this beach, so don't feel guilty. Just... love me now." I swallowed hard. "Make me forget about everything for a moment. Free my heart so I have the strength to free them tomorrow. Please," I begged.

"Yes," he replied, his voice husky, and he lifted me. I wrapped my legs around his waist and our lips met, crushing together in a heated kiss.

He lifted me higher, kissing his way down to my breasts, tasting them, teasing my nipples into tight buds, as the tip of his cock brushed against my opening. With a sigh, I gently rocked my hips, rubbing myself over him, teasing his length between my slick folds.

"Oh, yes." I let my head fall back and savored the heat growing inside me and his strong arms, holding me as if I was weightless.

He dragged his teeth over the tight bud of one aroused nipple, licking the tip before pulling back. "Have you ever coupled in the water before?"

I'd tried once, long ago, in a backyard pool. It had been stimulating at first, as my boyfriend at the time had stripped away the bits of my bikini, tossing them onto the patio. Then we'd played for a bit before he'd discarded his swimming trunks. But after that it had just gotten awkward as he'd tried to tread water and fuck at the same time. It had been good for him. But I hadn't gotten anything out of it.

That memory had soured me on the thought of sex in the water in general, but then again... Del was a triton. The water was his domain, and just like the sky was Rion's and having sex with him while flying had been incredible, I knew it would be just as incredible to have sex with Del in the water.

"Show me your world," I murmured. "Show me what sex with a triton is like."

"With pleasure," he chuckled and carried me into the water, my legs still hooked around his waist, his length still nestled between my folds, shifting with each step, teasing me in the most delicious way.

We headed farther and farther away from the shore. The warm water took some of my weight, helping me float, while Del took the rest, his movements becoming more fluid as he switched from legs to his fish tale.

Which brought back the memory of the first time I'd seen him and his jaw-dropping erection, appearing from nowhere from his tail. I didn't think I'd ever forget how shocked and turned on I'd been.

Finally, when the fire from our camp was just a speck in the distance, he stopped and rocked his hips, sliding himself against me, the movement slow and sensual, his tip drawing closer and closer to my entrance until he gently pushed inside me.

I gasped, and leaned back, stretching my arms out, giving him my body, knowing he'd satisfy me in the most incredible way.

He leaned over me, flicking his tongue over my nipples, sucking on them, worshiping them, all the while carefully working me up with slow, steady thrusts.

Heat pooled in my core and my breath picked up. A whisper of an orgasm shuddered through me and I gasped out a low throaty moan, drawing a masculine chuckle. But much to my disappointment, he fully withdrew, turning me so he could whisper in my ear.

"Float," he commanded, his hot breath teasing my sensitive skin.

I spread my arms and legs, the anticipation of what he planned next trembling through me, ratcheting up my desire. The water lapped around me, and for a moment I was alone, drifting peacefully in the waves, looking up at that amazing velvet sky with its silver moon and stars.

Then, he drew up under me, his chest pressed against my back, his tail swishing and sweeping down near my legs. His strong arms wrapped around me as I floated, his hands caressing up my belly to my breasts, a strange mix of relaxation and building tension heating my insides.

"This is incredible," I breathed.

"You're incredible," he replied, sliding his fingers back down my belly, through my curls, and into my folds.

My breath hitched and I released it on a moan to let him know how much I appreciated what he was doing. He nibbled on my ear, his fingers building up my need, the pace languid, as if we had all the time in the world.

And even though we didn't, even though my heart still broke over my missing bonds and I was terrified for my other guys, I let Del sweep me away with soft, warm sensation, just for a little while

Then his cock pressed between my butt cheeks and the idea of taking him there, of feeling the incredible pressure of him filling me, stole my breath completely.

"Oh yes," I gasped, shifting my hips and encouraging him to push inside me. "I need you."

"As my lady wishes," he replied, his voice thick with desire.

He swept his hands to my rear and spread me, his tip slowly pushing past the tight ring of muscle with a glorious lick of pain.

He entered me slowly, carefully, giving my body time to adjust to him. It felt like it took forever for him to burry himself completely within me, and I was gasping, trembling and more than ready for him by the time he was done.

Then he started to move, slowly at first, twisting my desire even tighter. His hands slid back around me, one coming up to cradle my breast while the other went down between my legs and rubbed circles on my clit.

I was already teetering on the brink from just having him enter me, and it didn't take long before another, more powerful orgasm washed over me. I cried out as my body shook, and he paused, his erection buried deep within me.

"More?" he whispered mischievously.

"Oh, gods, yes!" I huffed, my chest rising and falling as I sucked in great gulps of air.

He pulled halfway out and pushed back in again, his fingers still teasing my clit and pinching my nipple, sending aftershocks, rippling through me.

I sighed and moaned and trembled, loving every second of him filling me.

"You make the most incredible sounds," he gasped, his pace picking up as his desire started to overwhelm his control.

With a groan, he pushed two fingers inside me, matching his thrusts in my rear, his thumb grinding down on my clit, and his breath rushing past my cheek. His chest heaved against mine, his groans vibrating through me, and then he thrust hard, his cock swelling with his release.

He cried his pleasure with a long satisfying moan as his fingers slammed inside me, hitting my G-spot, and his hand on my breast clenched tighter. The force of him coming threw me over the edge again, sending another incredible orgasm crashing through me.

I let my bliss carry me away for a second, away from the heartbreaking emptiness inside me and away from my fears.

In that moment there was just Del and me, the warm, undulating water, and the sparkling stars above us.

We floated there, locked together for a long time, joined in the only way we could be joined in the moment, neither of us wanting to separate.

But eventually we had to. We had a mission to accomplish.

We returned to the camp with the others just as Poseia was saying goodbye to Janice. The young princess looked over at us and rolled her eyes.

"Young love," she said as if we were the ones younger than her, not the other way around. Then, more seriously, she whispered, "Take care of each other." Looking to Janice, she added. "All of you." She gave us all a lingering look, her pearl-blue eyes intense, then she walked into the waves and dove beneath the water.

"Are we ready?" I asked Janice. Del and I made our way into the light of the fire where our troops were, some quietly talking, others asleep, and I sat in Del's lap with his arms wrapped around me.

"You two go for a swim?" Janice asked with a wink. "Do a little breast stroke, maybe?"

I was sure I blushed all the way down to my aforementioned breasts.

Janice just smiled. "Yes, we're ready. Tomorrow, we're getting your guys back. It's all planned out."

That reassured me, though, as I fell asleep in Del's arms that night, I had the words of my high-school history teacher rolling through my head, "No plan survives contact with the enemy."

CHAPTER 9

ANNIE

"Oh," I said a bit deflated. "That's the plan?"

Janice and I were walking down the beach toward the stones that would take us and our troops — boy it felt weird thinking that word — back to our world. She was telling me what she and Poseia had discussed the previous evening, and it seemed the plan, once we were back on our world, involved a bit of experimentation and exploration before we did anything.

Since everyone from this world would have some special ability in our world, we'd want to know what that was before we continued.

"That's the start of the plan," Janice said. "The hope is that among the thirty people we have here, there will be a few with abilities that might be useful for what we're planning. Our main liabilities at the moment are three-fold: first, we have to assume Hera is watching the portal so we won't have the element of surprise if we try to repeat what we did the last time. Second, we don't know where your friends are inside that building, or even if they are inside the building. And third, going in guns-blazing is a bad idea — as we've already figured out."

Yeah, I didn't want a repeat of the last time, but I'd hoped that between Janice and Poseia they'd have come up with an incredible plan, not 'take a moment and figure out what we've got.' Even if figuring out what the others could do was probably the best plan.

"Even if we don't count Hera, we're outnumbered and out gunned, so finding some other, more secret way in, even if we don't completely have the element of surprise would be preferable," Janice continued. "If some of those here have abilities which can help with either of the above problems that would significantly increase our chances of success, which means it's worth it to take a moment and find out what people can do. Besides we'll need clothes for most of them anyway. That's where your part of the plan comes in. As we're practicing abilities, and I'm figuring out whose abilities we can use, you'll be getting everyone clothes."

"I have no money."

"You've got a bank card."

"If I use it at an ATM, Hera will know where I am. Don't those things have cameras and stuff?"

"They do, which is why you'll take one of these new guys with you. If they use your card, it will look like you sold it or gave it away. They can empty your accounts and that would seem like the natural thing for some random person to do. They'll be the ones on camera, not you and Del. Once you have the cash, you can buy the clothes and get back to us, hopefully without being traced."

I nodded to that. It was actually rather smart.

"After that?" I asked.

"We'll see if anyone has any abilities to help us get in, then reevaluate from there. I've memorized the layout and blue-prints of Hera's tower and—"

"You did? Really? When?"

Janice smiled. "I've always had a good memory. I did it before we went in the first time."

"Oh."

"The only issue is, those were the official blue prints, she may have some hidden rooms we don't know about."

"Yeah, probably."

"Anyway, assuming we can get in without drawing too much attention, a small group of us will go and case the area tactically, then extract your friends and get the fuck out of there."

"I may be able to sense them, but I think I'd need to be fairly close," Del offered, as he approached from behind us.

"Oh?" Janice asked.

"Using my abilities with water, I can sense those I'm familiar with, their..." He frowned as if he was looking for the right words. "Their water-sense is different from others', unique. It's hard to explain."

"How close would you need to be?"

"I don't know," he replied. "Perhaps a hundred feet? With Annie the range was a lot greater, but I was also bonded to her. These are good friends, so I would hope I'd have a decent range, but I can't be certain offhand."

"That's good to know, but a bit uncertain. We'll see if one of the others can sense them from farther away, somehow. If not, you'll be our bloodhound once we're inside."

"Bloodhound?" Del asked.

"A type of dog with a good sense of smell," I explained. I'd seen dogs in this world so I knew that would make sense.

He nodded. "Bloodhound indeed."

"Any thoughts on the 'getting in secretly' part of the plan?" I asked.

Janice shrugged. "Let's hope one of them can help us." She indicated the group of twenty tritons and the mixed bag of ten others trailing behind us.

That reminded me. "How did things go with Naz yesterday? You seemed to be having a good time. I heard you laughing."

Janice blushed. I was fairly certain it was the first time I'd seen her do it. "He's charming and funny, yes."

"And?" I knew she'd slept alone last night.

She looked away, out over the sea. "He told me about... about our kind." She seemed to stumble over the word: 'our.' "It sounds nice, where he comes from, though, cold. It's high in the mountains. But his people spend hours on end soaring out over all these lands, high above, looking down." A heavy sigh escaped her. "A part of me... some part of me likes that idea, of soaring free, high in the sky, but..." She grimaced, and glanced back at me with a pained expression in her eyes. "That's not who I am... is it? I'm from our world. I'm an infectious disease specialist for the FBI. Aren't I?"

I could see the turmoil within her. She was going through an existential crisis, not knowing who she really was.

"Once this is all over, you can come and go between worlds as you like. Well, I might have to help you, but we can work that out. Maybe if you spend some time here, you'll work out who and what you want to be."

"Thanks," she said with a half-smile. "I'd appreciate that."

"With everything you're doing — and have done — for me, it's the least I can do."

Her smile grew. "I can remember when I thought you were a goddess."

"You don't anymore?" I asked, curious what she now thought of me, but not upset that she no longer believed I was a goddess.

"Now I have wings. Everything has changed. I don't know what I think about anything."

That was fair.

I turned my attention ahead of us to the tall black rocks and the invisible portal back to my world.

"Once we're ready, I'll want to go through first and scout the other side. There's a decent chance Hera will be expecting us,"

Janice said, before hurrying away from us to go find her clothes where she'd hidden them.

Del and I found where we'd stashed ours and dressed amid odd looks from our new troop of followers.

I looked them over as I dressed. "Is there any way they can look more... human?" I asked Del. "Those minotaurs and the cyclops would really stand out in my world. Can they change, like you can?"

"They can," he replied, "but some may never have done it before. They'd have little need to."

Here was hoping changing to look like a human wasn't too difficult.

I pulled on my coat and turned to address the group. "Attention everyone. Where we're going, everyone looks like me. I've been told that you all can possibly do that as well? If so, please do so now. It will be much easier to blend in. We won't attract as much attention, which is the goal."

After a bit of murmuring and shuffling, there was a shift in the group. The minotaurs seemed to shrink a little — probably just from losing their horns — and looked fully human, though all three of them — including the woman — were bald. They instantly seemed awkward, stretching out their jaws and feeling their face, and slowly kicking out their legs.

The cyclops didn't shrink, but closed her one eye and then her face seemed to shimmer and she had two... in the right places. The *panai*'s legs shifted to look normal, his horns vanished, and his square eyes rounded. The various nymphs remained mostly unchanged. They couldn't adjust the mottled color of their skin — just like that disease-spreading naiad hadn't been able to be anything other than blue. The wings on the *nephelai* and on Naz disappeared, but their odd skin tone remained unchanged as well. Although unless anyone looked really closely, it would be good enough, Naz looked like some bronzed Greek god while the *nephelai* just looked extremely pale.

"Thank you!" I called out and went over to the stone where Janice was waiting with her gun ready.

"We have to assume there are forces on the other side, so I may be coming back quickly. Be ready," she said.

"Got it," I replied, pressing my hand against the stone.

She sucked in a deep breath then rushed through the portal.

My pulse pounded as I waited for her to return, fully expecting her to come running back with bullets following her.

But she didn't come back, which made me worried that she'd been captured right away.

I was about to go through myself, when she calmly stepped back through.

"It's clear," she said, but her expression was grim.

"Really?" That was a surprise. I was certain Hera knew about the portal and would be watching it.

Of course, maybe she thought I was so shattered at having lost my guys that I'd escaped with Del and wouldn't come back.

No. It had to be a trap... I just couldn't figure out how, and given that we had no way of knowing if we were being watched or not, we just had to continue with the plan until Hera attacked.

Or maybe things were actually going right for a change?

Yeah, I wasn't going to hold my breath on that.

And really, we had no choice. If we wanted to get to my world, we had to go through this portal.

It took a bit of time to get everyone across and by the time I went through last, the alley was crowded with thirty naked men and women who huddled together and shivered in the cold.

"I'll take them down this way, toward the dead-end of the alley —" Janice started before she was cut off.

"Annie Chambers?"

I spun toward the voice coming from the mouth of the alley.

Del jerked in front of me, blocking me from harm, and I peeked around him carefully.

There was only one man. He looked like one of Hera's goons, but he had his arms out and up.

"I have a message," he said.

I bet he did and I bet I wasn't going to like it.

I didn't trust any of this. Everything within me screamed that this was the trap I'd been expecting earlier.

Janice ran up to the man and frisked him, but didn't find a weapon... not that he'd need one if he was from the other world. He could have some kind of magic and we wouldn't know until he used it.

"The message is in my pocket," the man said, nodding to indicate the location. Janice got it out and he turned and left.

That was it?

No strike team repelling from the roofs around us, ready to capture or shoot us?

"That was not what I expected," Janice said as she came to me.

"Me, neither."

She handed over the envelope and I opened it carefully and drew out the small piece of monogramed paper inside.

ANNIE,

I HAVE YOUR BOYS, ALIVE AND VERY UNWELL. IF YOU WANT TO SEE them again, surrender yourself to me. I'll let them go in exchange for you.

HERA

CHAPTER 10

ANNIE

I CRUMPLED UP THE PAPER, A MIX OF EMOTIONS CHURNING INSIDE ME.

A small, foolish part of me had hoped we'd be able to sneak back into my world and be able to free my guys, while the rest of me had expected an attack. Instead, I got confirmation that my guys were still alive — thank God! — and that Hera wanted to continue playing her sick game with me.

"Fuck." I knew she was a big cat, and cats liked to play with their prey, but fuck!

"This is... interesting," Janice said as she paced deeper into the alley then turned back toward us, her gaze turned inward in thought. "You must have something she needs. That's the only reason she didn't ambush us here. An ambush risks killing you and she clearly doesn't want to kill you. She needs you alive for some reason."

"Swell," I huffed. "I'd like to know why."

Janice shrugged. "I have no clue. We have to assume she's watching us somehow."

"Does that change the plan?" I asked.

"Yes. No. I don't know." She frowned and jerked around,

heading deeper into the alley again. "Let me think." She reached the far end and came back. "I think the beginning part of the plan is the same. We still need money and clothes only... I don't think you should be out there with just a small guard around you. She might try to grab you. So you stay here and I'll go get the money and clothes."

"I'll go with you," Naz said stepping forward.

"All right. Here," Del replied and he stripped and handed the guy his clothes so he wasn't walking around Chicago naked.

It was a testament to how befuddled Janice must have been that she just nodded at him.

"We'll go and get the clothes. Del, you walk the rest of them through how to unlock their powers and see what we've got. Annie, stay in the middle of the group, hard to get at."

It sounded like a good plan to me, all things considered.

"Come on, fly-boy," Janice said, in control and seemingly forgetting her awkwardness around Naz, and they left the alley.

I turned to Del. "Time to find out what our crew can do," I said, even as my stomach churned with a new fear.

Hera could strike at any moment and the waiting was killing me. But what was worse, she wanted me alive, and I knew that wasn't a good thing.

We spent the next couple of hours trying to figure out what powers everyone had.

There was a wide array of abilities, from the useful, to the odd and weird. One of the *epimelidai* could turn himself into living fire! That discovery caused a whole bunch of burns in the tight alley, which I then had to heal. The female minotaur could read people's thoughts and the *nephelai* had powers of wind, like Hera, so maybe he could counter her attacks? Though I suspected Hera would be stronger than someone who'd only just discovered their powers.

Most of the powers the tritons had weren't that useful. One

had a foul stench, and we were forced to make the poor guy stand at the far end of the alley. Another had an extendable and prehensile tongue, which might be useful in other circumstances, but not for combat, and a third guy began producing oily ink from his pores. The rest of the tritons simply didn't know what, if any powers, they had. Either they were too subtle to see, or not easily manifested.

The cyclops also couldn't seem to figure out what she could do, though she was strong to begin with. Similarly, one of the male minotaurs didn't know what he could do, while the other minotaur seemed to be able to sense people's emotions. He didn't seem impressed by this.

There were, however, a few useful abilities. The second *epimelidai* could blend in with any background, camouflaging himself, while the *panai* could shapeshift into anything — which might be good for scouting.

The *oreadai* could jump from place to place in an instant, and take others with him, which could get us into Hera's building quickly and undetected, and I knew he'd be coming with us for sure.

The other useful power came from one of the tritons who could seemingly sense through solid objects. He was confused as to exactly how it worked, but I realized it might allow us to 'see' what was on the other side of doors before we went through. He couldn't do it at any extreme range, but we'd still be bringing him along.

By the time Janice returned, I had a good idea of who'd make up our smaller strike-rescue team. Aside from myself and Del — and probably Janice and potentially Naz — we'd take the mind-reading minotaur, the teleporting *oreadai*, the sense-through-things triton, and the shape-shifting *panai*. The rest would be responsible for creating a distraction outside of Hera's tower in hopes of drawing some of her forces outside.

I wasn't concerned about learning the names of everyone here, that would be too much at once, but I did try to learn the names of the few who were going with us. Yelling, 'hey *oreadai*' in the middle of a fight might work, but it would be more polite to actually use his name.

The minotaur woman was Khyrys, the *oreadai* was Dorios, the *panai*, who seemed to be playing with how many different shapes he could take, went by Rhoumin or Rhou, and the triton was Ladon.

When Janice did return, it was with two shopping carts nearly overflowing with clothes, and a very ill-looking Naz.

"Please send him back to his world," Janice said, her voice tight with concern.

"What happened?" I asked as I activated the portal.

Janice helped the man stagger through. He could barely walk and he clutched his head as if it hurt. He seemed about to retch, or collapse, or both.

She returned through the portal a moment later, her expression grim.

"I don't know what hit him. It seems like this world was just... too much for him," she said. "Before he got too bad, he said he could hear and smell things. I think his senses went nuts or something. Eventually he got a headache and could barely walk. I hurried back here as quick as I could. Unfortunately, that means the clothes selection is a bit slipshod. I was just grabbing stuff off racks. We'll see if we have enough and who fits what, and how good it looks."

Luckily the most of what Janice had gotten was bulky cold weather gear, which covered most of the armor the men wore. In the end, most of our force had decent clothes, if looking a bit haphazard. A few didn't have pants, so we gave them the longest coats, while a few others looked like they were about to head to the north pole in all their bulkiness, but it would work. Rhou, the shape-shifter, didn't need clothes, he could seemingly create them when he shifted, which meant one of the tritons trying not to shiver, did get pants.

Then we were ready. A small force of the tritons would stay and guard the alley, while the rest of us piled into a series of cabs and made our way downtown. And I could only pray that this would work. If not, we'd be dead... or become Hera's prisoners, likely wishing we were dead.

CHAPTER 11

ANNIE

My heart pounded as I materialized in a utility room in Hera's building. For a moment, I hadn't been anywhere, lost in darkness, feeling like I was in a million places at once, yet still feeling Del's warm hand holding mine.

The *panai*, Rhou, fell to his knees and lost his breakfast. Ladon, the triton, staggered, but didn't fall, though he took a long moment to come back to himself, while Del swayed, blinking, but remained standing.

"That was..." Janice flashed a hint of a smile, seeming to have coped the best out of all of us. "That was fun!"

She had a strange idea of fun.

As the rest of us took a moment, Janice inspected the room. We were in a small space packed with shelves with cleaning supplies and boxes, on a sub-level of the building.

"Rhou, feel up for some scouting?" Janice asked.

The *panai*, though he didn't seem fully recovered from Dorios's teleportation magic yet, nodded. "Of course, Miss Janice."

"Take the form of a mouse and scout through the vents. See if you can find an *erinai*, a stone titan, and a satyr," she said, the other world's terminology easily rolling off her tongue.

Rhou nodded and an instant later was scurrying off as a mouse toward a grate at the base of one of the walls.

Now we had to sit tight and wait, just like the rest of our force outside. The plan was for them to hide for a couple hours before they attacked, drawing out the guards in the building. We could only hope those few hours would be enough time for Rhou to figure out where everyone was, return, and for us to come up with a plan.

No one said anything while we waited, and while I considered sitting, I didn't want to get caught on my ass if anyone found us. And from the way no one else sat, I suspected they thought the same thing.

My pulse pounded, my blood rushing in my ears, and my stomach churned. Without a doubt Hera was waiting for us. I could only hope that the magical abilities the others had gained would give us enough of an advantage to help Rion, Aethan, and Keph escape.

That was the main goal. As much as I wanted to bring Hera down for good, I had to get my guys out of there first.

I turned to Del, whose expression was hard, the muscles in his jaw flexed.

"Can you sense Rion and the others?" I asked, hoping he'd be able to feel the unique 'water-sense' of the other three men.

Del closed his eyes and after a long moment shook his head. "There's too much steel and stone around. I can't sense far. All I know is they're not close."

I'd assumed that much already. If Hera wasn't keeping them in the basement, it made sense for her to keep them in her apartment on the top floor.

But man, I wanted to free them now. Now now now.

Frustration twisted in my stomach as I fought to ignore the ache of my missing bonds.

"We'll find them," he said, caressing small circles on my back as if he could sense my frustration.

"I know," I murmured back while a part of me whispered, *but in what condition?*

Del shifted closer, as if knowing I needed more than a back rub, and wrapped his arms around me. "We *will* find them," he murmured. "We—"

But swift-marching, booted footfalls sounded in the corridor beyond our room cut him off and we all went quiet, tensing as the footfalls stopped just outside our door.

CHAPTER 12

ANNIE

CRAP. CRAP CRAP CRAP. SOMEONE WAS IN THE HALL RIGHT OUTSIDE the door.

Janice shot a hard glance at Khyrys, telling her to read the mind of whoever was out there, while the others clenched their hands, preparing for a fight, and I held my breath, praying we wouldn't get caught.

"It's me, Rhou," came a deep and resonant voice from outside, and Khyrys nodded her confirmation.

I frowned. It certainly didn't sound like the *panai*, but then, if he was in another form, it wouldn't.

The door cracked open and a tall man clad in black body armor and a helmet entered, his hands up as if he feared we'd pounce on him even though we had a mind reader in our group. Then he carefully shut the door behind him and melted back into Rhou's short, slight form.

I let out a heavy breath I hadn't known I'd been holding. "What did you find?"

"I found the men we're looking for," he said, his expression grim. "But they're not in a good way. They'll probably need our help getting out, and one of them is with a woman on the top floor. I'm assuming that's Hera?"

"Fuck," I hissed, my heartrate rising. "Of course, she'd told me to come, so she'd want at least one of the guys with her for insurance."

"But why not all three?" Janice asked.

"If they're all in one spot, they'd be easier to rescue," Del suggested.

Janice nodded at that. "True."

"Where are the other two?" I asked Rhou.

His expression grew even darker. "They're in rooms a couple floors below where Hera is. "They..." he trailed off and frowned.

What? They... what?

"Are they alive?"

Please be alive.

"They are, but they've been badly hurt."

I turned to Dorios. "Can you teleport us to them?"

Dorios turned to Janice. "Draw me a map so I can concentrate on it, just like how we got here."

"What floor were they on?" Janice asked Rhou.

"Ah... I don't know the number, sorry."

Janice paced for a moment in the small cramped space, the others leaning back against the shelves to make room for her. "You said a couple floors below Hera's suite? Exactly two floors?"

Rhou blinked a bit, then closed his eyes, perhaps trying to remember and retrace his steps. "Ah... well, yes and no. Two floors below where Hera was, there was a door. It led to a stairway, which was the only access to a floor below that. As far as I could tell, there was no other way to get to that third floor down, and that's where the men were being held."

"A secret floor in the building?" Janice paused her movement and her eyes scanned back and forth as if she was looking at something, except she didn't seem to be seeing anything around her. "Yeah, that's not on the blue prints. Damn. I'm not sure I'll be able to draw anything accurate."

She returned to pacing, muttering to herself. I watched her, silently praying she'd be able to figure this out.

"Rhou..." Janice said, slowly.

"Yes?" He leaned closer, his gaze locked on her. There was something in his eyes, something—

A faint smile curled my lips despite the grim news. He was looking at Janice the same way my guys looked at me. He was infatuated with her. And if we got out of this alive, I was going to make sure those two had, in the very least, a conversation and got to know each other.

"Dorios..." Janice said.

The young man perked up, waiting for his instructions.

Janice frowned, then turned to Khyrys, the minotaur with the ability to read minds. "Could you take a picture from someone's mind and share it with someone else?"

The minotaur woman, no longer looking like a minotaur at all, raised a single brow. "I don't know. I can read minds, but putting something into another's mind..."

"Just try," Janice said. "Try to speak into my mind or project some image or thought."

Silence sank over the room as the two women stared intently at each other. It seemed to take forever before both sets of eyes widened.

"Yes!" Janice gasped. "Great! Now Rhou, bring to mind where you found the three guys and share those thoughts with Khyrys."

I began to sense where this was going. If Dorios could be given Rhou's thoughts as to where the guys were, perhaps he could teleport directly to them.

Within a few minutes, the location images had been conveyed to Dorios and then the *oreadai* started talking with Rhou about how high the building was to try to get a sense for the location in space.

Janice came to me as the other two worked through this.

"Here's what I'm thinking," she said. "Dorios drops us off in a secluded corner of Hera's suites. Then he jumps in and frees your two guys on the lower levels, taking them to the alley, where they'll hopefully be safe until we can meet up with them."

I nodded. As much as I wanted to see them right away, it was better to get them out of danger first. Once everyone was safe, then I'd have a chance to reunite with them... as bittersweet as that might be with our missing bonds.

"Meanwhile," Janice continued, "we make our way to Hera, and wait for Dorios to return. Once he's back, we'll create a distraction, so he can jump in to free the last one. Hera will probably know the instant he's in the room with her, given her advanced senses. So, we make like we're going to hand you over, which will hopefully be enough of a distraction for Dorios to get in an out. There will be even more of a distraction if we time this to happen while our force outside is attacking." She checked her watch. "In about a half hour."

My heart pounded so hard I thought it would tear out of my chest. I didn't want to wait. I couldn't stand another minute of doing nothing. I needed to see them and heal them and—

I shoved those thoughts as deep down as I could. I couldn't let them distract me.

This was the best plan we were going to get given the circumstances and I needed to keep my head and follow it, no matter what my heart wanted.

"Sounds good," I forced out and Janice turned to confirm the plan with the others.

Del drew close again and wrapped his arms around me. "How are you doing?"

"Horrible," I confided. "I can't get my nerves straight. I'm so worried about the guys and about these folks and those outside. I don't want anyone to get hurt, but..." I was talking a mile a minute, shaking with urgency and fear.

He tightened his embrace. "We're almost there."

I nodded into his chest, but secretly there was a much deeper worry in my heart. With luck — gods, please give us luck — we'd have my guys all free soon, but my bond with them was still broken. Del and I had been very intimate a couple of times now and it hadn't reformed, and I was beginning to think that Hera had taken that away from me permanently. If so...

No. I didn't want to contemplate that, either.

I'd die without my guys. And just having them around, would be good enough. It had to be. Except I feared I'd still feel hollow without their bonds even if they were close. And if I couldn't get over that, how would that effect our relationship?

I tried to push those thoughts aside with the others as time inched closer to the moment when the rest of our team would create their distraction.

Then all of a sudden Janice looked up. "Ready?" she asked. "It's time."

I nodded with the rest, but in my heart — my desperate, thundering heart — I was terrified and not ready at all.

CHAPTER 13

DELPHON

DORIOS WHISKED US FROM THE UTILITY ROOM TO A HALLWAY THEN vanished again. The hall was short with a door at one end with a symbol that looked like stairs, and at the other end, the hall turned right and kept going.

"Where are we?" Annie asked in a whisper.

"One of the only unguarded places close to Hera," Janice whispered back. "We're one floor below her and next to the stairs." She pointed to the door with the stairs symbol then turned to Ladon who could see through walls. "How many people are around?"

He put a hand against the closest wall and closed his eyes. "Two just beyond that door to the stairs. Another two directly above them and a group of four down that hallway." He pointed to the open end of the hall then bent his finger to indicate they were down a little.

I stared at him. I knew he could *see through* things. I just hadn't realized he didn't need to be looking in that direction to do so.

"They must be at the elevators," Janice whispered as if she thought I was confused about the direction he'd been pointing.

Which I hadn't been, but now I was. I had no idea what an elevator was.

"There are a few more upstairs," Ladon reported.

"Del," Annie said turning to me. "You're up."

I clenched my jaw and gave her a tight nod. I wasn't happy about what was to come next. I didn't want to use my powers to kill people, but things were dire and I was the only one in our group with a magic that could be used offensively.

I crept to the door to the stairs. There was a small vertical window in it and I peeked through it. I could see both men on the other side of the door, wearing that same black armor and helmet as the rest of Hera's men, and I reached out with my water abilities.

The body was mostly water and I could feel everyone around me, but I focused on the two on the other side of the door and began pulling the water out of them.

I heard the gasps and groans from both of them as they must have suddenly felt... well I had no clue what that would feel like, but I guessed it was painful, probably very uncomfortable at the least.

Then both men fell with a heavy thud and I felt their bodies curling in on themselves as they lost more and more water. I halted before — what I hoped — was a fatal stage, then wrenched open the door and rushed inside, ready to finish them off in case I'd failed to incapacitate them.

But they weren't in any condition to attack. They lay at my feet, looking gaunt and surprised, squirming and unable to speak, the sight making my stomach churn. Gods, they looked horrible. And I'd done that to them.

"Quickly," I hissed, not wanting to kill men who were just doing their jobs like the soldiers who'd come with me from Galniosia. "They'll recover in time, but they're out for now."

Though, even as I finished saying this, I heard footsteps coming down the stairs from above.

The guards on the landing above us must have heard something.

I closed my eyes and reached out again.

This time I felt men both above and below us. There was one figure descending from above and another staying up on the landing, as well as two on the floor below us, one of them tentatively coming up a few stairs.

I reached out to all of them and pulled on their water.

In a moment, they were all writhing and incapacitated like the two before me.

Then something *popped* and agony screamed through my leg. I fell to the ground, hands clamped around my injury and forced myself to look up the stairs for whoever had attacked me. One of the guards had managed to reach the landing at the turn in the stairs just above me, and had used his *gun*. Though he only got off one shot and was now writhing and gasping on the floor, severely dehydrated.

Annie knelt next to me. "Let me see."

I started to peel my hand away, but blood, which had been oozing from my fingers, now gushed over my hand and down my leg, and I pressed back down on the wound.

Annie slapped her hands over top of mine and the blood flow eased enough for me to remove my hand. A moment later the small metal projectile was pushed out of the wound by Annie's healing magic and the pain faded.

"Thank you," I murmured.

"Let's go," Janice hissed. "They're using silencers so hopefully no one heard that, but I don't want to wait around to find out."

We hurried up the stairs, then waited at the door.

Time crept by before Dorios appeared with us as planned.

"The other two are safe," he said, and a pressure in my chest eased a bit.

Thank the gods! At least two of my friends were safe. Now there was only one left in dire trouble. And while I still feared what Hera could do, I had hope Janice's plan would work.

We hurried through the next doorway, keeping quiet, and I disabled the four guards down the hall, who stood in front of two odd-looking metal doors. Perhaps these were the *elevators* Janice had mentioned.

Then, just outside of Hera's rooms, we paused and Ladon and I felt for people.

"Four just inside," Ladon reported. "Another four in a room beyond, one on their knees. About a dozen more not too far away in this complex of rooms."

I could only feel the four nearby.

"Fuck," Annie hissed. "That's a lot."

"Let's do this quickly," Janice said. "Del?"

My turn again. I pulled water from the four on the other side of the door where we waited, then all of us, except for Dorios, charged in. He remained hidden, keeping one door open just a little to peer through since he needed to see where he was jumping to and there was a chance whoever was being held there had been moved since Rhou had last been there.

The room beyond was a large foyer area with a few chairs and a flagrant display of wealth: lavish tapestries, large pieces of art, and pedestals with vases or glass cases displaying valuables. It was meant to impress, and it did.

"Annie, so nice of you to join us!" Hera proclaimed. She stood holding one of Rion's wings to keep him upright — the *erinai* only seemed to have one — with a small *gun* to the back of his head. Two more men in armor stood behind her.

"Rion!" Annie shouted, her voice cracking with pain and concern. He looked horrible with cuts and bruises all over his naked body. He was barely conscious, held upright on his knees only by Hera's grip.

"My security tells me you've already freed your two other friends. I don't know how, but trust that this one will not—"

It happened so quickly we were all stunned. Dorios jumped in, grabbed Rion while prying Hera's hand off his wing, and teleported away.

My thoughts stuttered.

They were gone.

And *I* been expecting it.

Hera looked stunned, blinking at her now empty hand as if she couldn't figure out what had happened. "What—?"

She raised her *gun* as did the two men behind her, but the rest of us had joined hands by then. A spray of bullets roared from their weapons as Dorios popped in behind us and yanked us back to the alley. I was sure I'd been staring at one of those projectiles only inches away when we'd left.

My heart was racing as I staggered back. My shoulder blades hit the cold brick wall and I sagged to the ground.

"We did it?" Annie asked, her tone hesitant as if she didn't believe it.

And gods, it had happened so fast, I still wasn't sure we'd actually done it.

"Almost. We need to get the others away from Hera's tower now!" Janice said and Dorios was gone again.

Dorios brought the others back in small groups, but it quickly became apparent that their assault hadn't gone well. Far too many were wounded, dying, or dead and with Annie the only one able to heal and open the portal, she decided to save those who were critically injured instead of opening the portal, fearing they wouldn't last long enough to get to our world.

She helped everyone she could, jumping from one person to the next, as Dorios brought in group after group. She even managed to heal Aethan, Rion, and Keph, who'd also been severely injured, but not enough for them to regain consciousness.

She was staggering toward one of my fellow tritons, looking exhausted and barely able to stay upright when the sound of cars roared nearby.

Both Annie and Janice's gazes jumped to the mouth of the alley, and Annie jerked toward the wall where the portal lay.

"Back through the portal now!" she said.

I grabbed Rion, while one of the minotaurs lifted Aethan, and the two other minotaurs, the cyclops, and three tritons picked up Keph.

We staggered through and I handed Rion off to two other tritons then stood by the rocks, watching everyone else run through, and waited for Annie.

My heart pounded. I couldn't see or hear anything. Nothing from her side could be seen through the portal to our side and I didn't want to get in the way of those escaping to go check on her.

I hurriedly counted who'd already come through and who was left.

The last triton rushed passed me and then Annie staggered through, bleeding from several wounds. Her gaze lifted as if she was trying to look at me before her eyes rolled back and she collapsed onto the sand, unconscious.

CHAPTER 14

AETHAN

I screamed, jerking upright in a cold sweat, desperately looking around, but not able to focus on anything. Then my vision started to clear and I saw sand. A vast, warm stretch of sand with a large group of people nearby.

I was on a beach.

Oh thank all the gods!

I was safe... unless I wasn't.

My pulse leaped, pounding in my chest. I had to be dreaming. This had to be a vision my mind made up so I could escape the pain and horror.

Except if this was a dream, why were there so many people I didn't know wandering around.

"Aethan?" a familiar voice called out, and I dragged my gaze behind me as Del rushed over to me.

"You're awake. Good," he said, kneeling beside me.

"Am I?" I asked, my pulse trying to return to normal even though I still wasn't sure if I was dreaming or not.

Del frowned. "Are you what?"

"Awake."

He stared at me as if he had no idea what to say then grabbed me, wrapping his strong arms around me in a brotherly embrace.

"Aethan, you're safe," he assured me. "We got you out. No more danger. Annie healed you and we're in our world now."

More of my fear bled away, and I almost completely believed him. All that remained was a tiny voice of self-preservation that wouldn't allow me to completely hope and be happy just yet. I needed more proof.

I hugged Del back, then we released each other and I stood, my body complaining at the movement. But just being able to stand was astounding... which didn't completely add to Del's assurance that I wasn't dreaming.

Hera had been thorough in her torture.

A shudder swept through me and I tried to shove back the memory. I didn't want to recall any of it. She'd cut the tendons in my legs and done something to my hoofed feet, but there was no indication that I'd been hurt. My body was whole, if sore and aching.

Taking a tentative step, I easily found my balance even if the rest of me, my mind and emotions were unsteady. I'd wanted to die and I'd been terrified Annie had died. I still was terrified, even if Del had just said she'd healed me. There was an aching hollowness in my chest where she was supposed to be, and I was afraid it meant she was dead. My mate, my goddess was dead.

"She really did a number on you guys," Del said, his voice soft and grim.

I couldn't answer, not yet, maybe not ever. That would require remembering and I didn't want to remember. Instead, I gave a tight nod, unable to fully make eye contact and started shuffling around, trying to work out the pain in my body.

Except that made me think of being strapped to Hera's table and—

"How are the others?" I forced out, trying to change the conversation in my mind, but unable to really think of anything else.

"You're the first awake," Del replied, watching me walk in slow, unsteady circles.

I glanced around and saw Keph and Rion laying not far away... and Annie.

My pulse lurched. She lay beside them, still in her other world clothes, the fabric covered in blood even though her complexion looked fine, like there wasn't anything wrong with her. But something had to be wrong because I couldn't feel our bond.

"Oh gods, Annie," I gasped, jerking toward her and losing my balance.

Del caught me. "She'll be okay. She was hurt holding the portal open when we returned, but she's healing herself even though she's unconscious. She looks a lot better now than she did before. I'm sure she'll be awake shortly."

I leaned in his grip, unable to go anywhere else but to her side and Del helped me, as if he knew I had to go to her.

"I can't feel her anymore," I said, my voice tight with grief as Del helped me sag to the sand beside her. "Something happened just before she got thrown out the window. I thought she'd died."

"Janice, that FBI woman, caught her. Turns out she was a hidden *aurai* all along, and she sprouted wings and saved them both."

"Hidden *aurai*?" I asked confused. What was that supposed to mean?

"She's from their world, but I'm guessing a long time ago her ancestors got together with some *aurai*. It was in her blood, but dormant until a crisis brought it out. That's my guess. She was quite shocked about it for a while there."

"Hunh."

I had no idea what to say to that. I wanted to thank the gods that Annie was alive, but remembered what Hera had done to me and thought better of it. Better to just stick to cursing them.

I brushed a lock of soft red hair away from Annie's cheek, the ache of her absence inside me swelling as I looked at her, and cupped her cheek. She didn't stir, and if I didn't look at her damaged body, I could almost think she was just asleep.

"Why can't I feel her?" I might have been able to endure so much more if I'd felt my bond with Annie, but that had vanished, leaving a gaping wound in my soul.

"Hera did something to Annie which removed her bonds with us." Del sighed. "We've tried to get it back, but nothing has worked so far."

That didn't sound good at all.

A few feet away someone grunted, then grunted again, and Keph slowly sat up, his hands pressed against his temples as if his head hurt.

"Where...?" His gaze darted around and landed on us and Annie. "Annie?"

"She'll be fine," Del reassured, except I could hear the tension in his voice. She might be physically fine, but her soul was broken like ours was, her bonds missing. "How are you doing?"

Keph gave another heavy grunt. "Hera tried really hard to hurt me. It took a lot and tired her out. I don't think I was much fun." He rolled to his hands and knees, then slowly climbed to his feet, not looking as effected as I was. "What happened to Annie?"

"She got hurt when we left the other world. She's healing. She'll be fine," Del insisted.

Keph sat heavily on the other side of her and nodded. "Good." He looked over at us. "You two? How are you?"

Del glanced at me and I grimaced.

"I..." I didn't want to say how I felt. I was weak and terrified. "I'll be well. Eventually."

Del nodded at that. "I wasn't taken. I'm well enough." He

looked around at the others on the beach not too far away. "But I'll be paying back my mother for the rest of my life," he murmured.

I didn't understand what that meant and was about to ask when Keph spoke up first.

He pressed his large hand over his heart and frowned. "What happened to our bond?"

Del explained it to Keph, and even hearing it for a second time, it still felt wrong. It was even worse to see Keph's expression fall, his heartbreak clear on his face, the same heartbreak I felt.

"It was rough being separated from her," he rumbled.

"Yeah," I agreed.

Del swallowed, the muscles in his jaw flexing. "I know."

We didn't say much after that, just watched Annie, or the others on the beach, or the distant waves.

After a while of silence, Keph finally drew in a deep breath and squared his massive shoulders. "What do we do now?"

I didn't know about the other two, but I'd been waiting for Rion or Annie to wake up and hadn't thought much beyond that.

"I think we rest and heal and..." Del shrugged. "I don't know." He opened his mouth as if to continue then shook his head. "I don't know. Hera seems unstoppable." The fight seemed to have gone out of him. He just kept shaking his head. "I'm just glad we have all of you back."

"How did you do that anyway?" I asked. "I was only half aware of what was going on. I was there then... not."

Del glanced around then pointed at an *oreadai* talking with a triton and a female minotaur. "See that *oreadai* over there?"

I nodded.

"We all have powers in the other world. We found that he could jump from place to place. Annie called it *teleporting*. That's how we got you out. Another fellow... Ah... Rhou — that *panai* over there." He pointed at another man standing a few feet away from the first one. "He can change shapes and did some scouting around to find you. Then the *oreadai* pulled you out. You two were easy, Rion... was with *her*. That took precise timing and we almost all died."

There was something he wasn't saying, but I wasn't going to push him on it and Annie let out a long, drawn-out groaning breath, stopping whatever else he might have said.

"Fuck me," she groaned as we all turned to her. "That hurt."

"What happened?" Del asked.

She raised her arm to shield her eyes from the late day sun, her gaze jumping from him to me then to Keph, a warm, sad smile pulling at her lips. "Soldiers arrived as the last of us were going through. I was shot several times as I ducked into the portal. I can safely say I don't want to be shot ever again."

She half rose, sitting propped up on one arm and looked down at herself. "I can still feel it even though the wounds seem to be gone." She sat up fully, rolling her shoulders and moving around a bit, flinching with some movement. "It may take a bit to get rid of that remembered pain, I think."

"But you're alive." I wrapped my arms around her, pulling her to my chest in a tight embrace, never wanting to let her go. "I'm so glad you're alive."

She weakly returned my hug as if even though she was awake she was still exhausted. "I missed you, too. All of you. Is Rion...?"

"Not up yet," Keph rumbled looking back over at the still prone form of our last brother.

She sighed heavily. "He..." She shuddered and something sad and angry darkened her expression. "Gods."

I wasn't certain I wanted to know what was going through her mind. Annie had healed me, so she'd known what Hera had done to me, and I had a feeling what Hera had done to Rion had been worse.

"I... I need to walk." She extracted herself from my reluctant-to-let-her-go embrace and stood. I was up next to her in a flash as Keph rose as well.

"No," she said, seeing all of us ready to go with her. "I can't... not everyone, not right now." She pressed her hand to her chest, as if she too felt the emptiness of our missing bond—

Gods, she was missing all four of us.

If missing just her was bad, missing all four of us had to be horrible.

"You shouldn't be alone," Del insisted, a strange fear in his eyes that I'd never seen before. "You're still weak. If something happened..."

She sighed. "You're right. Just one of you then," she offered.

We all looked at each other. The desperation I felt to stay close to her must have shown in my eyes, because the other two nodded at me, agreeing I should be the one to go with her.

Thank the gods.

Annie stripped away her bloody clothes and began a brisk walk toward the hills, away from the beach, as if she wanted to get away from everyone. I got the feeling she wanted to be completely alone but had let me come along as a compromise, so I kept my mouth shut. And even if she had wanted to talk, I wasn't sure what I could say. I didn't want to bring up what had happened or the empty ache inside me. Yeah, perhaps not talking was best right now.

Once we were well away from the beach she finally slowed. She gave a half-hearted chuckle, which didn't last and didn't seem to particularly reflect her dour mood. "You're not as fast here."

I gave a similar short, breathy laugh. "No, I'm not. If I were in horse-form I'd be much faster."

She turned to me then, one brow raised. "I don't think I've ever seen you in horse form. Would you mind showing me? Can you talk in horse form?"

I shifted for her. It was easy enough. I didn't spend much time as a horse, but there was something about the more powerful form which made me feel more confident, less like an empty, bondless failure. "Yes, I can still talk."

"You sound a little funny though," she giggled and drew up next to me, running a hand over my long neck and flank. She slowly came to embrace me, her hands around the base of my neck, and I rested my large head lightly on her back, not able to do much else.

We stayed that way for a long time, just touching each other before she started softly weeping.

"Annie?" I murmured.

She sniffled. "I'll be okay." She didn't sound like she would be.

"What do you need?"

"Can you... stay like this for a while?"

I wasn't sure why. "Of course."

Silence stretched out again as we simply stood there, her arms wrapped around me.

Finally, she drew in a shuddering breath and released me. "Can I..." She came around so I could see her more easily, sliding both of her hands along my snout. She had an odd look. "Can I ride you?"

I whinnied — which was my horse version of a laugh. "Of course."

Just those two small words and her eyes lit up. It made my heart sing that I was the one to bring her such joy with something so simple.

Carefully, I knelt so she could straddle me, and once her legs were clenched tight to my sides and her hands digging into my mane, I rose.

"Is this okay? Am I hurting you?" she asked.

A little. Her grip in my mane was a little too tight, but I wasn't going to complain. "No."

I began to walk slowly.

"Oh!" she said and her legs squeezed tighter, as did her hands in my mane. I tried to ignore the pain. My flanks could take it, but my mane felt like it was going to be torn out.

"Are you stable?" I asked. Turning my head to look back. She seemed to be faring well enough. She looked like a queen, proud and tall, riding bareback. I was momentarily distracted by the movement of her breasts as I walked, but I turned away eventually.

"Faster?" she said, and I eased into a slow trot.

Again, she tightened her hold on me.

"I want to feel you run, feel your power. I want to feel free and unburdened, to forget everything!"

I picked up the pace slowly, from a fast trot to a canter. I felt her duck lower, pressing herself against my back, one hand reaching around my neck.

"Yes!" she whooped, close to my ear, her voice filled with joy.

I slipped into a full gallop for a moment before slowing again to check on her. There was a wildness in her eyes as if she was determined to force away the bad memories and feelings and just be free.

"More," she whispered, and I ran.

Annie whooped and shouted, wordless cries of joy and grief and release.

I was a bit lathered by the time I stopped, and Annie slid off my back quickly, stumbling, and leaning against me to keep her balance.

"Oh! My legs are sore," she laughed, but her voice was edged with something else, something desperate.

I glanced back at her, her hair was windswept and wild, her complexion flush with the exertion of riding.

"Switch back," she said, the desperation thickening. "I need you."

I didn't need to be told twice. I was in my satyr form again in an instant. Annie had her body up against mine, and captured my mouth with hers. I responded in kind, already well aroused and ready from having her ride me in my horse form.

The wild, needy kiss lasted only a moment before she urged me to the ground and straddled me yet again, this time in a way I much preferred. Grabbing my erection — with perhaps a bit too much force — she positioned it and lowered herself onto it with an exhalation of breath through her bared teeth.

Stones dug into my back, but I didn't care. The pain was a small price to pay for this pleasure, a pleasure she seemed to desperately need.

I reached up to hold her breasts, cupping and caressing, feeling their weight, and her already aroused nipples.

She tossed her head back, arms up, reaching skyward, as her hips ground and rocked against me. It was raw and desperate sex, no emotion other than a raging need. She was gasping and moaning, her body tensing as she pleasured herself on my cock.

"Harder," she moaned, and since she was already in control and grinding hard with her hips, I took her words to mean the work with my hands. I tightened my grip on her breasts, grasping and kneading the soft skin a she pressed more of her weight down upon me. "Yes!"

A hiss of breath escaped her lips and with eyes full of burning lust and desperation and heartache she looked down at me, capturing my soul. Gods, she was almost scary in her intensity, except I understood it, understood she was trying to fill the emptiness of our missing bond the only way she knew how.

I could tell she was nearing her peak, her motions quickening, frenzied, and I could feel my own release build.

"Come with me," she said, a demand, as her breath caught and her body stiffened. Her hips rocked one last time, forceful and jerking and I did as she commanded. I felt her muscles tighten around my cock, squeezing so hard I could feel her pulse, and my release crashed over me.

"Yes!" she gasped. "Yes."

Tears misted her eyes and she slowly sagged forward and lay on top of me. I wrapped my arms around her, her head on my chest tucked under my chin, and she cried again. This time her tears turned to heavy gaping, heartrending sobs as she cried out her heartache.

I didn't know what to do. There wasn't anything I could do. Del had said they'd tried to fix their broken bond and couldn't. Our bond hadn't reformed either with our kiss or during sex and I didn't know if I would ever be able to fix it.

I held her close, murmuring soothing noises. This wasn't the reaction a man hoped for after sex, but I knew it wasn't me. I'd given her something she'd desperately needed and now, only now, could she allow herself to release what had been pent up within her.

"I'm going to need to move soon," I whispered. "There's a rock digging into my butt and given your... intensity, I think I might be bleeding."

Her now quiet sobs shifted to a jerking, awkward laughter.

"I'll heal that for you," she said through her sniffles. Lifting herself up, her sunrise pale-red hair a curtain around us as her face hovered over mine.

"Thank you," she whispered, then lowered herself to kiss me lightly. As she withdrew, she said, "Sorry. I was a little... aggressive. My knees and thighs are killing me."

I laughed a little with her, and she smiled, the look in her stunning golden eyes filled with love and warmth and gratitude and sadness.

CHAPTER 15

HYPERION

I WOKE WITH A START, MY HEART POUNDING FOR A SECOND BEFORE grief swept through me. I'd lost my wing. I'd lost Annie. I'd—

My thoughts stuttered. I wasn't strapped to Hera's table, I wasn't in pain, and I wasn't on my stomach. Right. I vaguely recalled being freed and whisked away from that horrible place.

I lay on my back, a warm breeze sweeping over my naked skin, staring up at a brilliant blue sky that called to me, begged me to take flight.

Except I couldn't. Hera had cut off my wing and if Annie was dead than an injury like that couldn't be fixed. I was flightless and that, added to the emptiness in my soul where Annie should have been, threatened to consume me. I couldn't push past the grief. And usually when my thoughts were too heavy, I'd fly. There was something about soaring high above everything that helped to clear my mind.

I knew I should have been happy. I was back on my own world and...

Back... on my own world?

But the only one who could open the portal was... Annie.

She had to be alive!

I looked around, but couldn't see her. Del and Keph spoke quietly nearby, but I couldn't see Annie or Aethan. Still... if I was here then...

I jerked up and pushed my wings out of my body. Both wings.

My pulse froze.

I had both of my wings. Somehow, by some miracle, I could still fly.

No.

Not a miracle... because of Annie.

She'd saved me twice. Somehow freeing me from Hera and then giving me back my wings, and yet my soul was still shattered at what had happened, at how helpless I'd been. I, a trained warrior, had been useless. I hadn't been able to stop Hera, hadn't been able to protect my friends, or my mate. And even though Annie had to be alive, I still felt this aching emptiness in my soul where my bond to her should have been. It was gone. Had Annie done that? Had Hera? I didn't know. I knew only that something was terribly wrong and I needed to fly.

I moved away from the crowd, not wanting to talk to anyone, swept my wings out, and took off, trying to leave the world and everything, especially my churning, consuming emotions behind. But it didn't matter how far or high I flew, I couldn't escape myself.

Movement to my left and slightly behind me caught my attention and I turned my head to see an *aurai* shadowing me a few body lengths behind and above me.

My frustration twisted into rage. I wanted to be alone. If I'd wanted to talk with someone, I would have gone over to the group of strangers and said something.

As if looking at him gave him permission to speak to me, he flapped his larger, squarer wings, and leveled out next to me.

"Glorious day!" he called out.

Was it? It didn't feel like it even though I could still fly.

I was sure I didn't know him, but I nodded an acknowledgment, not wanting to be rude. "It is, yes. But I'd like to be alone if possible."

"I was told to keep an eye on you. Something about you having a rough time in the other world and people being worried about you." The *aurai* shrugged. "But if all you needed was some space, I can give that to you. Just don't throw yourself into the ground or anything." He peeled away, slowly soaring higher, off over the seas.

Who'd told him to keep an eye on me?

At least the *aurai* had seemed to understand that I needed some space. Apparently, there were others who were worried about me. I guess that didn't surprise me. I was worried about myself.

A shudder wracked through me and I fell a few feet, my wings not supporting me for a moment, before I caught myself again. It would be so very easy to just fold my wings and fall — *throw myself at the ground*, as the *aurai* had put it — then there'd be nothing. Maybe I should. What did I have now? I couldn't claim to be a warrior. But I did have friends, men who were like brothers to me, and Annie...

My chest tightened with grief. I was so empty, so hollow. The bond was gone and even though I'd been saved and returned to this world, it hadn't been restored. Why hadn't Annie rebonded with me? Perhaps I'd needed to be awake? Maybe she was rebonding with Aethan now?

My jaw tightened and tears leaked from my eyes. I couldn't forget the pain, the horror. It stuck with me like a niggling infection, poisoning my heart and soul. And where there should have been my bond with Annie to help quell these sickening memories, there was nothing.

I circled back, angling to fly inland, in hopes of seeing Annie and Aethan. My keen eyes picked them up, wandering back toward the beach.

Suddenly I needed to talk to her, needed to know what had happened, needed to have the bond restored.

I folded in my wings and dove.

Some part of me — much larger than I wanted to admit — pondered simply not reopening my wings, but I flared them out as I drew close to land, flapping them to land lightly near Annie and Aethan as they reached where the beach met the hills beyond.

"Annie," I said, but couldn't say more past the lump in my throat.

She squeezed Aethan's hand, which she'd been holding, and gave him a look. He nodded and moved off as she came to me, throwing her arms around me, holding me fiercely.

"Rion. Oh gods, I'm so sorry for..." She couldn't say it, but I knew she was talking about what had happened, about my wings.

I still couldn't speak. I just held her as tightly as I could as well, locking our bodies together in a desperate need, as if the tightness of our grip could somehow replace what was missing.

We stayed that way for a long moment before I finally found words, though they were broken and choppy, spoken around heavy breaths and a throat choked with emotion. "The bond... I need it... I need you... I—"

"I need you too, Rion," she said squeezing me tighter for a moment before moving back enough to look up at me. "But I don't know how to reforge the bond. Del and I tried and nothing worked. I fear..."

My heart lurched, following her train of thought.

"No." I couldn't say more. All I could think of was that one word. No. No no no. There had to be a way, there had to be something we could do. If I was determined enough, I could fix everything. I had to fix everything.

Plucking her up, hands under her arms, I lifted her to kiss her. She responded in kind, our need desperate and intense, but as the kiss drew out longer and longer and no feeling came to me of the bond reforming, my soul started to tremble, threatening to shatter.

I set her down and fell to my knees head in hands. "It can't be."

Hot wet tears welled and rolled down my cheeks. I didn't care how unmanly they were. I didn't want to feel like this forever. I couldn't.

Annie knelt next to me. "There's a way. I have to believe there is. But a simple kiss or even sex can't do it this time."

"What happened?" I managed to force out. I couldn't look at her, couldn't let her see my shame, couldn't look into her golden eyes and see the same heartache, so I focused on the ground and the patch of earth below me that was slowly soaking up my tears.

"Hera happened."

I flinched at the name, a name I never wanted to hear again.

"She took all of our bonds."

"No." I hugged myself.

"Oh, Rion, please." Annie wrapped her arms around me and held me close.

She stroked my back between my wings, but I flinched, unable to stop myself. Her touch reminded me of the horrid cuts Hera had inflicted, and I curled into her, my head on her shoulder, pulling her close — as awkward as that was with both of us kneeling.

This was all that was keeping me sane, all that was keeping me from flying back up, as high as I could, then simply falling. This embrace, her touch, her warmth, her body next to mine.

I felt a warmth flowing through me from where she held me.

Not having the words or capability to ask what that was, I guessed she was simply trying to heal me more. But the pain I felt wasn't physical. It couldn't be healed in that way. I needed my Annie back, my bond, my life and meaning, my everything!

I had to try bonding again. Looking up, I grabbed her face and mashed my lips to hers. I needed this, couldn't live without this. I pressed us together as hard as I could. Annie squirmed. I knew this wasn't what she wanted. She was trying to push me away, trying to speak, but unable to with my lips hard on hers.

But with all the force and drive and will I possessed, there was no bond, no life, nothing.

I was a failure as a warrior and now as a mate. Except I didn't stop, couldn't stop, wouldn't stop. I just kept holding us there.

Strong, vise-like arms pulled me off Annie, and I squirmed and screamed, heaving against whoever held me

Annie fell back gasping.

"You were killing her," someone snarled. "She couldn't breathe!" I didn't quite know who or what was around me, I was losing myself. Some distant part of me registered Del's voice and Keph's arms holding me, but I couldn't make my mind work past the need to reform my bond with Annie.

"Relax, Rion. It's going to be okay. We'll find a way to make this work," Aethan said, but I couldn't relax. I was lost. The world had faded into a blur, and I was consumed with pain and emptiness.

Keph slapped me... hard. Then again.

I gasped, stunned, the tang of blood on my tongue, then he set me down, and I went limp, sitting hard on the ground, then collapsing onto my back, instinct making my wings vanish at the last second before I crushed them. I stared at the sky, feeling blood ooze down the back of my throat, everything, body, mind, and soul, numb. I was pretty sure my nose was bleeding, but I couldn't quite register it. My mind was retracting, sinking away into darkness and I let it go. I didn't want to be awake. Awake meant pain. Awake meant being without Annie.

And I couldn't be without her. I couldn't, so, I embraced the darkness, letting it consume my consciousness.

CHAPTER 16

ANNIE

"Is he okay?" I hurried over to Rion and checked him. He was unconscious with bruises showing up on his face from Keph's slaps, but other than that okay. Or at least okay physically. I pushed a little healing magic into him and faded away the bruises, but couldn't do anything else to help him.

"Sorry, I didn't know what to do," Keph said, his voice a low soft rumble. "He wasn't well, screaming and flailing like that. It seemed like the easiest way to get him to stop."

I didn't know if it was the best way, but it was the fastest. Rion had been having an all-out panic attack and I hadn't been able to break free of his grip.

I sighed heavily and sat back on my heels. I was all for a little rough play, but Rion had been so desperate, pressing so close and hard, I hadn't been able to breathe. One thing was certain, that sort of a kiss was not going to restore the bond.

"What are we going to do?" I asked of no one in particular.

The guys crouched or sat around me, looking as worried and confused as I felt.

"We haven't had any luck coming up with anything," Del said.

"Let's just remove all the variables," I said, rising quickly, and going to Keph.

Sitting on the ground, the big man was still more than half my height with his head reaching my chest.

"You're the only one I haven't kissed yet," I said, bending down to kiss him.

Nothing.

Fuck.

I hadn't really expected anything, but a small part of me had still hoped.

"That confirms it," I sighed as I straightened. "Just kissing isn't working."

Keph reached up and laid one of his massive hands gently on my arm. "It's well, Annie. We'll figure it out." His deep voice was still low and soft, as if he was trying to be reassuring, but I was starting to get antsy again. I'd thought I'd gotten all my anger and frustration and pent-up agitation out while riding Aethan, but it was beginning to return, and I could completely sympathize with Rion's breakdown.

"Perhaps we need an outside perspective," I said softly.

"Oh?" Del asked.

I turned to him, thinking as I spoke. "You three stay here and watch over Rion. See if you can come up with anything. I'm going to have a talk with someone who doesn't know anything about bonding." I shrugged. "We've tried everything else, so why not."

They seemed reluctant to let me go, but they all nodded and I went off to find Janice.

She and Naz stood a short distance away from the others, who were mostly grouped up on the beach, quietly talking with each other.

Evening was falling, the last remains of another stunning

sunset coloring the sky, and I was getting hungry. It looked — and smelled like — someone, most likely the tritons, had done some fishing and were cooking their catch over the fire. But my bonds were more important so I continued toward Janice and ignored my stomach.

"Janice?" I asked.

She turned and looked at me, a hint of blush coloring her cheeks and making me smile. The woman still seemed out-of-sorts around men.

"I'll grab some food for us," Naz said.

"Thanks," she said to him before turning back to me. "Is it easy for you to just... bare it all, now?" Her gaze swept over me. I hadn't even really registered that I was naked. I'd woken up clothed, felt far too warm, and had simply taken everything off, then hadn't thought of it.

"I guess so," I said, giving Janice a once-over in return.

She still wore her pants and a light shirt — whatever courage she'd had for her mostly-naked trip into Masia now gone — and had probably been warm when the sun had been out.

"Naz says it's mysterious and alluring when I wear clothes." Her gaze dipped down at herself. "Even these clothes. I don't get it. This place is... odd."

"You will, in time. Can I talk to you about something?" I asked moving closer and lowering my voice.

"Sure. What is it?"

I drew her a little farther away from the others, and we sat, our legs stretched out, our toes dipped in the warm water where the edge of the surf lapped the beach.

"Do you know anything about the magical bonding that happens in this world?" I figured I'd just go ahead and start there.

Her blank stare with one raised brow was answer enough.

"Yeah, didn't think so." I pulled up my feet a little, letting my toes play in the damp sand as I hugged my knees. "It's what happened between me and my guys. We were... connected in some deep spiritual way and because of that I could use their super-powers."

Her other brow rose.

"Hera took that away from me and now I can't seem to get it back."

"What happened?" she asked.

"Just before she tossed us out the window, she... I don't know... she touched me and... it felt like she was tearing the life out of me. But it wasn't my life. It was my bond with the guys. Except it was so much a part of me it felt like she was ripping out my heart, my soul."

"Fuck," Janice breathed. "That's awful."

"Yeah." I shook my head. "Now it's gone." I put my chin on my knees. "Before, we just had to kiss and that was it. Kissing on the lips means so much more here than it does for us, and somehow that connected me and the guys. But now that doesn't seem to work anymore."

"Kissing?"

I gave a short laugh. "Yeah, I know right? Apparently people on this world don't kiss on the lips, not unless they're deathly serious about each other. That's what signifies a bond between them. It would be like a guy giving you a ring in our world."

"Really? Wow. And when they do it, magical stuff happens?"

"Ah... well no. Not for normal people of this world. I think magical stuff only happened for me because I'm from our world? Or perhaps, I'm special somehow?"

"That you are," she said, a hint of a smile tugging at her lips, and she pulled her knees up, hugged them, and set her chin upon them, mirroring me.

"Well anyway, that doesn't work now. I've tried kissing them, I've tried... other forms of intimacy?"

"Like when you and Del fucked your brains out at the safe house?"

"You heard that?" Gods, I was so embarrassed.

"Oh, yeah. Howling monkeys in heat don't make as much noise as you do." She grinned, her smile breaking through.

Heat flushed my cheeks and I was sure I turned beat red and could only hope she wouldn't be able to see it in the growing darkness.

"Sorry, didn't mean to embarrass you. It was a joke, nothing more." Apparently, she could see just fine.

I drew in a long breath to try to get back some sense of balance. "Anyway, nothing's worked. The bond won't come back."

"Ah."

"And I'd hoped talking to you about it would help me figure something out, but this isn't working. So I should just—" I began to rise, but Janice reached out and grabbed my shoulder sitting me back down.

"Annie, I'm sorry. I'll stop making fun and listen. I want to help, if I can."

"Thank you." I resumed my previous position, hugging my knees.

"So, what have you tried?" I could tell she was trying very hard not to grin again. "Be specific." A giggle broke through and she sucked in a sharp breath, trying to get it under control. "It's okay. Don't be embarrassed. I'll just listen, no comments."

I told her the various things I'd tried with the guys. Her eyes widened a bit at some of my explanations, but she was true to her word and kept silent. When I was done, she nodded.

"It seems you have been... thorough." But then she quirked her head to one side. "Though there *is* something you haven't tried."

"Oh?" I was quite curious. "What?"

"Some other guy."

"No," I said instantly. "I don't want a bond with some other random guy."

She sighed. "I get that, but if you *did* kiss a different guy and a bond formed that would tell us whether or not you could form one at all, or if you just can't form one with your guys. That's a distinction that's worth noting."

She was right. But still— "I don't want to risk bonding with some guy I don't care about. That almost seems worse than living without the bonds." My shoulders fell. "But you're not wrong. I just don't know how to test your theory."

We sat in silence for a long moment.

Janice finally spoke, a bit hesitant. "Ah... you could... kiss me?"

I looked at her, one brow raised. "I'm not..."

"No, I'm not really into that either, but... we're friends, yes? It wouldn't be horrible to be bound to each other would it?"

I drew in a long breath. She wasn't wrong. Still, I hesitated. Were we friends? We'd only known each other a short time, but a lot had happened in that time and we were fast becoming dear friends.

There was a certain connection between us already, just knowing about this other world and the strange things that were happening because of it.

She blew out a breath. "Yeah, sorry, bad idea. I'll—"

"No, it's not a horrible idea," I said cutting her off. "Just give me a moment to think about it?"

"Yeah, sure."

"I don't even know if the bond would work with a woman," I mused.

"Exactly."

I sighed. She was right. It was a way to test the theory and it wouldn't be the worst thing. "Let's do it."

There was an awkward moment as we tried to figure out how to just... be close.

"How about we stand," she offered. "It might be easier that way."

"Yeah."

We stood, then stared at each other for another long, awkward moment.

"I guess, we just... kiss, then?" she said.

"Yeah." I was still having second thoughts and my mind was whirling. What if it worked? Would it work? Janice was from my world not this one. Did that make a difference?

Man, I didn't know anything about these bonds other than I'd had them and lost them and desperately wanted them back.

She stepped in, laying a hand on my shoulder, an understanding look on her face. "Annie, you are a dear friend, and dear friends can sometimes kiss." Her eyes softened and she drew a bit closer.

I leaned forward a bit as did she, her hand softly sliding up from my shoulder to my jaw as our lips met.

It was a new experience for me. Her lips were softer than the guys, more tentative. I kept thinking, *she's a dear friend. I love her — in a best friend sort of way — a dear friend.*

The kiss lingered, somehow no longer feeling awkward now that our lips were pressed together. I had my eyes closed, and in some ways, it felt like kissing anyone really. I stepped in and embraced her as our lips began to part, but then...

I felt a flicker of something.

"Oh!" Janice said, our lips still close.

I opened my eyes to see her blinking, but this close all I saw was one large eye.

"You felt that too?" I asked.

It hadn't felt like it had with the guys. This had been different.

My connection to them had been a whole body feeling... I think — it was hard to recall now that I'd been without it for a while — and with her it was a spot of warmth in my chest. I didn't know what that meant, but if she'd felt it too, it had to mean something.

"I did." She drew in a long breath.

We remained there, close, as we both took a moment to understand what had happened. Then Janice dipped forward and pressed her lips to mine again, the kiss becoming a bit more impassioned. A strange new connection started to unfurl, warm around my heart, then I felt a full and resounding vibration through my soul, like I was a gong, and I'd just been rung.

Janice broke off and immediately backed away.

"Oh, wow!" she gasped. "Wow." She reached up and touched her lips. "That was..."

Telling.

So, I *could* create new bonds.

Though what I'd just formed with Janice didn't feel like what I'd shared with my guys. It *was* a bond. But it was different, not as consuming, not as soul deep. A bond of friendship perhaps?

I touched my lips as well.

Janice was staring at her fingers, the ones she'd pressed against her lips. "I hadn't expected..."

Neither had I.

"I feel..." She looked up at me. "I feel powerful!"

I wasn't quite sure what that meant.

She turned away and began to frantically search the beach. I just watched her, curious what she was thinking. She plucked up something and returned to me. She held a broken shell in her hand.

Her eyes met mine for a long moment, then she looked down, pressing the shell into her palm, drawing blood.

"Oh, what...?" I was too shocked to do anything. I didn't have a clue what she was doing.

Then she closed her eyes and drew in a breath... and the small cut healed itself, closing up.

She had my healing powers!

"Fuuuuuck," I breathed, drawing out the word in astonishment.

She opened her eyes and looked at me. "Yeah... exactly. I'd say we shared something, all right!"

CHAPTER 17

ANNIE

I didn't know what it meant. My first thought was... did I still have my healing powers? Had she somehow taken them from me?

I grabbed the bit of shell from her hand and did the same thing, cutting my palm. I didn't even have to close my eyes. I summoned my healing, second nature to me now, and the wound closed.

"Oh, good."

Janice quirked a brow. "You thought I'd stolen your powers?"

I shrugged. "I don't know what to think. This is new. Even the guys never shared my powers, but Hera said she could take them from those she bonded with."

"Ah." Janice nodded. "I wish I knew what to say, but I don't."

"Well, we can be certain that something happened and that I can still bond. But to be clear, this doesn't feel like what I shared with the guys. This is different."

"Oh? Really?" She looked away. "I can't stop shaking. I'm trembling. I feel like I need to run a mile or something! Is this what you feel like all the time?"

"Not at all, no."

"So, what does that tell us?" She began to pace.

"I don't really know. I can bond, but this was different. So... does that mean I can still bond with the guys? I have no clue."

"Yeah, I guess this wasn't that helpful. Well, it was for me. I feel great, but for you, not so much. Sorry." She was rambling and I could tell she was agitated, though apparently not in a bad way. She suddenly stopped pacing. "I wonder..."

"What?"

She didn't answer. Instead she marched away suddenly. I followed. Despite being taller than her with my slightly longer legs, I had to jog to keep up with her fast pace.

"Janice?"

"I was just thinking that if I have your healing powers, perhaps there are other things I can do now," she said, her words coming out in a rush.

"Such as?" But then I realized where we were heading. Janice was making a bee-line straight for the stone... the portal. "You think you can open the portal?"

She shrugged. "Don't know. Thought I'd check."

I didn't know what to say. I was fairly certain the transfer of power hadn't gone that far, but I really didn't know for certain.

She reached the stone. "How do you do this?" she asked, leaning forward a bit.

Her hand hit the stone, or should have hit the stone, but it wasn't solid anymore and she fell through the portal.

"I guess that answers that," I muttered.

Janice came scrambling back through, on all fours, her eyes wide with surprise. "Holy fuck!"

"What happened?" I asked.

"Heal me," she gasped. "I was shot and..." I knelt next to her and put a hand on her arm but couldn't sense any wounds.

"They missed you," I said.

"No." She grabbed her shirt, showing me three holes in it that hadn't been there before. "They hit, I felt it..." She lifted the shirt. The skin beneath was fine, unmarked, not even a drop of blood. "But..."

For a second I thought maybe the shots might have gone through her shirt and out the other side, missing her or grazing her and that's what she'd felt, but when she laid her shirt back, it was fairly tight on her torso and those shots — the holes in her shirt — were right on her stomach.

She kept lifting the shirt to check. "There's no blood, no holes. How is there no blood?"

"You're bulletproof?" I asked. It seemed crazy at first, but then I remembered she was at least part *aurai*, from this world, and that would mean in the other world — earth — she'd have powers. "You must be, that's your power in our world!"

"Ah... no, it isn't. I've been shot before and it was painful and bloody and horrible. Not bulletproof. But..." She kept putting her shirt down, then lifting it. "I can't explain this." She looked at me. "Maybe you're bulletproof?"

"Oh no. I can heal, but I'm sure I was shot when we came through the portal the last time. Are Hera's men still out there?"

"Yep."

"That's going to make going back tough."

"Yeah," Janice replied, her expression a mix of shock and grim resignation. She sat in the sand and took several long breaths. Finally, she looked at me. "This is fucked up."

I couldn't argue that point.

I'd hoped talking to Janice would help me figure things out, but now I was just more confused than ever.

I'd bonded with Janice.

But it was a very different kind of bonding than the one I'd had with the guys, and she now shared my powers and could open gates.

Except what did that mean?

I had no idea.

I double checked that I could still open the portal and yes, I could, confirming that she hadn't taken my powers. Which meant she shared them? Was that all that had happened for the bond? I didn't know. If she had a power, I didn't know what it might be, so I didn't know if I shared it as well. Her wings and flight were innate to her, not a power, just like my guys' shifting abilities, and she didn't seem to think she was bulletproof.

"Are you sure you don't have any powers in our world?" I asked.

She shrugged. "No clue." So, if she did, she didn't know what it was. Though... something had happened with those bullets. But what?

Fuck! I had too many questions and not enough answers.

I thanked Janice for all her help and returned to the guys. They had a meal waiting and I hunkered down and ate in silence, my thoughts spinning. Thankfully they didn't ask about what I'd been up to and I guess my demeanor was clearly saying, 'don't talk to me now.'

I didn't even really know what I'd eaten I was so distracted, and didn't register much of anything until I put down the plate—

Plate?

"Where did we get this from?" I asked.

"A group went to Masia to collect supplies this afternoon," Aethan answered.

Right. Of course. There were more of us than just my guys and Janice and they were more than capable of taking care of themselves.

I glanced at my guys. Their expressions were all tight with worry, with the exception of Rion, who was still unconscious. Which was probably for the best since I didn't want him freaking out again. And despite that, none of them of asked about what I had or hadn't figured out when I'd gone off to talk with Janice.

I sighed. "I'm sorry, guys. I found some things out, but I only have more questions now and I don't even know if I got any answers." I grimaced and put my head in my hands. A large hand settled softly on my back and began rubbing slow circles. Keph.

"If you'd like, you can tell us what you found out, and perhaps we might have a different thought on it?" Aethan sounded hopeful.

I sighed again and nodded, drawing my gaze back up to him. "Yeah, you're right. Maybe, if we keep talking this through and experimenting, we'll get somewhere." Blowing out a breath, I told them of my talk with Janice and the ensuing — if different — bonding with her.

"You say you don't know how it was different. Can you try to describe it?" Del asked.

"Sure." I dug my toes into the sand stared at the fire, comparing the bonding with Janice to my bonding with them.

It was only then that something clicked for me. "Oh!"

"What? Del asked.

"I just realized, and this is going to sound bad, don't take it the wrong way, but... when I bonded with Janice, I felt this deep and resounding vibration within me."

"Yes, that's what we felt," Aethan said.

"But that's just it," I said. "When I bonded with you, I don't think I felt much at all." I scoured my memories. Those times were a bit fuzzy for me, but there had been something. "There was... it felt like a shock on my lips, and a warmth in my soul, but it hadn't been much more than that, not in the initial moment of bonding. Afterward, I'd felt the connection to you all and felt it grow over time, but in that bonding moment, well, what I felt with you wasn't the same as what I felt with Janice. That might mean something." I wasn't sure what it meant, but it felt significant.

"You didn't feel something?" Aethan asked, sounding a bit put out.

I smiled. "Well, yeah. I mean, I felt things afterward. I came to feel connected with you all, I could... sense you, how you were feeling, and there was a..." How could I describe it? "There was a sort of tingling sensation at times, which I knew was my connection with you. So, there was something, but in that first moment, the actual bonding kiss, I didn't feel too much beyond the kiss." My grin turned a little sloppy. "And all the wonderful sensations that went along with it."

"Oh," Del said softly. "What I felt was like..."

"Like a bell rang in my soul," Keph finished.

"Yeah," Aethan agreed. "It shook me and resonated within me. It felt amazing!"

"That's what I felt when I bonded with Janice," I said excitedly. Though I could see they still weren't thrilled to hear I'd had more of a reaction to her than I'd had to them. I pushed on. "And it sounded like Janice felt something like that as well. So, I guess the other end of the bonding was the same. I don't know why I felt something with her and not you guys."

"Did you do anything different with her than you did with us?" Aethan asked.

Another good question. I thought about it.

Here again, remembering back to my first bonding with the guys — and I don't know why I hadn't thought of this earlier — I recalled that there had been words, a ritual that had gone with it. With Rion, it had been short and sweet, but with the others I'd drawn it out, made it a formal thing, like wedding vows. How had I forgotten that?

"Yeah, there was a difference, a lot of difference in how it happened..." Now that I thought about it, I felt like I was on the verge of a realization and excitement bubbled within me. "With you all there had been a ritual. I'd asked if you wanted to bond —

though in Rion's case he'd been the one asking and I'd accepted. But there had been that verbal agreement before we did it. With Janice there wasn't anything like that. We talked about it, but then just did it. We... Oh wait!" That was interesting. We *had* talked about being friends and being bonded and how that wouldn't be the worst thing. And I'd been thinking about my sisterly love for her when we'd bonded. So...

"What?" Aethan asked, his eyes bright with hope.

How could I put this into words? My thoughts were still tumbling around in my head and not quite fitting together yet. "I was thinking of bonding with her, of bonding with a friend and we'd talked about it as friends, as..." My skin tingled. "As... equals." That was it! "Perhaps that's why it affected me too! We bonded as equals. But when I bonded with you... you all still thought I was a goddess at the time, you were giving yourselves to me wholly and I was... well I was accepting that. I was taking your bond but not truly giving you mine? No, that doesn't sound quite right either, but there's something in there I think."

I trembled. I could feel the answer just out of reach. If I just stretched a little farther, just a little more... "When I tried bonding with you the second time, it wasn't the same at all. There was need and desperation, there was passion and intimacy, but there wasn't that full agreement, not like the first time. Perhaps that's essential to the bonding process?"

"Yes!" Aethan said, moving around the fire to me. "Let's try it. I, Aethan of—"

"Wait," I said holding up a hand. "That's part of it, but I don't think it's all of it. Let's not do this until we have a better idea. I don't want us all to get our hopes up and be disappointed."

Aethan stared at me, a mix of emotions flashing across his face: sadness, disappointment, hope, then he gave a tight nod. "What do you think we're missing?"

"I'm not sure," I said.

Del inched closer to me. "Let's go over it again."

"We're close," I said. I could feel it. There was just one piece to the puzzle we needed to figure out.

CHAPTER 18

KEPHAS

I FELT MY HEART QUICKEN AT THE THOUGHT THAT MY BOND WITH Annie might be restored. We hadn't come to a conclusion yet, but I felt like we were drawing close. After we'd gone over a few things, we had a short list of what might be required.

A formal agreement.

A mutual desire to be connected as equals.

A kiss. There had been a lot of discussion around this, about emotions as well. Apparently there had been a fair amount of intimacy between Annie and Aethan, and Annie and Del in recent times.

"I'd felt something when we kissed," she said to Del. "When we were saying goodbye on the beach, and you were going off to your home and Janice and I were headed to Masia. I think it may have been something connected to bonding."

Her expression softened and I could see her love for him in her eyes. It was a look she'd shared with us all at one point or another.

"I think perhaps that kiss was our purest, the closest we'd gotten to the state we needed to be in to bond," she continued.

"Something about giving of yourself to the other without restrictions or limits. Only love."

"Yeah," Aethan murmured. "In all the turmoil and pain of the last few days. I think we've forgotten what forged our bond. It was love. Love for you and for each other. We've had so much else on our minds..." He glanced at Rion and his expression turned glum.

The *erinai* slept peacefully. I was sorry I'd had to hit him to get him to finally rest. It had been one of the most painful things I'd ever done, but I didn't think he would have stopped otherwise. He'd been beyond reason and I could only hope when he woke he'd be calmer.

I turned my attention to the sea and watched the dark waves lap against the shore in the distance. Stone Titan's had exceptional dark vision and I could see out over the waves, and the sea beyond, especially with the stars out. I couldn't look at the others for a moment. They had endured so much, while I...

Hera had been able to hurt me. She'd borrowed my own power and become strong enough to hit me so it would hurt, but that hadn't really done that much. There'd been bruises, but not much more. She'd tried using tools on me, but with how durable I was in that world, and the force she'd needed, those tools usually broke before my skin did.

She'd given up on me after a while, simply leaving me in isolation, which in itself wasn't great because I could occasionally hear the screams of Aethan and Rion, and knew they were probably taking the brunt of her frustration because I hadn't provided any outlet for the mad goddess. I hadn't had it half as bad as they did and my heart hurt with guilt about that.

"Keph?"

I turned back at Annie's voice.

"Are you okay?"

I raised a brow. "What does that mean? Okay?" I asked.

She grimaced. "Sorry, other-world-speak. Are you doing well? You seem distracted."

"I am. But don't worry about me, please. Let's go on. Where were we?" I smiled for the others, hoping to ease their worry even though I knew I wasn't really the cause of that worry.

"We think we're ready to try bonding," Annie said. Then that look of love and intensity filled her gaze as she looked at me. "And I want to try it with you first."

"Me? No, you don't have to, the others—"

"We..." She looked at the other two. "We've tried and I don't want those previous attempts to influence me. With you there haven't been previous attempts. Well, there was that one kiss from earlier, but... yeah. I don't think that really counted. I think we can do this fresh and clean and see how it works. What do you think?"

My pulse picked up.

Annie's gaze dipped to my lap, where my cock must have stirred. "Ah, I see you think this is a good idea?" she purred, a mischievous grin sparkling in her eyes. "Great. Come on, let's step away a bit and have some privacy." She rose and offered me her hand. I didn't need it, but I took it as I too rose.

I nodded to Aethan and Del, who both looked eager and a bit envious.

Annie led me into the darkness, though with my stone titan eyes, I could see well enough in the dark. We moved inland a bit until she stopped and glanced back at our fire, now a good number of paces away and partially hidden by a dune.

"I think that should be far enough." She turned to me, looking up with her heart in her eyes. "Thank you, Keph. You're always so willing to help, so kind and gentle and tenderhearted."

She stepped in and kissed my chest. This brought her body pressing close to my erection and the tip of my cock brushing the bottom of her breasts.

"Now come down here so I can kiss you," she said reaching up to cup my cheek.

I knelt, both knees on the ground, to be roughly eye-to-eye with her, and took a moment to simply take her in, appreciating her fine red-blond hair that framed a speckled face with large, soft golden-brown eyes, her wide, free smile that was always warm, and her full breasts and hips, and slender waist that made me hot with desire. She was a wonder and it was clear in the way she looked at me that she loved me as much as I loved her.

"I love you, Annie. You're..." My words vanished for a second. There was so much I wanted to say and yet none of it seemed smart enough for someone like Annie. "You're unlike any woman I've ever met. So strong and fierce, but not a warrior. You're soft and yet hard, delicate and yet strong, terrified and still brave. You're a whole lot of perfect opposites."

She huffed a soft laugh at that and stepped closer still, cupping my cheeks in her small, delicate hands. I was reminded of our first kiss in that strange closet at the conference center with Rion watching. Again, as she drew in to press close to me, she was forced to straddle my erection, and I felt her wetness as I brushed her opening. Her breath caught, then quickened as her gaze on mine became intense.

She kissed me lightly on the mouth, only a brief brush of her soft lips.

"That wasn't to bond," she murmured, "that was just... for you being you." Then she swallowed hard and a hint of fear and need darkened the softness in her gaze. "Let's do this before I get too aroused and just want to ride your amazing cock."

I rumbled a laugh. "We can do both."

"Yeah, good idea, but let's do the bonding first."

I nodded.

She drew in a steadying breath, even as her hips swayed slightly, rubbing herself on my erection.

"Kephas Vathia Spiti," she began.

I was a bit surprised she recalled my clan name. Most people didn't care to remember it. Even I wasn't particularly fond of it. I thought it sounded a bit harsh. But Annie always made it sound soft and warm.

"Will you accept a bond with me, Annie Chambers? There will be no going back from this. I will be yours entirely, and you will be mine. There will be others who will join with us, and together we will be one. Equals in love, one body, one soul, one heart. Is this what your heart desires?" Her breath was heavy and hot, her face so very close to mine, so close her lips would brush mine when she spoke again. She was more than ready to go through with this and so was I.

I found my own breath catching as my heart thundered within me. This was everything I wanted. Having a woman like Annie — a woman like no other — and to be a part of something powerful with her and my truest friends.

"Yes," I breathed, my lips teasing hers. "I Kephas Vathia Spiti do wish to bond with you, Annie Chambers, for now and for always. To be one with all of those who I hold dear in this world. To that I commit my body, my heart, and my soul. One with you, equals with all."

"Wow," Annie said softly, nibbling on my bottom lip. "Let's do this." And then her lips pressed to mine.

The kiss quickly deepened as we opened to each other. She tilted her head to one side, pushing deeper still, not forceful or demanding, but insistent and loving.

And I felt something... several somethings.

My immediate physical reaction was a swelling of my cock. Annie's breath caught mid-kiss as I lifted her a little. This had happened before as well. She was making all manner of amazing noises, as her hips started rocking, moving over me.

But there was a deeper reaction as well. I felt it, soft and subtle at first, a ringing in my soul, a... knowing.

It grew, spreading through me, growing stronger, louder, ringing me like a bell. Annie seemed to undulate and tremble. Somehow, I knew I wasn't the only one feeling this ringing connection, that Annie was feeling it as well.

She pushed back, breathing hard.

"Did you feel that?" Her eyes glistened with unshed tears of joy. "Oh, Keph! It worked!" Her gaze shifted from elated to hot with passion. "Now let's get to that cock-riding."

I wanted that, intensely, but I didn't know if she was ready yet. I slid one of my arms around her, then down between her legs to the slick opening there.

She gasped as I probed and played, our kisses becoming hard and intense. She had reached down as well, grasping the end of my cock, grinding against it, pleasuring herself.

With our desperation, it wasn't long before she was crying out with her first release, her warmth rushing over my fingers and her muscles contracting then relaxing even more.

I withdrew my hand and she went to her toes to align my tip with her entrance and slowly take it into her. She was still in the throes of her first orgasm, and she gasped and trembled all the harder as I started to enter her.

"Oh Gods, yes!" she breathed. She kissed me, hot and wet and hard. "I want you, all of you, inside me."

I wasn't sure if that was a good idea. There weren't many women her size who could fit all of me. But even as I considered what to say, she was slipping farther down on me, taking more of me into her than she had before.

I grabbed her butt with one large hand and her back with the other, cradling her. She rose a bit and wrapped her legs around me, and I crouched a little so she could rest her legs on my thighs, laying her back a little as I took control, slowly pushing deeper within her. She threw her head back, mouth open and gasping as I did.

It took a long time, a long and painfully slow time, since I didn't want to hurt her. And I grew more and more surprised that I *wasn't* hurting her. In fact, she seemed lost in bliss, eyelids half closed and fluttering as her body twitched and trembled. She let out low deep moans and sharp cries of pleasure. I hit a spot where I didn't think I could go deeper, but it was Annie who pulled herself down with her legs, clasped around my thighs, past that point and farther.

Then, somehow, I was fully inside of her.

She didn't even seem to realize how astonishing this was and simply began grinding herself upon my base, gasping and letting out high keening noises.

I began slow, careful thrusts. Usually I wouldn't even dare such a thing, letting the woman do all the movement, just to be safe, but with Annie... Perhaps our bonding had truly changed us, and made this possible.

"Yes, harder," she gasped, voice hoarse. Her skin was glistening, the moonlight catching in her sweat, and she slid her hands up her body and fondled her own breasts, squeezing them, ratcheting up her pleasure. I wished those were my hands, and from her hot and mischievous look, I think she knew it. Except I was supporting her. She lay upon my hands like a bed as I bent over her and... as asked... I began to pick up my pace.

Then her hands moved up, to tangle in her hair as her gaze went from playful to eye-rolling bliss. I moved her over my erection with ever quicker and harder thrusts, losing myself in passion, which I'd so rarely been able to achieve.

"Yes," I grunted. This was so new for me, it was astounding and exciting and amazing.

"Yes!" she echoed, crying out into the night with all her heart and soul, her body arching back, stiff and trembling as she convulsed in the throes of another orgasm.

I was lost in the pleasure now. I didn't know how this was possible, to be so hard and needful and rough with a woman and not... break her. But with Annie, it seemed anything was possible.

"Come," Annie breathed, her gaze catching mine. "I want to feel you come." Even amidst her current peak, it seemed she was aching for more.

I didn't need any more of an invitation. I was ready and I let out a feral roar as I released within her.

"Holy, fuuuu..." she cried out, voice rising in pitch. Her eyes rolled up as she shook wildly in my grasp, but I made sure she didn't fall as we came together — violently and far too loudly — in the night.

CHAPTER 19

ANNIE

I LAY, STARING UP AT THE STARS, MY BODY TINGLING AND ALIVE. I'D never felt so amazing before, but then, I'd never had sex like that before either.

I couldn't quite explain how it felt with Keph, like my body had somehow adapted to his, opening more, taking him in deeper. I hadn't thought I could take him fully inside me, but apparently I'd been wrong. He'd gotten as far as I thought he could go, but I'd wanted more, and with my legs hooked over his, I'd pulled myself down, experimenting, and I think I'd surprised us both when that had worked.

I still didn't quite believe it. Nor did I believe how much he'd let loose, unrestrained and hard. It had literally shaken me to my core, but in a good, amazing way, in the amazing raw power mixed with tenderness way which was sex with Keph.

On top of that was our bonding moments before. Just the memory of that mind-blowing moment made my whole body tingle.

"I felt that," Keph said, a low, soft rumble. He sat next to me, his legs pulled up, head resting on the bulge of a muscled arm atop his knees, looking at me.

"And I felt you," I whispered, referring to our time together. So deep and large and hard and wonderful.

He chuckled again.

"Holy fuck," I giggled. It *had* been a rather divine fuck after all.

I didn't even know if I'd be able to walk! Though, I felt... fine. More than fine. I felt incredible!

When he'd withdrawn from me, I'd felt a moment of being hollow, but then that had faded and I'd seemed to... shift.

I couldn't explain how it felt. It was like I'd somehow adjusted to fit him, then once he was gone, I'd gone back to how I was. Except, that didn't make any sense at all. How could I do that? I wasn't even really sure it had happened. I'd have to have more sex with Keph to find out. And that seemed like a very good idea... but later.

Right now, I was exhausted from a long and draining day and from truly world-shattering sex with this amazing man.

I began to rise and Keph moved quickly to help me up, but I didn't need help. There wasn't any soreness or stiffness, no awkward bow-legged wobbling. I was strong and firm.

"Holy fuck," I whispered again. I felt like I should be as awkward as a newborn foal, but I wasn't. What I was, was tingling and so very satisfied. So, I just kept whispering, "holy fuck." Then we both giggled, Keph's a low rumbling from deep within him.

We made our way back to the others and Aethan came running up to us.

"Did..." He blinked, perhaps noticing the blissful looks on both our faces. "It worked? It worked!"

"Yes," I replied.

"I told him as much," Del said strolling up to us. "You two certainly made a racket out there. I figured that wouldn't have happened if you'd failed."

"And I told him you were just too hot and no man would be able to resist you, success or failure. Perhaps he was consoling you," Aethan shot back with a grin.

I laughed. "Yes, it worked. We're bonded, and you two are next." I was tired, yes, but also felt like I wouldn't be able to sleep just yet. Perhaps more mind-blowing sex would do it.

Del gave a relieved laugh. "Aethan, you can go first, if you like."

"I would yes," he said. "That's big of you."

I gave Keph a look. He nodded. There was an understanding between us now, like there had been before — a knowing of how each other was feeling — and he sat at the edge of the fire, peaceful and still. He'd rest well tonight.

As would I, eventually.

I took Aethan's offered hand and we moved away from the others. I could practically feel the excited energy radiating off him. He was like a kid on Christmas morning.

And he should be... I was quite the present.

I gave a short laugh. Thoughts like that, so confident and empowered, had been so rare and fleeting for me since I'd lost the bond.

"What?" Aethan asked.

"Nothing. I'm just feeling a whole lot better than I was."

He nodded. "Earlier, when we went for a ride, you were..."

"Lost, desperate, confused, terrified, dejected?" I said, shooting off the list, the words rushing out.

"Yeah." He squeezed my hand, his expression softening and turning serious. "I'm glad you're feeling better."

I stopped, turning to him. "Shall we?"

He nodded, energy and enthusiasm in his eyes, but his body was still. "Guide me."

Of all my guys, he was the closest to my height, just a hair shorter than I was. I stepped in, cupped his face with both hands, and brought him close but didn't kiss him. Instead, I rested my forehead on his.

"Aethan of the Theophylian Plains," I whispered, my own hot breath washing back upon me.

I was going to say what I said for Keph, but realized those words would be a disservice to Aethan, to all of them. This needed a unique touch. And I knew just what Aethan needed. Of all my guys, he had been the least confident, the least self-assured.

"You are an amazing partner," I said. "Always there to help, whether it's me or any of the others. You're a dedicated friend and a giving lover."

He let out a shuddering breath, not of impassioned heat, but close to tears. "Thank you," he murmured.

"Never doubt yourself, Aethan. I don't doubt you. I love you, deeply and truly." I quirked a smile as my mind turned a little dirty. For some reason, with him, it seemed fitting. "Every time your cock has been inside me, I've hit incredible heights of passion. I can't wait to have it again." I reached down and ran two fingers along the top of his rigid erection, and drew my lips to his, nipping his lower lip.

"Oh?" he breathed, his body trembling.

"Oh, yes." I gave a breathy laugh. "And I know you have such incredible patience and control as a lover. But I won't prolong this any more than I have to." I cleared my throat. "Will you accept my bond, Aethan? This is a final and binding seal between us. We, together with the others, will be one in body and heart and soul. We'll be equals. Do you hear that? You and I, and the others, will be equals. No more worshiping me." I gave another quick laugh. "Unless I'm worshiping you too. This is my bond. Do you accept it?"

A tribute to his patience, he didn't respond right away.

Everything that I'd said had been true, no exaggeration or lies.

I needed this to be a pure moment and it was, and I think he was soaking it all in.

"Annie," he began softly, slowly, bringing a hand to my waist as if to help steady me. "I love you with all my heart and soul and being. And I love Del and Keph and Rion dearly as well. There is nothing more in this world—" He gave his own quick laugh. "—or any other, that I want more than to be one with you and them. I give myself to you, and to them, heart and soul and body. And I accept you, and them, as equals." He paused. "Equals," he repeated with more confidence as if he'd needed to see that truth and finally had.

Good.

I lowered my lips to his, teasing, tasting them tentatively, before pushing deeper. He too played and teased before our mouths — and souls — opened to each other.

It came slowly, building, radiating out from my core to my entire body, that resonant vibration. I shook and felt him shake in tune with me. And as that bond formed and deepened, so too did our kiss.

My arms encircled his neck as he pressed a hand against the small of my back and pulled me closer. His other hand, the one on my waist, slid up my side and cupped my breast.

I pushed my belly hard against his, capturing his cock between us, and sensed his passion, love, and burning desire, as I opened my own emotions up to him.

When our lips finally separated, I brushed mine along his cheek, pressing close as I whispered into his ear, "This afternoon I took you. Since we're now equals, I think it's time you took me just as hard."

"Yes, my goddess," he whispered back. I was just about to chide him for 'worshiping' me when he then said, "I'll be your god."

That was more like it.

He spun me around roughly. I was a bit surprised and gave a

clipped cry of confusion and excitement. His hands, firm and forceful on my hips, pressed me to him, his erection between my ass cheeks. Then he slid his hands over my waist and sides, and around to my breasts, grasping, holding, fondling, owning.

I moaned and relaxed back onto him, grinding my butt against his cock as forceful as he kneaded my breasts, my need to have him inside me swelling. I ached for him, but not with the heart-breaking emptiness of before. This was deep, throbbing desire born from the renewed connection between our souls.

He trailed a hand down my belly, skimming my abs, teasing into my curls, and dipping into my wet folds. A whisper of a climax teased through me as he dipped his fingers in my wetness and teased it over my clit.

Oh, yes.

I ground back against him, savoring the delicious torture of his fingers on my clit and inside me, working me up.

Then he shifted, bending his knees to slid the tip of his cock up between my legs. He teased my entrance, his fingers helping to guide him to where I needed him, sending another whispering climax rushing through me.

"Yes," I moaned, desperate to have him inside me.

But he continued to tease me, shallowly pushing inside me then withdrawing, again and again.

Oh, God.

His hands slid to my thighs and he urge me to close them on him. Suddenly his cock felt twice as big inside me, hitting all the right places, torturing me with a glimmer of what I really wanted: him driving inside of me, riding me like I'd ridden him.

I squirmed, pushing back into him, trying to take him deeper, faster, harder.

He hummed his pleasure, a pure masculine sound of desire that sent shivers rushing over me, and pressed a hand on my back, bending me forward and making his cock hit another, incredible spot inside me.

I shuddered. This would be a core workout indeed, but God did it feel amazing.

But then his hands moved around in front of me again, helping support me, as he used my own weight to put the most divine pressure on my breasts.

He captured my hardened nipples between his thumbs and forefingers, pulling and pressing, sending spikes of pleasureful-pain as he slowly moved inside me, working up, building me to a soft, exquisite climax that was wonderful, but not at all what I craved.

"Aethan," I moaned. "Please."

"I can't have you coming just once," he said.

I huffed. "I'm beginning to regret praising your patience as a lover."

"You did want me to take control."

"Not that kind of control."

He chuckled, the sound low and sensual, seized my hips, and thrust into me.

The impact sent a shuddering after shock rushing through me and stole my breath in the most delicious way.

I opened my mouth to encourage him, but he jerked halfway out and thrust back in, just as hard, then repeated the action again and again. His pace was hard and fast, his fingers digging into my skin. I gasped and cried my pleasure as he pounded into me.

He grunted as he jerked my hips back to meet his powerful thrusts. Our bodies crashed together, the sound of flesh slapping against flesh joining our gasps and moans, and my desire twisted tighter and tighter.

This was what I wanted, what I needed.

It was perfect and wonderful, and felt so much better than the last time because our souls were bonded together again.

His thrusts grew wild and with a feral scream, he slammed a final thrust home, hitting the perfect spot inside me and sending me crashing over the edge.

All my muscles contracted and I screamed my release. He grabbed my chest and hauled me up, clutching me against his body, as our orgasms tore through us, wave after wave of glorious, trembling muscle contractions.

We stayed, frozen and trembling, in that position for some time, until we were both spent, then he eased his iron grip, but still kept his arms around me.

"Ohhhhh," he drew out the word, and I felt one final shudder rush from him, then he slowly pulled out of me.

I turned quickly and pressed myself to him, kissing him intently. "That was amazing," I whispered. "Thank you, my god."

He smiled and touched my cheek, freeing some hair plastered by sweat, brushing it behind my ear. "Anytime, my goddess. I will always be here for you."

CHAPTER 20

DELPHON

ANNIE WAS FLUSHED, HER HAIR WILD, AS SHE AND AETHAN RETURNED to the light of the fire, making me smile. I was happy for Aethan and Keph. I'd had Annie all to myself these last few days while they'd been in a much worse situation. They needed this, and so did Annie.

Aethan nodded to me with a confident grin as he sat at the fire beside Keph, and Annie came to me.

"Your turn." She sounded tired and a little drunk. After what I'd just heard in the night from her times with Keph and Aethan, I could understand her slightly giddy nature.

"Come," I said softly. I swept her into my arms and had been about to say 'let me carry you,' but she spoke first.

"Oh, I have. Lots of times." She giggled. "Are you going to give me more?"

Except even as she said this, she snuggled against my chest, her eyelids drooping as I walked away from the others to give us privacy.

"Perhaps," was my only reply. It hadn't been my intent to pleasure her, only to rebond with her, but we'd see how things played out.

She seemed semi-delirious, dozing as I carried her past the larger camp of the others who'd helped us rescue Rion, Aethan, and Keph to the water's edge. There I laid her gently in the shallow waters, angled so her head would be on the beach above the waves but her legs would be well in the surf.

"Oh," she murmured, her eyelids flickering open. "Water?"

"Yes," I laughed. "I figured you could use a nice warm bath after your... escapades."

"Oh?" she said, blinking, then she relaxed. "Yeah, that would be lovely."

I caressed her, moving the water over her, using a bit of sand to softly scrub some less-sensitive places, starting with her legs and slowly moving up. Once I reached places where the water didn't lap around her, I cupped it in my hands and brought it to pour over her: belly, breasts, then carefully rinsed her shoulders, face, and hair.

"Hmmmm," she said, her lids starting to slid shut again. "We should bond before you put me to sleep."

"I can wait if you need the rest."

Her lids snapped open at that and I could see the heartache of our broken bond in her eyes. "I can't wait. Even if I need the rest."

"I understand." I lay on my side next to her, propped up on one arm. My other hand traced delicate patterns on her stomach and occasionally up around her breasts or down over her hips. "Go ahead," I murmured.

She drew in a long breath, letting out a contented sigh. "Thank you for that. Now, to mix some business with our pleasure. Delphon of Galniosia, will you bond with me?"

"I will," I said softly

She blinked and laughed, "I wasn't done yet!"

"Oh, go on."

She slid an arm under where I was propped up and snuggled closer to me. "Where was I? Right. Delphon of Galniosia, will you bond with me?" She shot a sidelong look at me, and I pressed my lips tight in a promise that I wouldn't interrupt her again. "This is an irrevolvable... irrevobakle... irrerev..." She paused, drew a breath. "This is a binding bond..." She giggled. "I'm getting so tired I don't quite have the words. Let me say this simply. I love you, Del. I love you and all the others with all my heart and soul and body... especially my body." Another giggle. "The bond will make sure that we are one, all of us are one, equal in all things. Is that what you want? If so... kiss me." She grinned.

"Annie of Chicago, yes. All I want is to be one with you and the others. I want to be one in body and soul and heart, equal with you and them, together forever, bound and committed. I'm yours and you are mine. We are theirs and they are ours. This is my pact and bond with you." I lowered myself, leaning over her. But I stopped before my lips touched hers. "I love you, Annie."

"I love you too, Del," she said, all giddiness gone, her gaze intense and solemn.

I kissed her softly, gently. Slowly, we opened to each other, though there wasn't any hard passion, just tenderness and love, and I felt my body tremble as the bonding took me.

It was soft at first, like our kiss, but then grew and spread, rocking me with its intense vibration.

Annie was trembling too, moaning softly, her breath picking up, chest heaving.

We shook together as the bond solidified, then quieted. I could feel her exhaustion and relief.

Lifting back a bit, I asked, "We've bonded. What would you like now?" My hand went back to tracing soft patterns on her belly.

"Stay close," she whispered, sleepily. Then she lifted her head — it seemed to take some effort — to look at the waves upon her lower body. "Make sure I don't drown. I want to fall asleep in your arms."

That was fair.

I pulled her close, rolling her a little to lay atop me, my chest as her pillow even though the tide was going out and there was little chance she'd drown before she woke. I stroked her back, washing off the sand, then held her. Her breathing quieted and evened out, and then she started snoring.

I smiled. I was dedicated to her now, snoring and all. I drifted off as well, eyes closing on the star-splashed sky above feeling complete and whole.

I woke to water lapping against my toes and opened my eyes, immediately regretting it as the sun blinded me.

Wincing, I blinked, but couldn't raise an arm to shield my eyes as both were pinned down by Annie. She lay atop one of them and was reaching over, holding the other, and if I moved, I could wake her, and she'd had a... busy night.

Instead I rolled my head to one side, blinking until my vision normalized. It was only then that I saw Aethan sitting on the sands not far away, his knees pulled up, his chin resting on them.

"Morning," I whispered.

He looked over, noting me and the still sleeping Annie, and smiled. "I was sent to find you and tell you we have a meal prepared when you're ready." He kept his voice low, then he rose and left.

The tide was coming in, which meant we had slept for nearly twelve hours.

My stomach rumbled.

Then Annie's rumbled, sounding even more empty than mine, and she squirmed, starting to wake.

I kissed the top of her head. "Morning, my love."

She groaned. "I have sand everywhere."

"That's what happens when you sleep on a beach. Luckily there's a sea nearby where you can wash it off. Shall I bathe you again?"

"Oooh," she said, her squirms gaining more energy. "That was nice. So relaxing." She shifted raising herself up a little to look at me. "But I think that's part of what got sand everywhere." She blew a few strands of hair from her face. "It's in my hair and in my mouth." She stuck her tongue out.

"So, is that a yes or no to a bath?"

She grinned. "A yes to having your hands all over me, a no to doing it while lying on the beach."

I returned her smile. "I can accommodate that."

We rose and I escorted her into the waves until she was chest deep. Then I washed her, moving my hands over her wonderfully speckled skin. We kissed and played, though it didn't go any further than that, before our stomachs were rumbling again.

"I'm famished," she said. Then she looked up at me, her eyes large and innocent, and fluttered her eyelashes in an over-exaggeration of innocence. "You carried me down to the beach last night. Could you carry me back? That way I won't get sand all dried up in my toes."

I scooped her up and she gave a yelp of glee.

As I carried her out of the water and back to our camp beyond the beach, she said, "You didn't get any last night. We should rectify that."

"There will be lots of time for that," I replied. "I think you need to bond with Rion first."

She nodded, face falling a little. "You're right. He wasn't doing well yesterday at all."

"No."

Once we reached the camp, I set her down and both of us were given a plate with sweet-pastries, some slices of fruit, and freshly roasted meat.

Annie quickly finished her first plate and was given more.

"How long were we down there?" she asked.

"It's past noon," Aethan said in answer. "A while."

We all looked over at Rion. He was still out cold.

"Are we sure he's well?" Keph asked.

Annie put a hand on his chest, and closed her eyes. "His body is well, and he's breathing fine. He went through a lot. Perhaps he just needs time to recover."

She went back to her meal, and we ate for a few more minutes before Aethan sighed and met all of our gazes one by one.

"Once we're all bonded again," he said, "Then what?"

Annie licked the last of the crumbs and fruit juices from her plate and set it down. "I don't know. We still have to face Hera. There's no way she'll just let us go, even if we're willing to turn a blind eye to all the horrible things she's done and will likely continue to do. But I don't know how, not yet." She smiled, despite her grim words. "But we figured out how to bond again, so I know we can figure that out, too." She rose and stretched and we all marveled at her proud, beautiful body.

She noticed us and blushed a little. "What are you all looking at?" she asked playfully.

"The most beautiful woman in the world," I said softly.

She blushed more, it spread down her neck and chest in the most alluring way. Gods, she was even more beautiful when she blushed so deeply.

She finished her stretches and turned away kneeling next to Rion. "Let's see if we can't wake him and get him bonded again." She looked back over her shoulder. "Then all four of you can... show me exactly how beautiful you think I am," she added with a wink.

Through all the bathing and intimacy last night and this

morning, I hadn't truly gotten aroused, but now, with that mischie-vous look in her eyes, I felt my cock stir and rise.

Annie eyed me. "Exactly," she chuckled. "But first Rion!" She turned back to him and leaned down to whisper something in his ear.

CHAPTER 21

HYPERION

"I love you, my angel," the voice — Annie's voice — filled my being and shredded the nightmares which threatened the edges of my dreams.

I drew in a long breath and opened my eyes to see Annie leaning over me. She smiled and kissed me softly. "Hello there, sleepyhead."

Instantly, I recalled how I'd forced myself on her, and my chest tightened with shame and regret.

"I'm so sorry," I said, tears coming to my eyes. I was so fragile, so confused, my soul broken, that I couldn't control myself, even if I should have. "I lost control. I still—"

"I know," she murmured, kissing the tears off my cheeks. "You were just trying so hard to get our bond back. I don't mind a little rough play. I just couldn't breathe. It's well, you're well, and..." She smiled and I felt my whole soul ease and spring to life with that look. "We know how to bring the bond back now. Would you like that?"

I nodded. More tears leaked from my eyes as my emotions

welled up and overwhelmed me. "Please, yes. I need you, Annie. I'm lost without you."

She quirked an odd grin at that. "I know," she replied, pressing a hand over her heart. "I feel that way, too. Let's get you up and go for a walk."

I nodded and she leaned back so I could rise.

The other guys were all there, watching, and my face heated with shame. I turned my head away from them, not wanting them to see me like that, all those years with my father reminding me that men didn't cry, they didn't show weakness, they were strong, they didn't get taken prisoner, rushed through me.

"No," Annie said, touching my face. "There's no shame here. Tears are always welcome. Emotions are real and powerful things. We all need to be able to express them. None of this manly-man bullshit, got it?"

I nodded.

The other guys got up and surrounded me, slapping me warmly on the shoulders.

"It's well," Aethan said. "I know— well I don't know what you went through, but I know what I went through and I know that wasn't easy. But, as you're about to find out, we're stronger together. We're all here for each other. Whatever you need."

"Exactly," Annie said. "Thank you, Aethan."

Del handed me a plate of food and I ate hungrily as the others stood nearby. They all seemed to be so content and serene. I wanted that, and knew it came from being bonded with Annie again. So, I bolted down the food, handed the plate back to Del then turned to Annie. She put a finger to my lips, perhaps seeing my desperation.

"Hush, I know." She took my hand and began to lead me away from the others. To them, she said, "Give us a little privacy, yes?"

The others went back to their fire, and Annie led me off, over the next hill into a small valley.

Then she turned to me and rested both of her hands on my chest, her expression serious. "There is something you need to hear before we bond."

My pulse stuttered. This sounded like it was going to be bad news, and I tried to brace myself, but I had no inner fortitude. I was just too broken and fragile after everything that had happened.

"What?" I asked, my voice rough and just a little too harsh.

She looked up at me, her eyes intense, but not hard, then she cupped my cheeks with her warm hands. I leaned into her palm, comforted by that touch.

"Rion," she said, "we're going to bond, never doubt that. But before we do, I wanted to ask you something."

"Yes?" I waited on a razor's edge. She said she'd bond with me, but I couldn't help but fear if I said the wrong thing, I'd ruin my chances.

"Are you whole?" she asked, her voice edge with worry and grief.

I frowned. "Whole?"

A shudder swept through me and the memory of *that woman* — I couldn't think her name — digging out my wing rushed into my mind. I'd already flown, but I still suddenly needed to know that my wing was there, that flying hadn't been a dream. I pushed them out, both of them, and stretched them out to either side.

Still there.

Thank God.

I could still fly.

I could still take Annie flying.

And yet, even knowing my wings were back, I still felt unsteady, broken.

Because I'd failed. I was the warrior among my brothers and not defeating *that woman* had been my fault.

"I know what she did," Annie murmured. "I saw. I healed you."

"Oh." I didn't recall that. There had been a hazy moment of pain fading away in a cold alley, but that was it.

She let her hands wander over me. "I'm... very aware that you're whole in body," she said with a slightly mischievous look. "I intend to test that out once we've bonded, but that wasn't what I was asking. How's your spirit?"

Ah.

For a long moment I couldn't respond, my whole body trembled with fear at what had happened, at the emptiness inside me, with the worry that Annie wouldn't accept me, no matter what she'd just said, because I wasn't the man she'd first met.

I couldn't get the memory of what *that woman* did out of my mind, and I couldn't shake the feeling that even though I had proof, my wing was still gone.

She put a hand to my cheek again. "It's okay, you can tell me."

"I—" My throat tightened. Annie wouldn't want me to lie. Even though we weren't bonded, she'd probably be able to tell if I lied. How I felt wasn't something I could hide from her or the others. They knew me too well.

"I'm a failure," I forced out, trying to swallow back a sob at saying the truth out loud. "I'm broken... and afraid."

I was a soldier. I was supposed to have become the next Sky General. And now I was nothing, terrified of ending up back in *that woman's* hands, of losing my wings for good, of losing Annie.

And while I didn't care if I was anything to my people, and I sure didn't care if I was anything to my father, it broke my heart that I was no longer a warrior for Annie.

But rebonding with her would fix that. It would make everything right. It had to.

"I'm—" Tears burned my eyes and I clenched my jaw, fighting to hold it in, unable to resist what had been beaten into me as a child.

"It's okay," she murmured. "Just sit with me."

She guided me to the ground. I made my wings vanish to make it easier to sit, and she wrapped her arms around me, holding me close.

"I know that wasn't easy to say. And I'm sorry I had to make you say it," she said.

"But I'll be whole again once we bond, I—"

"No, Rion, you won't, that's what I wanted to get across to you."

"I—" I blinked.

She wasn't going to bond with me? She didn't think I could be fixed?

What little was left of my heart began to crumble.

"Rion! Stay with me, listen to me, please." Her grip on me tightened and an urgency filled her voice.

I sucked in a breath, fighting the overwhelming loss flooding me. I could hold it together for her, for my Annie, even if only for a moment longer. I nodded as tears came again. Gods, I was such a mess.

"Rion, joining with me isn't going to make you whole. Yes, it will fill in the emptiness you feel, but your spirit is and always has been yours, not mine. I can't give you back what she took from you, from your spirit. When you join with me, you'll be exactly as you are now, but bonded. Do you understand?"

I shook my head. What was she trying to say?

Annie sighed and leaned in to kiss me lightly on the cheek. She stayed close, one hand on my face, caressing, calming. "I can't give you your spirit back," she repeated. "I can give you a bond, yes, but only that. It will fill part of what you feel is missing within you, but not all of it. I can't fill that remaining part, only you can. I needed you to know this before we bonded. I need you to understand that there will still be work you'll need to do, on you." She swallowed and sighed. "I know *she* took a lot from you. More than the others."

I nodded, my throat tight, grateful that Annie hadn't used the woman's name. The mere thought *of her* sent me to near panic.

"Some of that, I can give back," Annie went on, "but most will be up to you. You'll need to claim your power back from her. That's all I'm saying. I didn't want us to bond and have you feel like it was... incomplete. It won't be. We'll be one, together, in heart and soul. But your spirit will be up to you to reclaim."

I nodded. She was preparing me. And I understood why. I'd been going on about how lost I was, how I needed her. I did, but part of what I was feeling wasn't my need for her, but my need... for me, for what *that woman* had taken from me. "I understand."

"Good." She remained close. "Then Hyperion of the Phyllidian Forest, will you bond with me?" she pressed a finger to my lips as I was about to respond. "Not yet, there's more. I, Annie Chambers would very much like to bond with you. This would be a life bond, a commitment of your heart and soul and body to me and to the others who have bonded with me. We would be one. We would be equal, Rion. *Equal.* Each of us our own person, bringing our own strengths and abilities to this bond. Each of us helping each other in areas where we're weak. As Aethan said, we'll be stronger together, but we must be strong ourselves first. Knowing all of this, will you bond with me, Hyperion?"

She was close and I dipped in for a quick kiss, my heart filling with joy at her words. Her soft lips were responsive, eager, and I knew what she was asking.

Our first time bonding it had been so quick, so informal. She'd kissed me and I'd asked if she meant it. She hadn't even really known what she was doing then. It was very clear to me now that she was fully aware of it.

And knowing that... I had to ask myself if I was aware, if I was ready and capable of being in this bond, with her, with the others.

I pulled away from her slightly, making her eyes widen in surprise.

"Rion?"

"I'll answer you, but can you give me a moment?"

She nodded and I rose and brought forth my wings.

"I need to fly, to think, to... remember myself," I said softly. "Can you give me the time to do that?"

She smiled as if understanding that I couldn't bond with her so emotionally unbalanced... of course that had been what she'd just told me, that our bond wouldn't fix what had been broken, that I had to find that myself.

I took off and quickly climbed high into the sky. Once there, I flared my wings out and soared, drifting so I could think.

Yes, my thoughts and feelings were still in turmoil. Yes, I was... broken... as hard as it was to admit that. I'd been helpless.

I shuddered, but forced myself to think back on the pain, the horror. My jaw tensed, clenched hard, and my body was wracked with tremors, but I forced myself to remember the pain of *her* digging out my wing.

I flinched, and fell for a second then steadied my flight.

I had my wing back.

I was whole.

I had proof. Why was it so hard to believe?

Rolling my shoulder, I flapped a bit harder, reassuring myself of that. I gained a bit of height, then set to glide once again.

She had done this.

She...

I had to say her name. If I was ever going to face her again without fear — and without a doubt Annie would want to face her and end her evil plans once and for all — I needed to be able to at least say her name.

"Hera," I choked out, that one word sickening me.

I forced myself to say it again. "Hera."

My jaw tightened and I fought a scream, then realized that was stupid and released it.

"I hate you, Hera," I snarled, tears welling in my eyes again. "You tried to take everything from me, *Hera*. You tried and you failed. I'm whole again. The pain. Is. Gone." And it was... physically. There were emotional scars still, but I knew I didn't have to face them alone.

That realization stunned me.

Against everything I'd been taught by my father, I didn't have to do it alone. Annie and the others would help me through this and it wasn't a sign of weakness.

"You failed, *Hera*." More tears leaked from my eyes even as my body still trembled at her name. Why was I afraid? Why did her name shake me? Why did the very thought of her bring me to my knees? Yes, she'd inflicted so much pain... but that was gone now. And at the time I'd thought she'd also, somehow, taken my bond with Annie, but that could be restored as well.

"I won't fear you. I won't live in your pain," I insisted.

Except there was more around that. There was the fear that I'd be captured again. The fear of more pain and suffering. The fear that she'd inflict that suffering on Annie.

If I was going to face her again, I'd need to face that fact, face that fear.

Pain was nothing new to me. My father had been a harsh man, sometimes physically so, when I'd been growing up, although the wounds he had inflicted paled in comparison with Hera's. I knew pain was fleeting, that wounds could be healed, as they had been this first time, but that did nothing to abate my fear. There was that nagging voice inside me saying, 'what if she hides you better?'

'What if you aren't found the next time?'

'What if the pain doesn't end?'

But... it would. One way or another, the pain would end. If I was captured again, I'd either die or I'd be rescued. Death might be long in coming, but it would be an end. And I didn't think that was the likely outcome anyway. Annie had rescued me once, she'd do it again. I'd never doubt her again. She'd found me the first time, and I'd thought that impossible. Now I knew. Nothing was impossible.

The pain would always end.

Annie would always come for me.

And I... I would always fight for her, and for myself. I'd fight all the harder to make sure I wasn't captured again.

Yes, I'd face Hera again, and I'd do everything in my power to repay my debt of pain to her. Did I still fear her? Yes. But I couldn't let that fear overwhelm me and endanger everyone I loved.

I smiled, a hard and cold thing.

My love for Annie and my chosen brothers was stronger than my fear. I'd just needed to be reminded of that.

I folded in my wings and dove down to where Annie was waiting for me. I stopped my fall with a flourish, then vanished my wings and landed gently on the ground.

"I'm ready," I said, firm, decided, and I wrapped my arms around her tugging her close.

"Oh!" she said, a bit startled, as if she hadn't expected me to take charge so completely. But she leaned into my embrace and looked up at me with desire and love and confidence, giving me no doubt that she didn't mind my determination.

"I, Hyperion, no longer of the Phyllidian Forest — for you are my home now — do accept your bond, Annie Chambers. I will become one with you and with the others. One heart, one soul, one body." I shifted my hips, pressed my hard cock against her belly, and made her eyes heat with desire. "All that I have is yours, and I accept all that you are to me. Let us be so bound and committed, for now and forever."

She pulled my head down to hers and we kissed.

I felt the bond bloom within me, growing until it shook both myself and Annie, which I didn't recall happening before. This time was stronger, that much I could feel.

And in that moment, I also felt... three others warming my soul, strengthening it with their love. My brothers. They were a part of this bond as well, and I knew if any of us doubted or faltered, the other would lend strength unconditionally. I hadn't felt that before either. Truly this was a bond no one could break. Not even Hera. Let her try.

Annie drew back, breathless and shaken.

"I can feel all of you," she whispered.

"As can I," I replied.

She blinked. "Truly?"

I nodded.

She smiled, a breathtaking, sensual smile, and reached down to stroke my semi-aroused cock. "I promised you we'd 'test' out how... whole you are."

I grinned. "And we will, but I can wait for just a moment." I looked up and somehow knew I'd see the other three guys cresting the hill behind Annie. "I think we'd all like to show you exactly how we feel about you."

She raised a brow, then half turned. "Oh? Oh!" She waved her free hand for the others to join us. "Yes, I think that could work too."

CHAPTER 22

ANNIE

I COULD FEEL THEM, EACH OF MY GUYS, THEIR WARMTH INSIDE ME, wrapped around my soul. And I could feel their desire. It was glorious. They were aroused in more ways than simply physically, excited and filled with life. They wanted to celebrate the completing of our bonded group.

I closed my eyes as they drew near and drank in their love and excitement, their desire and joy. It lifted my spirits to new heights and turned me on.

We'd been together once before, all four of us, but my memory of that time was a bit fuzzy. I hadn't wanted to think at all in that moment and had just turned off my brain and enjoyed the sensations. I recalled only a few moments, Aethan's vibrating cock, hands everywhere, kneeling on Keph because I couldn't take him fully inside me... which didn't seem to be an issue anymore.

This time I wanted to remember everything, every aching, loving moment of this encounter.

As they had before, they stood close around me, and I slowly turned, taking in each of them.

Del, tall and broad, with his glistening blue-black hair falling to below his shoulders and those clear sea-green eyes shining with the warm and tender smile that brightened his face.

Aethan, swaying with anticipation, an eager grin on that ruddy face, his mane of red-brown hair bristling like a mohawk and his soft brown eyes filled with anticipation and desire.

Rion taller than Del and leaner, with stunning chiseled muscles. His long, pale-blond hair always seemed perfectly windswept and flowing, and his smile was sure and confident, his intense blue eyes taking me in as well as the others, his dearest friends.

Last, but certainly far from least, was Keph, with his mountainous frame of hard rolling muscle, from shoulders to arms and chest, abs, and legs. His onyx skin glistened as he smiled, wide and relaxed, a playful glint in his silver-rimmed, black eyes.

These were my guys. My glorious guys. Gods, how I loved them. And I was more than ready to be with them again, all as one.

"How do you want us?" Rion asked, his voice husky with desire.

Every way, all the time. Unfortunately, we weren't in my world and they didn't have their powers. Aethan couldn't vibrate and Del couldn't play with water in fun ways. Still, I knew this was going to be a moment I'd never forget.

I knelt, thinking I'd start the guys off with a little oral teasing, but as soon as I was on my knees, I noticed a problem. We were in a field. The grasses were soft, but the myriad stones and rough earth weren't pleasant. Even if the guys were kind enough to shield me from it, it wouldn't be comfortable for them.

I rose again. "Perhaps we could go to Masia, get a room?" I offered. "It's a bit... natural here."

"If it's the little stones you're worried about, I can get rid of those," Keph said.

"You can?" Del asked, staring at Keph in surprise.

Keph nodded with a shy grin. "I probably mentioned my father is the stone-speaker of the Ophion Mountains. But I don't think I ever told you what he did."

"He speaks with stone?" Aethan asked.

"Ah... yes."

"And you can to?"

"Well, yes. In truth my father speaks to the earth itself, the mountains, the stones, the dirt and what lays below. He's much more practiced than I am. I only ever learned a little of this. But it's enough to flatten out this area and remove any offending pebbles."

We all stared at him for a long moment.

"What?" he rumbled, a bit defensively.

"Why didn't you ever tell us you could do that? Between that and your ability as a seer, you're full of surprises," Rion said.

He shrugged. "I can occasionally see the future — which has generally only gotten me in trouble — and I can move pebbles. I never thought either trait was that impressive."

No, perhaps they weren't, but still.

"Please," I said, laying a hand on his massive chest. My heart quickened just with that one bit of contact. "If you could clear out this area, I think we'd all appreciate that."

"Stand back," he said. "Things are probably going to get a bit... shaky."

Del scooped me up, holding me firm as the others braced themselves. Then the earth did shake and more violently than any of us were prepared for. Rion's wings sprouted and he took flight, hovering, while Aethan became a horse and bolted a little farther away. Del, to his credit, didn't drop me, but he did fall to one knee in the short time Keph took to do his thing.

Then it stopped.

Rion landed, and Aethan returned, flashing back into his satyr form.

"I was twenty feet away and didn't feel a thing," Aethan said in wonder.

"I just cleared this area," Keph replied, indicating a radius of perhaps five to ten feet out from where he stood.

"Amazing," Rion said as Del laid me upon the soft grasses.

"Well," my triton asked. "How is it?"

It was... I snuggled a bit into the grasses and ground. Not only was the grass lush and soft, but the earth below was free of stones and felt like it had been... tenderized. "It's lovely."

I made to rise, but then Del knelt and indicated I should just lay back. "If it's that nice, then just relax. Let's begin this with our lips upon your perfect skin." And he bent to kiss me, mid-stomach.

The others knelt as well and did the same. Keph kissed the tops of my feet, then began working his way up one leg. Rion, kneeling above my head, leaned down and kissed my forehead, then began peppering my face with kisses as well, while Aethan took up an arm and began by sucking on each of my fingers.

It was glorious and so very soothing, at least at first. Then Rion found my lips and Del sucked on my nipple and Aethan flicked the other one with his tongue and my need started to tighten into what I knew would become amazing molten desire low within me.

Keph's lips teased up my thigh, inching closer and closer to my core. He reached the crux where my legs met, oh so close to where I wanted him, but tauntingly switched to my other thigh instead.

I squirmed in my guys' grip. I didn't want him to move down the other leg, I wanted him to stay in between my thighs, using his powerful tongue to twist me tighter.

I opened my legs wider in invitation, praying he'd get the hint since Rion's lips still fully possessed mine in a powerful, demanding kiss.

Keph huffed, a low, sensual rumble and shifted, settling between my legs and sliding a hand under my ass to lift me, making it easier for him to drive me crazy with his tongue. With another low rumble, he traced my folds, drawing out the sensation then swept his tongue over my clit.

My hips jerked in anticipation and the heat inside me spun tighter. If I hadn't been fully aroused before, I was now.

But I was done being passive, so I reached out to the sides and found Del's erection, then Aethan's. They were both hard and ready and I grasped them tightly, stroking them.

Aethan groaned, while Del drew his teeth over my nipple, spiking a flicker of delicious pain that coincided with a vigorous series of flicks by Keph's tongue. Together they sent a small rushing orgasm sweeping through me, and I gasped into Rion's mouth, sucking in his breath.

He pulled away, concern in his eyes, and check to see if I was okay.

"Enough foreplay!" I managed to gasp out and thank God they didn't need any more instruction than that.

I didn't know how they communicated, it certainly wasn't with words. Perhaps there were significant glances? Or perhaps the bond — even between them — was that close.

Del laid back, and the guys lifted me with strong and caressing hands, and helped me straddle him. I took a long moment, drawing it out for both me and Del, and eased myself onto his magnificent cock, enjoying every inch of it as I slowly took him deeper and deeper inside me.

Finally, with a shuddering breath, my desire ratcheted tight, I had him fully sheathed and could feel him throbbing within me with his rapid pulse.

Again, with a delicious torture for both of us, I started moving, grinding down as I rocked my hips, making our breaths pick up with our blossoming need.

Del cupped my breasts, caressing them, as Rion pressed a hand against my back, urging me forward so he could tease my other opening. He took a long time to fully ease past that tight ring of muscle, adding to the incredible pressure and heat building inside me, while Del kneaded and caressed my breasts and our lips mingled in a teasing, tasting dance.

I had another shuddering moment, a whisper of another climax with the promise of something amazing in my future, as Rion finally buried himself inside me, his body tucked up tight against me. Then he wrapped his arms around me and urged me to sit up, shifting where both of them rubbed inside me, hitting nerves wound tight with anticipation.

Then the guys started a slow, sensual rhythm, building a glorious heat within me.

On either side of me, Aethan and Keph watched, their eyes dark with desire, their cocks hard and erect and ready as they patiently waited their turn, Aethan a little less patiently with his hand wrapped around his cock, slowly stroking himself in anticipation.

Precum glistened on his tip, begging me to take him in my mouth, and I lifted my gaze to his, licking my lips as I reached out, and wrapped my hand around him.

He drew close and I flicked my tongue over him, making his eyes roll back in pleasure.

"Gods, you're so beautiful," Rion murmured in my ear, and I took Aethan fully into my mouth until he bumped the back of my throat, then slowly slid him out, relaxed my throat, and took him deeper.

He grunted in pleasure, his body trembling, and I worked him faster and harder, matching Rion and Del's thrusts into me.

Out of the corner of my eye, I saw Keph kneel and press his hands to the ground. I wasn't sure what he was doing, but a few seconds later, the ground started to tremble. It wasn't as violently as before, but enough to vibrate *everything* sending rippling tremors rushing through my body and exploding into a wave of bliss.

I moaned my release around Aethan's erection, my body tensing then relaxing and flooding with more liquid heat. Del and Rion picked up the pace, Del capturing my hips and holding me steady, while Rion teased my oh-so-sensitive nipples, building on my orgasm and twisting me higher just like the other times I'd made love with them.

I took out my pleasure on Aethan, teasing and sucking and stroking, my desire making me wild. He trembled in my grip and I raised my gaze, wanting to watch him while he came.

Heat and need and love filled his soft brown eyes, rushing more heat through my body and making my soul thrum. This was right. This was the way things were supposed to be with my guys, us joined together like this in a primal dance of pleasure.

He tensed and groaned and his salty warmth rushed into my mouth. Pure pleasure filled his expression and I held him tight until he was done.

When I finally released him, he staggered back, grabbing his cock and bringing it back to full erection with little effort. I watched it rise again, shocked with how fast he recovered. But then Aethan wasn't a normal human, none of my guys were. They were magical and powerful and incredible.

Rion pulled me back a little, leaning against him, and Del ground his thumb against my clit, in slow, delicious circles. His own thrusts grew harder and faster, and my body blazed with the promise of another, more powerful orgasm.

He gave a few more, powerful thrusts, then let out a feral yell and swelled even larger, filling me completely with Rion in behind. My near-constant orgasm ramped up another level at this and I cried out with him.

He shuddered and groaned, while Rion held me still, letting us ride out our release, then, with my muscles still trembling, Rion grabbed my hips, released his wings, and lifted us off Del. He thrust long, hard strokes inside me, bringing me back up to a trembling, aching need, and brought me face to face with Keph.

I leaned forward, my lips meeting his in a devouring kiss, while Rion slowly pumped inside me, keeping me primed and thrumming.

Keph drew in closer and his massive cock brushed against me, sending another whisper of an orgasm rushing through me. I didn't know how much more my body and heart could take, but if I was going to die, I was certainly going to die happy and thoroughly satisfied.

Keph held out his large hands like a shelf, and Rion helped me settle my thighs on them, giving the large man more control of my body. He continued using his cock to tease my already well aroused and ready opening, while Rion kept thrusting in time with the slow beat of his wings.

"Soft or hard?" Keph rumbled, his stunning black, silver-rimmed eyes capturing me, body, mind, and soul.

"Hard," I gasped out. Now that I'd had him fully and knew I could take it, I didn't want him to hold back. I wanted him to have everything the others had without fear of hurting me.

He grinned and pulled me onto his cock with one powerful thrust. Once again, my body — miraculously — made room for him, although with Rion in behind, I was stretched to my limit, my pleasure verging on pain in a delicious, shuddering way. The joining of that massive cock inside me must have over-stimulated Rion, because he cried out and tensed, released in that same instant, filling me with warmth and pressure and making my muscles shudder and contract.

Oh, yes. Oh, Gods, yes.

There was something incredible about bringing these powerful men pleasure, about feeling them let go and love me, just like I was letting go and loving them.

I cried out as another wave of bliss crashed over me. Rion pinned me against Keph's hard body, their cocks buried deep inside me, as he gasped his pleasure, his body trembling. Then he carefully pulled out of me and sagged to the ground, leaving me entirely to Keph.

I wrapped my arms around his neck and met his gaze again.

"Hi," I purred.

He smiled, and thrust into me. "Hi, beautiful."

I moaned back as he thrust again, harder and faster, encouraging him because I knew he'd never been like this with a woman before, had been afraid he'd hurt his partner with his strength and size.

"Yes!" I cried, throwing my head back, trusting Keph to satisfy me, loving every powerful second I was in his arms. I'd never had sex like this before. Such a large man, so strong, so filling, thrusting deep inside me. It was every sinful fantasy I'd ever had and the look on his face, the lust and love and need, all for me, was a drug like no other.

I cried out with another release, or perhaps I'd been coming this entire time and was just reaching a new plateau, I didn't know. But with one final, incredible thrust Keph swelled and released as well.

I let out a prolonged scream of pleasure as my body convulsed, waves of bliss crashing over me, rushing through my whole body as if even my hair and toenails were hypersensitive and reacting to my orgasm.

When Keph finally set me on my feet, his arms still wrapped around me to hold me steady, I must have been a sweaty-bedraggled mess, and I didn't care. I'd had the most amazing sex with my amazing men and they all looked at me like I was the goddess they first thought I was, even though they knew I wasn't.

I found it odd that my legs weren't quivering at all. I was strong and oh-so-very fulfilled, and — holy shit! — my desire was far from quenched.

A giggle bubbled up inside me. It was like I'd become some sex goddess... or sex demon? I didn't know if that was possible. Maybe I was just so in love with these guys and my magical healing gave me incredible stamina.

Whatever it was, I wasn't going to look a gift horse in the mouth.

I glanced mischievously from Keph, to Rion, to Aethan, to Del.

"More?" I giggled.

"Truly?" Del gasped. "After Keph, I... I've never seen him like that."

"It was incredible," I half moaned half sighed. "Let's do it again."

They didn't need to be told a third time.

Aethan was there, all furious kisses and caressing hands as he ducked and nudged his cock up to brush my opening. I lifted one leg, resting it on his hip as he adjusted his position and entered me in a smooth, powerful stroke.

Surprisingly, after having been gloriously punished by Keph's massive erection only moments ago, Aethan's much smaller cock still felt incredible. Again, somehow, I was adapting to each man as they entered me.

I wrapped my arms around him rubbing my body on his as we pressed close, undulating against each other as he thrust into me.

"I don't think any man has been ready for a second turn with me so quickly," I breathed into his ear. "You're incredible."

"I love you, Annie," he groaned back. "I'll give you whatever you want whenever you want it."

"I want you," I replied, meeting him thrust for thrust, crashing our bodies together in the most delicious way.

His pace was incredible. He didn't have super-speed in this world, but his hips were still powerful and fast. I jumped up into his arms, wrapping my legs around him as he supported my ass, and relentlessly plunged into my depths.

The bliss of an orgasm shivered through me and I grasped him tighter with my arms and legs. I was high enough that he had his head buried in my breasts and I pushed him closer still, his teeth nipping my tender skin with delicious licks of pain.

Then pressure at my other opening, drew my attention and I glanced back to see Del, close behind me. He was a bit tall to get a good angle with Aethan holding me, but he seemed to be half-crouching so he'd be able to get in.

"I want to feel all of you," he murmured, as his teasing turned to shallow penetration, and I moaned my pleasure, giving him permission.

I felt his tip first and with Aethan's unceasing rapid driving it was enough to push me over the peak of another orgasm. Apparently, that was exactly what I needed to loosen up a little and Del pushed fully inside me soon after that. His strokes were slow and long, a counterpoint to Aethan's speed, my body captured between the two of them on the precipice of another incredible orgasm.

I kept waiting for Aethan to finish, but recalled — as my body thrummed tighter and tighter — that some men lasted much longer their second time around.

Keph joined us. Raised as I was, I was nearly at a height to meet his lips. He only had to duck a little to join in with a kiss.

Rion, flew in as well, and I turned from Keph's lips to Rion's cock and grabbed it from the air to taste and pleasure.

My mind seemed to explode, overloaded with sensations, Aethan's driving need, Del's slow rocking strokes, the hard intensity of Keph's lips, and salty sweetness of Rion's cock.

Keph knelt again, the ground trembled and all the men within me were suddenly vibrating in all the right ways.

Del's strokes quickened as his erection swelled. I knew, in one glorious moment of connection, that all my guys were going to climax at once. A moment later, Aethan's final hard thrust matched Del's as they released. Rion cried out as well, filling my mouth. And for me... it was a high like I'd never experienced before, a heavenly orgasm so sweet and overpowering my muscles locked me into stillness, my release sending me spinning, lights flashing across my vision.

Eventually the moment passed. Rion landed, breathing hard, and Aethan and Del removed themselves and set me down. Like the last time, I wasn't weak or exhausted. I was empowered and strong. As they all collapsed into sweaty, exhausted heaps, I was filled with strength and drive.

It still took me some time to regain my voice, but when I did, I said, "That was the singular most amazing thing I've ever felt. Thank you. All of you."

They all smiled wearily, groaning and humming their satisfaction.

"How are you not tired?" Keph asked. He, out of all of them, seemed the least weary.

"I don't know," I giggled, my elation overwhelming me. "I'm a little baffled myself. All I know is, right now, I feel like I could take on the world."

"What about Hera?" Del asked.

I put on an eager smile. "Her, too."

CHAPTER 23

ANNIE

As the guys rested from their oh-so-amazing exertions I, feeling empowered, went to a nearby stream to wash up, then went looking for Janice. I couldn't find her on the beach, and when I asked the assembled men, a few smiled mischievous grins and pointed to the towering set of black stones where the portal was.

"She went to the other world?" I asked, suddenly concerned.

"No," Naz said, with a sheepish smile. "I believe she's just hiding on the other side of those stones. She... needed a moment to herself."

I didn't know what that meant but went to find her.

I came around to the other side of the stones to see Janice hiking up her pants. She looked flushed.

"Janice?" I asked, wondering if I was interrupting a private moment.

She jumped. "Oh, good, it's just you." Though her tone then shifted. "You little minx!"

I raised a brow at that and joined her in the small alcove of rocks where she was hiding. "Minx?"

"What were you doing?" she demanded, waggling her eyebrows suggestively at me.

"What? Oh!" I gave her a silly grin. "I was able to re-establish my bond with the guys and then we... ah... celebrated."

"Fucked like bunnies?"

Heat warmed my cheeks, although not as much as before. I wasn't ashamed of what we'd done at all. They were my mates, and I loved them. "Yep. Could you hear us?"

"Oh, there was the occasional cry from the hills, but... ah... no..." Now she was blushing, her cheeks a soft pink.

"What?" I asked.

"I could *feel* it!" she hissed. Her eyes intense and accusing.

"You could?" I asked, shocked.

Oh, shit. We were bonded. Could she feel what I felt? Would I when she found *her* someone... or someones?

"Really?" I don't know why, but I flushed even more.

"Yes!" she hissed. "Last night I kept waking up feeling really horny. I even..." Her face went from flushed to beat red. "I think I cried out in my sleep a few times and ah... well it turns out, women can have wet dreams too, it seems. I had to take a fully clothed dip in the sea this morning to cover that up. Then, just now, I... well, for a while I felt really relaxed and mellow, with a pleasant—" She cleared her throat. "Well, all the guys in camp said I had a glow about me. But then suddenly I needed very much to... ah... give myself a little release. And I wasn't about to do that in front of all those guys... especially Naz!"

"Oh." I pressed my lips together, trying not to smile or giggle. Giggling would be bad given how upset she was. It seemed my bond with Janice went so far as to share some of my feelings with her, though it sounded like the transfer was more than just emotions, but physical sensations as well. "Sorry about that."

"Yes, well, I'm... good now." She rolled her eyes and chuckled. "So what did happen out there?"

"Only the single best moment of my entire life. An orgasm so divine it defies description."

"Fuck? Really?"

"Yep," I said, actually bobbing on my toes, a silly grin on my face.

"Ah... well next time warn me when you are about to have a divine orgasm so I can find somewhere private to ah..." She cleared her throat again.

"You know, you could invite a guy along — or more than one — to help you with that," I suggested, making her cheeks red again. "Maybe Naz?"

"I'm not at that point with Naz, yet."

"Oh? I'm sure all you'd have to do is ask and he'd be there for you."

"Well, I'm not ready to ask," she insisted, but her tone said she was seriously considering it.

I shrugged. "Your call."

She straightened. "Now I should probably get back out there before those guys think something strange is happening between us."

I hated to tell her, but— "I think they already think something is happening. The few who saw you leave were all a bit... odd about it," I chuckled.

"Fuck, not Naz?"

"Yeah, him too."

"Ah, fuck! I'll never be able to look at him without blushing ever again!"

I put an arm around her shoulders and accompanied her as she walked around the rocks and headed back to camp. "Don't worry, you look lovely when you blush, I'm sure he won't mind at all."

She elbowed me in the ribs... hard.

I grunted, tears coming to my eyes half in pain and half in mirth. "Ow."

"You're a healer," she huffed. "Heal."

I blinked the tears away. "Yeah, I guess I deserved that. So, anyway, to the real reason I came to find you. I'm feeling like I want to go after Hera again. At the moment, I know we can defeat her, but I'm curious what you think on the matter."

"We have the same resources we did last time," Janice said, as we headed toward the surf, away from the camp, in part to discuss our options and also to avoid the guys who might be curious about what happened to Janice. "And she'd be ready for us."

Which was something I feared and the reason I'd asked Janice for her thoughts on the matter, hoping she'd have a solution to the problem.

"We have to assume she isn't just waiting in her penthouse. She knows we can teleport in and out now. She'll have moved to someplace secret and safe. And — and this is a big one — she probably still has the portal staked out. Anyone who walks through there, is gonna get shot up really darn quickly."

Right.

Fuck.

"There's no other portal that you know of?" she asked.

I shook my head. "Not that I know of."

I thought about that, a whirlwind of questions rushing through my mind.

"Here's a question," I said, thinking out loud. "Hera should be able to use the portal, so why hasn't she come through with her goons and squashed us?"

"That's a horrifying thought. But... you're right," Janice replied. "Why hasn't she? With the forces she has at her command — and those she could buy — she'd have no trouble wiping this world clean. Assuming guns worked here. Have we tested that?"

"No, I've never had a gun with me."

"I do," Janice said. She pulled out her handgun and fired a quick shot down into the sand, proving it worked well enough.

I jumped a little at the roar as it went off even though I'd expected it.

Janice holstered her weapon. "I don't get it. Some of these folks can fly or turn into animals, but they don't have the amazing powers they have on the other side, so why not face them here?"

"Maybe she can't?" I said, although it was more of a question than a statement, and I had no idea why she wouldn't be able to.

Janice raised a brow at that.

My mind spun faster and faster. Perhaps it was the amazing sex which had cleared the cobwebs, but I felt like I was quicker, more lucid. Hera should have come through by now. She'd have the advantage of numbers and superior weapons here. There was no reason for her not to come and wipe us all out... unless she couldn't.

And, the last time we'd gone back, there had been that strange man — one of her agents — waiting for us, for me. She'd wanted me to go to her, as if there was something I had which she didn't.

Except I couldn't figure out what that could be. She had everything, including stronger powers than me, but if she'd lost her ability to cross between worlds, then that would be something I could do that she couldn't.

"I think Hera's lost her ability to cross between worlds," I said. The more I mulled it over, the more it made sense. "If she could, she'd be here. She has all the advantages here, assuming she brings her small army with her. It also explains why she wanted me to surrender myself. There isn't anything I have that she doesn't have, except maybe that."

Janice nodded. "Well, let's be thankful for that then, otherwise we'd probably all be dead by now."

I nodded, grateful indeed.

"But still," Janice said. "Assuming she doesn't care about that anymore, anyone who goes through that portal, even potentially you, is dead."

"Except you," I said, realizing it as I said it.

"Me?"

"You went through, got shot several times, and weren't hurt."

"That was... I don't know what that was." She frowned, her expression a mix of fear and uncertainty.

"It must be your superpower."

"But I'm not bulletproof. I've been shot before."

Right. Perhaps we could try a different approach to figuring that out. "Assuming you do have some sort of superpower, you've probably had it your entire life, since you've always had *aurai* blood in you. Is there anything you can do better than others, like, a lot better?"

Janice gave a quick laugh. "Drink."

I didn't see how that was a power, but it could be a clue to something else. "Tell me about that."

She shrugged. "I started drinking young. My dad thought everyone should get a taste for alcohol early. It would either dissuade them or prepare them. For me, well, I sort of liked it. I come from a larger family, one younger sister and four brothers, only one of whom is younger. My sister was the girly-girl, not me. I was more like my brothers, rough and tumble. I drank like they did, even though I was half their size." She gave another laugh. "The first time I tried to match them drink for drink, oh God, was I sick, it was nasty! But after that, I kept up with them just fine, in fact I began to be able to outdrink them, usually with little or no side effects." She frowned and cocked her head to one side. "Hunh, now that I say it, that does seem fairly extraordinary. Perhaps that's my power?"

"Incredible drinking ability?" Maybe, but I knew she'd been shot and somehow come away unscathed and had a strong suspicion there was more to it. "Anything else?"

We walked in silence for a long moment before she said, "Sleep."

"You think your super power is sleep?"

"No, not sleep, but being able to go without it."

"Go on," I prompted.

She made a bit of a face, as if more and more of what she was saying — what she'd probably taken for granted — now seemed... odd when analyzed.

"It's sort of the same story. In university, I studied hard, like really hard. I stayed up for three days straight once and then crashed, just before an exam actually. But ever since then, I haven't had any problems going a day or two without sleep. I hardly notice it. I can stay out drinking all night and still feel refreshed in the morning even when the FBI guys I was drinking with were all bleary-eyed and half dead."

"That sounds less like a power around drinking and sleeping, and more something to do with fortitude or stamina."

"Yeah, it does, doesn't it?"

"And maybe that transfers to being shot as well." My clearer-than-ever mind was starting to work once again.

Janice raised a brow at me, skeptical.

"No, listen." Words tumbled out as I thought this through. "You had a bad drinking experience, then after that, you were an amazing drinker. You had a bad sleeping experience, then you were okay without sleep. You got shot once, and now, maybe you can't get shot again?" Before she could refute this, I asked, "Has there been anything else in your life that went badly once, but has been great since?"

She opened her mouth, then closed it, thinking. After a moment she said, "Well, yeah, sort of."

"And?"

She quirked her mouth. "Well I'd thought it was just because I was in top physical condition, but this matches what you're saying." She sighed heavily. "When I was training for the PFT, I—"

"PFT?" I asked.

"Sorry, the FBI Physical Fitness Test. PFT."

"Ah, okay."

"Anyway, when I was training for the running portion, I wanted to really challenge myself so I borrowed all the gear from a firefighter friend of mine. I suited up with all fifty pounds of it, then for good measure added a few ankle and wrist weights and set off on my run." She grinned. "I finished the one-and-a-half-mile run, but then collapsed and blacked out. Luckily, I had a friend there and they got me to a hospital. I nearly died from heat stroke and extreme exhaustion. It took me days to recover, but I was stubborn and determined to try it again. The next time, I was a bit more careful, but the second time was a breeze. I hardly felt tired at the end. And when I ran the course for real, without all the gear, I did it in record time."

She looked at me, but I didn't reply. It seemed so obvious to me, but I had a feeling she needed to say it to really believe it.

She huffed. "Yeah, okay, it seems you're right. I guess, I just... adapt well, to... anything and everything. Even apparently being shot."

The way Janice said it, sparked something for me. This last sex-capade with the guys, I'd seemed to be a perfect fit for all of them, even massive Keph, who I'd never been able to take in fully before. But now I could adapt to his size then to Aethan and the others. If Janice had my abilities, perhaps I'd gained hers as well. It seemed logical.

But I wanted to confirm that was what Janice's power was.

"There is a way to test our theory," I said with a shrug. "You do have a gun with you. I can heal you if it doesn't work. Actually, you have my powers now too, so you can even heal yourself."

She looked at me like I had two heads. "Shoot myself?"

"Someplace non-vital. Only if you want to be sure." I shrugged.

"Fuck." But she took out her gun and grimaced at me. "This is a terrible idea."

"But the only way to know for sure." I didn't like the idea of her shooting herself, either, but we needed cold, hard — possibly painful — evidence.

"Fine." She removed her pants, sat, and aimed for the fleshy part of her thigh. Her breath picked up and her hands trembled, and she sucked in big breath after big breath.

Then, with a scream, she pulled the trigger.

The weapon roared to life and she screamed in agony, but she didn't gush blood. She didn't even weep blood. There was no wound at all and we had no idea where the bullet had gone.

For a second I wondered if she'd missed, but tears leaked down her cheeks and she panted, confirming she'd been hurt.

"Fuck fuck fuck," she hissed. "Fuuuuuuck! That hurt."

"But you're not bleeding."

She stared at her leg. "I'm not."

"That's got to be your superpower," I said. "You're adaptable."

"Well... fuck me," Janice groaned.

CHAPTER 24

AETHAN

"I DON'T LIKE IT," NAZ SAID, SHAKING HIS HEAD. "I DON'T CARE IF you're immune to their weapons, you'll still be in danger." He looked at Janice with all the intensity of devotion that I and the others looked at Annie.

A small group of us had gathered to discuss our plan for going back to the other world. Annie and all of us bonded to her were there, as was Janice, Naz, Khyrys the female minotaur who could read minds, Rhou the *panai* who could look like anything or anyone, and Dorios the *oreadai* who could— what was the word Annie used? *Teleport.*

The first part of the plan was simple. Janice would go through and distract or fight the men waiting in the alley, since she couldn't be hurt by their weapons. Keph would be in the front line as well since bullets pretty much bounced off him.

The next part was me.

"She only has to distract them for a moment," I said. "Just long enough for me to get through and start running. Once up to speed, I'm sure they won't be able to hit me and I can snatch away all their weapons. Between the three of us, we should have them dealt with quickly."

Naz still didn't look happy. He didn't want to go back at all. I wasn't sure what his power was, but whatever it was, it made him sick with a pounding headache.

"Fine," he huffed, his expression turning resigned as he realized he wasn't going to convince Janice not to do this.

In my mind the real problem wasn't dealing with the 'gate guards' so much as finding and dealing with Hera. Annie seemed upbeat and positive about our chances, but I wasn't sure why.

"Once we're safely on the other side," Annie continued, "Khyrys and I will see if we can get information from any of Hera's 'gate guards'. That will determine our next move. If she's at her building, then Dorios will teleport a small group of us to see if Del or I can sense Hera using our water sense. We've been close enough to her now that hopefully we can identify her."

Del nodded. He didn't look certain though. He said he didn't have a great range with his abilities, and he wasn't able to practice in our world where he didn't have them. Again, though, Annie was hopeful.

"If she's not there, we'll regroup at the safe house and plan from there," Annie said. "Wherever she is, everyone focus on her guards. I'll be the one to deal with her."

Annie hadn't said how she was dealing with Hera yet, only that she had an idea. I would have liked more information or more than just 'an idea,' given what had happened the last time, but that's all she'd given us.

There were serious faces all around, including Annie's. Everyone knew this was dangerous.

"There is still the matter of payment," Khyrys said, her voice gruff.

"My offer still stands," Annie replied. "You can loot whatever you want from Hera's house."

"That didn't happen last time," Khyrys shot back.

"This time we're dealing with her for good. I'll make sure you get your chance to take what you wish."

Khyrys frowned, but didn't press the issue.

"Are we set then?" Janice asked.

Everyone nodded and the group broke up to settle in for the night.

One night's sleep and then we'd go back to Annie's world. The idea made my stomach hurt and my heart pound. I didn't want Annie going back. I didn't want to risk Hera getting her hands on her.

"Annie," I said, jerking my chin, indicating I wanted to talk to her. Just her and the other guys.

She nodded and we stepped away from Janice, Naz, and Khyrys.

"What's this idea you have?" Rion asked her, before I could. "We need to know. I want to face Hera again and repay my debt of pain, but she's powerful. I— *We* can't risk you."

She wrapped her hands around his biceps and drew him close as we wandered back to our little private camp just beyond the beach.

"It's still only half formed," she replied, then held up a hand before the rest of us could argue with her. "I know that's not reassuring, but I just know that we can beat her this time." She looked at each of us in turn. "This new bond is different from the last. It's stronger. The way I feel all of you is incredible."

I couldn't disagree with that. Before I'd had a good connection with Annie, but now it was incredibly close. I could feel her confidence and calm, and beyond that, I could feel a connection with the other guys as well. It was hard to explain, but I just *knew* things about them. A simple look conveyed so much now. It was... intense. Annie was right about that much.

"My idea... well, it... I need to get close to Hera, touch her.

There was something that passed between us the last time when she touched me and broke our first bond. I... don't think this new bond will break so easily. But I think when I was connected with her, that I took her ability to open portals. I can't be certain about that, but I know... something went from her to me while we were connected and I was trying to fight her. The more I think about it, the more I believe that's what happened. And if I can take that... I think— No, I *know* I can take more. She said she could take the magic from her bonds. I think I can take her magic from her. It'll be a battle of wills between us but I know with the strength of our bond coursing through me I can defeat her."

A battle of wills.

With an ancient goddess.

It was crazy. And yet, Annie felt different to me now. Powerful. Supported by the four of us.

"I know you can do it," I said and the others nodded and grunted their acknowledgement as well. Keph was firm, reassuring, like me. Del was less so, but willing to go along with the plan. Rion was the least convinced, but he nodded, and Annie invited him for a 'walk' to help calm his nerves.

I was half asleep when they returned. Rion seemed stronger, more confident, and Annie was glowing with life and energy. I don't know if they'd talked, but I was certain there had been more than just walking happening. I smiled, glad Rion was on board, and fell into a peaceful sleep.

Annie woke me early with dawn only a smudge of light on the horizon.

"Come with me," she said.

I did, rising quickly. "What is it?" I asked, although I had a strong suspicion what she desired.

"I always feel stronger and braver, more confident after I've been with one of you," she said softly, confirming my suspicion.

"Today is a big day. I want to have a moment with each of you to make sure I'm on my game."

I was more than happy to go with her. Once we were far enough away, she turned to me, pressing close and capturing my lips in a long, passionate kiss.

"I liked the way you did it the last time we were alone," she murmured against my lips before turning and pressing her behind against me, my hard cock between her cheeks.

I obliged her, pushing into her tight, slick, warmth, drawing a throaty moan of satisfaction, then driving her to gasping, moaning heights of pleasure.

The coupling was quick, but thoroughly satisfying, filling me with strength and energy and certainty.

"Now I'm ready," she said, through heavy breaths, grinning at me.

I escorted her back to the camp, where she woke and left with Rion. I winked at him as he left, then I began preparing a meal.

The others woke and had their time with Annie, returning to a large meal of fruit and roasted meat, and I could feel certainty and vitality radiating from all of us.

We joined Janice and the others at the portal. Everyone looked nervous, but Annie and Janice's confidence was contagious. We may have been worried, but we were also determined.

Hera needed to be stopped and whether we wanted to be or not, we were the ones best suited to stop her.

With a quick nod from Annie, Janice stepped through the portal then Keph followed a moment later.

I counted down slowly from ten, then drew in a long breath, and stepped through.

The frozen Chicago air slapped me in the face, but I leaped into action, taking in the scene as I ramped up my speed. Keph and Janice were moving toward the mouth of the alley, both moving as fast as they could toward the men with guns firing at them. Neither was moving fast. Keph was slow to begin with and Janice seemed to be in pain from all the shots she was taking.

A bullet zipped past my head.

I gritted my teeth and pushed myself to move faster. Suddenly everyone was moving in slow motion. Even the bullets slowed to a speed where I could see them coming and avoid them.

I reached the guards at the end of the alley before either Keph or Janice. Plucking their weapons from the hands of the guards, a couple at a time, I ran back to place them where Keph was about to step so he'd crush them.

There were a dozen men there, and in an instant, they were harmless.

Then I sped away, running to disarm the other men stationed farther away, in buildings or on roofs.

The fight was over quickly, as Annie had anticipated, and we rounded up Hera's men and identified a leader among them. Once all our troops were through the portal, Annie and Khyrys went to interrogate the leader to learn where Hera was hiding.

"Where is Hera?" Annie asked pleasantly. "Or June Olympios as she might be known to you."

"I'll never tell you, bitch!" the man spat.

Khyrys turned and nodded to Annie, indicating that the minotaur had read the man's mind and gotten useful information.

"How many guards are around her?" Annie asked.

"Go to hell!"

Khyrys nodded again.

"When is she the most vulnerable or have the least guards?"

"Fuck you!"

Khyrys snorted and rolled her eyes, trying not to laugh.

"Anything else helpful we should know?"

The man grinned and Khyrys shrugged. Guess there wasn't much more they could learn. Two tritons marched the man over with the others, while Khyrys reported to the rest of us what she'd learned.

"Hera is in a house, outside the city," the minotaur said. "From the picture in the man's mind, it's a vast house. There are over a hundred guards in and around the place. There's a lot of open land around the house as well, and we'll be seen approaching it. It'll be difficult to get past them. According to the man's thoughts, he believes she's most vulnerable when she goes for a run. She only takes a few guards with her and there are times when she may be far removed from the guards at the house, but she will also be somewhere on the vast property, perhaps hard to find. As for helpful information, I got only a strange word: pump-er-nickel?"

"It could be a pass phrase of some sort," Janice said. With that, Dorios teleported us to Janice's safe house in small groups to plan for the next phase of the mission.

This was it. We were going to get another chance to end Hera, and this time, I wasn't going to go down easily.

CHAPTER 25

KEPHAS

THE FIRST PART OF THE PLAN WENT OFF WITHOUT ANY ISSUES AND we'd regrouped in a house that Janice referred to as a safe house. Then Janice and Dorios — disguised in the armor we'd taken from Hera's 'gate guards' — along with Rhou — who could disguise himself with his magic — went back to the alley and took one of the large cars used by Hera's guards. They drove to Hera's estate to scout out the location, get a better idea of the layout of the house and grounds, and check out where Hera did her running, in preparation for our attack the next day.

Even though we knew Hera might become suspicious if her guards didn't check in during the day, we didn't want to rush the attack. Better to have more information and be prepared than not enough.

The next morning, Annie once again had a moment with each of us. I was last, and by the time she got to me, she was already radiant. I'd felt the incredible arousal of each of the other men before me through our bond and was more than ready when she climbed up into my arms.

It was also wonderful to know that I didn't need to be slow and careful with her — which still astounded me. I could just let go and enjoy the moment with her.

Once everyone was ready, Dorios started teleporting us in small groups to Hera's estate.

He moved me and the other guys, along with Annie, into a forested glade, and then Aethan was off in a flash, scouting the area. Janice and Rhou were already there in their stolen armor, looking like Hera's soldiers, while the others had been ferried into other parts of the forest, spreading us out to make our attack.

It wasn't long before the soft pounding of running foot falls started coming closer and everyone tensed, ready to make our strike.

Hera was supposed to have six men with her on her run, but when the troop came into view, there were many more than that. A full dozen ran ahead of her, a line of six ran to either side of her, and another dozen came after. There were thirty-six, where there should have been six, but given that Hera probably suspected something was up, the extra guards weren't surprising.

Everyone tensed but we wouldn't call off the attack. We'd already established we would go ahead no matter any changes. The plan was essentially the same. The only thing that could have thrown us off was if Hera had decided not to go for her regular run. But both Annie and Janice figured Hera was too cocky to do that. And they'd been right.

One of the *epimelidai* in our group turned into living fire and charged into the guards at the front of Hera's party.

The guards yelled out, some screamed, and rushed to face the attack, but Aethan zipped in stealing their guns, while Del concentrated on 'stealing people's water,' and Rion blinded them with his light. I leaped in, rushing toward a group near Hera, determined to take out as many as I could, as fast as I could.

A rapid crack-crack-crack erupted through the yells, and my

chest stung, telling me one of them had gotten some shots off. The bullets hurt like Hades — these guns must have been more powerful than the ones used before — but they still didn't do a lot of damage to me, and I pushed on, barreling through the group, shoving them into each other and bowling some of them over. I rammed my fist into one man's face, sending him flying, then kicked another. He screamed and crumpled to the ground.

Chaos rang all around. Men screamed, some in pain, others calling orders. Shots roared around me, and through it all, Hera laughed. She stood in the center of it all, her head thrown back, laughing as if our attack was the funniest thing in the world.

I spun on her, slamming my fist toward her face. But she borrowed my strength, easily caught my hand, and threw me back over her head like I was a ragdoll.

I crashed through the trees, landing hard, but that hardly hindered me, and I was up a moment later, charging back in.

Fewer and fewer of the enemies had *guns* as Aethan did his job, and I tackled three more men, taking them to the ground as I reached the group on the other side of Hera.

But she wasn't looking at me anymore. She was staring down Annie, who'd moved with incredible speed to get up next to her.

This was what we'd planned. Annie just needed to touch Hera, engage with her and...

Crack-crack-crack.

Dark blood blossomed on Annie's chest as the three shots tore through her. Her eyes widened with shock and pain, and she dropped to the ground, her body suddenly limp.

I screamed, along with the others, as agony tore through me. I could feel what she felt and it staggered me, bringing me to my knees.

I wanted to go to her, *had* to go to her, but I was too slow. Time stuttered and stretched as I tried to rise and run to her.

I felt so weak. Perhaps this was the downside of this greater bond we shared.

And the question that hung in my mind as I stumbled toward the woman I loved was simple: if she died, would I?

And if I didn't, would I want to?

CHAPTER 26

ANNIE

THE BULLETS TORE INTO ME, ONE JUST UNDER MY LEFT BREAST, another near the center of my chest, and the last high on my right side, near my shoulder, then I dropped to the ground

Except there was no pain, just stillness, my body too numb with shock for my brain to register what had happened. My warmth rushed out of me and a soul-numbing cold threatened to consume me.

Not that far away, on the other side of Hera who howled with laughter, Keph staggered. He seemed so weak and awkward as he tried to rise and stumble forward. I saw this, but didn't really know what it meant. My mind was muddled, hazy, my senses growing dim. What had been sharp sounds and scents a moment before were now dull.

I was sure I knew what was going on. I'd just thought about it, thought about—

I coughed and tasted the metallic tang of blood on my tongue. That didn't seem like it was a good thing.

Darkness swam across my vision and my soul drew further

and further back from everything as if I was shrinking... or being yanked away or...

I didn't know.

I was cold and getting colder.

The world grew dimmer, the darkness swelling, consuming all thought, all feeling, all—

"No!" The voice was distant and it sounded odd, like a mixture of voices all at once, and oddly, one of them sounded like mine. "Get up Annie! Heal yourself!"

Heal...

Myself...?

But I wasn't in pain. Why did I need healing? Here in this darkness, everything was serene... and empty. I didn't need healing. There wasn't anything left of me, no body, no thought.

No body...

I was sure I'd had one before... hadn't I? I couldn't remember. Was that a good thing or a bad thing?

It was so peaceful here, but so... empty. I was missing something, something important, something I didn't want to live without...

My guys. My guys were gone.

My soul lurched at that.

No—

They weren't gone. Hera hadn't taken them again, they were just too far away... no I was too far away. Then four faintly glowing shapes appeared in the darkness. One small and lithe with weird looking legs that ended in hooves. One massive, a giant of a man in all proportions. One broad and strong but with the tail of a fish. And one tall and lean with chiseled features and wings.

Did I know them?

"Annie!" they called. And again, my voice seemed to call with them.

They seemed to know me. They were... I *knew* who they were. I did. I just couldn't find that knowledge in the darkness.

"Yes?" I responded... only I didn't. I didn't speak, I didn't have energy or breath. I was sure I'd spoken and yet I hadn't.

Of course not, said some distant part of my mind. *You can't speak without a mouth, without a body.*

That made sense.

"I've lost my body," I said to the glowing figures, realizing as I did, that once again I wasn't actually saying anything.

"Come back to us, Annie!" the figures called.

Back?

Back where?

They certainly seemed insistent. I had to know them, and I was more and more certain that I was indeed this 'Annie' they were talking to.

"Do I..." I stopped myself this time. I'd been about to ask if I knew their names. I felt like I should. It was on the tip of my... except, I didn't have a tongue right now.

Names...

The figures were reaching out for me and I felt... love? Yes, love. It was so intense it radiated like the light around them, growing stronger and brighter and warmer.

One of them brushed the cheek I no longer had, caressing my soul and in an instant I knew.

Hyperion. Rion. A winged man. An Angel. A man of light. A man I loved deeper and more binding than anything else in the world.

Another brush of light. Aethan. Fast and lithe. A vigorous and eager lover. And I loved him just as much as I loved Rion.

I reached out to the last two, connecting with Delphon, at home in the waters. Broad and strong and loyal. And Kephas. A giant with a tender soul. Hard body. Stronger than anything or anyone, yet gentle and kind.

Together, with the others, they were mine. My guys. I loved them all and they loved me.

I felt their pull, their desire and hope and longing. I didn't know what I was being pulled toward, but I desperately wanted... needed to go to them.

I blurred into their light, joining with them, became one shining beacon. Then... I was slammed back into screaming agony.

Back into my damaged body.

I had so little energy left, I was weak, and fragile, and dying. But I knew I could heal this. I could fix these wounds. And even though I was so very low on life, I was being fed power from my guys, my loves, my bonded.

I grasped my healing power and shoved it into my wounds, slowly returning to myself, my mind clearing, my breath steadying. And it was only then that I realized I hadn't been breathing. I'd been dead.

I sucked in a long, gasping breath, and the laughter nearby stopped suddenly.

Hera.

I grinned a manic, furious grin, and opened my eyes. My guys were all feeding me so much power, I felt like I floated to my feet— No I *was* floating, using Del's water power to lift myself.

I didn't know what look was in my eyes in that moment, but Hera's eyes went wide with shock.

She scooped up a nearby gun with her wind powers, setting it in her waiting hand then pointing it at me, and fired.

Agony slammed into my head, and I slapped my palms over the point of impact.

"Fuck! That hurt!" I snarled, then realized I wasn't bleeding and I sure as hell wasn't dead.

Well, shit. I'd been right. Janice had shared her adaptation powers with me when we'd bonded and now that I'd been shot once, I couldn't be harmed again.

A manic giggle escaped my lips. I hadn't really wanted to test that theory. It had been far too dangerous since I'd almost died, but hell. I'd been right!

Hera's eyes widened even farther, and I stepped toward her, moving with Aethan's speed.

One minute I was a few feet away, the next I was right beside her.

"Come to me," I said, laying a hand on her cheek.

"How...?" she gasped.

I dipped forward and kissed her. She stiffened and I captured her head in my hands. I couldn't let her get away. I had to finish this now.

She screamed and clawed at my wrists, her grip enhanced with Keph's power.

But I had Keph's power, too, and I clung to her, bonded with her, and then pushed through her resistance somehow on instinct, and sucked out her powers, just like she'd sucked out the powers of her bonded so long ago.

I had no idea how I was doing it, how it had come so easily to me when I thought I'd have to struggle to succeed at this part of the plan, but I wasn't going to question it. My guys were with me, feeding me their life and power, and right now... I could do anything!

She heaved and writhed, clawing and punching, screaming into my mouth as I took everything from her.

Then a matching pressure swelled inside me, as she desperately clawed at my power, trying to take mine away from me. The bond went two ways and she was strong.

But I had something she didn't. Hera had never truly cherished her bonded. She'd used them for their powers, nothing more. And when she'd drained them, she'd taken their powers, but she'd also lost something. Her connection to them. She'd lost the strength that came from that bond, but I hadn't. I was stronger. Five times stronger. And I had the force of will and power of five hearts and souls behind me.

Strength from Keph.

Vigor from Aethan.

Water from Del, to physically drain her, weaken her.

And Rion's light to overwhelm her with its purity.

Even my bond with Janice, allowing me to adapt, made me stronger.

Hera gasped and moaned, her body weakening, and I could feel through our bond that she now knew her mistake. She'd tried to take my bonds, tortured my guys, tried to take everything from me, and hadn't finished the job. She should have made sure I was dead, because I'd come back stronger and now it was my turn to take everything from her and end this.

I pulled my lips away, taking the last of her power with me and felt a thousand feet tall as I released Hera.

She stumbled back, emaciated and weak, her eyes wild.

"It's not possible," she gasped as she sagged to her knees. "I'm the only one who can take powers. How could you...?"

"I still have friends and lovers." I knelt beside her. "I don't want them just for their powers. I want them for everything they are and that bond makes me stronger."

"No," she gasped again.

"Yes." I still didn't know exactly how I'd taken her powers. Yes, I'd bonded with her, but there was no love there. It had been a brutal and forced thing — probably what she'd done with her bonded, and now she knew what it felt like.

I rose and glared down at her.

"Now you have nothing. Your immortality is gone and you'll soon wither and die." I didn't know if that was true, but even if she didn't, she still only had an average human life left.

She sneered. "I'm still the richest and most powerful woman in the world! There won't be any place you can go where I can't find you and when I do, I'll—"

A shot rang out and Hera jerked back, her eyes wide and empty.

I blinked as Janice stepped into sight holding her gun, her expression hard with determination. "She was right. We couldn't let her live. She'd escape any justice we tried to put her through. She was too powerful, to wealthy."

I stared at Janice unable to fully comprehend what had happened.

It was over.

Just like that.

Janice had killed Hera.

"You..." I murmured.

"Did what had to be done," Janice replied, "something I knew you wouldn't. Your heart is too good."

I glanced back at Hera, her expression blank, her body already starting to shrivel with her impossible age.

Janice may be right, but still...

I shoved that thought aside. It was done now and there wasn't a chance Hera would return. Janice had done what Hera should have done to me and hadn't. Finished it for good.

"Thank you," I said, although my voice was hollow. As much as she may have been right, I still couldn't shake how horrible I felt that I was responsible for Hera's murder.

Then strong arms wrapped around me, four sets in a massive group hug, and I folded into my guys, melted into their love, as Janice turned and walked away.

It was done.

Finally done.

CHAPTER 27

ANNIE

THE FEW REMAINING GUARDS SPREAD THE WORD TO THE REST OF those on the estate. By the time we got to the main house, it was empty, and already partially looted. Some of the mercenaries from the other world began to pick the place clean, but both Janice and I suspected Hera wouldn't keep her most valuable items out in the open. We went on a bit of a treasure hunt with Ladon, the triton who could sense through walls, and soon enough, in Hera's massive office, we found a secret room. We searched a bit for the hidden mechanism that would move the bookcase out of the way, but we didn't want to waste too much time in case someone had alerted the authorities, so Keph just smashed through the wall for us.

On the other side was... I didn't have the words to express the amount of wealth displayed in the large room. We each selected a few prized items, most of which were inlaid with gems or made of gold, then we stuffed our pockets with some of the smaller, more portable loot. After that, the surviving mercenaries finished cleaning it up for us. Several had died in the fight, including Khyrys the minotaur and all but one of her crew, which made my chest hurt just thinking about it. So many had died for our cause and there wasn't any way I could repay them for their sacrifice.

By the time we left, Hera's house was picked clean.

Then Janice called in the FBI to take charge of the scene and by the time they got there, the rest of us were long gone.

I moved to Eytheron, and the guys and I built a house just back from the beach near the rocks and the portal. It was fairly simple in design, many square rooms, as part of a larger square around a central courtyard. There were six bedrooms, two bathing rooms, and the southern side of the house was an open concept kitchen, dining, and living area, with no outer walls, just a spectacular view of the sea.

We each had our own room with a bed and a chest of drawers for our few items — since clothes weren't a thing, and my room had a particularly large and sturdy bed, since it needed to be able to hold all of us.

The house had gone up quickly, in roughly two weeks. The villagers from Masia had helped, supplying some materials, food, and labor. They'd been a little disappointed that we hadn't built in the village, but we were close enough they could make the trek out if they ever did need the miracle healing of 'Anichambers' as they called me.

That was another major shift in my life. My dream, since leaving university, had been to be a virtual assistant, living on a beach.

Well, I had the beach part, but the virtual assistant part was impossible in this world.

I suppose I could have made it work, returning to my world for jobs, but... when I'd started trying to set that up, I realized I didn't want that anymore. I had a much more hands-on way of helping people now, as a healer. And I loved it. People came from Masia — and all the surrounding lands — for help with things as simple as cuts and bruises, to much more serious and severe issues like complicated child-birth and deadly illnesses. Some people came to me who'd been crippled for years.

It was hard some days, seeing the pain and suffering of people, but then... they were always so happy and joyous when they left and that made it all worth it.

During that time, I also went back and forth to Chicago a fair bit. There were many things I'd needed to tend to, like giving my notice for my apartment and taking what I'd wanted from it.

Which had been an odd moving party, lugging my furniture down the street and into an alley... where it vanished!

We got lots of strange looks from passersby, but I didn't care. I was moving to paradise with the men I loved.

I'd put my financial situation in order and visited my old job, explaining that I'd had some harrowing life circumstances that I didn't want to talk about and wasn't coming back. I'd hugged Diane and wished her well, saying I was moving to the tropics like I always wanted and would be out of contact for a while.

Most of the loot I'd taken from Hera's place I'd given to charity. I hadn't felt right keeping it. It felt like blood-money. Some had gone to paying off my credit card debt — which I'd only racked up because of Hera, but the rest went to charity. Once my cards were paid off, I cut them up and withdrew what little remained in my bank accounts. I bought myself a couple nice items to take to the other world — or to wear if and when I returned to this one — and that was it. I had nothing, no "earthly" wealth... and I was just fine with that.

The final step was the hardest and I put it off for six weeks hoping I'd figure out the right way to do it. I had no idea what to tell my family, but I couldn't just disappear on them. That would be cruel and while they didn't understand me, I still loved them.

Now, six weeks later with spring having returned to Chicago, I stood in the alley with my whole family — my father, brother, and sister — my stomach churning with uncertainty because I had no idea what to say to them and this wasn't a conversation we could have over the phone.

No one would believe me if I just told them. They needed proof.

"Why are we in an alley?" Sheri asked, her tone hesitant and worried, something I couldn't blame her for because we *were* in an alley.

I considered saying, 'I live here now,' but that seemed like a cruel joke. Instead I said, "I have something I wanted to tell you all. But I knew if I just told you, you'd think I was crazy and lock me in an asylum somewhere. So, I thought I'd show you."

"Show us what?" Sheri's frown deepened.

"This," I said and I walked through the portal. To them it would look like I just walked through a brick wall, so I returned almost instantly before one of them had a breakdown.

Three stunned set of eyes stared at me.

"See, crazy, hunh?" I said, trying to keep the situation light.

"Wha...?" my father tried.

"Did you want to try? I promise it won't hurt." I took my father's hand and led him through the portal. He shied away from the wall as I pulled him closer, but I had Keph's strength now and I easily tugged him through.

He blinked at the shining sun in the other world and the brilliant blue sky.

"Wha...?" he repeated. "Where...?"

I laughed and said, "I'll be back in a moment, I'm going to go get the others."

I led them through one by one, each of them stunned at the sunny beach, a mix of shock and wonder filling their expressions.

"Welcome to Eytheron, the Okanid Islands." I threw out my arms to indicate the world around us.

"Those names don't mean anything," my father said, the first to recover — probably because he'd been staring at his surroundings the longest. "Where are we?"

"On another world," I said grinning. "This is where I live now."

"L-live?" my brother stammered, his body shaking with what was starting to look like serious shock.

"Yep. Isn't it nice?" I pointed to the large, squat structure nearby. "That's my home."

They all looked. Then several of their eyes went wide.

My sister gasped. "Oh!"

I looked, thinking I knew what they were seeing and... yup, there was Keph and Del, standing in the open-sided living area completely naked.

A man-shaped shadow passed over us and I sighed. Apparently, the guys had decided to ignore my suggestion that they stay hidden for the first part of this, until I'd gotten around to explaining them to my family.

Rion landed with a flap of his white wings and all eyes turned to him. At least he was wearing the leather wrap-skirt he'd had on when we'd first met.

"An angel!" Sheri gasped.

"Hello, my name is Hyperion. But for Annie's family, you can call me Rion." He held out a hand as I'd shown him. My father shook it, but I think that was more on instinct than actual acceptance.

"Are you..." my sister began, whispering to me. "Is he... your... he's gorgeous!"

I grinned and waggled my eyebrows at her unable to help myself. Yes. He was.

"So, ah, yeah," I said. "I now live on another world and also... I have four live-in lovers that I'm pretty much married to."

"Polygamy?" my brother blurted.

"Ah... no, probably not in the way you're thinking of it. It's more polyamory, or polyandry." I'd spent some time researching the terms knowing this would probably come up.

"You're... married... to all three of them?" my father said, his voice tight as if the shock was starting to strangle him.

"Four," I corrected. Aethan wasn't around at the mome—

A horse neighed off in the distance and came galloping along the beach toward us. Aethan. Well, that would need to be explained as well at some point. Might as well just rip all the bandages off and do it now.

"Where's the other one?" my sister asked, looking just a little too eagerly at Del and Keph, devouring them with her eyes as Aethan trotted up to us and shifted to his satyr form.

"Hello!" he said jovially.

Everyone gaped, mouth open, eyes wide, and I burst out laughing.

My sister glared at me and I tried to suck it back in, but if their expressions had gotten any bigger they would have looked like cartoon characters.

"You were a horse—" my brother gasped.

"H-his legs—" my father stammered.

"He's naked too—" my sister said, her cheeks turning bright red.

I sighed. "Aethan, I thought we talked about how I was going to make the introductions and explain everything before we showed them your other forms. Remember that conversation?"

He just grinned and snorted, sounding very much like the horse he'd just been.

"Other forms?" my father asked.

"Yeah, it's a lot to take in. Why don't you come inside where it's a bit cooler and I'll explain everything."

Once we were all up in the living area, I made the formal introductions. "This is Delphon, Kephas, Hyperion whom you've already met, and Aethan." To my guys, I said, "This is my father,

David Chambers, my brother Daniel Chambers, and my sister Sheri Chambers."

They all stared at each other, the awkward silence stretching on and on and—

"Can I get anyone a drink?" I asked.

It was a long and arduous afternoon as I slowly explained everything to my family. My sister took it the best, I think. Though she kept not-so-subtly looking at the various swaying bits of my guys. My father was confused, then angry, then confused, then shocked, then just seemed dazed and worn out. My brother didn't seem to like any of this. Of course, I also had to explain about his wedding, since he recognized a couple of the guys from that disaster. So I didn't blame him for being upset, at least for now. I guess we'd see if he ever forgave me for that debacle.

As evening fell, I escorted my family back to the portal, while the guys trailed along a good few steps behind.

"What do we tell people?" my father asked. "If they ask where you are?"

"I've been saying I'm moving to the tropics and I'll be hard to get ahold of."

"Yes." He nodded. "That should work."

"How *do* we get ahold of you?" my brother's tone still held a bit of scorn. He was too straight-laced and high-strung to accept my new life situation so easily, or forget about the mess I'd made of his wedding.

"That will be hard. I'm working on something, but I haven't got it figured out yet. For now, I'll call you whenever I return to your world."

"Your world," my father said, still sounding dazed. "Other worlds." He just shook his head.

"Think of it like Narnia," my sister said, taking my dad's arm to help him along.

I took them back through the portal and made sure they were safe in taxis before I returned.

"I like your family," Keph said in his low rumble where he and the others had waited for me to return by the rocks. "We should visit them in your world sometime."

Yeah, that would be interesting.

"Sure," I said and continued on up to the house. That hadn't gone quite as well as it could have, but the guys consoled me that night and by the time I fell asleep, snuggled with all of them in my bed, I was quite relaxed and already forgetting the incident.

CHAPTER 28

ANNIE

THE NEXT DAY, JANICE PICKED ME UP FROM THE ALLEY AND DROVE ME to a café nearby. We didn't speak much in the car on the way there, and it wasn't until we were settled at a table, coffees in hand, that she finally spoke.

"I'm sorry Annie," she said a bit sheepishly. "I…" She shook her head and because of our bond, I got the sense that she was still trying to apologize for killing Hera.

I reached over, taking one of her hands in mine.

"The more I think about it, the more I realize you were right, and had to make a very hard choice." I gave her a reassuring smile. "I couldn't have done it. I hated her, but I still couldn't have."

"I know," she said softly. "And I could." She pressed her lips tight for a long moment. "I was worried you'd hate me. You've been out of contact for so long, I…"

I squeezed her hand. "I just had a lot to do, and while I did it, well, you were always in the back of my mind. I didn't know how to say what I needed to say until now. And what I need to say is: thank you, Janice."

She sighed heavily, nodding, her gaze dropping to our joined hands. "Good. 'Cause I just kept thinking about it, running things over and over in my head, and I can't see any way she wouldn't have rained hell down upon us if she'd lived. She still had far too much power and wealth at her disposal, and we had no idea how long she'd survive with her immortality gone. I know I did the right thing, even if it wasn't the moral thing."

"Hey," I said, giving her fingers another squeeze and drawing her gaze back up to me. It was clear she'd tortured herself over this and it broke my heart that she'd think I hate her for it.

"Thank you," I said, willing her to *feel* through our bond how much I appreciated what she'd done for us.

She gave me a tight nod and a soft smile. Yes, it had been six weeks, but killing Hera wasn't something she was just going to be able to get over.

"Okay then," I said brightly, determined to change the subject to something happier. "I had another reason for wanting to speak to you."

"Oh?"

"Ah, yeah. I was hoping I could give my family your number to contact you if they needed to get ahold of me. They... I told them about the other world. Showed them actually."

Janice snorted. "How did that turn out? Did they meet your hot as hell, buck-naked harem?" she chortled.

"Yeah." I rolled my eyes at her. "And it went as well as could be expected."

"Oh, the price you have to pay to live with those guys in paradise," she said, her sad smile turning into an all-out grin.

"Which is where you come in. Since you can open portals, I thought you'd be the best go between if my family needs to get ahold of me. I know that's a bit of an imposition, but—"

She waved at me, cutting me off. "Of course I will."

"Wonderful. Thank you again. And," I said, drawing out the word, "that will give you an excuse to come and visit."

"Ah, yeah," Janice quirked an odd smile. "I may visit more often than that, we'll see." I was about to ask what she meant when she said, "I left the FBI."

"Oh?" That was news. "Didn't you like it there?"

"I did, very much, but... I've changed just a little too much to go back to my old life."

"Because of me," I said softly.

"Yes," she said and it was her turn to squeeze my hand. "But not in a bad way. I'm still trying to accept some things about me. Like my wings, but overall, I feel a lot more... empowered now than I did before. I don't know what I want to do, but I feel like I can do anything I put my mind to." She shrugged. "I was thinking I might try my hand as a private detective. Not sure though."

"Janice... P.I...." I blinked. "You know, in all the time we've known each other, I don't think I've learned your last name."

"It's Leoni."

I tried again. "Janice Leoni, P.I. That has a certain ring to it."

She gave a bit of a laugh then sighed heavily. "Yeah, we'll see if I go that route. I don't know what I'll do. I think I'll take a bit of time and figure that out. And while I do, I may want to visit the other world a bit more often and... find out more about... me."

"And see Naz?" I asked mischievously.

Her blush and grin told me everything I needed to know. "Maybe."

"We'd be happy to have you. We have one dedicated guest room and most nights there are other rooms available as well. You could stay with us—" She gave me an odd, slightly apprehensive look. "Or not."

"Ah... yeah, thank you for the offer, but if you're going to be bumping-uglies with those guys of yours, just remember little old me can *feel* it when you do. When I'm a world away, I'm fine, but staying in your house... might be a bit awkward."

Awkward to say the least. "Right, well, no worries. You can stay with Naz and bump-your-own-uglies."

Her blush deepened and swept down her neck. "Ah, yeah, no..." She rolled her eyes and laughed. "Well... maybe. We'll see."

I laughed with her. I wouldn't push her toward Naz, but I had a good feeling about him and Janice, and with everything that had happened to her, she deserved some good, other-world sex with a hot guy.

CHAPTER 29

HYPERION

A FEW DAYS AFTER ANNIE TALKED WITH JANICE, I DECIDED IT WAS time for me to finish things with my father. I'd been avoiding the conversation because I knew it wouldn't go well. But I also knew if I put it off for too long, my father would send men to look for me, and I didn't want to face him from a weakened position.

No, better to confront him, show him my bonded mate, and be done with the monster once and for all.

Now we stood in front of my old house. The deck around the house was a large expanse of wood, which projected well out from the trees to give an amazing view of the Syltheorin River — where it cut through a lush and green valley — and the Ophion Mountains beyond. There were no railings on things in the *erinai* world, high in the trees of Phyllidian Forest, but I wasn't worried about Annie falling over the edge. She could float using Del's powers if she needed to.

"Gods, this view..." Annie said, her voice hushed and reverent.

I nodded. It was an amazing view, but everything to do with this house, this place, was tainted for me.

Annie looked at me then, perhaps because of my silence. She

slid her hand into mine. "You are stronger than you know," she said softly. "I know this isn't easy for you."

It wasn't, but she was right. I had her... and the others — though they were back at our house at the moment. And I did feel stronger. The flight here had been quicker than any other time before.

Usually it took me the better part of two days to fly across the large island, resting occasionally and sleeping at night. I hadn't been certain how long it would take while carrying Annie, but she'd used Del's powers to make herself lighter, and through our bond, she'd shared some of Keph's strength and Aethan's speed and endurance. Because of that, I'd felt refreshed the entire way and made the trip in one long day of travel, and despite the sunset with its oranges, reds, and purples staining the sky and draping the forest in deep shadows, I knew we'd return home once I'd said my piece. I drew myself up and went to the door to the house in which I'd grown up and firmly knocked.

It was my mother who answered. Hades would turn cold before my father ever did anything as mundane as answer a door.

"Hyp?" My mother's eyes went wide and she strode out to embrace me. "It's so good to see you."

"Hyp?" Annie asked behind me.

I extricated myself from my mother's hug and stepped back. "Mother, this is Annie, my bonded." To Annie, I added, "I like my other short form better, but I couldn't convince my family to use it."

My mother stared at Annie, stunned for a second, then she smiled. But I knew that smile. It was the awkward smile which said, 'I don't like this, and I don't know what to say, so I'll smile a bit too brightly.'

Annie approached my mother and embraced her. My mother followed suit after a long awkward moment of standing there. It was clear she was surprised that I'd bonded to a non-*erinai,* but I'd known this would be her reaction and I'd warned Annie before we'd left.

"I've come to talk to Father," I said stoically. "And introduce Annie."

Oh, the feathers I was about to ruffle.

Mother's eyes went wide behind Annie's back. She shook her head ever so subtly. "Ah... Annie? Nice to meet you." My mother's words were a bit halting. "Your father is... unavailable."

I doubted that, and I wasn't coming back. I was getting this over and done with and then moving on.

I'd never lived up to my father's expectation and knew he wouldn't accept Annie. But I wanted to make it clear she was my bonded, she wasn't a lie I'd made up to get out of my responsibilities, and that I was never going to be the *erinai* he wanted me to be.

I strode past my mother into the large house and called out, "Father! It's Hyperion! We need to talk."

My mother gasped and I smiled. I'd never been so forthright with him because I'd been afraid of what he'd do. And now I didn't care.

Heavy footfalls sounded on the floor above me letting me know my father was indeed around, and he strode down the stairs with all the pomp and arrogance I'd come to know from him. His pristine white hair fell in perfect waves down to precisely an inch above his shoulders. Even at his age, he was fit and well-muscled, as tall as I, but larger through chest and shoulders. A consummate warrior.

His pale blue eyes were hard as he stared me down, and for the first time in my life I matched that stare without fear. I even smiled, knowing it would infuriate him.

"Father," I said with the exact amount of respect someone of his station deserved and not a bit more.

"Hyperion," he growled. "You've been gone too long. You have duties here you've ignored. There will be a reckoning for that." His lips grew tight, his jaw tense. "I thought I'd taught you more respect."

"I don't care what you think I should be doing. I never accepted the position of Sky General, you just assumed I would. And I haven't come back to take it either. I've come back to introduce you to my bonded."

His brows furrowed. "You've been nowhere near the forest. Where did you meet an *erinai* woman?"

I couldn't help but smile even larger. "Oh, I didn't. She's not even from this world. This is Annie." I half stepped back and waved to introduce her.

She strode forward radiating all the stunning, confident power that I knew she possessed.

My father's eyes widened. "What... is she?" he hissed.

"Beautiful, strong, loving, intelligent, passionate, independent, caring. She's defeated a goddess. Can you say as much, Father?"

He was sputtering, his mouth opening and closing, so angry he couldn't form a coherent sentence. "She's not one of us!"

"Oh, dear," I heard my mother say, now hiding a little behind the open door. She knew how angry my father could get.

"Hello, General Eonas," Annie said, keeping with the same respect I'd shown him, and she dipped her head in a slight bow. "It's not at all a pleasure to meet you. I can see now why you left home, Rion."

"How dare you come into my home and—" My father stalked toward her with an arm raised to slap her. With Aethan's speed and Keph's strength Annie landed a solid blow to the man's jaw before he could hit her and he went down in a heap.

He sat there, blinking for a long moment.

"Don't you ever presume to lay a hand on me, sir," she said softly. As he rose, she continued. "Now, I think Rion has some words for you as well."

She turned her back on him and made for the door, but stopped in the open entranceway and turned back.

"Oh, and you should know, Rion has already impregnated me. We're going to have a litter of half-breed babies. But don't worry, we won't name any of them after you." She smiled beatifically, then left.

I knelt next to my still recovering father, not waiting for him to stand and regain his composure.

"She's something, isn't she?" I chuckled. "Now, here's the plan. I'm going to leave and probably never return. There's nothing for me here. You drove my sister to her death, sapped the spirit from Mother, and the only friends I had were ones mandated by you in the military. I have new friends now. A new family. We have a home on the beach near Masia. Perhaps someday, you can come and visit and see all your grandchildren, but I suggest you get your attitude straight before you do. Step one foot inside my house in belligerence, hatred, and anger, and you'll face so much more than that little tap Annie gave. Do you understand me?"

My father glared at me. "Get out!"

He spat at me, blood leaking from the split lip Annie had given him. She hadn't held back. Good.

"Happy to." I stood and strode to the door. There, I spoke loud enough that my father could hear. "I have a loving home, in which you'd be welcome, if you like, Mother. You don't ever have to see him or face his rage again."

She stared at me, her eyes wide with shock and fear.

"I won't be back," I added, "but know that my door will always be open for you."

"How dare you!" my father roared from inside. "Get out!"

I waited for my mother's response, hoping, praying, she'd say something.

We stared at each other. I didn't think she was aware that I was waiting for her response, she was so used to father speaking for her.

Finally, she blinked, realization flashing through her expression. "Oh... Hyp, I..." She glanced inside at the hulking form of the man I no longer considered to be my father. "I... can't leave him."

And there it was. I didn't know why she chose to stay, but it was her choice.

I nodded, then gave her a kiss on the cheek. "Goodbye, Mother."

I turned away from her, a part of me hoping that someday she'd find her way to Masia. I wanted to be there for her, but I couldn't stay. I wouldn't have that monster involved in my new life with Annie in any way.

Annie waited for me at the edge of the long balcony, and I picked her up, and flew away.

"How did that feel?" she asked once we were well away.

"Horrible," I said, the weight that I was sure would always be there, heavy in my chest. "But it was necessary." And as I said the words, the weight shifted to sadness, edged with relief.

I'd done what I'd never had the courage to do, freed myself to live my life, not the life that had always been expected of me.

Annie nodded, holding me close. "It felt good to clock your father," she murmured against my neck. "Sorry if I stole some of your thunder doing that."

I shook my head. "I don't think he's ever had anyone stand up to him, let alone a woman. It was... the most perfect thing I've ever seen."

She giggled. "Good."

"One thing," I asked, leaning back to look her in the eyes, more than a little curious. "Was that true what you said about being pregnant?"

Her face lit up with a brilliant smile. "Yep. I'm fairly certain I am. It can't surprise you, given how much I've been with all of you guys. Though I have no clue whose child it is. I guess we'll see when he or she comes."

A stunning swell of pride and joy swept through me. I hadn't realized how much I wanted to be a father until that moment and while I hoped the child was mine, I realized I didn't care. Even if he or she didn't have wings, they'd still be my child. All of ours. Another member to our amazing family.

I smiled and hugged Annie a little closer, surging higher into the sky, speeding home. I was sure the others would want to hear this amazing news as well.

CHAPTER 30

AETHAN

R ION HAD RETURNED WITH A NNIE LOOKING HAPPIER THAN I' D EVER seen him, and while I knew he was thrilled with Annie's news about having a baby, I also knew it was because he'd closed the book on his relationship with his father.

Something I felt I needed to do. I didn't have a terrible relationship with my family, but that was because I didn't really have one with them. And while I didn't have someone I needed to confront, a part of me wanted to show Annie where I came from and why I didn't belong.

So, a few days later, I invited Annie to join me, shifted into my horse form, and we took off.

It felt good to let loose and gallop, and it was even better with Annie riding bareback on me. I didn't fully understand it — something about the power she shared with Janice — but she was a far better rider now, easily moving and staying in place while I ran full-out in my horse form.

She let out whoops and calls every now and then, sounding so free and excited, and it made me run just a little bit faster, just to see if I could make her call out again.

But there was a point to this ride. I was taking Annie to see my home, such as it was, and soon she'd see why I'd wanted to leave. Something I knew I had to share with her, but didn't really want to.

I took comfort in knowing that I'd found my herd, that I was no longer a misfit among the people who were supposed to love me, but this was still a journey I hadn't wanted to make.

And then I crested a hill and we were there. The great plains where I used to live.

Off in the distance stood a massive shifting heard of horses, meandering slowly over the plains, and moving among them were perhaps a dozen satyrs.

"These are my people," I said. It was always just a little awkward speaking in horse form, too much lip and teeth.

"There are so few of them," Annie said softly.

I swung my large head around to look at her. "It's not just the satyrs. All those horses are my people, too."

Her eyes widened. "Oh."

"Now you see," I said, shaking my head. "They prefer this form. Easier to graze. They don't want to worry about the world of men. They wish only to live wild on the plains."

"Oh."

"Exactly. I don't mind my horse form. It's a part of who I am, but only a part. It gets me places quickly, but I don't want to be an animal all the time. I want to be a man. I want to hold myself to a higher standard of intelligence and awareness."

Annie dismounted, easily hopping off and landing lightly, and I shifted back to my satyr form.

Together we watched the slow, shifting herd out on the plains for a long moment, letting the warm breeze sweep over us and the clouds lazily drift by.

"They never really understood me," I said softly. Annie's hand slipped into mine, giving it a squeeze. "Oh, don't get me wrong, I don't really understand them either. I was happy to get away and I don't think they really missed me."

"It's still sad," she said softly. "They're your family."

I looked at her. "No, Annie. You and Rion and Del and Keph are my family."

She kissed me softly on the lips, an action I was still getting used to after all this time. When she stepped back her hand rose to stroke her stomach.

I smiled. A child was on the way, though still some time off, and it made me happy beyond reason.

"Soon, our family will be a bit larger," she said with a soft smile. She looked up at me. "Thank you for bringing me here. I don't think I fully understood, until now."

I nodded. "The people here are in many ways stuck in the past. I want to move into the future."

She nodded. "Do you want to talk to anyone?"

"No." There wasn't anyone who'd understand. They never had.

"Then let's go home," she said.

I shifted back to a horse and she was quickly on my back.

With a whoop and holler from Annie, I was off, galloping once again.

I was glad I'd shown her where I'd come from, glad I'd said goodbye to the part of me that had been a part of my people, but I wouldn't trade anything for the family I shared now. It was everything I ever wanted, and I couldn't wait to see what our future held.

CHAPTER 31

KEPH

THE EVENING AETHAN AND ANNIE RETURNED FROM THE Theophylian Plains, Annie took me for a walk on the beach and asked if I wanted to introduce her to my family, since my family was the only one she had yet to meet.

"Are you certain you don't want to go?" Annie asked me.

I nodded. "It's a long trip back to see my family and I have no quick way to get there, like the others. By the time we got there and back, you'd probably be due." I replied. "We can wait until after the child is born. Though I fear it would be a bit of a let-down for all involved."

"Why would you say that?"

I sighed and turned my gaze to the sunset, the beautiful end to another warm, calm day. "You have to understand, my people are a lot like stone itself. We're hard and unfeeling about a lot of things. They're set in their ways and don't change easily. That's not to say they wouldn't welcome you, but their welcome would be... cold. Not because they don't like you, but because everything they do is cold. It's just who they are, distant and..." I gave a bit of a laugh. "Stony."

"Oh," she said softly.

"I'm sure my father and mother would love to meet you, but their love and reception would seem like a hard, cold indifference to you."

"Really?"

I nodded. "And you to them would be so vastly different from anything they know. You're so warm and welcoming, and... soft." As I said this, I reached over to trace a finger down her shoulder and arm, then slipped my hand around her waist and hugged her gently against my side. "They wouldn't understand you. They'd try to love you for my sake, but you'd be so foreign to them. I can see it now. When we leave, they'd just shake their heads and shrug, and go back to their lives."

"It sounds like a lonely and distant life." Annie leaned into me a little as we walked, snuggling close in my embrace.

"It was. That was one of the reasons I wanted to leave. I could have been at home there, but I'd always expressed my feelings a little more than the others, which made me odd. I was curious, another odd trait. So, they let me go and explore the world. I found so many wonders. I couldn't understand why they wanted to stay buried deep in their mountains. I love my family, but this new family with you and the others is so much warmer and more welcoming."

We were silent for a long time until Annie asked, "If this child is yours, what would your family think of that, a half-stone-titan?"

I chuckled. "They wouldn't be upset or curious. They would accept it with the same stoic coldness they accept everything. No shock or horror, like I suspect Rion's father would have if the child was his, just a nod and then back to their lives. They'd love it, but... not in a way you'd feel from them."

Annie shivered next to me. "So cold."

"Exactly."

"I'm glad you're so warm," she said, kissing my biceps.

That, more than anything she'd ever said, struck my heart.

"Thank you." But still... "I sometimes wish I was softer and not as big. I feel awkward at times and... well I know I can't really hurt you since you have my own powers of durability, but..." I didn't really have the words. "I just want to be a bit more like the rest of you some days."

"Oh, Keph, no! You should be proud and happy to be you. I like your... hardness," she said that with a hitch and a silly grin. I felt her shiver with satisfaction and snuggle even closer. "You're wonderful as you are."

"But I'll never be able to visit Del's home, or Rion's, I'm too big, too heavy, too awkward."

"From what I saw of Rion's home, you're not missing much. As for Del's you could get there eventually by just walking. But that doesn't matter. You're wonderful just as you are. You are a part of our family now and we accept you with love and openness and wonder."

I smiled and drew in a deep breath, letting that sink in for a long moment. She was right. I was welcome and accepted with them, not just with the cold acceptance of all things like my family, but with a warmth and joy that I'd never known elsewhere. I could be proud to be me.

"Thank you," I murmured.

Annie tried to reach an arm around me, but only just managed to get to the other side of my broad back. She gave it a vigorous rub and pressed closer.

"We all have each other," she said a bit dreamily. "That's all that matters."

And with those words, for the first time, in my entire life, I finally felt like I had a home.

CHAPTER 32

DELPHON

AFTER RION AND AETHAN HAD DEALT WITH THEIR FAMILIES, I KNEW I'd be happier dealing with mine. Except I didn't want to say a far-off goodbye like Aethan had, or have a confrontation like Rion... even though I knew a confrontation was inevitable. I didn't want to lose my relationship with my sister, brother, or father, and I was afraid my mother would force the issue, which was why I'd been avoiding the trip home.

Annie had also insisted on coming with me, and that she was going to do it without a huphelopoid. So, it was even easier to put it off until after she'd given birth to little Petra — a not-as-tiny-as-Annie-would-have-liked stone titan girl.

Then Annie announced that she needed to drown herself, saying the powers she'd gotten from Janice meant she would adapt and be able to breathe water.

Which had been a horrible idea!

But she'd insisted, and I'd been there to pull her out — after she'd nearly died, of course!

We'd resuscitated her in a panic, the other guys just as frustrated with her as I was, and she'd rested for a day and tried again, and sure enough, after almost drowning, she could now breathe water.

Except I was pretty sure I'd aged at least a decade from the experience.

We left Petra in the care of Keph, Rion, and Aethan, along with a wet nurse from the town, and Annie escorted me back to Galniosia.

She'd become an amazing swimmer in the short time that we'd lived in our seaside home. She still couldn't compete when I had my tail, but without it, she was nearly a match for me, lithe and graceful and the most beautiful thing I'd ever seen in the water.

And, even though I didn't have my powers over water in this world, she still did, and could use that to jet through the water even faster than I swam with my triton's tail.

It was amazing to watch her move with such ease, but, as we drew close to my old home, my mind turned from my attractive companion to the 'battle' ahead.

I'd been going out nearly every day over the past nine months, sometimes for most of the day, searching for pearls, and I'd managed to collect a little more than a half a dozen so far. I'd hoped for more, but I knew they were rare, hence why they were so valuable.

Seven tritons had died during the two attacks on Hera, which meant I owed my mother and Galniosia three hundred and fifty pearls, and I had a long way still to go. At my current rate, it would take me well over fifty years to repay the kingdom.

But I was bringing another gift which I hoped would diminish my debt, the item secured in a long box made of treated wood, which resisted water. This was the one trophy I'd taken from Hera's estate. It was a bit awkward to swim with the box, but we'd still made good time.

Poseia met us outside of the Hall of Light and her eyes widened at the sight of Annie without a huphelopoid.

"How...?" she asked.

"Long story," Annie said. "The short version is I can breathe water now."

Poseia huffed a half laugh, deciding to just go with it, then turned to me, her expression darkening. "Mother is in a foul mood today. Be careful."

"If I was careful, sister, I'd never have gotten myself where I am today, as good and bad as that is."

She nodded to that. "If you can't be careful, be wise."

"Good luck with that," Annie said softly.

That made Poseia chuckle. "Fine, if you can't be careful or wise, be..." She searched for a word. "Daring."

"That," I said, squaring my shoulders, "I can do."

We entered the Hall of Light with its spectacular ribbons of light coming from the surface, and even from a distance I could see the displeasure on my mother's face, and the exhaustion on my father's. This was going to be a challenge indeed.

Luarnon floated a bit farther to one side than usual as if trying to stay out of my mother's line-of-sight and therefore her line-of-fire. There was a young triton woman with him, and I took this to be the bride I'd avoided and he'd acquired. I didn't know if they'd been married yet or not, but they seemed happy, staying close to each other, whispering and keeping to themselves.

"What do you want, Exiled One?" my mother bellowed down the hall before we'd even made it halfway to her throne.

"That's what she's taken to calling you," Poseia whispered, still escorting us.

"Be quick and be gone. I don't wish you in my sight for any longer than necessary."

"I really want to slap her one," Annie hissed, low enough that only I and Poseia could hear.

"Let's not," I said. Then we were close enough that I stopped and bowed. "Dearest Queen and King of Galniosia. I bring to you part of what is owed."

My mother raised a brow at that.

Even Poseia, still in the water not far away, turned back to me. She mouthed the word, 'already?' and I drew forth a pouch.

From it, I withdrew the seven pearls I'd found so far. "This is only a small sum of my payment," I said, giving the pearls over to Poseia who took them to our mother.

"Seven?" Mother said with distain. "You owe us fifty times as much!"

I did indeed.

"That's not all I brought," I said and sank to the floor of the hall, my tail brushing its smooth tiles, to set down the long box and undo the clasps holding it closed.

My mother remained silent, which hopefully meant she was curious. Even my father perked up a little.

I made sure, when I opened the box, it was facing away from the thrones so they couldn't see the trident which lay within, and when I pulled it out, I held it up saying, "Behold the trident of Poseidon!"

Poseia and Luarnon gasped and my father's eyes went wide.

My mother to her credit, showed only the barest moment of shock, then was stony-faced once again.

It was a magnificent weapon, made from a strange green-blue metal. Tracings on the three sharp prongs and down the long haft were intricate, depicting all manner of sea-life, and inlaid in the handle, were a few aquamarine gems, and pearls, dozens of them.

I swam slowly toward the thrones, the haft across my open hands, unthreatening, and presented it to them.

I knew it was Poseidon's own trident as it had been labelled as such in Hera's treasure room.

"We found this when we defeated Hera. Something she'd claimed from the God of the Sea long ago. I give it to you, the rightful rulers of the sea." Well... only of this part of the sea, but I wasn't going to quibble.

My mother rose slowly and reached out to lift the trident from my hands and inspect it.

"It's magnificent!" she whispered. "The detail and the material, so light, yet strong." She gave it a few test strikes, then looked at me. The awe on her face was slowly replaced with disdain once again. "This will go a long way toward repaying your debt," she said, voice proclamatory.

"Oh Hades, Hanea! You're still going to ask for more?" My father had risen from his throne. "This gift is priceless! Surely it repays his debt."

She shot him a long, hot look, her jaw tight. "Do you so easily dismiss the lives he so casually threw away?"

"Of course not. And if you're going to proclaim he was so casual then state their names, each of the fallen seven, right now," the king countered.

I tried not to smile at his bravado.

My mother's expression turned sour. She didn't know their names. "Still their lives—"

"Are irreplaceable, yes. They are priceless, yes?" the king said.

"Yes!"

"As is the gift you're holding. One priceless gift for another should suffice," he huffed.

"I won't let him off that easily." She turned back to me.

It was at that point that a quick current of water brushed past me and Annie was suddenly in front of my mother, barely inches apart. Her hair floated behind her like a pale red cape and she was well flushed with emotion.

"I have stood by and listened to this for long enough!"

"You!" my mother countered. Then she blinked. "How are you... You're not..." It seemed she'd only then begun to pay any attention to Annie and realized she didn't have a huphelopoid.

"You want to know how I swim as I do? How I breathe water? It's simple. I'm the one who defeated Hera. I have powers over water and can adapt to any environment. I'm not a goddess. I don't seek to be worshiped. But I have killed a goddess and let me tell you, you are nothing compared to her."

My mother's eyes widened and she shied away, her back bumping the back of her throne.

Annie backed off then, composing herself and drawing herself up.

"Tell me," she said softly. "What is it you hold against Delphon? Why do you despise him so much? He's your son."

The fire returned to my mother's eyes. "Exactly. I knew my duty! I gave everything for this kingdom, and yet he always shirked his responsibility. He didn't take anything seriously. He's a lazy, simpering, worthless child."

"Is he?" Annie asked, her expression eerily serene. "That's not the man I've known at all. He's loyal and responsible. He's strong and dedicated. He risked his life to save two worlds, not just your small kingdom. And those seven tritons you throw in his face, they did the same. They gave their lives for this world and another. I think that deserves a little respect. And I think this gift shows Delphon's respect for you and for the sacrifice those seven tritons made."

My mother sneered at her. "I can see you're a strong woman, such as myself. Don't worry, he'll disappoint you, fail you, betray you."

"He never has and never will," Annie replied with certainty, making my heart swell at her love.

"Does he do everything you tell him to do?" my mother shot back.

Annie took a long pause before answering. She looked back at me, smiling, then at the others in the room before turning back to my mother. "I don't tell him to do anything. I make no commands. I ask and he is more than willing to help, because... he loves me."

Oh Hades! She just told my mother that I didn't love her.

My mother's eyes went wide.

Poseia nearly choked.

My mother sputtered for a moment and Annie kept going. "If you had shown him the love of a mother instead of the harsh hand of a queen, perhaps he'd have been different. But then... you'd never have driven him away, and I'd never have met him. So I guess I do have something to thank you for. Did I mention we were bonded, mother-in-law?"

My father's eyes went wide. He looked to me for confirmation and I nodded with a grin.

Annie pushed on, her voice even and calm, revealing just how powerful she really was with her relaxed confidence. "I do hope, that in the years to come, you'll come to see him differently, as I have. I hope you'll come to our home, on the beach near Masia. I hope you'll want to visit your grandchildren. We haven't had any half-tritons yet, but I'm certain we will. And when that day comes, if you wish to reconcile and make peace with your son, I'm certain he'll forgive you."

I approached with an air of penitence. I didn't want this battle to continue and I didn't want the rest of my family to have to pick sides. "There's no need to wait for that day. I know you were only doing the best you could, and I know I wasn't the son you wished you'd had. But I've come to learn what it means to love and be loved, what it means to serve instead of being served. I understand your sacrifice, Mother. I forgive you."

My mother blinked, looking back and forth between me and Annie. Her gaze settled on me and it wasn't entirely displeased. "You've... changed."

Annie must have been shifting the eddies around herself with my water magic as she didn't otherwise move, yet she drifted back, away from the queen, to give me more room.

"I have," I said, bowing my head in respect.

When I looked up again, my mother's stern look had returned and she drew herself up. She looked at the trident and said, "This is a most precious gift and it shall repay the most precious sacrifice of our people." Well that was a start. "And..." this in a softer tone I'd so rarely heard from her. "I should like to see my grandchildren, when I have some." She looked back and forth from me to Annie again. "Even if they are with a fiery, god-killing, human woman." She sighed then. "One whose heart is true and who loves my son. That much I can see plainly."

Annie smiled. "Thank you, your majesty."

"Good!" Suddenly my mother was all business once more. "And thank you for this precious gift. Will you be returning to the shore immediately?"

That was a surprise question, implying that we didn't have to make a hasty retreat as I'd expected. "Would you like us to stay?" I wouldn't mind spending a bit of time with my family, if the option was on the table. I turned to Annie. "Would you like to stay?"

She nodded, giving me a warm smile. "Of course."

My mother gave a tight nod. "I think I'd like to get to know this new daughter of mine. She's... full of fire... like me." My mother returned to her throne and sat, the trident across her lap. "Please stay for a bit." And then she actually smiled.

A small, intimate dinner was prepared — my mother was willing to meet Annie, but not publicly announce her to our people — and during the meal I learned Luarnon would be returning with his newly bonded to the Atargatine Merfolk kingdom and Poseia had taken the mantle of heir and would succeed my parents when they died or stepped down.

I congratulated them both as Annie chatted up the foreign princess, giggling together for half the meal, and for the first time in a long time, I felt comfortable in the palace.

Something that never would have happened if I hadn't met Annie.

CHAPTER 33

ANNIE

A LITTLE LESS THAN A YEAR LATER, I LEARNED THAT THE ADAPTATION power I'd acquired from Janice included the rigors of childbirth. Petra had been more than ten hours of sweaty, screaming, painful — very, very painful — labor. She hadn't been a small baby. She was half stone titan after all, but when little Cupid was born — our half-*erinai* bundle of joy — it was a breeze.

There'd only been enough pain to let me know things were happening and when to push, and only for barely an hour's worth of time. The tiny child had the cutest little wings, which were completely ineffective, thank the gods, since I couldn't imagine what a flying newborn child would be like, and I recovered quickly.

A week later we invited all our friends for a party in celebration of the new baby.

Janice came and brought Naz as her plus one. She'd been visiting him frequently, often stopping in at our house because we were so close to the portal. Poseia, Del's sister, had come as had a few people from Masia with whom we'd become close, one of whom had been the some-times wet nurse for Petra, a *nereia* woman named Zona. She'd had a child around the time I'd had Petra, and had just had another, so there was a good chance we'd be keeping her on as a wet-nurse for Cupid when I wasn't available.

My father and sister had come. Daniel, my brother, still wasn't over my odd relationship with my guys, nor me ruining his wedding. He'd sent a card, though, which I hoped was a first step in reconciliation.

The others had brought gifts as well. The guys had made Cupid a crib. Well, they'd made a *new* crib, since we already had one for Petra. And since they'd learned from the making of the last one, this one was sturdier, so we'd moved Petra into it — her being a much heavier and larger child.

My father had bought the new baby a bunch of onesies — that were adorable! — only to then notice how no one was really wearing much of anything. He said he'd return them and get something else, and I told him the bonus to that was that we'd get to see him again, sooner than usual.

Zona made a beautiful sling-wrap in which I could carry Cupid. She was wearing one herself with her new baby asleep inside, and my sister had brought a variety of small tropical plants. Less a gift for the child as it was something to spruce up the area around our house.

She also showed off her diamond ring and my guys made the appropriate noises — once I'd told them what the ring had meant. She was engaged to a baker who had a shop down from hers in the same plaza.

But Janice had brought possibly the best gift of all: chocolate. It wasn't something I could get in this world and I knew I'd truly treasure and savor every last bite. Poseia brought several beautiful shell-based pieces of jewelry, that the queen had insisted she give us. She said she knew I probably wouldn't wear them, but we could use them to barter in the town for supplies as our family grew, which made me laugh, because it was Poseia being practical as ever.

Now we all sat in the covered living area, drinking fruit juices and chatting, while little Petra toddled around on the porch moving from person to person loving all the attention. She'd grown a lot, not even twelve months old yet, and was now over three feet tall. She was going to be big like her father. If it hadn't been for the strength I'd acquired being bonded to Keph, I probably wouldn't have been able to pick her up anymore. She was heavy and ate... a lot. I'd been horrified the first time I'd found her eating dirt and pebbles.

Keph had been watching her playing outside, and I'd come to join them and nearly fainted. But Keph assured me that such things were actually a part of a growing stone titan's diet. He then proceeded to pop a small stone in his mouth and chew on it, quite happily. Apparently, there were some things about this world I still hadn't gotten used to.

As evening set in, my father and sister left, but everyone else stayed. Poseia was going to stay the night as it was a bit of a trip back to Galniosia, and she chatted with the others, while Janice and I went for a walk.

Even though she still lived in the other world and we didn't talk often, we still shared a bond and I felt closer to her than anyone else other than my guys.

"So," I asked. "How are things?"

"Not bad. My P.I. caseload is slowly building, and I'm actually starting to get clients referred by previous clients, so that's a good thing."

"That's great!" I said.

"Yeah. This new role is certainly interesting." Janice had built up a business as a private investigator for the last sixteen months or so, and the job had morphed into a semi-permanent gig with the Chicago police as a consulting investigator. She was often hired by others to look into things the police didn't have time for, cases of lower importance. When she solved them, she'd hand the case over to the police all nicely wrapped up and they'd take it from there. She got a bit of a stipend from the police and often a bit from those who hired her, and it added up to enough to live off of.

"But I feel like it's still doing what I did at the FBI, just for less money," she said. "It's good work and I like helping these people who otherwise wouldn't be helped, but it's still not... quite right."

"Maybe that's because you're not quite where you're supposed to be yet," I said.

She glanced at me. She must have sensed what I was thinking because her cheeks turned pink before I could even ask.

"Like with Naz?" I teased. "How are things with him?"

Her blush deepened. "Good. He's joined up with one of the minotaurs and Rhou, the *panai*, and they've formed their own little mercenary company. He's been away a lot on jobs."

"And when he gets back, I'm sure he's excited to see you?" I knew this much because he'd occasionally come to me, asking to send messages to Janice.

"Unhun," she replied noncommittally.

Gods, but she was tight lipped.

"And?"

"And?" She turned to me, an innocent look in her eyes.

"How's it going. Have you two...?"

She groaned. "It's going well enough. I'm not like you Annie. I'm not a... passionate woman. I was a tomboy most of my life. I like guys, in that I prefer them to women, but I've never been really close to anyone. I was dedicated to my schooling, then my job. I didn't have time for guys in my life. Now that I do, I... I don't really know what to do with him."

Oh, there was so very much she could do with him! But I could see her discomfort and unease, which made me wonder...

"Are you...?" How to word this and not be insensitive. "Have you been... intimate with anyone before?"

"No," she said, the word tight and clipped.

"Ah." I sighed. "Then I'm sorry if I seemed to have been pushing you. I just thought... he's handsome and interested. I don't know him that well, but he doesn't seem like a jerk."

"No, he isn't. He's kind and sensitive, but also strong and well... yeah... you've seen him."

"I have." I reached over and rubbed her back. "Don't be afraid to let things happen. And don't be afraid to make things happen if that's what you want. I guess, don't be afraid to wait, either." I wouldn't. I hadn't. But I wasn't her.

She nodded. "Thanks. Honestly, I can't imagine what life must be like for you, with four big, handsome guys. It must be exhausting! And now you're pretty much constantly pregnant. Isn't that rough?"

I laughed. "Not really. The first pregnancy was rough, yes, but with our powers, we adapt well. Cupid was a breeze. And I don't mind having four hunky guys constantly wanting to make me happy in every possible way. It's a dream."

"Yeah, I guess, when you put it that way."

"If you ever need any advice on anything, I'm just a portal away."

She huffed a laugh. "I might. Naz has been exceptionally patient with me, but he's suggested a couple things — sexual things — we could try that are... not kinky things, but... beginners' stuff and..." Gods, she was so awkward and stilted talking about anything to do with sex. Poor girl.

"I get the idea, yeah. I'm here if you need me." I meant it. I felt for the woman, only now experimenting and growing in her sexuality. She wasn't old, but she wasn't young either, mid-twenties or so, and I'd been experimenting since my late teens.

She nodded, blushing furiously.

We returned to the others. Naz gave Janice a chaste kiss on the cheek, which she returned in kind. It was growing late, though, so we all retired. Poseia slept in Del's usual room. Janice said goodbye to Naz and returned through the portal, and he flew off soon after.

Zona said she'd stay the night and take care of Petra and Cupid, which meant I had a night alone with my guys. Before they'd come along, I'd always prized my space in bed, but now, I was a consummate snuggler.

We all curled up together, Keph behind Rion on one side, Aethan on the other, and Del tucked up behind Aethan, his feet tangled with mine. It was warm and intimate, but relaxed and peaceful. I reached out to each of them, stroking a shoulder or hip, arm or leg with a few words of love before we all closed our eyes and slept.

I had everything I'd ever dreamed of: a tropical house on a beach, and not one, but *four* men who loved me, and a meaningful life as a healer.

I slept well that night.

And every night thereafter.